BLOOD NEXUS

JJ PORTER

Published by JJ Porter
Santa Cruz California 2018
Copyright © 2018 by JJ Porter

This is a work of fiction. Any similarity between an imaginary character and a real
person, living or dead, is purely coincidental. Where companies are mentioned, the
events, products, and characters associated with them are purely imaginary, and none
of these fictional creations should be construed as depictions of real events, products,
people, methods or things.

Printed in the United States of America

Library of Congress Control Number: 2018909744
ISBN 978-0-693-17202-5

Covers designed by Geneva Porter
Edited by Peter Sterbach and Mary Karlton, GiG Productions, Inc.

Dedicated in loving memory to
Wendy

BLOOD
NEXUS

List Of Main Characters
(in order of appearance)

Communication Station 4

Jed - *Communication Station 4 Technician*
Sergio - *Communication Station 4 Super Technician*
Sulof - *Chief of Data Collection and Processing Center*
Karlin - *Geologist, Jed's Friend*
Tamtira - *In Orbit Pilot, Jed's Friend*
Melf - *Geological Research Director, Sulof's Friend*

The Hunt

Batu - *Adabuma Hunter*
Sanisi - *Adabuma Wise One*
Jenkins - *V.I. Earthling*
KC - *V.I. Earthling*

San Francisco

Jacqueline - *KC's Friend*
Triton - *Jacqueline's Friend*
Rabiu - *KC's Friend*

Leaving Earth

Krella - *Jaylex Ortan*
Zanatu - *Jaylex, Ortan Jump Questioner/KC's Evaluator*
Volgarth - *Jaylex, Venuvian Jump Questioner*
Zareg - *Jaylex, KC's Ortan Evaluator*
Morbred - *KC and Krella's Friend*
Jubley - *Morbred's Mate, KC and Krella's Friend*

Dome City

Samtatu - *Travelers' Guide*
Tagu - *Dome City Helper*
Joe - *Pediglide Converter*
Javita - *Joe's Mate*
M'ase - *Tambuki Sign Watcher*
BB - *KC's and Krella's Son*
Jov - *BB's Friend*
Gogandu - *BB's Companion*
Ogba - *BB's Elder Teacher*
Plorv - *Anti-Venuvian V.I.*

Proxsina

Miltoc - *Erlonian Stargazer*
Rima, TaRupi, and Kolord - *Zoltoc V.I.s on Erlon*

Libchic

Libchic - *Ortan BioDroid*
Treyak - *Northern Raider Herder*
Valiya - *Erlon Scran*
Losstuv and Mossyek - *Nortern Raider Herders*
Karlin - *Northern Raider Hunter*

Spaceship Lumkof

Welvek - *Third Family Ortan, Lumkof Navigator*
Stuven - *Third Family Ortan, Lumkof Navigator*

Valis

Luku - *Onkor, Elder Hilltop Sky Watcher*

Orta

Loosk - *Fluid Technician*
Moric - *Loosk's Assistant*
Primis - *Third Family Fluid Specialist*
Zremus - *Primis's Friends*

COMMUNICATION STATION 4

It was the 207th day of the 82nd year on the Titan settlement. Titan, Saturn's largest moon, was the site of a multi-national mining operation. Jed Leos was starting his shift in the Transportation Tracking and Communication Center. Jed was about to start the routine systems check procedure, but he hesitated. Instead, he activated the in-house communication system and buzzed Sergio's living quarters.

"Sergio, are you available?" Jed tried to sound as serious as possible. "Serg, please—this is Jed."

"No, I am not available," an irritated voice responded.

"Serg, it will only take a few minutes. I just want to show you something." No answer. "Serg?"

"Do you have an order from management?"

"No."

"Will the company pay me for the extra time I spend in that crap hole?"

"Serg, I just want to ask you about some weird signal I keep getting from Station 4." Station 4 was the communication satellite that Titan used to track ships traveling between Earth and Titan. Station 4 had to clear every piece of traffic entering or leaving Titan's airspace.

"Okay, if you really want me to leave the warmth and comfort of my craphouse-sized cubicle, I'll be right over."

"Thanks, Serg."

Sergio was a top-notch technician. He knew every piece of equipment in the center, inside and out. And, even though he had never seen it up close, he knew everything about Station 4. He was never at a loss for words when it came to belittling what he thought was an inferior and incorrectly used device. What Sergio really wanted to do was to work at the Data Collection and Processing Center. It dealt with the information gathered from all the planets in the solar system. It also processed information gathered from scanning deep space. Sergio knew that, someday, someone would find something new out there in the universe. He did not know what or when; he just wanted to be there. Sergio constantly complained about working with station 4.

"That pea-sized satellite is as old as dirt. When are they going to send some modern equipment?"

Sergio stepped into the control room. His tall, thin figure contrasted with Jed's short, stout one. Sergio's straight, pure white hair hung unkempt from his balding head to his shoulders. In contrast, Jed had short, black, tightly curled hair, which he kept well trimmed. Despite the physical differences between Jed and Sergio, they had a good relationship. They were not friends. No one at the center could be called Sergio's "friend." His acid remarks and blatantly irreverent responses were more than most could handle. Moreover, Sergio's unmasked contempt for under-qualified "short-timers" was downright alienating. "Those slobber lips need to be on Earth where they're harmless," Sergio would say. No one knew why Sergio called these managers "slobber lips." They were the ones who were near retirement on Earth and had enough pull to get transferred to Titan so they could say they had worked on the distant moon. Neither did Jed know why Sergio treated him with such deference. No other tech in the communication center could talk or even bribe Sergio out of his living quarters. Jed knew that, when he mentioned "weird signals," Sergio's interest would be piqued. In addition, Sergio knew that Jed would not call him in for some stupid question.

Jed certainly had not made the decision to call Sergio into the communication center quickly. Jed was a good tech but not great like Sergio. For the past two months, Jed had looked, listened, and studied, but he could find no explanation for what was happening. He knew that, if anyone could understand what Station 4 was doing, it would be Sergio.

"This place smells like fungus farts," said Sergio, now standing in the Communication Center. "Show me this rat-shit signal that's so weird!"

"Why hello, Sergio, how are you?" asked Jed.

Sergio just grunted.

"Serg, this is really weird. It only happens on this shift, and I can only get it to happen once. It's right at the end of the systems check procedure. At first, I hardly noticed it, but it kept getting stronger. I measured it two months ago and again yesterday. There has been a distinct increase in intensity. I also looked at it and recorded it on the scope. It's obviously at an extremely high frequency. It took me days to slow it down enough to be legible. I did a compare, and the signals are the same. I don't know if Station 4 has a glitch or what. I told Central about it, and they said it was some kind of outside interference."

"Those turds don't know the difference between a malfunction and a failure," said Sergio. "Show me this crap."

Jed put his finger on a flashing red button. For a second, doubt entered his thoughts. What if this was some simple malfunction and Sergio just gave him a cold look and said, "Oh that, it's nothing." No, Jed knew it was something coming from Station 4 that should not be. He pushed the button. Sergio sat down with his legs crossed and his feet on a desk. Jed stood near the audio output, a frown on his face, as if listening intently. The audio system emitted a series of beeps. After the last beep, there were three short blasts of what sounded like static, then another beep.

"Did you hear those three blasts?" asked Jed. "What the hell was that? It's not part of the programmed response, but there are no response errors generated. I've been looking closely at those signals for several months. Over the past three months, their energy level has increased 23 to 24 percent. The frequency is higher than anything I have ever seen. I tried slowing it down, but nothing here is fast enough to trace it. Sixty teras is as fast as I can punch the counters. That catches the carrier signal, but my guess is that's less than one percent of the info signal."

"Data Collection has units that are fast enough," Sergio said in a matter-of-fact tone.

"Does Station 4 have the capability to generate that high of a frequency?" asked Jed.

Sergio looked up and slowly rubbed his thumb across his fingertips. He was deep in thought.

"It could, but those slobber lips would have to stick some special units in that pea ball. I can't see why they would want to do that. If someone wanted to go to a lot of trouble, they could probably load some high frequency crap into Station 4's program. But why waste all that time on that piece-of-crap station?"

"One other thing—and this really throws me—the signals happen only on the morning shift.

"*Yeah, right. Slobber lips' morning,*" mumbled Sergio sarcastically.

Sergio had never liked the idea that this whole sector was on the same hour, day, month, and year as was corporate headquarters on Earth. Officially, local time did not exist.

"I've been checking other shifts, but nothing," said Jed.

Sergio looked straight at Jed and said, "I don't see how that could be."

Jed was now beginning to feel the excitement of finding something. "I'd like to look into this some more, but where do I go from here?"

"I don't know," said Sergio. Then he got up abruptly and left without another word. For the next few days, Sergio spent many extra hours in the center, especially on the morning shift. No one bothered to question his presence. Sergio was always working on some pet project. If anyone did ask him what he was doing, he would answer "Nothin' much," or "Just fiddle fartin'."

Jed watched the signals with renewed interest. There was not much more he could do besides calculate the change in the energy level.

Sergio just looked at the signals without saying a word. Then one day, he said to Jed, "Next morning shift, I'm going to try and record that high-frequency bull crap."

"I didn't think we had anything fast enough to do that," said Jed, knowing that Sergio must have done something to get around that.

"I thought I'd try something," said Sergio.

And, for the next 30 minutes, he explained what he had planned to do. Jed understood very little of what Sergio said. Something about referencing the high-frequency signals to quark vibrations.

"When did you learn that quark vibration technique?" Jed asked, not because he understood but rather to let Sergio know he was listening.

"Oh, I've never done it before, so it might not work the first time."

It did not work the first time, or the second time, or the third time. Sergio tried 17 times to capture the signals. Every time the capture failed, he would mutter a few choice expletives and begin doing more calculations.

Then, on the 18th try, "Got ya!" said Sergio with a sense of triumph, slapping his hands and laughing the way only Sergio could laugh.

"Did you get it?" asked Jed.

"I think so," said Sergio.

"What now?" asked Jed.

"I'll take it to Data Collection and see if Sulof can figure it out."

Sulof felt like he was getting old. Had he come to Titan to die? It was Corporate that had decided he was needed on Titan. It was his extraordinary genius that sent him to the Saturn moon. Sulof had the ability to cull garbage from the multitude of data collected. From shift to shift, there were billions of bits of information per second coming from the outer reaches of space. Sulof had to dig through this information and pick out the pieces that were important. It was not Sulof himself but his use of data-gathering equipment. The Data Collection and Processing Center daily recorded trillions of bits of data from outer space, which was only a fraction of the emanations from the cosmos.

Sulof sat down in front of his morning meal with a sigh that could have been fatigue or could have been boredom. It was both. Sulof had been on Titan for 21 years. When he came to Titan, the Data Collection and Processing Center—then called Space Scan—was a small dome 60 kilometers from Freedom Sector Central and accessible only by some kind of land craft like a lunar rover. Sulof had fought with the company for two years. He argued that it was necessary to have the scanners some distance from Central, but it was not necessary to have the control station remote from Central. He finally convinced them that the cost of new equipment would be covered by the savings they would reap from not having to support a remote station. When it came to increasing the number of land scanners and deploying three satellite scanners, the company ignored his arguments. The company received government compensation for the Space Scan project and the Data Collection and Processing Center project, so most of the costs were covered. The company felt that what little was not covered by the government was money well spent toward image building.

"Why does the universe have to be so meticulously scrutinized?" company management constantly asked Sulof.

"'Out there,'" Sulof would reply, "can not only tell us about the past, it can tell us about the future! The future!" No one seemed to be that interested in the future or the past.

In 2202, things changed. Earth became re-fascinated with space outside of its solar system. The government established what amounted to a reward for new information about what's out there. The company gave Sulof his satellites, land scanners, and the data processing equipment he needed.

He began in earnest to collect information coming from the unending ocean of the outer reaches. Collection was only half the job. The information had to be sorted, categorized, examined, compared, and saved. Nothing was discarded. Sulof had his data processing equipment to do most of those jobs. Even with all his equipment and all his assistants, he knew that all his detectors could capture only a small fragment of the out-there stuff. "We are a grain of sand in the universe trying to reach out and grab a sea of information," he would say.

Sulof toyed with his meal, wondering if he was just wasting his time. In all the years he had spent gazing at the beyond, he had found nothing, at least nothing he felt was of any importance. There had been a few things here and there, enough to get some support from the government and keep the company happy, but nothing exciting, and nothing new. "Some day we must find something," he muttered to himself.

"Sulof," announced an assistant. "Sergio from TTCC to see you."

Sulof brightened despite himself. Sergio bothered him. He was disorderly, always engaging in projects that had no destination. He wanted to know how everything worked and why things were done a certain way. His questioning stimulated Sulof to think and study and calculate and dig. Sulof had to admire Sergio's wonderful mind. He knew that

Sergio wanted to work in his department, and probably, someday, he would. Not only because he wanted to study space but also because he needed the use of Sulof's data processing equipment. Sulof knew that the company was wasting Sergio's abilities at TTCC. Despite the man's unruly and unconventional procedures, Sulof looked forward to the day when the company forced them to work together. Sergio sauntered into Sulof's sparse quarters. Even though Sulof had lost interest in his meal, he pretended to be eating. Looking up in feigned disinterest, Sulof eyed Sergio. "Yes?" Sulof asked, with hidden anticipation.

"I have some high-frequency data I want you to look at," said Sergio.

Was that it, just some high frequency data? Sulof felt a letdown. He was almost angry. "You have equipment that can analyze signals. What do you want from me?"

"These signals are too fast. I had to use the quark reference procedure just to properly record them."

"That referencing procedure is outdated and practically useless," said Sulof antagonistically.

"With your equipment, it isn't," said Sergio, ignoring Sulof's nastiness. "And I don't have your equipment."

Sulof's attention was beginning to rise. Signals that fast did not occur naturally, and he knew of no equipment that generated such signals.

"Where did these signals come from?" Sulof asked.

"Our com sat," answered Sergio.

Again, Sulof felt a rush of disappointment. "Your communication satellite?" asked Sulof incredulously. "Someone must be playing a joke. Well, I don't have a lot of time to spend on your pet projects." Sulof pushed his meal away and stood. "Let's go have a look at your com sat signals."

The Data Collection and Processing Center was large—even by Earth standards. It was packed with equipment. There was only one dimly lit aisle between the banks of equipment, and it was not wide enough for two people to walk side by side. From the left and right of the main aisle were even smaller aisles leading to areas where Sulof's assistants worked. The equipment modules rose five meters with little evidence that they were anything more than big, square, neatly stacked boxes. An occasional green or red LED would flash, indicating that some process was taking place, but, other than that, there was little to show what, if anything, was happening. The main aisle ended in a circular area 15 meters in diameter. There was one mobile chair in front of a semicircular control console, some writing boards on the desk area of the console, and one writing tool. There was nothing else to show that Sulof ever used the area. The consoles were dead silent. This is where Sulof had spent most of his life. Sulof sat.

"I am sorry, but I don't have a chair to offer you," said Sulof.

Sergio grunted. Sulof touched a few spots on the console, and a display monitor came to life. He activated a few more terminals, and then he turned to Sergio.

"Okay, let's have the data packet."

Sergio produced a black, shiny disk. Sulof placed the disk in a recessed area on the top of the console.

"First, we will make a frequency count to see how fast this data really is," said Sulof.

Sulof touched a few more spots on the console. A small light flashed on—the only indication that anything had happened. Seconds later, the light flashed off.

"Doesn't seem to be much here," Sulof remarked.

"Oh, there's a lot there," said Sergio. "It's just fast."

Another monitor came to life, and Sulof's chair glided around the console, stopping in front of it. One look and Sulof's bushy eyebrows shot up, his eyes widened, and his jaw dropped. He turned to Sergio, who grinned.

"What is this?" Sulof asked.

"I don't know. You tell me."

Narrowing his eyes, Sulof said, "Glory Sector, New Life Sector, and here are the only places on this moon that could produce frequencies anywhere near this fast. And you say they came from your com sat?"

Sergio shrugged. "That is correct. Jed says they have been slowly increasing in amplitude since he noticed them."

Sulof's demeanor changed. He moved with urgency. "And you recorded this with your quark reference procedure?"

"Correct again," said Sergio. "And, if you turn me loose on your equipment, we could speed up those monsters fast enough to decipher this signal."

Without a second thought, Sulof said, "I will see that the company transfers you immediately. I think you have something here."

"I know we do," Sergio replied confidently.

◆

Jed and his two friends, Lota and Maira, sat in Jed's quarters musing over the events of the past few days. Lota was a huge, unruly man with locks of unkempt, peppered gray hair strewn about his rounded head. He was in the habit of staring at his Associates with his gray-green eyes—a hard steady gaze that some found unnerving. He was a powerful man, not only in his physical build but also in his approach to life. He was honest and straightforward and never minced his words.

Jed asked Lota, "So what do you think is going on?"

"I think Sergio and Sulof are a couple of brains playing with their complicated toys," Lota said.

Lota was a builder and designer, constantly trying to make more efficient use of the limited spaces available on Titan. When he worked, he worked incessantly, forgoing any off time until a task was completed. The results were always remarkable. In the few years he had worked in Freedom Sector, he had transformed a cramped, unorganized area into a relatively comfortable and efficient living and working space. On his off time, he usually traveled to other sectors and spent his time walking wherever he could. At times, he imbibed heavily in whatever intoxicants were available. It seemed that people he encountered—especially women—either admired or detested him. His friends were close, his non-friends antagonistic. There were many of both.

Maira was a short, dark, compact woman. She was on the small side, but she was definitely not petite. The form fitting outfits she was fond of wearing revealed her excellent physical condition. She was a strong, dedicated woman, but, having been on Titan for less than one year, she was still adjusting to the newness of things. Maira dealt with the necessities of Titan. Food, air, and water were her specialties. She made sure that waste was almost nil and that most everything was recycled. Food, an object of perennial complaints, consisted mainly of some combination of the 153 varieties of Titan-grown mushrooms. The cooks flavored the fungi with everything from local minerals to genetically designed bacteria. Vegetables were of the type that thrived on low energy light.

Purifying air was relatively easy. Keeping the use of that purified air to an absolute minimum required meticulous management. A person sleeping required much less air than someone who was rearranging wall panels. Maira knew what every warm body in the sector was doing and when. She was also in charge of water. There were three types of water: drinkable, useable, and waste. Waste was near nil.

"Who knows what Serg might be up to?" said Maira. "But, as we know, Sulof is nothing but business when it comes to his computers."

Jed fingered one of his many precious rocks as he listened. He had a rock specimen collection as complete as most geologists on Titan, and he shined his own rocks. His room had an abundance of plants—Maira's idea to produce more oxygen. Agricultural scientists had genetically engineered plants to produce maximum foliage in minimum light. Maira was working on the production of edible plants for living quarters.

After his guests left, Jed mused over the events of the last few days. That signal must mean something or Sulof would not have shown up. Sergio, without explanation, had asked Jed to keep quiet about the signals. Jed was glad to comply. Even though he had "discovered" the signals, he was not anxious to admit that he had no idea what the significance of the signals was. He just knew they were getting louder.

"There is definitely an increase in amplitude," Sulof said, looking at one of the monitors.

"Jed coulda' told you that," Sergio answered quickly. "What I want to know is what-in-the-name-of-god's gray rock do they mean? Those are not just random bursts. I want to slow them down and feed them to your units so they can tell us what this stuff is."

"Don't get ahead of yourself Sergio," said Sulof. "My interest is in finding out how these signals got into your com sat and maybe, more important, who put them there?"

"Then why don't you get your slobber lips to investigate?" snapped Sergio.

Sulof ignored the question. "Today I will talk with Melf at corporate," said Sulof. "I am sure he will let me examine the instruction and maintenance records. A com sat will not send a signal unless instructed to do so. I am sure that, upon close inspection, we will discover exactly what those signals mean."

◆

Jed decided to do a little investigation on his own. His geologist friend Karlin, who was the main contributor to his rock collection, kept company with an in-orbit satellite repair flyer named Tamtira, a friendly, easy-going woman who enjoyed talking about her work. Jed decided to use his off time to visit Karlin, and perhaps have a conversation with Tamtira. Although Sulof and Sergio had hardly spoken a word to Jed, he had overheard many of their conversations concerning the strange signals. He knew that one theory was that someone had planted a device inside the satellite and it was transmitting the signals. They both had strong reservations about that idea but Jed wanted to check for himself. When Jed contacted Karlin, he was delighted to hear that Karlin would be at Tamtira's quarters. Jed gladly accepted the invitation to stop by.

The flyer's quarters were more spacious than Jed's and Karlin's combined. Unlike Jed's one cubicle with attached shower, Tamtira enjoyed a four-cubicle-size open room, one-cubicle sleeping quarters and a half-cubicle bathing area. The only real piece of furniture was a hanging chair. There were custom-designed rocks of various shapes—Jed's work—which served as seats, tables, and counters.

Tamtira's flowing gown clung to the front of her body as she moved through the open room and trailed her in a wake-like fashion. Her almond eyes smiled at Jed. "Would you like something to drink?" she asked.

"Water would be wonderful," Jed said enthusiastically.

"How about something stronger?" teased Tamtira.

"We know how you love that Raingale," threw in Karlin.

Jed did love that particular beer. Water use above your daily allowance was considered a luxury, but intoxicants, even those made on Titan, were costly. Jed overcame his trepidation. "I will of course be forever in your debt," he said, somewhat shyly.

"Great!" said Tamtira. "I'm thinking about getting another rock. You can work your magic on it."

"It's a deal!" said Jed.

Tamtira pulled three containers from a vat containing useable water. Carefully she wiped the containers dry, removed the seals, and placed one container in front of Jed and one by Karlin. Jed put the container to his lips, took a large swig, and leaned his head back with his eyes closed, savoring the liquid with obvious satisfaction. Karlin and Tamtira followed suit.

"So, Tam, how are your efforts with satellites going?" asked Jed.

"Just fine," replied Tamtira.

"I have a new rock for you, Jed," injected Karlin. "We hit a vein yesterday. It hasn't been analyzed yet, but it is definitely an igneous type. I think it's mostly a combination of minerals, but it has a yellow tint that I can't explain."

"Wonderful, wonderful," said Jed, not exhibiting the usual enthusiasm Karlin expected.

"Are you interested?" asked Karlin.

"Yes, of course," answered Jed. "But first I would like to ask Tamtira about her work with satellites."

"Fire away," said Tamtira, always happy to discuss her activities.

"I guess what I really want to know is if it would be possible to attach or insert any device in a com sat without your knowledge?"

"Want me to blow up your com sat so you can have more off time?" replied Tamtira jokingly.

Jed smiled. "Well, just between us, we've been getting some signals from our Communication Satellite 4 that we can't explain. Either the instructions have been modified or something has been placed in or on the satellite."

"Couldn't these signals just be transferred through your com sat?" asked Karlin.

"It would be highly unlikely," said Jed. "If the signals were beamed in, other receivers would pick them up. No, there seems to be no other way our com sat could pick up those signals."

Tamtira frowned. "Well, I don't know about changing the instructions. Those can be manipulated from Titan. But a device, I don't think so. Not in this sector. Only Jerio and I fly missions to the satellites."

"This is only a hypothetical question," said Jed, picking his words carefully. "Could you place a device in or on a satellite or somehow change some instructions manually?"

Tamtira raised an eyebrow. "I have only the slightest idea of how satellite instructions work and practically no idea how to manipulate them," said Tamtira. "Even on my own ship I need to be prompted through the simplest changes."

Jed persisted, "Could you replace a module or add a unit to a satellite?"

Tamtira stiffened and glared at Jed. "Do you think I've been playing with your communication satellite?"

"Oh, Tam, no. I know you better than that." Jed smiled. "I just want to know if it can be done. Besides, if you get nailed, who would supply me with Raingale?"

Tamtira relaxed. "Okay. I don't see how it could be done. Someone would need specialized tools and equipment. They would have to store everything in the bay, pull the correct module from the satellite and exit the cockpit to do the work. I have retrieved and exchanged modules before, but most of the time I just dock the ship. The ground takes care of everything else. Sometimes I retrieve a module, work on it, and replace it, but I have to study identification procedure for days, and someone on the ground prompts me through every step."

"But, if you had the equipment," Jed said eagerly, "and knew how to use it, could a module be changed?"

"I suppose so," Tamtira said slowly.

"Could someone plant a device in a module while it was in the bay?" Jed could feel the intoxicant spreading through his body. He knew he had better finish his questions before his mind drifted away. "Could you do it without the company knowing?"

"The company knows everything," giggled Tamtira. The potent liquid was starting to affect her. "No way could you get equipment in the bay without the company knowing," she continued. "A device would have to be very light to get by weight control. The land crew takes the ship's exact weight before launch so they can calculate trajectories. A slight variation in weight would surely be questioned."

"So the company would have to know," said Jed.

"The company knows everything," injected Karlin.

"Could the company take a ship without you knowing?" asked Jed.

"Maybe without me knowing," answered Tamtira, "but the dock crew would have to know, and re-entry and deceleration would have to know. I cannot imagine anything like that being kept quiet. Besides, if they wanted to make any changes, they could bring back a module, do whatever they wanted, and then send it back."

"Do you know if our com sat has pulled any modules lately?"

"No, but I can find out."

◆

Sulof sat in front of a large desk in a spacious, well-lit, fourth-level room. Plants draped the walls and hung from the low ceiling. At the end of the room opposite its entrance, a transparent bubble, large enough to stand in, protruded into the dark, brownish-orange, airless atmosphere of Titan. From his vantage point, Sulof could see points of light radiating from different parts of Freedom Sector. Some might have considered the lights spectacular, but the lifeless dark gray structures presented little to please his eye. To the right of the bubble on top of a sculptured rock was a rectangular tank containing various forms of water life. Sulof watched as fish swam lazily around the tank. What a waste of drinkable water, he thought. Sulof suddenly felt weighted down with fatigue. Everything seemed so pointless. He had spent years of his life on this dead rock. And why? His work seemed meaningless. For the first time in years, Sulof thought about Earth. There were few things there he missed, and he had never planned to return. The entrance of Melf, his longtime friend and Geological Research Director, interrupted his thoughts.

Melf was a tall man. His straight, well-groomed hair framed his dark, square face. His clothes were what Sulof assumed were the latest fashion. They were certainly not the drab gray-green outfits worn by many of Titan's inhabitants. Melf's one-piece suit was white with the vaguest blue tinge and was loose fitting, except at the neck, wrists, and ankles. Sulof had first met Melf at the Space Life Institute on Earth. Sulof liked Melf. If Sulof was a genius in astronomy, Melf was a genius in everything. Melf's structured art, although not outstanding, had won awards. He had mastered piano and delighted Titan audiences with his electric keyboard performances. He had excelled as a long-distance runner and was a chess master. Physics, mathematics, and Earth sciences came easily to him but his true love was geology.

Melf knew all about rocks. At a young age, he had studied most of the available information dealing with the geological formations of Earth, which he called "creation rock." Titan was a natural extension of his intellectual curiosity with new and different mineral combinations and rock formations that were unique to Titan. Of course he studied in depth the geological structures that contained one particular substance—the reason for Earthlings on Titan—the almighty runan. Runan, the mineral that, when added to steel in small amounts, rendered the steel 100 times stronger. Melf was happy to be alive in this time. He was part of the new discoveries and able to take a firsthand look at new rock samples. Of course, if the company felt there was no possibility of hitting a runan strike, work would cease in one area and move to another. Melf was frustrated whenever the company had abruptly shut down an area where he was working. Fortunately, there were so many projects and so much research that Melf did not worry about the infrequent interruptions.

As usual, Melf's face wore a confident and impish smile. "Sulof, wonderful to see you!" Melf extended a warm hand. "Why don't you visit more often?"

"I guess our worlds are so far apart they just don't touch very often," said Sulof shifting uneasily in his chair.

"Well, why have our worlds crossed today?" queried Melf.

"I need to ask a favor of you."

"Anything I can do," Melf replied, beaming with sincerity.

Sulof came right to the point. "I need to look at some records on a com sat over at Serge's place."

"Ah yes, Sergio Laskestes. I've heard about him. He likes to tinker. Great mind but not focused. What's he up to?"

"We're getting some strange noise periodically." Sulof was purposely vague. "We want to see if we can figure it out."

"What's your interest in this noise?" Melf laid stress on "noise."

"There's a high frequency signal I don't understand. I just want to figure it out."

Melf raised his eyebrows, giving Sulof a penetrating look. His face, serious and thoughtful, suddenly brightened. "Of course, I'll tell Conrad to expect you. He is the data control person and should be of help. But you must promise me one thing."

Sulof stiffened. "What would that be?"

"Come to my party."

Jed looked at the information module Tamtira had given him. Fitting easily in his hand, it contained the logs of the two Satellite Maintenance Ships. These two orbital spacecraft routinely checked the satellites assigned to Freedom Sector. Jed toyed with the module, and then slipped it into his jacket pocket. He would have to go to the library to view the logs. Jed decided to wait until they served first meal. The library would be empty. He did not want anybody around while he was studying the logs. Why am I being so secretive? he had asked himself. He did not know why; he just was.

The library was deserted as Jed had hoped. Quickly, he sat in front of a viewer and inserted the information module (or info mod). He had hoped Tamtira would bring him a data pack. With a data pack, he could do a computer search and come up with all the info on the com sat within seconds. With this info mod, he would have to scan all the logs to see if any mention of Communication Satellite 4 came up. He began to scroll the information. Each entry contained date, destination, orbital vehicle assignment, and outcome. Jed focused on destination. He increased the scroll speed. Satellite this, orbital that… Communication Satellite 4. Jed stopped the scroll. The date was the same as the first day he had noticed the signal.

Until now, without admitting it even to himself, Jed had known the first day of the signal. His ears were acutely tuned to the sounds of his instruments. One day, before he had noticed the signal, he was going through his preliminary checks with Communication Satellite 4. There was the usual sound of beeps, clicks, and buzzes when, for a second, there was a pause. With the exception of the pause, everything seemed normal. On his next shift, Jed had paid very close attention to the instruments. That was the first day he had seen the signal. Now Jed looked at "assignment" and "outcome" on the monitor. Both were completed with the same code. Jed quickly pulled out his personal memory bank and took a photo of the incomprehensible letters and symbols.

The codes were used to save space, not for secrecy. If Sergio or Sulof could not get them decoded then Jed would visit Tamtira again. One thing was for sure, Jed now had a fix on the day the signals first started.

◆

Sergio did not care when the signals started or even where they came from, he just wanted to find out what they meant. The signals were codes that had to be broken, and Sergio intended to break them. His use of the quark reference method had helped to record those signals, but now he needed Sulof's computers to slow the signals so they could be deciphered.

Sulof had given Sergio the full use of his computers. Sergio had his quark reference machine performing a series of complicated tasks. Essentially, he fed the machine data that the machine sampled at different intervals. The machine then fed data into the computers, again with the smallest possible shift in the time base. The computer combined the samples and then checked to see if there was any pattern. Finding patterns, that was the big problem. The machine saw many patterns, and Sergio accepted or rejected each. He combined, compared or otherwise manipulated the patterns even as new samples were being continually incorporated. If an answer was to be found it would depend on the machine's ability to sample, Sergio's ability to separate garbage from patterns, and luck. Even when an answer was obtained, its validity would be questioned. Sergio was sure he would come up with something, but he knew there would be no way to verify its correctness. There was also the matter of time. Sulof had been even more generous with his equipment than Sergio had hoped. In the past, Sulof had advised Sergio to return to projects that were more productive. It had happened before and Sergio had angrily retreated. This time was different, very different. Sulof had immediately regretted accepting Melf's invitation to his party. He felt uncomfortable around all those important company people. He knew no one. He toyed with the glass of champagne he held with both hands. Anything but local brew was unheard of on Titan, and Sulof was having his second glass of premium wine. It dangled awkwardly from his fingers. The room was enclosed by three-quarters of a geodesic dome. The remaining quarter of the dome was made of a transparent material. The triangles that made up the dome were outlined in an orange brown that blended with the stark atmosphere outside. The view was unmoving and monotonous, but Sulof had to admit that there was a certain rugged beauty about Titan's surface. Saturn setting behind the rock-strewn horizon dominated the western view. Behind Saturn and to the right hung another moon, Enceladus, looking pale next to the giant planet. Melf had no doubt planned the gathering so the guests would be treated to this natural spectacle. Melf had furnished the room with simple but precious Earth furniture. No rock chairs, no rock tables—no rocks. Even the circle of plants growing through the floor in the middle of the room had no rock decorations. About 15 people sat on wooden chairs at a wooden table, lounged on stuffed sofas and chairs, or sat cross-legged on a thickly carpeted floor.

Melf and Sulof were the only two standing. Sulof looked idly at Saturn as it slowly disappeared, while Melf floated from guest to guest, pouring champagne. "More champagne?" Melf asked, beaming at Sulof.

"Why not?" answered Sulof, extending his glass.

"Well, what do you think?"

"Think about what?" asked Sulof, forcing a slight smile.

"The gathering, the view—everything." returned Melf.

"Very impressive," Sulof said heavily, not even feigning enthusiasm.

Melf grinned. "If you need a roommate again, just let me know," said Melf.

Sulof shrugged. "Great idea. I'll start moving my things into your place tomorrow."

"Yeah, you need to move into this dump," said Melf.

The wine and Melf's infectious warmth was starting to have an effect on Sulof.

"Of course, if you need someone to look after your place here, I could really help you out," said Sulof.

"You would do that for me? You're such a pal."

Sulof and Melf both laughed. They hadn't laughed like this since the time they spent at the Institute. It seemed so many years ago.

Sulof was beginning to feel much more at ease. Maybe it had not been such a bad idea to come to Melf's party.

A woman who had been sitting on the floor was now standing next to Melf. She looked straight at Sulof with her dark, hazel eyes. Then she turned to Melf. "Melf, we're having an argument—well, not an argument, a discussion. Daniel and I were wondering. How many lifers came to Titan, and how many people were born here? I think there must be more lifers, because there are so many people here. Daniel says that all those people must be doing more than just looking at each other." She rolled to her tiptoes and then rolled back. She smiled at Sulof with an innocent look on her face as if it were an academic discussion and had nothing to do with what men and women had a habit of doing with each other. "What do you think, Melf?"

Melf, as usual, had the air of an expert. "Well, of the approximately 3600 inhabitants in this sector, 1500 relocated here from other sectors. Currently the net increase of Earthlings in Freedom Sector is 1600. So, that makes about 500 native born. Now, determining how many lifers there are is a much more difficult proposition. Up until 20 years ago, all personnel were required to return to Earth after a four-year tour. Since then, even though we are still required to have return passage, there are no limitations on how long one can stay in any sector. There is a handful, less than 20, who have been here more than 20 years. It really depends on how many years it takes to become a lifer."

"Daniel and I settled on 20 years," she said.

Sulof chuckled. "I guess I became a lifer a year ago, and I didn't even know it," said Sulof.

"So you've been here for 21 years?"

Without waiting for an answer or the end of Melf's discourse, she grabbed Sulof's hand, almost causing him to drop his champagne, and pulled him toward the other guests.

"Oh, Sulof," said Melf, "this is Jodi. Jodi, Sulof." Melf lifted an eyebrow and grinned devilishly.

Jodi stopped, looked Sulof squarely in the face, and said, "It's a pleasure," and gave him a firm kiss on the cheek. She turned and, holding his hand firmly, pulled him toward the others. The rest of the evening was, as Sulof would later describe it, delicious. The champagne had loosened his tongue, and people were truly amazed by his anecdotes of life 21 years ago when Titan was first changing from an outpost to a community.

For the rest of the evening, Sulof and Jodi were together. She leaned against him, touched his arm, and held his hand—anything that required contact. When their eyes met, which they did many times, Sulof could feel himself drawn to her. Her long, slender neck was like a magnet. He wanted to get closer to her, to touch her, to hold her, to…

Jodi and Sulof held hands as they walked down the common hall toward Priority Transportation. Melf's personal vehicle was to carry Sulof to his living area. The vehicle was rumored to be quite luxurious. Earlier, Sulof anticipated zooming down the priority rail in Melf's elegant personal vehicle and, after being dropped off, slowly sauntering into his living area through the priority entrance. Now thoughts of the fancy ride and his impressive entrance were lost. He could only think of the woman next to him. Even though there were only a few hours left before his next shift started, he felt more alive and awake than he had in years.

They stopped in front of the transport entrance. Jodi grabbed Sulof's free hand with hers. She moved close to him and, in a whisper, said, "It's been wonderful."

Sulof impulsively or instinctively released her hands, wrapped his arms around Jodi, and kissed her. The kiss started soft and warm but quickly turned passionate as their bodies pressed and their hands explored. When they stopped, Jodi looked into Sulof's eyes.

"I want you to see my quarters," she whispered.

Sergio paced back and forth in front of the terminal. A metal box, one meter square, sat on the floor. Four cables attached it to terminals on Sulof's computer. It was Sergio's quark reference device. The technology was old but had never been used in any practical way. It was slow, initially inaccurate and, more important, unnecessary; but it was the only known method that could decipher very high frequency signals. It had never gained much recognition. No such signals existed naturally or in the man-made realm—at least until now. Sergio impatiently waited for the computer to indicate that it had an answer. It might take minutes, it might take days. Sergio heard footsteps, undoubtedly Sulof's.

Sulof was uncharacteristically late. He entered, looking tired but relaxed and contented. "Anything exciting happening?" asked Sulof. His question lacked its usual negative tone.

"Just waitin' for your computers to cough up an answer."

"How long will it take?"

"Oh, I don't know," Sergio said nonchalantly. "An hour, give or take a few days. Maybe never, if the data is incomplete."

"Incomplete? I thought you captured the signal."

"I think I did." There were a few moments of silence.

"Is this the quark reference device you rigged up?" asked Sulof gesturing toward the box on the floor.

"Yep." More silence.

Sulof was thinking about the strange signals. It seemed as if he were looking clearly at the situation for the first time. Even if the signal was decoded, the Communication Satellite was incapable of producing it. For that matter, as far as Sulof knew, there was no place on Titan capable of producing such high frequency signals. Then where did the signals originate? A tone indicating an incoming call broke the silence. It was Jed.

"Sulof? Sergio?" It was Jed's voice.

"Yes," said Sulof calmly.

"I got the data on the com sat." Jed sounded out of breath. "There was an inspection the day before the signals started. A friend of mine, Tamtira, got me the data but everything is in code—the problem, the solution, everything. I was hoping you could help me."

"Is there a reference code?" asked Sulof.

"Ah… " Jed paused. "Oh yes, Tam said when she wanted to look for particular data, she used the date followed by an eight-digit code… Are you ready?"

"Ready," said Sulof.

"One, two, one, six, four, three, C Clark, zero. There's code here for initialization, action, and outcome. Tam told me that this code is for the important stuff, everything else is routine. Something did happen to the com sat. You want me to run this stuff over after my shift?"

"Let me see what I can do with the reference."

Sulof remembered that Melf had promised to help him get anything he needed. He thought about the past night. He owed Melf. Last night was one of the most special times in his life. Nonetheless, he immediately called up Melf.

"Is that you, Sulof? You dog! Jodi really attached herself to you yesterday."

Sulof smiled with a furtive glance at Sergio. Sergio seemed uninterested.

"What can I do for you?" asked Melf.

"I need some code deciphered on a satellite maintenance record."

"That com sat you spoke of?"

"Yes."

"Do you have a reference number?"

"One, two, one, six, four, three, C, zero."

"No problem. I'll have that info for you in 15 minutes," said Melf.

Sulof wondered if the maintenance record would show a malfunction. A malfunction could not explain the high frequencies. Nothing on Titan could explain the high frequencies. They must be from somewhere else—Earth? Was there something secret going on with high frequencies? It would have to be secret or he surely would have heard about it. If he had not heard of it, undoubtedly Sergio had. But why? It was extremely expensive to generate, receive, and store these frequencies, and, once the signals were received, there was a limit to how fast the data could be reproduced. Although feasible, the use of frequencies this high was extremely impractical. For the first time Sulof had to admit to himself that there was no explanation for the high frequency signals. From the time he first met with Sergio and Jed, he knew he had wanted to believe it. Now he realized he was hoping, wishing, dreaming that it was true. Sulof lifted his eyes and thought about the vast universe outside this insignificant solar system. The signals must be from out there.

Jed rushed into the chamber obviously out of breath. Beads of perspiration were forming on his dark forehead. "Have I missed anything?"

"We're just waiting for Sulof's slobber-lips buddy to give us a call," answered Sergio.

Sergio's blatant derision of Melf irritated Sulof even in his semi-blissful state.

"Someone with fungus-fart breath shouldn't worry about people's lips," said Sulof.

The tension was obviously having an effect. Normally, Sergio would have just laughed and paid no attention to Sulof's remark. Instead, he stiffened. Jed, seeing the anger growing in Sergio's face, was about to say something when a dark monitor came to life: "Ready to transmit visual decode."

Sergio leaped to the console and made a frantic entry. All three men froze when the images appeared. Their eyes stared in disbelief. The intercom light flashed. Without taking his eyes from the screen, Sulof pushed a button.

"I have that info you wanted." It was Melf. "Not very interesting."

"I don't think we will need it," Sulof said, mesmerized.

"What is it?" Melf could sense something in Sulof's voice.

Sulof did not answer. What could he say? The outline on the screen was simple, but its meaning monumental. The high frequency signal had been decoded. There on the monitor, arms held slightly from their sides, fingers spread, were the outlines of a humanoid man, woman, and two children.

SCOUTS

Palto leaned back in his chair. He was happy. He, Marsua, and the Venuvian were to be the first to make contact with the new aliens. Excitement had reached a fevered pitch on the small scout ship two days ago. A transmission from a moon the aliens called Titan had confirmed that the aliens had indeed deciphered the Venuvian signal.

The moon, Titan, had transmitted a very quiet news release: "Unusual signals are being received by a Titan communication satellite, origins unknown. The signals indicate that they were transmitted by an intelligent life form. These signals are currently being investigated by the International Space Confederation."

Marsua had been skeptical about the aliens' ability to do anything with the Venuvian signals.

"Although they are a clever little people, all indications are that they lack sufficient technology to receive or decipher the signals," she had said.

"What do you mean '*little people*'? asked Palto. "It's the little people who do all the best work around here." He smiled.

Compared to Marsua and the Venuvian, Palto was short. Palto and those from Muga, his home planet, were all the height of the average new alien. Palto did not mind the occasional ribbing he took about his size.

"Well, the '*little people*' seem to have the technology to read the signals after all," Palto said, mocking Marsua. "It seems they are even organizing a search team to try and locate the origins of the signal."

"More like a lynch mob," said Marsua. "Some of their ships are armed with weapons, but I doubt if the little brutes can make it outside their own solar system. They remind me of your oversized planet before the Venuvians arrived."

"Yes, they are a bit like us—clever, hard-working, and very good-looking!" said Palto.

"You Mugans think anything vaguely humanoid is good-looking," said Marsua.

"If you mean we don't turn up our noses at anything that isn't tall and skinny, then you're right," said Palto.

"Ha!" said Marsua. There were a few moments of silence. Both Palto and Marsua were contemplating what would happen next.

"What if the Earth people do decide to attack us?" said Palto reflectively.

"The Elders have given strict orders to avoid any conflict with the aliens," said Marsua. "Besides, we have the protective shield, and nothing they have can come close to our speed and mobility."

"The Earthlings have nuclear fusion devices that are powerful enough to breech our protective devices." It was the Venuvian, the third member of the crew. He seldom spoke.

Palto and Marsua both froze. They watched the Venuvian, wondering if he would speak again. He did not. He just stared through the observation port as he had the entire time since leaving the mother ship.

Little was known about the Venuvians. They rarely spoke. No one had ever seen one sleep or eat. Their origin was a mystery. They would arrive in a solar system, establish contact with intelligent beings if any existed, establish a series of worldwide academies, and construct more mother ships. The original mother ship would remain in the solar system. As each new mother ship was completed, it headed for another solar system to continue the process. Most star systems had no higher life forms, but, in most instances, the Venuvians were able to create at least one ecosystem capable of supporting life. Venuvians transformed lifeless planets, moons and even large asteroids into ecosystems with plant and animal life. This process took under 200 years. Venuvians' knowledge seemed to be limitless. They established information and training centers throughout the star system at Venuvian academies. Extensive data on everything from agriculture to interplanetary travel was available.

Life with the Venuvians was very livable. Two areas of Venuvian mastery were more mysterious than even the Venuvians: travel and communication. When the construction of a mother ship was completed, and 10,000 adventurers were secure, the craft would set out for another star system. It accelerated for 20 months. As it approached the speed of light, a collision with the sun's forces seemed imminent. Just when the ship's situation seemed untenable, it vanished. Within 24 hours, Earth had established communication with a star system many light years away. Venuvian Space Travelers, also known as Travelers, reported that there was a slight feeling of movement and an indeterminate period of conscious darkness—then they were in a different star system. When a spacecraft traveled from one system to another system—referred to by everyone as a "jump"—some Travelers reported that they had visions. Occasionally, a Traveler suffered from mental problems after the "jump." Information from systems light years away was available on a daily basis. Not only were videos and coded data available, personal messages arrived from vast areas of the galaxy on a regular basis.

In 2.5 Earth cycles, the scout ship planned to become detectable to the new aliens. History had shown that contact with new people was usually peaceful, but occasionally aliens met scout ships with hostility. Palto and Marsua spent most of their time on the scout ship absorbing the data that they collected as they sped toward the new system. They analyzed cultures, geography, and languages—anything broadcast from inhabited areas. Since the Earthlings transmitted a huge amount of information about Earth via airways, they knew a great deal about this blue planet. Palto had learned the languages, cultures, and history of 16 groups. Marsua had studied another 16. The official language of Titan was Jaral, the world language on Earth, but hundreds of languages were spoken on the moon. Palto and Marsua were ready for the first encounter with Earthlings.

THE HUNT

Batu gazed into the fire. He felt Dream Smoke starting to take its affect. His whole body was falling under the spell of the powerful vapor. Light was coming into Our Place. Soon, Sun would appear again on the outside of Our Place and begin to float into Sky. Now the sounds were few. The night ones had fallen silent, and the morning ones were awake but still quiet. Soon the winged ones would begin to tell their story. Aguagus would squawk and talk of going to Big River to dive for the swimming ones. Hatua would let out his long cry as he swooped from tree to tree searching for small ones to eat. When the Magutes find their first nest of Begeeli bugs, the Magutes would chatter like excited women. Soon Our Place would be awakening to the sounds of another day, but now it was quiet.

Batu's brother, Blegwa, nudged him. Batu's gaze moved to the pipe in Blegwa's hand, the pipe with Dream Smoke. Batu took the pipe from Blegwa, slowly put it to his lips, and inhaled deeply. He would soon be ready for the Big Hunt. He would not be hunting Buru or Makira or Latrumba for their meat. He would not be hunting Mirika, a powerful and crafty cat. Possession of Mirika skulls gave the Hunter great powers. Batu already wore Mirika's teeth around his neck and had three of Mirika's skulls on his waist. Some excellent Hunters had one or two Mirika skulls, but most had none. Batu, with three skulls, was hailed by Story Tellers as one of Our Place's greatest Hunters.

Today he was preparing for the greatest hunt of his life—not for meat, not for skulls, but for the Invader who had been trespassing on Our Place. Batu knew that, if he and his brothers could capture the Invader, its spirit would bring great power to Our Place. The wise one, Sanisi, stood and began the Dance of Grugru—Grugru the worm. Grugru would hide under the leaves of Kintura and become invisible to its prey. She would then wait for some unsuspecting small one to wander into her trap. Grugru was very patient. She would wait and wait and wait; sometimes she would wait from Moon to Moon, not moving, not eating… waiting.

The wise one fell to his knees, and then he laid face down on the ground. He began to undulate, mimicking Grugru. He moved around the fire, half crawling and half moving like a worm. Periodically his painted face would stare across the fire into the eyes of one of the Hunters. Then Sanisi began to chant. His words told the story of the first Hunter to feel the presence of the Invader. Mataku, who had walked with Batu's grandfather, had been many days with Dream Smoke. He became one with Grugru, crawled to Kintura and covered himself with her leaves. He lay still beneath the leaves of Kintura for many days. Then one night, after Sun had left Our Place, Mataku felt the presence of the Invader.

"Invader," said Sanisi, "can see at night like a cat and can hear like Blind Flyer. He leaves no scent, can see through trees, and lives in Big River. He is very clumsy, his feet step heavily on the paths. However, he cannot see through the leaves of Kintura."

Then Sanisi said that, to capture the Invader, the Hunters must be like Grugru. They must crawl like a worm, bury themselves under the leaves of Kintura and lie in wait for many days without eat or drink. They must not move, not even their lips or eyelids. Even breathing must come close to stopping. Like Grugru, who waits for his prey to come near and then sinks his poisonous stinger into the unsuspecting victim, Hunters must come to life and immediately pursue the Invader with the passion of a young Hunter on his first Chase.

Batu became aware of Sanisi gazing at him across the smoldering fire. The wise one cocked his head to one side, and he stared at Batu with steady, piercing eyes. A band of white circled each one of Sanisi's eyes. Red bordered Sanisi's black stained teeth from under his nose to halfway between his lower lip and his chin. His bare torso and chest had six black stripes on either side. His arms and legs were painted black.

Sanisi was Grugru. The wise one abruptly removed his trance-inducing gaze from Batu and again did the Dance of Grugru.

Sanisi began to chant the praises of Hunters. "They will bring great power to the village," he declared. "The Invader, who violates Our Place, will be captured. The great Hunters of Our Place will lay in wait like Grugru until the clumsy-footed Invader comes near. Then a Hunter will leap from his hiding place beneath Kintura's leaves and pierce the Invader's scale-like skin with a dart tipped with the body-numbing Anuu juice."

Sanisi alternated between drawing one of the Hunters into a trance with his hypnotic eyes, chanting praises of the Hunters and crawling on the ground like the Grugru. The seven Hunters could feel themselves changing into Grugru. Batu bent to his right and put the palms of his hands flat on the ground. He rolled to his side and then, with his hands in front of him, he moved to his stomach and began crawling like Grugru. One by one the other Hunters followed suit until they were all mimicking Sanisi's Grugru Dance. Batu, the leader, stopped at River Path. He knew that the Invader lived in Big River. The Invader would come from that direction—but when and where? Batu began crawling down River Path. Periodically he would stop, raise himself up and scan the horizon. Each of the Hunters, in his time, would repeat this action. Sanisi was the last to leave the campfire. He was no longer crawling. Instead, he ran low to the ground, monkey style—legs bent, back bent, hands on the ground. He approached each of the Hunters and put his head close to theirs. He spoke softly to each Hunter, as if telling a secret. Then he slipped something into each one's hand. Batu was last.

"Batu, you are the great Hunter," said Sanisi "You have Makira bones in your hair and three Makira skulls tied to your belt. This is your hunt. You are Grugru, quiet and patient while you wait, quick and powerful when you attack." Sanisi put Life Seed into Batu's hand. "When you hear the clumsy-footed Invader and rise up to capture him, eat Life Seed immediately. It will give you great strength."

Batu took Life Seed in his hand and continued to crawl. First Light was beginning to spill into Sky. Batu was scanning the horizon when he saw, to his left and many steps from River Path, an opening between two giant Bakuyus. Some force drew him toward the opening between the trees. He knew that someone coming from Big River who wanted to stay off River Path might pass that way. He knew that he must go in that direction to find his spot. Some Hunters had already left River Path to look for their spot while others continued. Soon all Hunters would be in various spots between Big River and Home Circle… waiting.

The thick brush and coarse grass prevented Batu from crawling on his stomach, but he kept low as he moved, crouching and using his hands. He passed through the giant Bakuyus. He could smell Big River. Then he saw Kintura. Batu knew that was his spot. When he reached Kintura, he began digging away layers of leaves. Although the leaves on top were dry, he continued digging until they became moist and decomposed. When he had dug out an area large enough for him to lie, he gathered dry leaves from around Kintura and piled them around his spot. Batu lay down on his back, and began to move his arms from side to side causing Kintura's dry leaves to cover him. When Batu had covered himself with leaves, he became very still. He relaxed and let Dream Smoke take him. His breathing slowed to imperceptibility. Then Batu waited.

V.I. Charles Jenkins sat in the submerged, two-person, underwater craft. KC and Jenkins were both V.I.s. The only qualification for becoming a V.I., or Venuvian Integrate—besides the dreaded Monthly Full Body Inventory, otherwise known as Monthly—was to hold a Venuvian position. KC was officially an Advanced V.I. To become an Advanced V.I., in addition to taking the Monthlies, one had to complete a 4-year course at a Venuvian Academy and pass a vigorous physical requirement every year. The great majority of those seeking to enter the space travel program accepted low-level positions just to become a V.I. and qualify for the space travel program. They were looking for adventure or, for some reason, they wanted to escape from Earth.

Jenkins scanned the control panel studying three monitors. One monitor displayed the satellite's view of KC—whatever it could pick up through the thick vegetation. KC, who was the V.I. on the ground, had to find the unit that recorded and transmitted native activity and re-place its power supply. It was difficult to get decent video images, but, with the help of the transmitters in KC's suit and some computer en-hancement, Jenkins could follow the reddish-yellow shape as it moved through the tropical rainforest. The second monitor displayed what KC saw through his night-apparatus. Jenkins could see blotches of color, each a warm-blooded creature that inhabited the forest. Some were noc-turnal and scurried about in search of food or mates. Others had bur-rowed in for the night, waiting for the next rays of the sun. The third monitor showed a 360-degree picture of what surrounded KC. During these retrieval missions, one fear was that a V.I. would get a surprise visit by a big cat. Even with the 360-degree scanning device mounted on KC's headgear, Jenkins might not detect a big cat until it was dan-gerously close. However, the biggest concern during a retrieval mission came from humans. The Adabuma, the tribe that inhabited this area, were fiercely territorial and would not hesitate to kill and devour anyone caught trespassing on their territory. Two Venuvian academies studied every detail of the Adabuma in the Amazon Basin. They had somehow remained isolated from the rest of the world. There were only two other isolated groups on Earth that had managed to avoid the encroachment of the more technically advanced societies—both were located in Central Africa. The academies stressed that, although as much information as possible should be gathered, detection must be avoided.

Even though there had been one near detection here 150 years ago, Jenkins felt that the chance of KC running into any of the local inhab-itants was slight. The area had been totally scanned by satellite for 48 hours prior to KC's arrival. The Environmental Data Collection Module had monitored the Adabuma, and there was no trace of any unusual movements. In fact, the Adabuma had been unusually quiet for the past four days.

KC peered through his night-vision apparatus. He had trained six years for this assignment—three years at the academy and three years in a rainforest. There had even been simulated attacks by big cats, but this was different. During training—when the Base Operator suddenly alerted KC to a red condition and KC's instruments detected a large, warm-blooded object's approach—he had merely followed procedures. He turned toward the attacking animal, armed and aimed his stun device, and dropped the big cat at 30 meters. Training was like a game. This was the real thing, and KC knew that reality had a way of being unpredictable. This recovery mission only required replacing the power module in the Environment Observation Unit. Few of the V.I.s, who had studied isolated cultures, actually got a chance to walk on a path, or see the trees, or feel and smell the thick jungle of the people they studied. KC knew as much as a V.I. could know about the Adabuma and now he was actually there, walking, breathing, and seeing. "Jenkins, you see anything I don't see?"

"All clear."

"It was more fun at V.I. School. Then at least I'd get jumped by a big cat or fall into a pit or even get attacked by a night-walking Adabuma."

"All clear," Jenkins repeated dryly. "Just get in, exchange the power supply, and get out."

"I just wish something would happen." KC would never forget that wish.

◆

Batu felt it. It was not the small insects crawling over his body—sometimes stopping to rest and accepting his subdued warmth, sometimes burrowing under him, sometimes biting. It was not the dryness in his mouth, the gnawing hunger pangs in his stomach, the aches in his muscles, or the stiffness in his bones that awakened Batu's senses. He felt movement, soundless vibrations. It was not a movement of Our Place. Batu did not know how long he had been lying under Kintura's leaves, not moving, willing his senses and bodily functions to slow, almost stop. Nevertheless, there was still that inner spot that was awake, wound like a tightly coiled spring, ready to explode and bring his near comatose body to life. The movement was coming closer. Each vibration was like a silent scream. Then it happened. It was like an uncontrolled eruption inside Batu's entire body. In one motion, Batu rolled to his stomach, sprung to his feet and let out a blood-chilling scream.

Jenkins was leaning back in his chair nervously tapping his fingers on the desk as he watched the monitors. Jenkins was a worrier. Nothing had gone wrong, nothing should go wrong, but he still worried that something would go wrong. He worried that a cat would charge KC so suddenly that Jenkins would not have time to warn him. He worried that KC, who was avoiding the main path, would trip over an unseen branch and would need Jenkins to exit the underwater craft and come to his aid. He worried he would make a mistake, the mission would fail and it would be his fault. He worried an uncharted meteor would crash through the jungle canopy and the whole area would explode. Jenkins was a worrier. Now, as he studied the monitors, he was not worried about the local tribe. The monitors were mostly pale green with light and dark outlines. Small specks of red appeared everywhere on the monitors—insects. Occasionally larger streaks of red scurried into view—night rodents and small animals. Jenkins carefully studied the monitors looking for any sign of change. Then he heard it. It was somewhere near KC but barely audible. The sound sent a chill through Jenkins. It could have been a weird audio feedback, but Jenkins knew instinctively that it was not. The Venuvians trained him to recognize every known jungle sound. This sound was human.

"KC, I think you have company."

"Animal, vegetable, or mineral?" KC asked jokingly.

"Human."

"What do you mean 'human'?"

"Homo sapiens, walks upright on two legs, has a brain. Human."

"The only humans around here are Adabuma."

"What about *you*?" Jenkins asked dryly.

"C'mon, Jenkins, you know what I mean. So, let's get back to that company you mentioned. Where are they?"

"They're in front of you somewhere; I haven't picked up a visual yet."

At that moment, there was another yell, this time much closer. Jenkins saw the figure before KC did. It was in front of KC, definitely human. It just suddenly appeared out of the ground, sprung to its feet; stumbled, regained its footing, yelled, and then it began to run toward KC. Then another figure appeared, already running, and then another, and another, and another…

"Abort," ordered Jenkins. Jenkins's adrenaline was starting to flow and there was a definite edge to his voice.

"Abort?"

"Abort!" This time Jenkins yelled.

"What about... " KC stopped midsentence. Fifty meters in front of him something or someone appeared. The figure had suddenly stood up, stumbled, hesitated for a few seconds, and then let out a fierce cry. KC knew that the cry signaled the beginning of a hunt. He saw the figure put a hand to its mouth and began to run in KC's direction, but not directly toward him. KC realized the figure had not yet seen him. "How many?" asked KC.

"Seven so far, but we're not detecting them until they stand up."

"Where are they?"

"All in front of you, so far."

"How far to the module?"

"Get the hell out of there, KC. Abort! Abort!"

"How far to the module?" KC's voice was calm and hard as runan tempered steel.

Jenkins knew KC was not yet ready to abort, and to try to convince him otherwise would be a waste of time. "You've got 614 meters—your best time for changing and resetting a module is 6.3 minutes. Then you have 1500 meters back to the craft. How will you get past the Adabuma?"

KC slowly knelt to one knee and crouched. He had a better chance of going undetected if he did not move. His mind raced: *How could the Adabuma get so close without being detected? Would they blindly run past him or methodically check the bushes?* At the academy, KC had prepared for what the Venuvians had considered every possible emergency. None of the possibilities had included an encounter with seven undetected Adabuma. Now, as he crouched near a bush, an Adabuman hunter passed within 20 meters of KC, and at least six others were in the vicinity. The Venuvians, supposedly the bearers of a scientifically advanced civilization, had miscalculated. A group of Hunters was closing in on him with the intent of capturing him—or worse. KC had a few seconds to decide whether to abort or to complete the mission for which he had trained the last six years. His first job was to survive.

Pain shot through Batu's body. His mind ignored the pain. The Hunt—that was his focus. He began to run. He did not know where he was going or even what he was Hunting. The Chase had begun, and knowledge of the Hunt would come. He was chewing on a Life Seed and he knew that soon the pain in his arms, and legs, and chest would fade. He knew that the darkness in his head would leave and that Spirit would return. The Chase would not wait. Batu heard the cry of another Hunter to his left, then another to his right, and another, and another. Batu let out another yell, one that was slightly different from his first. A chorus of yells responded. Batu knew the sounds well. The Net was complete and all the Hunters were running. The Chase was on. As he chewed, Batu could feel the fire of Life Seed shooting through his body. His legs grew stronger and his pace picked up. He could feel the life giving air rushing into his chest. His heart beat harder, pumping hot blood through his veins. Batu was the strongest and fastest Hunter and he knew it. Batu felt good. Batu cried out again and all the Hunters came to a complete stop.

Everyone listened for the slightest movement, hoping to hear a sound from their prey. No one breathed. Each Hunter leaned his head back and silently dripped the liquid from the seed down his throat. The bitter juice was food and liquid for their starved and dehydrated bodies. Batu's trained ear heard nothing, not a twig snapping, not the swish of a bush swinging back into place—nothing. Batu's mind had a flash of clarity. It was his ability to clear his mind that had made Batu the great Hunter. The Prey—what was the Prey? How did the Prey think? What would the Prey do? The Prey, the Invader. Batu realized that he had made a mistake.

KC broke into a fast jog, hoping that all the hunters had joined the Chase.

"Jenkins."

"Here," replied Jenkins.

"In about one or two minutes, one of the hunters will yell. I want you to track his every movement and sound. If there is a second yell, track him too, and tie their sound into my audio." KC accelerated into

a full sprint, thankful for the rigorous training he had gone through after accepting this assignment. He knew he could keep up this grueling
pace for at least 10 minutes but certainly no more than 15. Plenty of
time to get to the module, change and reset the pod, and get back to
craft. That is, if there were no obstacles. But there were obstacles, seven
of them—seven strong and swift hunters—and KC was their prey. KC
knew that, even with his equipment, he was no match for an Adabuman
hunter. His equipment, which allowed him to hear in the distance and
see in the darkness, was the only edge he had. If he could not outrun
the Adabuma, he would have to outsmart them. KC had heard the yell,
which meant that all the hunters would stop and listen for any sound.
KC stopped and tried not to make any sound. Even his heavy breathing became controlled. If a hunter heard anything, he would signal the
leader and the chase would continue; if not, the hunters would wait for a
signal from the leader. KC was hoping the hunters would keep running
toward the river, so that their sounds would muffle the sound of his own
movements. Still, he suspected their paths would likely cross.

Batu stood erect. He felt the light breeze. He sniffed the air. He listened
for the slightest sound that might indicate the whereabouts of the Prey,
the Invader. Batu could feel it. He knew that the Invader was no longer
in front of him. He was too clumsy to outrun the Hunters. He could not
move smoothly when he was off River Path to Big River. He could not
feel Our Place, but he was clever. He would not try to outrun the Hunters: he would try to outmaneuver them. He would try to trick them. Batu
must retrace his steps. What should his next command be? The Invader
was not Big Cat who had slipped through the Hunters' net. If the Hunters reversed the Chase, they might pass the undetected Invader again.
Batu thought about Fake Bush, the small animal that boys would chase
before they were Hunters. Fake Bush, when being chased, would often
curl into a ball and disguise itself as a bush. The boys would usually
run past it before they discovered Fake Bush's trick. As a boy, Batu had
always been the first to discover Fake Bush's deception and call for the

others to retrace their steps. It had been an early sign that Batu would be a great Hunter. Batu now gave the only command that might catch the Invader. He cried out for his men to retrace their steps and search for Fake Bush.

◆

Jenkins heard the command. Although he was familiar with the Adabuma language, he only heard a few words. He did not want to spend any time trying to analyze fragments. His immediate focus was on tracking the lead hunter. The monitors picked up the sound, and within seconds he was tracking the leader visually and audibly. "They're heading back in your direction. The leader said something about 'bush.' I've got you tied into his audio. Now let me get you the visual."

Immediately KC could see figures of the hunters. They were moving toward him in a zigzag fashion. This time they were looking more closely. The net was growing tighter. KC began to run toward the module again—running, thinking, calculating. How could he get past the net?

"Jenkins, we have to create a distraction."

"What do you mean 'we'? There's not much I can do from here."

"Think of something." KC was talking more to himself than to Jenkins. "An explosion, a flash of light—do you think Central could provide us with fireworks?"

"If Central finds out you ignored an abort command, you might as well forget your nomination to the space program."

KC's breathing was starting to get heavy. "Nomination? How do you know I was nominated?"

"I heard that Kinkade has a little party planned for you. What else could it be for?"

KC felt a surge of joy. He knew he was well qualified, but he also knew that he had a habit of breaking Venuvian rules, like disobeying an abort order, which could disqualify him.

KC's elation over his possible nomination to the space program was short lived. A loud beeping indicated he was approaching the buried module. All thoughts of the Adabuma, the space program, and his escape evaporated. He went into a well-practiced routine. He pressed the activation button on his utility belt. A bright red spot appeared on his vision monitor indicating the position of the module, just 15 meters in front of him. At the same time, the Environmental Data Collection Module pushed its way out of the ground with one meter of soil above it. "I have module contact. Power-supply-exchange procedure in progress." KC fell to one knee, and within seconds he had opened the access hatch and disconnected and removed the old power supply. He removed the new one from a pocket on his chest, inserted it into the module, made the connection, re-checked the connections, checked all the readouts, rechecked the readouts, closed the access panel, then hit his utility belt again. The module sank back into the ground. KC put the old power supply in his pocket. "Power supply exchange complete. Good for another 75 years." KC expertly rearranged the ground coverings so the area looked undisturbed, removed a small spray canister from another pocket, and sprayed the area with an odor neutralizer. The whole procedure had taken under 5.9 minutes, a record for KC. He was about to replace the spray canister when he stopped. "How much time before the Adabuma arrive to take me home for dinner?"

Jenkins made a quick calculation. "At their current speed, between five and seven minutes."

"Is this spray neutralizer flammable?"

"Slightly," said Jenkins without enthusiasm.

"How much pressure does my oxygen supply have?" KC knew the answer: 500 bars. Again, he was talking to himself.

"Five hundred bars," said Jenkins. "Don't forget, the Venuvians want us to leave no evidence of our visit."

"Would they consider a captured V.I. evidence of our visit?"

"Probably."

"This power supply must still have enough energy to create a spark."

"More than enough. I don't know what's on your mind, but it sounds dangerous."

"Just a diversion," KC said casually. He removed the old power supply from his pocket. "How do I get this power supply open without totally destroying it?"

"I give up," said Jenkins. "How?"

"If I could create a spark, I could start a fire with the odor neutral-izing spray."

"No doubt. You think a fire would be enough of a distraction?" Jenkins felt like he was talking to himself.

"I could use the fire to burn through the hose on my emergency breathing apparatus."

Jenkins saw immediately where KC was going. Once the fire had burned through the hose, the escaping oxygen mixture, which was under 500 bars of pressure, would turn the oxygen tank into a projectile. KC removed the oxygen tank from a side pocket. He began using it like a hammer, trying to break open the power supply.

"Is there any chance of this exploding?" asked KC.

"Slight, very slight."

The power supply was cracked and was close to opening when KC heard another hoot.

◆

Batu was beginning to fear that he had somehow let the Invader escape when he heard it. The sound of the Hunters jostling the bushes almost drowned it out, but Batu's finely tuned ears detected something that was not of Our Place. With one soft command cry, Batu ordered the Hunters to stop and listen. Silence. With a series of birdlike cries, Batu told the Hunters to run 20 paces, then stop and listen. Batu did not move. He heard the unfamiliar sound again. This time, he got a better sense of what direction it had come from. The Hunters had stopped and were listening. Batu began to sprint toward the sound while giving another series of cries telling the Hunters to follow him and tighten the Net. The Chase had resumed.

◆

"I think they've spotted you," said Jenkins. "The leader is heading straight for you. They'll be on top of you in about two minutes."

KC began to work feverishly. "I'm going to light up when I get a spark," he said.

"Judging from their direction and speed, I think they already know where you are."

KC's night vision did not work on cold objects. One more smash with the oxygen tank and the power supply opened. "The lights are on, and somebody's home." KC flipped up his night-vision apparatus, ripped out wires and touched two of the wires to each other. He jumped as a larger than expected spark leaped from the wires. "Yep, still plenty of spark," KC said, as he pulled out the odor neutralizer.

"Watch out or you'll singe your eyelashes," Jenkins said in a monotone.

"Thanks for warning me." KC smashed the odor neutralizer.

"One minute max," said Jenkins.

KC could see a green mist escaping from the odor-neutralizing dispenser. He touched the two wires together again—another flash, a flame, but no fire. KC cursed under his breath.

"What?" Jenkins asked, with obvious concern in his voice.

"Flame but no fire," answered KC.

"You'll have to completely saturate the hose to get it to burn," Jenkins said firmly.

"Could you have those hunters slow down? I can feel them breathing down my neck."

"Thirty seconds."

KC watched as the green mist began to form a film on the hose. He knew he had only one more chance. If he did not wait for enough mist to escape, there might not be a fire. If he waited too long, the Adabuma hunters would be joining him. KC touched the wires. The hose ignited.

"We have ignition," KC said. He lowered his night-vision apparatus and said, "Lights out. Help me get around these guys before the tank takes off." He took off in a sprint.

"Fifteen degrees right, quick!" said Jenkins. There was some relief in his voice but it was still tense. "Which way do you think the canister will head?"

"I don't know. Away from me I hope."

Even while running at full speed, KC's voice remained steady. There was a small explosion, and KC could hear the hiss of escaping gas and the sound of the oxygen canister shooting through the brush. It was getting louder.

"I can't see it," said Jenkins, "but audio tracking says the canister is heading in your direction, and the hunters are following it."

KC could hear the cries of the hunters as the hissing got louder.

"Reverse direction," Jenkins ordered. "Now!"

KC could see the Hunters through his night-vision apparatus, but they could not see him. He heard the canister pass him within a few meters. He was still 300 meters from the river.

"It looks like the hunters have taken the bait," said KC.

"All but one," said Jenkins.

"What?"

"The leader is still between you and the river."

Batu saw the light. It was not of Our Place. He heard the strange explosion and the snakelike hissing. He also heard the bushes being smashed by... by what? It was a different sound than the Invader made. The Invader was clever—too clever to make such a light, too clever to cause such noises. It was a trick. Batu stood his ground while the other Hunters continued their Chase. The sounds of Hunters faded—and then cries of victory. Batu still did not move. Then he heard it. It was the sound of someone running at a fast pace, but it was not a Hunter. Hunters did not make such noise. Batu knew it had to be the Invader. He assumed a crouching position close to the ground and waited.

"You're heading straight for him," said Jenkins. "He's about 50 meters ahead. Turn 90 degrees right."

KC made a sharp right. He heard a cry from the leader.

"The leader is on the move again," said Jenkins. "He's on a course to intercept you before you reach the river. The other hunters are heading back in your direction, but they're too far away to worry about. The leader looks like he's locked in on you. Can he see in the dark, or what?"

"Don't know." KC's breathing was getting heavier.

"Be careful, those guys carry poison."

"Yea." KC was conserving his strength.

"Maybe you should get your stun gun ready," said Jenkins.

"Deadly," said KC.

The stun gun was set with a charge strong enough to put down a big cat. It could kill a man.

"You're on a collision course," said Jenkins. "He should be visual any second."

KC saw a figure approaching on his right. He could not help but marvel at how swiftly and smoothly the figure moved. KC knew he could not win a footrace. He stopped abruptly and watched the figure run a few steps and stop as well. The figure began moving slowly toward KC.

"Damn he's good," muttered KC.

"You can't hang out too long," said Jenkins. "The rest of the gang is heading straight for you."

KC waited. He could hear the others coming.

"Move KC!" yelled Jenkins.

Hoping the sound of the approaching hunters would cover the sound of his movement, KC sprinted a few meters to his left and stopped again. The figure, the leader, must not have heard him. He kept going in the same direction. KC made another dash straight toward the river. The leader stopped to listen. The other hunters were near. The leader turned and headed straight for the river.

◆

Batu had made another mistake. He knew the Invader was heading toward River but, instead of heading for Big River himself, he had tried to cut off the Invader. Now Batu headed for Big River, ignoring the noise made by the Invader. He hoped to catch the Invader before he could escape into Big River. The Hunters' Net should keep the Invader from retracing his steps, so he would have to go to Big River. Batu reached the Big River, crouched low to the ground, prepared his poison dart, and waited.

"You've got six hunters behind you, and the leader is between you and the vehicle," said Jenkins.

"I've got a visual on the leader and the others," whispered KC. "I'm going to take out the leader." KC headed straight for the leader.
Batu could hear the Invader approaching. The Invader was almost on him. Batu leapt up, numbing poison dart in hand, ready to drive it into the Invader. For a fraction of a second, he could see the silhouette of the Invader. That was the last thing he remembered before he was blinded by a flash of light.

KC raised his night-vision apparatus and activated his emergency torchlight. He stopped—face to face with the leader. KC had seen visuals of the Adabuma hunters, but none compared to the real thing. The hunter was half a meter shorter than KC. His highly developed arms and legs had been momentarily frozen by KC's light. KC would never forget the leader's eyes—strong, steady, wise. No hatred, no fear, just a hunter seeking prey. KC immediately delivered a blow to Batu's chest. It could have been deadly, but KC had no desire to kill his crafty adversary. The blow, delivered with expert accuracy, was powerful enough to knock the hunter to the ground and render him temporarily unconscious.

"Ready to come aboard," said KC.

He jumped into the river just as the craft pushed its way above the water. On shore, the other hunters arrived and surrounded Batu just as the craft submerged with KC on board. KC stepped into the main compartment dripping wet.

"Okay Jenkins, let's go home. I have to get ready for a party."

THE PROGRAM

Kinkade dropped the folder on his desk in front of KC. He gave KC a cold, hard look. "There seem to be a few irregularities in the report on the power module exchange in the Adabuma Reserve."

KC squirmed a little in his chair, gave Kinkade a weak smile, cast his eyes downward, and made no reply.

"It seems you returned to base without your emergency breathing apparatus and odor neutralizing canister, and the old power supply has been damaged beyond repair." Kinkade paced back and forth behind his desk. He was well into his nineties and, thanks to Venuvian technology, still an active healthy V.I. His wiry two-meter frame, which stood erect, and his steady gait conveyed firmness and authority. "You also made physical contact with the Adabuma." Kinkade stopped with his back to KC. He spun around, bent forward slightly and placed his hands firmly on his desk. His iron gaze locked on KC. "You know the Venuvians want contact with study groups to be kept at a bare minimum?"

"Yes sir." KC tried to look as innocent as possible.

"You not only left physical evidence of your presence, you allowed a subject to see you, and you struck and possibly injured him."

KC tried to sound charming. "I'm sure I only put him down for a few seconds. He probably only remembers a flash of light and—"

"Quiet!" Kinkade shouted as he glared at KC. "The Adabuma have been under observation for 200 years. The intention was to watch them in their natural state." Without interrupting his speech, Kinkade resumed his pacing, his shoes clicking a steady beat on the hard floor. "They were to be kept completely free of outside influences. The slightest change in their normal activities could change the way they react to their environment and jeopardize the entire project. You know how demanding the Venuvians can be."

"Come on, Chief," said KC. "I just gave the hunters something to talk about around the fire at night. The tank is just another trophy they can hang in the shaman's hut. Maybe they'll pull it out during some feasts and brag about the Chase." KC was beginning to warm up to the idea of being a part of Adabuma legend. "You see," he continued, "Adabuma society has mechanisms to deal with minor outside influences."

Kinkade interrupted KC again, this time less abruptly. "KC, I know you are an expert on the Adabuma society. But this is a Venuvian project, and we are here to follow Venuvian guidelines." Kinkade's expression softened. "I know you think the Venuvians are a little restrictive in their directives, but you have to admit their results have been outstanding. We now know more about quote-unquote *primitive* societies than we ever could have hoped for without the help of the Venuvians."

"Well, that quote-unquote *primitive* society was able to outsmart the Venuvians' quote-unquote night-vision apparatus." There was an obvious note of disgust in KC's voice. "The Adabuma are an intelligent people. I don't know if the Venuvians fully appreciate what they're dealing with."

"Maybe they do know what they are dealing with. Maybe that's why they are making such painstaking efforts to avoid introducing anything foreign."

"Well, I just wish they wouldn't get their spacesuits all in a knot over one little canister. The Venuvians need a little more imagination."

"If you think so little of the Venuvians, why do you work for them? You are smart enough to make it as an Associate. I'm sure you wouldn't even have a problem making it without Venuvian help, although I can't imagine why anyone would want to work or live without Venuvian services."

"Let's face it Chief, the Venuvians are the only game in town," said KC.

Kinkade stopped and again faced KC. This time he had a smile on his face.

"KC, the Venuvians know you are good, but they don't leave much room for individuality. Their programs are quite demanding."

"Chief, I've been a V.I. for 17 years now. And I spent two years as an Associate. You don't need to tell me about the Venuvians."

"If you are going to spend the rest of your life working for the Venuvians, you need to learn how to deal with them."

"The rest of my life?" KC's face had a quizzical look.

Kinkade's smile broadened to a giant grin. "You have been accepted into the space program. We are arranging for you to start training for Deep Space. Congratulations. We will miss you."

At first, KC sat dumbfounded and speechless. Then he smiled. "Deep Space." He began to laugh. "Deep Space!" And his laughter became uncontrolled. KC jumped to his feet, grabbed Kinkade's hand, and shook it vigorously. "Thank you, sir, thank you, thank you, thank you!"

KC left the office, and Kinkade could hear him repeating "Deep Space, Deep Space," as he continued down the hall.

SAN FRANCISCO

KC got off the transport in mid-city. He loved San Francisco. Today the fog engulfed the pre-Venuvians skyscrapers, hiding them in a cotton candy mist. He decided not to take another transport. As he walked, KC ruminated on the fact that someday—someday soon—he would never see this city again. It was late afternoon. A few transport vehicles floated by pedestrians strolling through town. Two hundred years ago, these walkways would have been streets crowded with harried drivers in noisy vehicles that belched poisonous fumes. One hundred forty years ago, after the necessity of large cities had decreased, the Venuvians transformed many streets into gardened walkways. The office buildings, once crammed with workers, were transformed into living quarters, amusement areas, restaurants, and small businesses. After the Venuvians upgraded buildings for safety standards, they created living spaces that varied from spacious upper floor penthouses to one-room subterranean cubbyholes. Jacqueline, KC's girlfriend, who aspired to be no more than an Associate, had a three-room affair on the bottom of a nondescript, two-story building near the bay. It was in an area where waterfront warehouses had once dominated.

KC walked slowly. He was in no hurry. His relationship with Jacqueline had cooled but he did not look forward to saying goodbye to her—goodbye forever. He had had some wonderful times with Jacqueline, he had even toyed with the idea of asking her to come and join him in the space program. KC came to realize that Jacqueline was content with her simple, uncomplicated life. She earned a few units and spent a few units. She wanted no more. She enjoyed the amenities KC was able to provide, but she could live quite happily without them. Today KC planned to take her to her favorite restaurant, one with live chefs and live waiters. Being a server herself, she appreciated the interaction between a live waitperson and a customer. BioDroids, which could pass for humans and contained biological systems, were starting to appear everywhere. The Venuvians said BioDroids, or BDs, which took 20 to 30 years to produce, would be commonplace within the next fifty years. Androids, or andys, which were completely mechanical, were already commonplace. But human waitpersons were still in demand. No matter how pleasant the face or how effective the voice response system, nothing yet had replaced a real person. Someday BDs would replace most people like Jacqueline. Until then, people's desire for the human touch allowed Jacqueline to live her unencumbered lifestyle.

KC stood in front of the building that housed Jacqueline's quarters. Her windows and door were located in the rear of the building. KC followed the narrow walkway down the side of the building that led to an entrance to Jacqueline's quarters. When he reached the rear of the building, he stopped and took in what was the most distinctive characteristic of her living area. It was a 20-by-30-meter garden. She had meticulously landscaped every square centimeter. A path of flat irregularly shaped earth-colored stones snaked between the building and the garden. At the end of the path were an ornately carved door to Jacqueline's quarters and the entrance to her garden. KC was about to activate her detector. He paused. He decided to have a walk in the garden before announcing himself. For some reason, he wanted to walk through the yard alone. It would be for the last time. Since Jacqueline had never favored electronic devices in her garden, KC felt his presence would go undetected. He marveled at what Jacqueline could do in such a small area. Of all the plants in her garden, not one was a duplicate. Not one was a native of Earth.

"Who's visiting my garden?"

KC heard Jacqueline's voice coming from some unknown spot. Jacqueline's distaste for detection devices had obviously been reduced.

"It's me, KC."

"Oh, yes, K." There was surprise in Jacqueline's voice and a sound of... of something KC did not recognize. Jacqueline never called him "K."

"When did you get detectors?"

"Oh, that. Well, I was worried about my plants."

"I'll come on in," said KC.

"Sure, no problem," said Jacqueline.

Something was definitely strange, thought KC.

Only two days ago, KC had linked with Jacqueline from base. She looked as alive as ever and seemed genuinely happy that KC would be coming to see her. Today she sounded tentative, different.

"Hello, K," Jacqueline said when she opened the door.

There it was again: "K" only. She gave him a stiff peck on the cheek, avoiding body contact. KC stepped into a sparsely furnished, white walled room. Sitting on a long sofa was a man about KC's age. He had shortly cropped, unkempt hair and wore loose-fitting, outdated clothing. Instantly, KC realized what was happening.

"K, this is Triton."

Triton struggled to get to his feet, shifted to gain his balance, and extended his hand.

"Hey," said Triton.

"Hi there," said KC. KC could tell by the glazed looks in Jacqueline's eyes and a faint acrid odor that they had been sipping on the popular intoxicant, bunti root tea. KC had imbibed a few times but only with Jacqueline. He enjoyed the warm free flowing feeling but always had a slight fear that he might lose control.

"Triton is a chef at Lidáques." Jacqueline said nervously. KC beamed with his most disarming smile.

"Well, Jacqueline refuses to eat anywhere she works, so why don't you get another job so I can try you out." Triton smiled broadly, and Jacqueline laughed, the laugh that KC had grown to love.

"Have a seat KC," Jacqueline said warmly.

"Would you like to put your head with Mr. Bunti?" Triton giggled.

"Thanks, but no thanks," said KC.

"Beer and water are the only things I have to offer," said Jacqueline.

"A beer would be great," said KC. Triton was noticeably more relaxed as Jacqueline left for the kitchen.

"Jacqueline tells me you're in the space program."

"That's right. I go into training on the newest mother ship in one week."

"Where are you headed for?" asked Triton.

"A system about 15 light years off. The target planet is not quite as technologically advanced as we were here on Earth three thousand years before the Venuvians. That's probably why I made it into the program. My field of expertise is what the Venuvians call 'primitive societies.' The Venuvians seem to have some sort of fixation with isolated peoples who have certain advanced social structures without the accompanying advances in technology."

Jacqueline placed a mug by Triton and handed KC a bottle of beer.

"Thanks," said KC.

"What are you going to be doing on Dramalthus?" Jacqueline struggled with the name.

"*Dramaltus*," said KC. "That's what the Kromians call their world. I will be studying the Kromians, an isolated group located just below the equator. The first thing my group will do is to install monitors to study them. The Venuvians don't want them to be affected by any outside influences, so all activities will be carried out without their knowledge. Another group will catalogue the planet's animals, plants, and minerals. Other groups are interested in making contact with the various peoples on the planet and updating their technologies. Then V.I.s, Associates, and BDs will start to work on new ships. That's the Venuvians' deal."

"Have you ever heard that the Venuvians are only fattening us up like cattle?" asked Triton. "Maybe we are just part of a breeding program. Go in, pump up the population of a planet, then the Venuvians come in for a big feast."

KC had heard that rumor before. He had always marveled at intelligent people who seriously believed such nonsense.

"Well, they certainly have increased the size of the herd, and there's no denying that, on average, Earthlings are larger than they were 200 years ago." KC did not try to hide his good-natured sarcasm.

"Two hundred years ago they thought people who saw extraterrestrials were crazy," smiled Triton.

"They were!" said KC, and all three laughed.

"But what's with the Monthlies?" Triton was again serious. "An Unattached says he has proof that, when you're hooked up at the Monthly, the Venuvians are actually replacing your blood. Yeah, I know it's farfetched, but sometimes I wonder why the Venuvians are doing all this for us. They show up one day, give us all this wonderful technology, quadruple food supply, and make us healthy, wealthy, and wise. Why? And the one thing they don't share with us is how they got here and how they get away."

"Maybe they just like to share," said KC.

"Sure, maybe that's why they smile all the time," Triton said, showing he could also be sarcastic.

"I have to admit," said KC, "I have wondered how they get to other systems."

"They say we are free to travel," said Triton. "But we're really trapped in our solar system. Their ships just head for the sun and then disappear. What if those Unattached are right? What if the ship is just vaporized by the sun and those people who return to Earth and say they have been to other systems are just android lookalikes?"

"Don't let him get started on androids," said Jacqueline.

"Don't let me get started on androids," smiled Triton.

"Don't you get started on androids!" said KC in mock horror. Everyone laughed. "The Venuvians do seem to have a fetish when it comes to androids."

"Uh oh, looks like we're going to get started on androids," said Jacqueline. "Would you like another beer, KC?"

"Please," said KC. He didn't know if it was the beer or the increasingly relaxed atmosphere, but he was feeling quite comfortable.

"How about you Triton, more tea?"

"I think I've had enough tea," said Triton. "How about a beer?"

"Coming up," said Jacqueline. Both men watched Jacqueline walk into the other room.

"Ten percent of Venuvian operations are dedicated to producing BioDroids," said Triton.

"The Venuvians say that BDs will be the modern slaves—servants to mankind," rebutted KC. "In another 100 years, machines and BDs will set us free."

"Set us free? Or act as guards for the Venuvians?"

"We control every aspect of the creation of androids. How would the Venuvians be able to control them?"

"It's all Venuvian technology. If they know exactly how they are built, they may also know how to take control of them. I hate to sound like an Unattached—but I can't help wondering—what if some android that looks like me comes into Lidáques and slips a huge dose of bunti into the soup? A crowd of Venuvians could sweep in for a banquet, with smiley Earthlings as the main course."

KC, Triton, and Jacqueline laughed at Triton's obvious witticism.

"Remind me to skip the soup at Lidáques," said Jacqueline as she handed beers to KC and Triton. "And what about me? What happens when some young BD shows up who can wait on tables? I'll have to apply for the space program and go to some planet that doesn't have BioDroids yet."

"Well, I have to be honest," said KC, "sometimes I wonder about the Venuvians. But even if all the rumors are true, what can we do? Become Unattached?"

"I hear Unattached don't taste as good as V.I.s," said Triton. Everyone laughed.

"Well, if I'm going to be some Venuvian's snack, then I'm going to be some Venuvian's snack. I haven't got time to think about it. I just look at the way things were 200 years ago, and I'm thankful for all the benefits we've gotten from the Venuvians."

"Yeah," Jacqueline mused, "like Monthlies. There's nothing more beneficial than being hooked up to some strange machine and being probed and tested from head follicles to toenails."

"Not to mention having all your blood replaced." Triton knew how to laugh at himself. "Aren't you worried that the Venuvian spaceship will just keep going straight for the sun and be fried? The Venuvians even admit that there is a slight possibility that a ship might not survive the 'jump' to another system."

"Why would the Venuvians go to all the trouble of building a ship just to burn it up?" asked KC.

"Fried Earthlings?" quipped Triton. More laughter.

"I do wonder why the Venuvians don't let us know how their ships escape our solar system," said KC. "Even though we build the ships, there is one area where only Venuvians are allowed. I'm sure that's where they keep their secret. Well, I guess I'll see." KC finished his beer. "Well, I'd better get going."

The smile on Jacqueline's face faded. KC and Jacqueline both knew this was their last meeting.

"Well, well, well," said Jacqueline, mocking KC.

They all stood. Triton extended his hand to KC.

"I really hope everything works out," said Triton. "It's been nice talking to you."

"Thanks," said KC. "I hope everything works out for you, Triton. And you too, Jacqueline."

"I think I'll grab another beer," said Triton.

"Seems like a nice guy," said KC, after Triton had left the room.

"He is. Sorry things had to end this way. But, well… "

"Well, well, well," said KC. They both smiled. "It's probably easier this way."

Jacqueline leaned forward to plant a kiss on KC's cheek. KC pulled Jacqueline to him. At first, she stiffened, then she relaxed as and their lips met for a long, slow kiss.

"Goodbye," whispered KC.

"Goodbye," whispered Jacqueline.

As they ended their embrace, their eyes met for the last time. KC turned and left, his last tie to Earth severed.

It was dark when KC stepped outside. The fog had retreated, and the city sparkled with lights from thousands of windows. Outwardly, San Francisco had changed little in the 200 years since the Venuvians arrived. KC walked casually toward mid-city. He felt lightheaded, more from his separation from Jacqueline than from the beer. KC decided, on the spur of the moment, to go to Bingos, one of his old hangouts. Drinks were expensive, the panoramic view of the city was spectacular, and the servers were human. KC squeezed the small stud in his earlobe.

"V.I. KC, identification confirmed," said a voice that was only audible to KC. "What service, please?"

It was a soft female voice. KC had programmed his Personal Information Unit, or Personal, with a voice that mimicked Jacqueline's. A Personal was an optional device that could be implanted into a V.I.'s body or an Associate's body. It contained all collected information on that individual.

"Transport," replied KC.

"Destination, please?"

KC had a sudden vision of being 15 light years away on Dramaltus, activating his Personal, and hearing this voice that was so much like Jacqueline's. Maybe he would reprogram his Personal. Maybe he wouldn't.

"Bingos, S.F."

"Shared or private?"

KC decided to splurge. "Private."

He did not want to take a chance on having to make small talk. He was not in the mood.

"That will be 40 units. You have 1,297 units remaining. Your transport will arrive in less than eight minutes. Shared transport is available for five units and would arrive in three minutes. By taking shared transport, you would save—"

"Stop!" barked KC.

"Transmission stopped."

KC waited on a nearby bench. The sky was clear, and the stars shone brightly. There it was, bright as the brightest star—Spaceship Jaylex. KC had seen hundreds of visuals of Jaylex, from the early stages of construction to its present form. From where he sat, Jaylex looked like a bright speck in the sky. In 10 days, it would be his home. In a year and a half, it would embark on the twenty-month journey toward the sun. When the Jaylex nears the sun, with its velocity approaching the speed of light, something would happen—something only the visitors from a distant planet called Venuvia could explain. The Jaylex would be hurled through time and space and mysteriously appear near a star system 15.3 light years away. KC thought about his conversation with Triton and the wild speculations of some Unattached. How could the Venuvians defy the laws of physics? Was he a willing participant or a duped victim?

Well, thought KC to himself, *whether I'm a pioneer on the new fron-*

*tier or an entrée on a menu, once the Jaylex starts its trip toward the sun
my feet will never touch the soil of Earth again.*

An amber transport vehicle zoomed up on an invisible cushion and
hovered near KC. A door slid open.

"KC, your transport to Bingos is ready for boarding," said the Jac-
queline-like voice. KC climbed in, and the door slid closed behind him.

"Safety units engaged," said a voice to KC. The vehicle slid away.
"You will arrive at Bingos in less than five minutes. Would you like any
more services?"

"No," replied KC. "Stop."

"Transmission stopped."

KC watched the buildings of San Francisco whiz by as the vehicle
silently began to ascend Nob Hill. The transport slid to a stop in front
of the historic Fairmont Hotel. The hotel had an old-fashioned elevator
enclosed in a transparent tube running up the outside of the building's
front. At this time of the evening, the elevator emptied on the top floor
of the building—Bingos.

"Bingos, enjoy your evening," said the transport.

KC exited the transport and entered the unoccupied elevator.

"Good evening, KC," said an anonymous male voice. "Long time
no see. Hope you enjoy your evening at Bingos."

KC made no response. He found himself slightly irritated that the
recognition system had already identified him. The recognition system
would flash KC's bio with his photo and profile to the servers. They
would see what his favorite drink was, what he liked to eat, what his
V.I. position was, and much more. One reason KC was willing to pay
Bingos' exorbitant prices was that the servers were human and would
not even bother to read most of his information, let alone memorize it,
whereas a BioDroid would retain everything.

KC stepped into Bingos. He had no idea it was going to be so crowded. He scanned the packed bar and decided that he did not feel like being
in a crowded room. He turned and was about to leave when he heard
someone call his name. KC turned and saw his longtime friend Rabiu,
who was wearing his usual half-inebriated grin. Rabiu was the only Unattached KC knew well.

"KC my friend, how are you? Let me buy you a beer."

"Rabiu, you never change."

"Whad'ya mean?" said Rabiu, feigning innocence.

Rabiu's M.O. was to buy the first round then sponge for as long as he could. KC, like most of Rabiu's V.I. friends, enjoyed his good-natured degeneracy and did not mind buying him a few beers, even at Bingos' outrageous prices.

"That's alright," said KC, ignoring Rabiu's fake look of hurt. "I'll buy. I don't plan on staying long."

"I've heard that before," smiled Rabiu. Rabiu yelled at one of the waiters, "Carlos, I'll take two Stars!"

"It's crowded tonight," said KC, surveying the room.

"Lotsa lovelies," replied Rabiu. "I love these female V.I.s, They're so healthy."

"We call unhealthy V.I.s 'Associates,'" said KC "and unhealthy Associates 'Unattached.'"

"What do you call unhealthy Unattached?" asked Rabiu.

"Dead," said KC.

Rabiu laughed.

"KC, Rabiu, your beers," said the waiter. "Should I put this on Marta's Personal, Rabiu?"

"I'll take care of the beer," said KC. "Thanks, Carlos,"

"Yo," replied the waiter, whose attitude verged on rudeness.

KC sometimes wondered why he preferred to have humans serve him. This was one of those times.

"Who's Marta?" asked KC.

"She's an Associate who works here. I do things for her and she lets me use some of her units."

"What things?" asked KC.

"Things," Rabiu said evasively. "Look! There's Minna. She's an old friend of mine. Minna!" Rabiu yelled out.

He gestured for Minna to come over. Minna headed for the table. A woman with wild hair accompanied her.

"Minna's not real smart, but she has a big butt and those wide, child-bearing hips," said Rabiu. "Minna! Come here!" yelled Rabiu again.

A full-figured woman, who had just entered wearing a dress that left little to the imagination, weaved her way toward KC's and Rabiu's table. She was followed by the woman with wild hair.

"Hi, Minna," said Rabiu, slipping his arm around her waist while looking lustfully at her companion. "Who's your friend?"

"This is Lisa. Who's your friend?" asked Minna, taking Rabiu's arm from around her waist and smiling broadly at KC.

"Whatsa matter, can't I give an old friend a hug?" asked Rabiu.

"I just want you to keep your hands where I can see them." said Minna. "Aren't you going to introduce me to your friend?"

"This is KC. Sit down, and join us," said Rabiu.

Minna shook KC's hand.

"We're meeting someone," said Minna. "Maybe later?"

She had not taken her eyes off KC and still held his hand warmly.

"Maybe later, Minna," said KC with a slight smile.

"Well, be sure to bring your friend," said Rabiu, eyeing Lisa lustfully.

"My name is Lisa," said Lisa, obviously irritated.

"Lisa," said Rabiu, correcting himself.

"We'll be seeing you, KC," said Minna.

"Goodbye, Minna. Goodbye, Lisa. It's been nice meeting you." KC's goodbye had a note of finality.

"They want us, KC," said Rabiu with a lecherous smile. "Minna is turbo hot. I saw the way you were holding her hand. Buy 'em a drink, and ask them to meet us later," said Rabiu. He took a deep swig of his beer.

"Not tonight," said KC.

"You still seeing that tea drinkin' lady?" Rabiu scanned the crowd as he spoke.

"No, she traded me in."

"I thought she was your main."

"She was my only."

"She was nice," said Rabiu.

KC knew Rabiu was not talking about Jacqueline's personality.

"Let's talk to those girls," said Rabiu. "Did you see that dress Minna was wearing?"

"I'm not in the mood."

"C'mon KC. I bet Minna could put you in the mood. I sure would like to play around with that Lisa."

"She didn't seem to be too impressed with you."

"Wait 'til she gets to know me. She won't be able to keep her hands off me."

"You mean her hands around your neck or her fist in your groin?"

"Hey, I know these V.I. ladies. They all have wild dreams about Unattached."

"They're not having dreams; they're having nightmares. Help! There's an Unattached in my quarters!" KC said in mock horror.

"Hey, spaceman, I bet I've seen the inside of more V.I. quarters than you have. And the screams were not for help." Both men smiled.

Although KC did not feel like socializing, his urge to leave Bingos was subsiding. He took another drink of his beer and had a flash of nostalgia—no more Bingos, no more nights trading barbs with Rabiu. He thought back to the days when he and Rabiu were both Associates.

"You think you could become an Associate again?" KC asked Rabiu.

Rabiu shot KC a look of disdain.

"I could be an Associate anytime I wanted to. I just don't want to. I have plenty to eat and drink. What do I need with the Venuvians?"

"Don't you get tired of always depending on someone with a Personal?"

"I get by," said Rabiu. "Don't you get tired of being hooked up to some machine every 30 days and being probed, scraped, and punctured? Just two days late, and your Personal becomes limited. I don't trust the Venuvians. I think they're up to something."

For the second time that day, KC had to admit to himself that he harbored a vague, nameless, uneasiness about the Venuvians. KC finished his beer and again suppressed his doubts.

"They've been here for 200 years," said KC. "We live longer and are healthier. Worldwide average age has gone from 85 to 145 and climbing. 160 years ago, there were still people who went hungry. Today starvation is unheard of. Since the Venuvians came, we are better off in hundreds of ways."

"Sounds like the Venuvian party line to me," Rabiu smirked. "I think that, along with sucking your blood at each Monthly, they also give you a good brainwashing. The Venuvians just want more people to hook up to their bloodsucking machines. Triple the population, triple the blood. Triple the lifespan, triple the blood."

"Sounds like the Unattached party line to me," replied KC, with an exaggerated smirk.

"Wait 'til that fake spaceship is burned to a crisp by the sun. Then you'll wish you were still an Unattached."

"Wait 'til you drop dead at 90, then you'll wish you were still an Associate."

Both laughed.

"How about another beer?" asked KC.

"Yeah, how about another beer!" yelled Rabiu at a passing waiter. "I'll be glad when they replace these humans with BioDroids or androids. All you have to do is whistle, and they're right there. And no dirty looks."

"Why don't you go to an android bar or an automated bar? Cheaper and no dirty looks."

"Oh, I don't know. Those people are... " Rabiu searched for the right word but failed to find it. "I don't know. When do you take off?"

"Ten days."

"Aren't you just a little afraid?"

"Of course. Even the Venuvians admit that occasionally a ship has left one system and has not shown up in another. But there's enough onboard energy to keep the ship alive for 300 years. So, even if a ship gets stuck in the void, it will outlive its passengers."

"Boy, that sounds like free-floating around the middle of nowhere for the rest of your life," said Rabiu.

"Ten thousand people, nowhere to go, not much to do? I guess we'd have to live it up."

"Whoopee," Rabiu said, finishing his beer and looking for their waiter. "Will there be BDs on your spaceship?"

"Venuvians sent a few androids for tasks that are considered too dangerous for humans—especially first contacts. You can never tell how some new group might react to space aliens. And I've heard that ships have at least one BioDroid passing as human to monitor the crew."

"*Monitor*? You mean *spy*."

"Yeah, I mean spy."

"See, those Venuvians are creepy: blood-sucking, brainwashing, spying. Who knows what else they have up their sleeves. Have you ever met one?"

"I never met one up close, but there were a few during training who spoke on the important projects."

"You mean *brainwashing*," said Rabiu.

"Okay, fine, brainwashing then," replied KC with a grin. "Once I'm on board the big ship I'm sure I'll meet one. I've heard that some of them are quite personable."

"I bet, probably sizing you up for the slaughter. I'd like to meet some Venuvian women. I see them on visuals. Not bad looking. I like those long legs. I wonder if they're any fun."

"Is that all you ever think about, having fun with women?"

"What's wrong with that? Can't have too much fun," said Rabiu, who was again surveying the room.

The waiter showed up with two more beers.

"Anything else?" he asked flatly.

"How about a little respect," said Rabiu?

"No Personal, no respect," shot back the waiter.

"See KC, that's why waiters are being replaced with androids," said Rabiu. "Who needs the aggravation?"

"You sure don't have to worry about an andy taking out your position, do you Rabiu," said the waiter?

"That's right! They haven't built an android that can replace the Great One," said Rabiu.

"The day the Venuvians produce something that looks like you is the day I turn in my Personal," replied the waiter.

Rabiu ignored the insult. "Did you see that lady in the almost suit over there?" said Rabiu to the waiter. "She ate up KC here with her eyes. That V.I. is going to help him forget the lost love of his life." Rabiu then turned to KC and said, "Right, KC, old friend."

Suddenly, KC no longer felt like being at Bingos. The boisterous chatter had turned into a deafening roar. The friendly crowd had morphed into a crushing mob. KC had to get out.

"Not tonight, Rabiu. I have to get going."

"What?" asked Rabiu, sincerely shocked. "I thought we were going to celebrate your last days on Earth."

"Sorry, not tonight." KC stood. "Put 200 units on my Personal for the Great One here," said KC to the waiter, "and 20 for you."

"Come on, KC, the night is young," said Rabiu. "Let's have some fun," pleaded Rabiu.

"Another night. Be good, old friend," KC said warmly, placing his hand firmly on Rabiu's shoulder and shaking his hand. He knew he would never see Rabiu again.

The cool night air felt wonderful. The San Francisco fog had returned to its ocean resting place and the moonless sky was clear. KC walked aimlessly toward the bay, feeling more invigorated with every step. The Jaylex hung high in the sky, mimicking a bright star. It would be KC's home for the next 36 months. KC thought that the Jaylex would be the start of the greatest adventure of his life, but his excursion to this new world would be a prelude to an even greater adventure—an adventure that would determine the fate of the galaxy. That night, under the San Francisco sky, KC had no way of knowing how important his life would become.

LEAVING EARTH

KC sat in front of the Shuttle Departure Center. The inconspicuous domed building gave no indication that it was the gateway to an underground complex used to launch shuttles headed for Jaylex or one of the other two mother ships under construction. Several groups sat or stood around the building's park-like surroundings. The well-wishers were saying their good-byes to V.I.s about to depart for spaceship Jaylex. The V.I.s displayed the gamut of emotions from boisterous laughter to tears.

KC could not help staring at the non-Earthling groups—Travelers from other planets who, for one reason or another, spent time on Earth and decided to take another "jump." They had left not only their home planet but also their own people. They had chosen to "jump" from system to system and ship to ship seeking new worlds and new people. The Jaylex would be 90 percent Earthlings; the remaining 10 percent would be a variety of non-Earthlings. All ships had a contingent of Venuvians.

KC stood alone. He had said all his good-byes. He had no desire to have people around mouthing sappy platitudes. This was it. He was about to board a shuttle that would deliver him to the Jaylex, and the Earth's umbilical cord would be cut. KC wished to make this transition in solitude.

KC was in one of the early groups to board the Jaylex. He would be working on the Jaylex for six months. Once every square centimeter of the Jaylex met exact specifications, and after the last V.I. had boarded and all auxiliary crews had returned to Earth, then the Jaylex would retract its modules and begin the 36-month trip toward the sun. For 30 months after the "jump," as Jaylex traveled toward the new planet, Dramaltus, KC would study the information that the scout ship had gathered prior to their arrival. By the time the Jaylex reached an orbit around Dramaltus' moon, KC would be an expert on the language, customs, and beliefs of a new group of people. That was what KC had planned, but, before he set foot on the new planet, KC's plans would be drastically altered.

KC touched his earlobe.

"V.I. KC, identification confirmed." Jacqueline's voice again.

"Shuttle boarding instructions," said KC.

"Proceed to port C307," said the Jacqueline voice. KC joined the other V.I.s in an elevator.

A male voice announced, "Those assigned to port C1 through C250 exit to the left. Those assigned to port C251 through C500 exit to the right. Work crew report to assigned stations."

KC exited to the right and went to port C307. He touched his earlobe and the port door opened. A dimly lit Travel Security Pod stood before him. The Travel Security Pod, or spinner, was a padded armchair enclosed in three quarters of an egg-shaped device. It was the same as the one used by V.I.s for simulated takeoffs. For the last week, every V.I. had spin simulations three times a day.

"Please be seated," said a voice.

After a week of repeated simulations, it had become a simple routine. KC sat in his pod, and restraints automatically secured his head, chest, biceps, wrists, thighs, and ankles.

"Please check all restraints. If any restraint is too tight or too loose, please use your right forefinger to press the alarm activation sensor. At this time, please press and release the alarm activation sensor for testing."

KC pressed his right forefinger.

"Your alarm activation sensor is functioning. If you have any problems, please press the alarm activation sensor. Keep sensor activated until the problem has been acknowledged. Restraint systems will now be deactivated. They will be reactivated 15 minutes before takeoff. Take off is in 53 minutes and 12 seconds."

Even though KC knew this was the real thing, it still felt like the many simulations he had already gone through. In 53 minutes, his spine would be spinning at four revolutions per second on vertical and horizontal axes simultaneously. The axes, which cross at his center of gravity, were driven by electro-magnetic forces. At KC's last three Monthlies, he had been injected with mutated electrolytic conductors to help counter the effect of the centrifugal forces that would be trying to pull his body apart.

"Fifteen minutes until takeoff."

This was not a simulation. In 15 minutes, the shuttle would be struggling to escape Earth's gravitational pull. Except for the spinning pod, takeoff was not much different from what astronauts had experienced before the Venuvians arrived.

The time for takeoff had arrived. KC began to spin. For five seconds he could feel his body being pulled apart in all directions—and then darkness. A rocket, using solid fuel, blasted the shuttle into orbit. KC's shuttle was on its way to a rendezvous with Jaylex.

KC jolted back to life. He had stopped spinning and he was ready to check out the shuttle. After the sensors monitored his vitals, the restraints would retract.

"Takeoff has been successfully completed. We will be docking with spaceship Jaylex in two days and seven hours. If your vitals are acceptable, restraints will be removed in two minutes and you will be free to go to the multi-purpose area. The observation deck is now open. You are now weightless. Please move about the shuttle with care. Use hand grips. You may proceed to the observation deck when your block is announced. Enjoy your trip."

KC had recovered from takeoff, but he still felt a little uneasy. He then realized what it was—he was weightless! He was free of gravity. KC remained seated even after the restraints had retracted. He was wondering what he should feel—fear or exhilaration. Then he realized he was smiling, a broad uncontrolled smile. He was on his way. He was a Space Traveler!

KC stepped out of his spinner. The corridor was already crowded with V.I.s using the handgrips to propel themselves toward the multi-purpose area and the observation deck. Everyone wanted to get a look at Earth. It would not be the last look. The Jaylex would be in Earth orbit for another six months. Then, during the trip toward the sun, Earth would fade until it became another speck of light in the sky.

"Isn't this exciting?"

KC turned to see a tall, slender man standing at his side. His angular features, which revealed a prominent nose and leathery tanned skin, gave little indication that he was excited. However, the sparkle in his eyes showed that he was indeed feeling a great deal of emotion.

"More exciting than my first date," smiled back KC.

"I can't wait to see Earth from outer space. They say it's a spiritual experience. My name is Vernon but people call me Fizz."

"Hi, Fizz, my name is KC, just KC. It doesn't stand for anything."

"Been off Earth before?" asked Fizz.

"Nope, first time."

"Me too," said Fizz. "What's your specialty?"

"I deal with pre… "

KC paused, recalling the blank stares he would get whenever he mentioned "pre-Avlon-structured, functionally isolated, Gavean-tooled societies."

"I work with isolated tribes that use simple tools and have no government."

"Gavean-tools?" asked Fizz.

"You know about Gavean tools?" asked KC, incredulously.

"No, not really. I had a friend who studied an isolated tribe in Central Africa. She talked about Gavean tools and African structures. I guess I didn't really listen to her. Last year she decided she didn't want to go to Dramaltus."

KC detected a note of sadness in Fizz's voice.

"I'm headed for a fishery project," said Fizz. "The Venuvians theorize that their fish population is in worse condition than Earth's was when they arrived."

The V.I.s entered the multi-purpose bay through a hatch that V.I.s called "Last Chance." In training, the Venuvians taught V.I.s that if there was a problem with the craft, they should enter the multi-purpose bay through one of four hatches. If the problem with the ship could not be resolved, the Last Chance hatches would close, the multi-purpose bay would become self-contained and, if necessary, separate from the ship. A V.I.'s last chance for survival would be to make it through a hatch before it closed.

The multi-purpose area had rows of stationary tables and benches that were mostly occupied, even though V.I.s were still entering the four hatches. There was light chatter. Most V.I.s were anxiously waiting to view Earth. KC and Fizz were heading for a table when the ship's audio system announced another set of numbers.

"That's me," said Fizz.

"Me too," said KC.

They entered the observation deck. There, through the observation port, shone mother Earth—bright blue, and partly shrouded in clouds. The view was breathtaking. KC, like the other V.I.s, was speechless. Fifty V.I.s were packed into the Observation Deck, and the only sound was the quiet hum of the air-filtration system. After five minutes, the sound system broke the silence.

"Please clear the Observation Deck."

KC felt like a kid whose parents were dragging him away from his favorite attraction. He could have watched his home planet for hours but it was time for his fellow Travelers to get a view of Earth.

"Quite a show, wasn't it?" said Fizz.

"Fantastic," said KC. "How about a cup of coffee?"

"Sure, I wonder if it's any good."

"Good or bad, I guess we'll have to get used to it."

The two V.I.s fell silent, examining their surroundings. They were the usual Venuvian-dull, utilitarian, plainness. Everything was made of gray, lightweight, indestructible plastic. Except for occasional color coding, the monotonous gray pervaded the entire ship. Even the snack and drink dispensers were a metallic gray.

A shot of Earth filled the video displays over the dispensers. On the beginning of day two, the video display split, and a bright object shared the display with Earth. It was the spaceship Jaylex. Even when the mother ship's intricate web of modules became discernible, Earth still occupied its spot on the display. After two hours of day two, the video displays showed only the approaching Jaylex. On the seventh hour of the second day, it was docking time.

At the center of the intricate web of interconnected modules, rested the mother ship. It was the residence of the Venuvians and the secret they would not share with Earthlings—the energy drive that enabled a spaceship with a mass of 15 million kilos to "jump" from one star system to another. The dull-gray colored, ellipsoid-shaped, plastic alloy mother ship was 600 meters long and 100 meters across the middle.

Venuvians were very tight-lipped about what was inside a certain part of the mother ship. One V.I. had calculated that 90 percent of the space inside the ship had to be empty in order to accommodate the modules that the mother ship would retract before takeoff. The remaining 10 percent contained the Venuvians and their secret power drive. Jaylex housed between 500 and 1,000 Venuvians. No one but the Venuvians knew the exact number.

The 43 modules that were tethered to the mother ship, revolved around the Jaylex at gravity-producing speeds. They were kept away from the Jaylex until their construction was complete. Consequentially, accidents that might harm the mother ship were avoided, and, if there was a problem with a module, it could be easily isolated. Eventually, they would all become part of the Jaylex. A few were still at the skeleton stage, but most of the others were complete.

Docking was uneventful. As the shuttle adjusted its speed and docked, gravity returned. Following the docking, it became another module revolving around the Jaylex.

After promising to look up Fizz after the "jump," KC joined the group of V.I.s that would be studying isolated societies on Dramaltus. He recognized a few of the V.I.s from the training program, but no one from his Amazon Basin group had decided to leave Earth. KC did not know anyone by name. Together, they boarded an elevator that transported them into the Jaylex. When the doors slid open, KC knew this was it—this was the Jaylex.

The multi-purpose room they entered was a much larger version of the multi-purpose room on the shuttle. It had the same dull Venuvian colors, the same food dispensers, and the same display units situated on various walls throughout. But the groups of V.I.s in the room were different from anything KC had ever seen. There were Earthlings everywhere, but groups that were not Earthlings or Venuvians also inhabited the room.

As they stepped off the elevator, the new V.I.s tried to look nonplused, but few could hide the amazement on their faces. There were V.I.s of every description: short, tall, thin, fat. The Earthlings who had just arrived wore standard Venuvian issue. Most of the Travelers wore clothing from their home planet. Some, who had bypassed adaptive surgery, wore protective eyewear, breathing apparatus, or some other type of equipment that protected them from the dangers of an Earth-like environment. The Jaylex residents, who had been intermingling with Earthlings since the Venuvians arrived, paid little attention to the new arrivals.

The fresh batch of V.I.s moved through the multi-purpose room as a group as they headed for another elevator. As KC approached the elevator entrance, he noticed a female standing nearby observing the new arrivals. She wore a veil, but KC could tell that she was looking at every V.I. as if searching for someone. KC found himself strangely drawn to her. She was tall by Earth standards—over two meters. Short, jet-black hair bordered her oval, green-tinted face. KC could not stop looking at her. She stopped when she faced KC. She lifted her veil and quickly lowered it. He had the uncanny feeling that he had met this woman, that he knew her, that he could feel her feelings. It was her eyes.

"This is the group that will be studying isolated groups, is it not?"

Her voice was pleasantly soft, and she spoke Venuvian with an accent that KC found completely charming. She stepped forward and gave a traditional Venuvian greeting—the palm of the right hand placed over the heart, and left arm extended with palm facing the other person.

"Krella," said the woman.

KC placed his right hand over his heart and extended his left arm. Their palms touched. Her hand was soft and warm.

"KC," said KC.

"I am with Jaylex agriculture," said Krella. She spoke without a pause. "I have much interest in isolated societies. My family is with on-ship agriculture. I have never been on a planet. I was born on spaceship Cluve as it entered system Arlus. Then spaceship Noraul went to system

Valkur to visit planet Lokar. Many of my family, they liked Lokar very much. It is primitive with many isolated societies, and there are many different plant forms, many. Many of my family stayed on Lokar. They are there today. You do speak Venuvian, do you not?"

KC realized that he had spoken no more than his name, but, before he could reply, Krella continued her sweet, non-stop narrative.

"But of course you speak Venuvian. You are a V.I., are you not? And all V.I.s speak Venuvian." Again, she did not wait for a response. "We left system Valkur on spaceship Salcura to come to your system. And we are here today, are we not?"

KC did not attempt to answer.

"We left spaceship Salcura and came to Jaylex," she continued. "All except my silly cousin Bryrif. He wanted to stay with some silly Earthling woman. I am not saying that you are silly because you are an Earthling, but that woman, Lizianna was her name, certainly was silly. And my cousin Bryrif was certainly silly, yes, very silly. They were always whispering and giggling and hiding from the family. They were both silly." Krella lifted her veil. This time she held it up a little longer. "Ortans and Earthlings are totally genetically compatible."

Krella blinked and then looked down but, before she did, KC saw the gold of her pupils expand to three times their original size.

Amazing, he thought. "Oh," was all he could say. The word came out a bit cracked and higher pitched than he had expected.

"After you get settled in your quarters, would you like to meet for mela?" asked Krella. "Mela is an herb tea from planet Locar. It contains a slight stimulant. Most Earthlings like it, as do Ortans."

"I would love to meet for mela," said KC, feeling a bit more in control. "How will I find you?"

"I would love for you to find me at this place at the 17th hour."

Again, KC saw the gold in her eyes expand.

"Kay Zee," she said, extending her palm.

"Krella," KC smiled, touching her palm with his.

Again, their eyes locked, and KC watched her golden eyes expand and then slowly contract. He reluctantly withdrew his palm from hers, relishing the last touch of their hands. Then Krella turned and left. He could not stop staring at the sumptuousness of her full figure as she gracefully moved away.

"She looks as lovely going as she does coming," he muttered to himself.

Then he turned and entered the elevator. His first few minutes on Jaylex had been more enjoyable than he had anticipated. He was anxiously waiting for the 17th hour.

The elevator opened to the module that was to be his home for the next 42 months. The module was nicknamed "Skull Searcher." Its colors were the typical Venuvian plastic gray. Except for a module map, the wall in front of him was bare. The narrow passageway led to living quarters on the left and to the multi-purpose room on the right. KC decided to retrieve his travel module from the multi-purpose room and then immediately go to his quarters. He wanted to be settled by the 17th hour.

Even though KC would have fewer units to spend, he was glad he had opted for private quarters rather than shared quarters or a dormitory. He had met someone in San Francisco who had spent time on the Jaylex as part of a construction crew. This person told KC that most V.I.s wished that they had tried to get private quarters. One could always trade with another V.I. for extra units, but, even if one did not trade, there were not many things to use units on anyway. Now that KC had met Krella... *Well, let's not jump to conclusions*, he thought to himself. *I've only said a few words to her.* KC just could not get those round, golden eyes out of his mind.

The Skull Searcher's multi-purpose room was small and crowded. All the V.I.s were Earthlings. KC went directly to the travel module dispenser. He touched his earlobe and looked at the detector.

"V.I. KC," said KC.

His eyes and voice were matched, and his 10.2-kilo travel module was dispensed. The display read, "Living Quarters 2127." He exited the Skull Searcher's multi-purpose room and headed down the narrow passage toward 2127. He passed the dormitories first, and they all had their ports open. The dormitories consisted of a rectangular room with a stationary rectangular table and benches running down the middle. The left and right walls had two bunk beds each, and the rear wall had one bunk bed, ten V.I.s in a seven-meter by three-meter room. They were all probably level one or level two V.I.s, barely above an Associate. KC, who was an advanced level five, could not imagine spending six years in a crowded room with nine other V.I.s of any level, especially with levels one and two. They were young and inexperienced with no special training, and they had little or no idea what they were getting into.

Every bunk bed had two spinners. They were exactly like the spinners on the shuttle. When the Jaylex blasted itself away from Earth orbit, each spinner would contain a V.I. Each V.I. would be strapped to the spinner and, as on the shuttle, they would be spinning on two axes. Now they acted as no more than a place where V.I.s could sit comfortably. The dorms were the same Venuvian color. Some V.I.s had covered the walls with their personal things to break the monotony.

KC went to the end of the corridor. The shared quarters were on the right, two to a cabin. The private cabins were on the left. KC turned left to 2127. The door opened automatically. The room was simple. There was a bed on the left, recessed into the wall. An adjustable stationary chair stood before a platform attached to the wall on the right. His spinner faced the door from the opposite end of the room. The whole affair measured three meters by four meters. It was smaller than he had imagined but quite adequate. He pictured himself sitting in his spinner talking to Krella—or more likely listening to her—while she lounged on his bed. *Whoa there, boy*, KC said to himself. *You haven't even had your first date yet.*

KC opened his travel module and began removing his few precious possessions. He had a pair of silk lounging clothes. He had protectively wrapped one around a crudely carved figure of a spear fisherman from the Amazon Basin. The carving was six centimeters tall. The right arm, carved with exaggerated proportions, held a spear that rose above the fisherman. Large wide-open eyes dominated the head. The rest of the figure was poorly detailed—legs together, left arm at its side. A strong arm and good eyes—that is what made a good spear fisherman. KC had found the carving during his training for the power module exchange. It had washed up near the area where he was practicing going ashore. KC knew exactly what it was. Every year the Adabuma had a ceremony next to the river in hopes that the harvest of fish would be bountiful. The carvings of spear fishermen were one of the offerings. The Adabuma believed that if they gave of their own, the river would give of its own.

The Venuvians considered the carvings artifacts. They were part of an Adabuma ceremony and as such should not have been removed from their natural site. KC knew that, in a matter of weeks, the jungle or the river would have devoured the fragile carving. Moreover, if an Adabuman ever found a carving, the tribe would consider it to be a bad omen, and the next offering to the river would likely be a human rather than a carving.

KC had sidestepped a few rules and secreted the carving back to camp. If the Venuvians had discovered KC's misdeed, they may have dropped him from the program. He may have even lost his level 5 status. The Venuvians were very strong on privacy, so, once KC had the carving safely stashed away in his quarters, his chances of the Venuvians detecting it were slim. Now his treasured carving sat facing him on his desk. It was not much to look at, but it represented the tribe of people that had been a major part of KC's life for seven years.

The silk lounge outfit that had been wrapped around the carving was a replica of a West African meditation riga. Pearl white in color, it had intricate pale gold brocade designs around the open neck and around the arm and leg cuffs. KC fingered the delicate fabric. He loved its feel. The brocade was one of a kind and hand designed. He had it made in San Francisco, and it cost him over a month's credits. The silk had gone through a Venuvian process that would keep it from deteriorating for over 250 years. The second silk riga had been made in San Palo. It had the same pajama-style design, but this one was jet black with silver brocade on the cuffs of the arms and the legs and around the neck. The stitching had been machine generated with a random program and, though KC liked the feel of it, it did not have the same look of originality as his white riga. KC folded the two rigas and placed them in a cubbyhole under his bed.

Next, KC removed a pair of slippers that Jacqueline had given him. He had considered leaving them because they made him think of her. They had been a just-because gift, and KC had loved the slippers from the moment he slipped his feet into them. He had decided that Jacqueline's memory would fade, but he knew the slippers would last a lifetime. Now, as he looked at the pale-blue slippers with soft, faux lamb's wool lining, he was glad of his decision. He put the slippers with his rigas under his bed. They were his only personal clothing. All other clothing he needed would be furnished—compliments of the Venuvians—for life.

He had also brought 40 visual-transmitting units he would use to give the walls of his quarters a personal touch. They ranged from holograms of friends and colleagues to pictures of works of art. He had only one photo of his parents, who still lived on Titan. He took it when he was 15 years old, before he left Titan to study with the Venuvians. Even though he usually had visual communications with his parents on a regular basis, KC always thought of them the way they looked in that photo.

KC had returned to Titan only once, when he was 25. His parents had not visited Earth since relocating on Titan. Since the Venuvians had synthesized runan on Earth, mining on Titan became unnecessary. All mining operations on Saturn's moon had ceased. But the Space Monitoring Program, run by Sulof, KC's father, remained. The Venuvians had increased the capabilities of the space-scanning operation by giving Sulof everything he had been asking for, and more. There was even a contingency of Venuvians stationed on Titan along with a few thousand people who called Titan their home. Sulof had told his son, KC, that the Venuvians were concerned that something would approach the solar system without their knowledge—very concerned. They were constantly checking on the program to make sure that the coverage was 100 percent complete. Sulof had told KC that the Venuvians were afraid of something, but they gave no clue as to what it was. KC had wondered what it was that the powerful Venuvians could possibly fear.

KC put all but one of the visual-transmitting units into his cubby. Now, all that remained in his travel module were two data packs containing all sorts of reading material. He plugged one of the units into the receptacle above his desk. A life-sized hologram of Jacqueline appeared. He decided he did not feel like reminiscing. The only one he wanted to think about was Krella. He pulled out the unit. Then, he touched his earlobe.

"Time."

"The time is 15:14," came an answer.

A chill went through KC. There was Jacqueline's voice again.

"Voice change—male, American-English."

"The change has been completed. Should I still save the custom female voice named Jacqueline?" responded the Personal in a non-descript male voice.

KC thought for a few moments.

"Save."

That was it. These few things from his travel module were now the only personal things he would have from Earth for the rest of his life. KC sat at his desk and ruminated on the path he had chosen. He had thought that separation from Jacqueline would be the hardest thing to do, but that had been taken care of without any effort on his part.

He had been separated from parents for so long that there was not much of a sense of loss. KC felt a closeness to his mother. He would miss her. His feelings toward his father were ambivalent. He and his father had never been close, but KC's father did not give the appearance of being close to anyone, not even to KC's mother. KC knew that, despite appearances, his father loved KC's mother deeply.

KC could still remember when his mother had fallen ill with a rare disease caused by a fungus in her lungs. In pre-Venuvian times, it would have been deadly. KC still remembered his father's face during the ordeal. His mouth had been twisted in anguish and the furrows across his forehead had been deepened in fear. The Venuvians had totally cured his mother, and KC's father, in his reserved way, had beamed with joy. KC supposed his father loved him too, but he just did not know how to express it. KC realized he would miss his father too.

"Time."

"The time is 16:17," came the nondescript voice.

KC did not like the sterile voice, and he had no desire to retrieve Jacqueline's voice—he was not even sure why he had saved it. Maybe he should have the computer speak Venuvian. He immediately rejected that idea. He wanted to keep that feeling of home.

What about Krella's singsong voice? Maybe someday, thought KC. "Voice change—male, English, Hindu accent." He had always loved the musical pattern of the Hindu accent.

"The change has been completed."

Better, KC thought. "Voice change—female, English, Hindu accent."

"The change has been completed."

"Yes," KC muttered. "Much better."

It was 16:95. KC peered through the crowded hall looking for Krella. At 16:98, KC shifted in the white riga he was wearing, even though he had spent minutes looking at his image trying to get the robe to hang just right. KC, who had always considered himself comfortable around women, found himself fidgeting with trepidation.

He had seen a few V.I.s that were obviously from Krella's planet. They all wore eye shields of some type. It was not unusual to see Travelers wearing eye shields, because they were sensitive to certain light waves. Krella had not been wearing eye shields when they first met. She wore only a translucent scarf. KC thought of Krella's beautiful golden eyes and realized how much he was looking forward to seeing them again.

"Kay Zee."

KC turned, and there stood Krella, tall and voluptuous. Her head was covered with a knitted cap, and a lacy veil hung from the cap to her shoulders. He could barely see her eyes.

"Krella," said KC. Their palms touched. "It is so good to see you."

He was disappointed that she had hidden her eyes.

"It is good to see you, Kay Zee," said Krella.

"Why have you hidden your beautiful eyes," asked KC.

Krella paused, seemingly at a loss for words. When she did speak, it was not with her usual exuberance. Even her voice sounded different. KC surmised that it was something she had repeated many times. Her words were speech-like.

"The eyes are the pathway to the soul. They reveal one's inner feelings and desires. To open one's eyes is to reveal one's self. We of Orta are blessed and cursed at the same time. Although we can read little in the eyes of our fellow Ortans, the eyes of others reveal many things to us. Unfortunately, when others look into the eyes of an Ortan, they can see into our soul. We can hide little of our inner feelings. That is our curse."

"I have seen others from your planet. Is that why they wear eye shields?"

"Yes. We only reveal our eyes to other Ortans." Her speech had obviously ended.

"You were not covering your eyes when we met. Why was that?"

"No, I was not. Not at all." She shifted uncomfortably. "I wanted to make a connection. I wanted to see and to be seen, to know and to be known. Other Ortans would find my actions very immodest. But I needed to make a connection. And I wanted to make the connection before..." she paused, "before the rumors. Silly rumors."

"What rumors?" KC was enthralled. "I hope you don't mind my asking," he quickly added.

"Oh, those silly rumors. Rumors that we can cast spells just by looking at someone." She continued with a little disgust in her voice. "Like we can cast spells? How silly! Our eyes tell only the truth. Yes, the truth. I wanted only to make a connection. Do you understand?"

KC smiled slyly. "Yes, I think I do. Do you know what I am thinking now?"

Krella again shifted in her seat. "We read only feelings, not actual thoughts. Only feelings."

"And what about *my* feelings? Can you read *my* feelings? What am I feeling now?" KC persisted.

"Of course I can. Don't be silly! Silly, silly."

"My feelings are silly?" KC felt a little hurt.

"Oh, no! No, no! Your feelings are not silly at all. You know what your own feelings are, do you not? You do not need me to tell you your feelings. Others often ask us to tell them their feelings. But, one always knows one's own feelings, does one not? Silly for you to ask."

"Well, maybe so. Still it's not fair that you know my feelings, but I don't know yours," KC said with mock indignation.

With a quick motion, Krella lifted the veil covering her eyes. She peered directly at KC. She had a smirk on her face, but her eyes—her eyes told a different story. She lowered her veil as quickly as she had raised it, but, in those few seconds, KC could see the warmth she felt. He could see something else in her eyes, something that exploded his already smoldering attraction.

Now I get it, I get it. I see the connection, he thought.

"How often do you reveal your eyes to others?" KC asked, trying—but without succeeding—to hide his sudden pang of jealousy.

"Every chance I get," she replied with obvious irritation. She raised her veil again and quickly lowered it.

"Cover your eyes if it makes you feel more comfortable," said KC, smiling.

He had seen the irritation in her eyes, and he had also seen something else—something that made everything else irrelevant. After only a momentary glance, KC knew that he had been the only one with whom Krella had made a connection.

"Krella, Krella, Krella," KC said, just to hear the sound of her name. "So what do you see when you look into the eyes of another Ortan?"

"When I look into the eyes of another Ortan, I see… " She hesitated. "I see myself, my own feelings. I do not see the feelings of the other Ortan at all. This is strange to you, Kay Zee, is it not?"

"Yes." KC, who could be pleasantly evasive, was surprised at his bluntness.

"Small children can easily be read, but they learn at an early age how not to reveal themselves," said Krella.

The time passed quickly. Krella described the agricultural projects that groups of Ortans were working on and invited KC to come and see for himself. She was mostly interested in what KC had been doing with the people he had worked with in the Amazon Basin and what he would be doing on Dramaltus. KC began describing his activities on Earth to her when, all of a sudden, he stopped.

"Let me look into your eyes again," he said.

Krella lifted her veil and gazed into KC's eyes. KC reached across the table and took Krella's hands in his. After several moments, Krella removed one hand to lower her veil, and then she returned her hand to his. Their hands remained together for the rest of the evening. When the time came to depart, Krella came close to KC. She lifted her veil, and their lips met. Although they felt the sweet electricity of the first kiss, there was also the feeling that it had always been and always would be. KC's first day on the Jaylex had been wonderful.

The next five months on the Jaylex were hectic. The 10,000 V.I.s who were headed to Dramaltus were all on board. Every V.I. had to take part in the inspection of the ship. The ship had to undergo an inspection and re-inspection to make sure it was ready for takeoff. Even though the areas KC had to inspect consisted only of his quarters and a section of the Skull Searcher, the work was painstakingly slow and time consuming. Several structural engineers did a thorough re-inspection. A construction engineer had lectured the V.I.s of Skull Searcher on the importance of exact specifications. A slight imperfection could result in a miscalculation that would cause the Jaylex to end up light years away from its intended destination. None of the V.I.s wanted to make a single mistake.

Questions regarding the Venuvians' source of propulsion went unanswered. The engineer said that, with the exception of the Venuvian quarters, he knew every centimeter of the Jaylex. The only sources of energy that he knew of came from solar conversion and rocket fuel. Most of the solar energy was stored. Jaylex's onboard systems used solar energy that was not stored. The Jaylex would use the rocket fuel to facilitate the ship's escape from Earth's gravity and initiate its journey toward the sun. How the Venuvians got the ship from one star system to another was still a mystery.

KC had formed only a few acquaintances with the other V.I.s. It was not that anyone was unfriendly; it was just that he spent every moment of his free time with Krella. He could see how others might imagine that the Ortans were able to cast spells. He had fallen so deeply in love in such a short time that sometimes he felt Krella had some magic control over him. KC knew in his heart that his feelings were real, but, even if they were not real, he did not care. A few months after he had met Krella, he asked her to come to his quarters. One look told KC that, although she had wanted to go with him, the time was not yet right.

"After we enter the new system, you shall meet my family. My father and brothers will not like you, not at all," said Krella.

"I can hardly wait," said KC sarcastically.

"There is no need to have concern. They will do you no harm. And my mother and sisters will love you, yes they will. We must wait until after the 'jump' to the next system."

As the departure date drew closer, excitement grew. The engineers had completed all final inspections. The Jaylex was declared to be in perfect condition. Twelve hours before departure, there was a general briefing. All monitors had a real-time display of Earth. Sharing the display was the Jaylex Council: Earth Co-Commander, Travel Co-Commander, and a Venuvian representative. The Earth Co-Commander was the first to speak.

"Hello. I am Ralph Marcon Duko, Earth Co-Commander of Jaylex. Take a good look at Mother Earth. It will be your last close-up view, ever. In three hours, a shuttle ship will depart Jaylex for Space Station Thornton. Any V.I. who has a change of mind had better be on that shuttle. It will be the last departure until we reach Dramaltus. Jaylex is a small city, and the Venuvians can easily replace most of you. In ten hours, module-retraction sequencing will begin. V.I.s will be restricted to their quarters while Jaylex retracts all its modules. In 12 hours, Jaylex will secure V.I.s in their spinners, and we will depart Earth orbit and head for the sun. For approximately 14 minutes, Jaylex will accelerate until it reaches initial velocity. After we have reached initial velocity, Jaylex will redeploy modules and release V.I.s from their spinners. For the next 37 months and 27 days, while we travel toward the sun, you will have few duties and much free time. Here to discuss a few of the multitude of options is Travel Co-Commander Vrueka Tacbas Ntubi."

Vrueka was a tall slender V.I. from some distant planet. Her voice was low pitched and smooth.

"Hello V.I.s, I greet you. Dramaltus will be the fourth system I have visited since leaving my home planet. None of you at this meeting have ever made a 'jump.'"

KC's mind drifted as Co-Commander Vrueka began reciting the litany of activities that would take place on the Jaylex during its plunge toward the sun. KC had covered all the information before, and Vrue-ka's monotone voice had failed to capture KC's attention. Then it was the Venuvian's turn to speak.

"The people of Venuvia would like to thank all of you who have chosen to help us explore a new solar system," said the Venuvian.

Although KC was completely at ease with the Venuvian language, when he heard the Venuvian speak, he realized how the language should really sound. The few Venuvians KC had encountered used local accents when speaking. The Venuvian's speech was short. Afterwards, all the V.I.s returned to their quarters and prepared for departure. In 12 hours, the Jaylex would be on its way toward the sun, and Earth—Earth would slowly fade away.

Departure was anticlimactic. Just as the Earth Co-Commander had said, leaving orbit had been little different from the shuttle departure from Earth. When KC emerged from two hours in his quarters, nothing had changed. There was no indication that he was now traveling at over 6,000 kilometers per hour. KC wondered if the "jump" to the next star system would be similar.

For the next few days, KC spent half of his time studying the various cultures similar to those of Dramaltus. The Venuvians had collected data on hundreds of them. The rest of his time he spent examining the agricultural project that the Ortans were involved on, all in the company of Krella. The time seemed to fly by. By the time the Jaylex was preparing for the "jump," KC had seen many Ortans, and Krella had introduced him to various agricultural techniques. Although he had seen several Ortans, all with their eyes hidden, he had not once spoken to one. Whenever he even hinted at meeting Krella's family, she would always demur, "After the 'jump,' yes, after the 'jump.'"

The last time KC had asked her why he had to wait until after the "jump" to meet her family, she lifted her veil—which she still wore most of the time—looked directly at KC, and said, "Sometimes people change."

For the first time since he looked into her eyes, he could not understand what he was seeing. He did not ask again.

Preparations for the "jump" were in full gear. Monitors no longer showed visuals of what lay outside the Jaylex. The only thing to see was the blinding light of the sun. The temperature outside the Jaylex had climbed to 1000 degrees centigrade. If the cooling system were to fail, the sun would vaporize the Jaylex and everyone aboard.

V.I.s had checked every square centimeter of the Jaylex, and structural engineers had rechecked everything. All was ready. The "jump" was in 24 hours. Among those who had never made a "jump," there was the expected air of heightened excitement. Some of those who had already made a "jump" become listless. A few appeared to be depressed. It was five hours to "jump" when KC saw Krella. He asked her about the gloomy condition of those who had already made a "jump."

"Sometimes the "jump" is not comfortable," said Krella. Then she threw her arms around KC and held him closely. They kissed. "It is time to go," she said.

"Please let me see your eyes, Krella," said KC.

"No," was all she said.

She pulled away from KC's embrace, turned, and left. That was the last time KC saw Krella before the "jump."

There had been 50 drills in preparation for the "jump." This was the real thing. All V.I.s had to return personal items to their transport modules. The modules were then stored in the multi-purpose rooms. All loose items, from large pieces of machinery to pea-sized items, had to be secured in such a way that there was absolutely no chance of vibration. At 30 minutes before the "jump," all V.I.s were secured in their spinners.

The ship's audio system announced, "All V.I.s are secure. All systems are operative. This will be the last communication before the 'jump.' Good luck."

Good luck? thought KC. *Why do we need luck?* Straps were tightly secured around KC's head, neck, forearms, biceps, chest, abdomen, waist, thighs, calves, ankles, and feet. The time-released substance he had received at his last Monthly was beginning to take effect. His muscles relaxed, and he felt a drowsiness overcoming him. Images of depressed Travelers floated by, and he could hear Krella saying "no" over and over again, and "good luck," and "sometimes people change."

A week earlier, a large-headed Ortan, who had already been through three "jumps," had informed the V.I.s in Skull Searcher: "Everyone's 'jump' experience will be different. Anyone crazy enough to take a second 'jump' will find that it will be different from the first. I won't try to make any substantive descriptions, but there are certain reactions almost everyone has. You will experience dryness in your throat and mouth. Your head will ache, and your vision will be blurred. You will be disoriented. You may not know where you are or even who you are. Some V.I.s experience panic, some pass out. I must tell you that, on some very rare occasions, a V.I. never fully recovers from a 'jump.' I've been told this, but on three 'jumps' I've never seen it. Jaylex will wait for all vitals to return to normal and then start to question you. If you have a problem responding verbally, use your finger touch pads. If you do not respond at all, Jaylex will assume there is a problem and react appropriately." KC had wondered what the appropriate reaction would be.

As KC's spinner began to spin on its two axes, the Jaylex stopped the rotation that had been creating the artificial gravity and completed the retraction mode. The walls of KC's quarters closed into each other until they almost touched his furiously spinning spinner. A perfect ellipsoid containing 10,000 spinners, the Jaylex then threw itself into a spin. Outside the Jaylex, the temperature had reached 5,000 degrees Celsius. The speed of the Jaylex had reached 300 kilometers per second and continued to accelerate due to the sun's strong gravitational force. Then, an explosion—silent in the vacuum of space—and the Jaylex was gone.

"JUMP" FROM EARTH SYSTEM

There were shadows, moving shadows, shadows everywhere. Almost shapes, but not shapes. Maybe the shadows were real or maybe they were... were what? What could they be? Were they close, dancing a few centimeters away, or were they in the distance, separated by infinity? Where were they? And there was something else, something unseen, something large and powerful, and... frightening. Where was it? Above? Below? Hidden in the undulating shadows? It was behind. Yes, behind! Out of reach. Out of view. Frightening!

Then a fragment of a thought form floated by in KC's mind: *Mother! Mother, I love you.*

Mother was there, but where? Her smile was there, her warmth was there, but... but where was she? Where am I? And the thing behind, the frightening thing.

Then the gray shapeless shadows were gone. Now there was nothing but white—antiseptic bright white. There was an Adabuman—wide-open focused eyes, spear in hand, strong muscular arm, motionless, beads of sweat glistening on his dark skin, and fear on his face, fear of something unseen. There was a deathly silence. The Adabuman's eyes were fixed on KC's. He had seen those eyes before. The eyes were trying to tell him something. There was anger and compassion and...

In an instant, the white room and the Adabuman were gone. There was a runner. KC was not the runner, but he could see through the runner's eyes. He could see a broad expanse of barren, parched land. The flat land gave way to gently rolling hills then to desolate mountains. He could hear bare feet pounding warm solid earth. He could hear the heavy solid breathing. They were not his eyes scanning the horizon or his feet running at a steady beat or his breath delivering air to this well-conditioned machine.

Was this thing running to something or from something?

Then he felt it, the unseen fear. As the fear grew, the runner that was not KC increased its pace. He wanted the eyes, which were not his, to turn and look upon that from which it ran. The eyes only looked forward. Its pace had increased to almost a sprint. Its breathing had become deeper and more labored. Then, abruptly, the running stopped, and KC could see the ground rushing toward its eyes in a surrealist slow motion. The runner was falling! Reflexively KC tried to put hands out to break the fall, but he was powerless. When it hit the ground, KC felt nothing. He was aware of a heavy thud and the face slamming into the dirt. But no pain—only fear, fear of something unseen and approaching. KC tried to look, but the runner's nearly closed eyes could only see the dust that was being fanned by its heavy breathing.

Turn! Turn and look! KC screamed out silently.

As if in response to KC's will, the runner, lifeless except for its heavy breathing, rolled to its side, then to its back.

Open your eyes, demanded KC.

The eyes shot open. There it was, the thing that was sending waves of fear through KC. It was a giant, prostrate gorilla. Though it seemed quite far away, he knew that its size was gigantic. It was not the beast's size, monstrous though it was, that was so frightening. It was its eyes. The giant gorilla was in some sort of stupor and its eyes were only partially open. Even so, KC could tell that they were not simian at all. They were large and round and would have been golden were it not for their bloodshot condition. The monster's glazed eyes fell upon KC. It shot up to a sitting position as if suddenly awakened. Its eyes widened. Fear tore through KC's body like a jolt of electricity. The giant monster's eyes boiled with rage and hatred. KC knew that the gorilla thing was bent on KC's total destruction. In seconds, it bounded to its feet and charged KC with a speed and ferocity that would not normally be expected of such a large creature.

KC wanted the runner, whoever or whatever it was, to get to its feet and run, run as fast as possible—escape. Then he remembered he was trapped inside of something that was not him. Arms, feet, legs refused to respond to his panicked efforts. The runner lay motionless as the monster raced forward. The ground trembled with each step. The approaching monster was beginning to block out the radiant sky and parched landscape. KC knew his time had run out. Even if the thing he was inside of immediately jumped to its feet and ran with all its might, there was no escape. Nowhere to run, nowhere to hide, nowhere. Nowhere. The beast was upon him, snorting hot, moist, acrid breath, bloodshot eyes blazing with wild destructive hatred. There was nothing else in KCs vision except the hairy beast that was ready to inflict unimaginable havoc.

Then, blackness. Nothingness.

KC's head ached. His stomach felt unsettled. He was disoriented. Where was he? What was he doing? Time—time seemed not to exist. Then he felt a jerk as though he had been moving and suddenly stopped. There was no sense of direction—no up, no down, no anything.

And then there was a dim light. He could see that his arms, legs, and chest were strapped in. He could feel the strap around his head. Suddenly, reality flooded in with thoughts of Krella, the Jaylex, and the "jump." Once he totally regained consciousness, all he could think of was Krella. For some reason, he feared that she was gone. What if he never saw her again? The thought horrified him. He began to struggle against his restraints. He tried to call out her name, but his throat was parched, and his mouth and lips were dry. All that came out was an unintelligible gasp. The sound, strange though it was, brought him to total reality. Again, he attempted to say Krella's name. This time it was not in a panic. He could not think of anything else to say, and he wanted to see if he could respond verbally. The first few times he tried to say her name resulted in the same gasping type grunts, but soon he could easily say her name. He touched the finger touch pad on the arm of his chair.

Okay, KC thought, *I'm ready for your questions, Jaylex.*

Jaylex's soft, reassuring female voice asked, "Can you hear?"

"Yes," responded KC.

"Is your vision functioning?"

"Yes," KC said again.

"Do you feel you have any injuries?"

"No."

"What is your name?"

"V.I. KC."

"Jaylex is now in expansion mode. Your restraints will be removed, but please stay in your pod until your quarters are fully extended. V.I. KC, did you have any visual or auditory sensations during the 'jump'?"

KC remembered the Brazilian fisherman and the giant gorilla. He remembered the sounds of bare feet hitting the parched ground and heavy breathing. The thoughts sent a chill through him.

"Yes," KC answered weakly.

"Did you have visual sensations?"

"Yes."

"Did you have auditory sensations?"

"Yes."

"Did you have any other physical or mental sensations?"

KC wanted to say he had felt fear as he had never felt it before, but he knew the voice response system would not understand and would ask him to repeat his answer.

He simply replied, "Yes."

"It is extremely important that all 'jump' experiences are recorded for future examination. Please recount all your 'jump' experiences in as much detail as possible. There is no time limit. When you have finished, wait three seconds, and say 'complete.'"

KC felt odd talking about what he had seen and felt, but the more he told, the more he realized that his experiences were already beginning to fade. It was like trying to remember a vivid dream upon waking. The images were fading. Only the picture of the giant gorilla and its round, blood-red, hate-filled eyes refused to fade. The fear—the fear KC had felt seemed distant and at the same time lurking nearby, ready to spring out and grab him.

"Complete," said KC.

"Expect to speak with a representative within one-half time unit. Thank you for your cooperation KC. Again, please remain in your spinner until your quarters have completed expansion."

KC wondered if the representative would be an Earthling, a Venuvian, or maybe even a Traveler. He remembered a director had mentioned during training that, after a "jump," those who had experienced anything during the "jump" would be interviewed. Now, as KC reflected back on this, he realized that there had been a very un-Venuvian-like lack of thoroughness on this topic. He would be meeting with a "representative" in one-half time unit. In one-half time unit, the Jaylex would have barely completed the expansion mode. He assumed that the Venuvians wanted to question him immediately, before his memories had faded. He would soon find out that his "jump" experiences would change his life forever.

The soft reassuring voice had told KC to report to area seven. Now KC sat in a room and looked at the wall in front of him. It was covered with a visual of a very large city. Some of the architecture was Venuvian, but most of it was not. Every area seemed to have its own unique style. Even the land craft that he could see, though they seemed to have Venuvian characteristics, were personalized. On the smaller wall to his left was a visual of a domed city that KC assumed was the same large city viewed from a distance. The huge dome had six much smaller domes, which were outside of the large dome. He could see passageways that connected the small domes to the larger one.

The transparent domes lay in a broad valley flanked on both sides by gently rolling, tree-covered hills. The big dome straddled a meandering river that continued past the city, went down the valley, and emptied into an ocean. To the left of where the river poured into the ocean, the coast curved around such that the shoreline jutted out into the ocean. Beyond the shoreline loomed a magnificent range of mountains. On the wall to his right was an entrance to another room and a small visual of a yellowish planet.

Home to the domed city, no doubt, thought KC.

Most of the "jump" side effects were gone, and KC felt a little silly waiting to be interviewed. His visions seemed so distant now. Only the sickening feeling of fear still lingered. The city on the yellow planet fascinated KC. He stood and was about to study the visual on the wall in front of him more closely when the door to the other room opened.

"V.I. KC?"

KC turned and froze in shocked surprise. He thought that he would be interviewed by some Traveler who had already made a "jump" or two, or maybe even by a Venuvian. It was neither. Standing in the open doorway was an Ortan. Even if KC had not seen his eyes, he would have known that this was an Ortan—he looked so much like Krella. With the exception of Krella, the Ortans that KC had seen had their eyes covered. This one made no attempt to conceal his. He looked directly at KC with his large, round, golden eyes, which were wide open. KC was taken with the strangeness of it all. He had looked so often into Krella's eyes and had seen what she felt, felt what she felt. Now, here were eyes, so similar to hers, looking at him. KC felt nothing.

"I am Zanatu," said the Ortan extending his palm. "Please step in."

The Ortan had a warm smile and, despite KC's initial uneasiness, KC now felt relaxed in Zanatu's presence. KC entered the room. It was not much larger than his living quarters. In the middle of the room was a small round table with three fixed chairs. Two of the chairs were empty, but in the third chair sat a stoic-faced Venuvian.

"This is Volgarth," said Zanatu. "We would like to ask you a few questions."

The Venuvian extended his palm. As soon as their palms touched, KC realized he had never actually touched a Venuvian before. He did not know what he had been expecting, but the Venuvian's palm was surprisingly soft and warm.

"Greetings, V.I. KC," said Volgarth in the usual Venuvian monotone.

Although Volgarth had all the appearances of a typical Venuvian, KC felt none of his usual trepidation. He felt the Venuvian's presence was almost inconsequential. KC had never feared the Venuvians, but he had always responded to their power and control. He was surprised at his relaxed feelings. He wondered if his attitude was somehow due to the "jump."

"KC," said the Ortan, dropping the title V.I., "we understand you experienced some visual stimulation during the 'jump.'"

"Yes, I did," said KC, with images of the gorilla, the out-of-body experience, and the Adabuma flashing through his mind.

"Yes you did," repeated the Ortan. "Describe everything you remember. Don't leave out any detail."

KC told the questioners what had happened as completely as he could, including the intense fear.

"Describe the gorilla," said Volgarth.

KC hesitated a moment, expecting the Venuvian to ask more specific questions. He did not.

"It was giant. Bigger than, than... " KC did not know exactly how to describe the beast. "At least 25 meters tall. It seemed to be awakening from a deep slumber. Maybe even a drug induced sleep. Its eyes were bloodshot and full of hate. The gorilla had focused all that hate on me. His eyes were full of more than just hate. There was anger, disgust, and a desire to not only kill me but to inflict upon me some unspeakable pain."

"Did the gorilla actually do you any harm?" asked the Venuvian.

A vision of the beast's face flashed through KC's memory. The fear he had experienced was painful but he could not remember the giant actually touching him.

"Nothing physical," said KC. "But...," he hesitated, somewhat embarrassed to admit how afraid he had been.

The Venuvian sat motionless with the characteristic lack of expression. However, the Ortan leaned forward in his chair looking at KC with an air of expectancy.

"Yes, but what?" asked the Ortan,

"Fear. I have never felt such fear in my life." KC felt an uneasiness in his stomach just thinking about that fear. "And it wasn't just a fear for my life. I had the feeling that the gorilla was going to inflict some unspeakable pain—something worse than death."

"Thank you, KC." The Venuvian stood and stiffly extended his palm.

KC stood, a little surprised that the meeting had ended so quickly. He extended his palm to the Venuvian. The Ortan was smiling.

"Yes, exactly. Thank you for your time," the Ortan said, standing and extending his palm.

KC extended his palm toward the Ortan. When he did, he looked into the Ortan's eyes. For a fraction of a second, the Ortan seemed to drop the guard that had prevented KC from reading his feelings. Just as quickly, his eyes became pinpoints for a flash and then had returned to their previously impenetrable stare. KC had seen something in the Ortan's eyes, if only briefly. He had seen great joy.

The "jump" and the meeting began to fade as soon as KC left the room. All he could think of was Krella. Only that feeling of total fear still held on to the edges of his thoughts. He also wondered how Zanatu, unlike any other Ortans he had seen, was able to conceal his thoughts without eye cover. He would have to ask Krella. Krella—he got a warm feeling just thinking about her.

KC thought he would head back to the Skull Searchers and check out his possessions. The Venuvians had said that the "jump" occasionally damaged things. When he got to the elevator, there was Krella waiting for him. She wore a veil, but then, after a long embrace, she lifted it. At first, there was a concerned look as she searched his eyes, then relief, then joy—the same joy KC thought he had seen flash across Zanatu's eyes.

"Are you fine? Yes, you are," Krella said, answering her own question.

"And so are you, very fine!" said KC flirtatiously. He was overjoyed and still surprised.

They embraced again.

"Krella, do you know Zanatu?"

"Yes, I know Zanatu. Yes of course, yes."

"I met with him after the 'jump.' And, surprisingly, his eyes were not covered. They…, they—"

"Yes," Krella interrupted. "He has studied at Tambuki. Did he speak to you of Tambuki?"

"No," said KC, somewhat perplexed. "Where is Tambuki? And why would he discuss it with me?"

"You did have visions during the 'jump,' did you not?" She also seemed perplexed.

"Yes I did. How did you know?"

"I can see it, yes I can. It changes some. Some it even destroys. But you, it has made you strong in ways you have not yet seen. Yes. You have powers. But if Zanatu has not yet spoken to you of Tambuki, I should say no more. He will want to speak to both of us together. Yes he will."

"What?" KC was more confused than ever. "Why both of us together? Did you see things during the 'jump'?"

Krella put a finger to KC's lips. Krella's eyes still spoke great joy. But there was also a tinge of embarrassment. Without asking, he knew Krella would say no more about the matter. He was dying to know why there was so much secrecy.

"Soon, Kay Zee, soon," said Krella softly.

She gave him a soft kiss and left. KC watched her walk away. He wanted to chase her and hold her and never let her go. He decided to go back to his quarters and digest his experiences.

◆

"He saw it," said Zanatu. "He saw it, and he feared the evil. And he has bonded with Krella, a sensible young woman. Not flighty like her cousin."

"He is a thief, and he broke strict rules about coming in contact with isolated cultures," said Zareg. "These Earth people are still a bit untamed. They act without thinking about consequences."

Zareg was tall, even by Ortan standards, and rotund. He popped a marble-sized delicacy into his mouth and took a sip of some hot beverage. He swiveled his chair around so that his back was to Zanatu.

"Remember how the V.I.s from Bugal tried to take over a ship? They were wild like these Earthlings."

"Yes, I have heard that story," said Zanatu, who had been slowly pacing back and forth on the opposite side of the table from Zareg. "It happened over 300 years ago, and the Elders have since put up protective measures to prevent such mishaps from recurring. You know that 'jump' analysis catches most misfits, and Elder screening at Tambuki is now so intense it's next to impossible for undesirables to be accepted for training."

"Yes, but there's still a chance, and I would hate to be responsible for getting another rebel in the system. What if a bad one should come under the control of bad forces? Our entire mission could be destroyed. I do not know," said Zareg, slowly shaking his head, swiveling in his chair and popping another sweet into his mouth.

Zanatu knew Zareg's little game by heart. He always expressed reservations about candidates for Tambuki so that, just in case there was a problem, he could claim that he had been opposed. Zanatu stopped and looked directly at Zareg.

"So, do you think we should suggest an Elder screen?" asked Zanatu.

Zareg returned Zanatu's gaze. Ironically, Ortans could look deep into each other's eyes and feel nothing of what the other felt, but Zanatu knew what Zareg's response would be, almost verbatim.

"Elder screens require so much fluid. I hate to be responsible for any waste. I suppose we should recommend candidacy."

Fluid was the element that was found in minute quantities in fresh blood. It was the element that gave the Elders their long lives and their psychokinetic powers. These psychokinetic powers could be used for almost anything—to move mountains or to explore the inner workings of the brain, but it was used primarily to move ships to different planetary systems.

Zareg's look of consternation was as practiced as his reluctance-to-accept-a-candidate speech. Zanatu had learned from experience not to challenge Zareg's sincerity. Zanatu just smiled.

"I agree," said Zanatu. "I think we should recommend KC for candidacy. If he and Krella should decide to unite, and I feel certain they will, she could accompany him to Tambuki."

◆

KC sat on his bed thinking about the last few hours of his life when he was surprised to hear his audio announce, "V.I. KC, you have a visitor." Though he felt friendly toward many V.I.s, no deep friendships had developed. This was primarily because he spent all his spare time with Krella. It was also because the cost of his private quarters absorbed most of his units. He could not afford to attend most of the activities with which other V.I.s occupied themselves. Consequently, KC got few visitors. He had the reputation of being an amiable loner.

KC was even more surprised when his port slid open and there stood a veiled Krella. He had once asked her to his quarters. One look into her eyes told him that, even though she desperately wanted to go to his room, she should not and would not. So her presence here and now was doubly perplexing to KC.

"Would you like to come in?" he asked, not knowing what her answer would be.

"Yes," she answered flatly.

"Have a seat," said KC.

KC motioned toward his computer chair, not daring to indicate the bed. She sat almost as if obeying an order—her eyes still covered, and her head down.

"Ah, what brings you here?" He was truly at a loss for words.

Krella's head shot up and she threw back her veil. "Kay Zee," she said firmly.

Then she seemed to lose her resolve, and her head dropped again. But KC had looked into her eyes. It was only for a second, but it might as well have been for an eternity. KC fell to his knees before her, took her hands and smothered them with kisses. Then he held her chin and gently lifted her head. He pulled back her veil, something he had never done before, and looked deeply into her eyes. She returned his gaze, her golden eyes revealing her innermost feelings. He knew no words were necessary, but he had to say the words.

"Krella, I cannot imagine one day without you. I want us to be together for the rest of our lives. I love you as I have loved no other. Will you unite your life with mine?"

Krella did not use words. She fell to her knees before KC and placed her lips on his. The sweetness of their kiss mingled with the salt of their tears.

◆

Krella and KC's meeting with Zanatu was short.

"Your visions during the 'jump' are a sign that you have certain communication skills and that you may have special powers, very special powers. There are teachers on a planet that can facilitate an enormous growth of your powers. We very much want you to go to that planet."

"I will never leave Krella," KC said immediately.

Zanatu turned to Krella. "Krella, we would very much like you to accompany KC."

"Only death will separate me from KC," said Krella.

"What will these teachers be teaching, and where is this planet?" asked KC.

"There is very little I can tell you about the planet. In many ways, it is similar to Earth, but you will be the first Earthling. There are many Ortans on the planet, Krella. I have been to the planet once and spent many years there, but I do not know where it is located. The teachers will teach you how to see, listen, speak, and move. You will experience a consciousness more profound than you can imagine. I assure you the experience will be life changing."

"What if we wish to return to Dramaltus?" asked KC.

"It is highly unlikely that you will be able to return," said Zanatu.

"There is a visual of domed cities on your wall," said KC. "Are they on the planet where you wish us to go?"

"Yes, they are. The name of the planet is Tambuki. You have 45 time units to make a decision."

Zanatu extended his palm to KC, then to Krella. His smile radiated warmth, but his eyes revealed nothing.

KC was numb. For the past seven years, he had been engaged in training that had prepared him for a life on Dramaltus gathering information on pre-Gavean-tool societies. Only one time unit ago, he had professed his undying love for Krella. He was willing to go anywhere with her, even if it meant joining a ship with her family and traveling to another system.

If Krella and KC had not met, Krella would have joined another ship with other Ortans. Ortan ties are very strong, and, although a contingency of Ortans had settled on Earth, Krella said she had chosen to join the Jaylex rather than stay on Earth.

"You didn't like my planet?" KC had asked, acting a bit hurt.

"Your planet's inhabitants are always fighting. Always."

"Not since the Venuvians came," said KC.

"There are still battles among your Unattached."

"But there aren't that many Unattached."

"And they continually fight."

KC had studied Earth's history and, although he only knew life with the Venuvians, he had to admit that when he studied Earth's history, he found that there was always a war or hostilities going on somewhere on the planet.

Zanatu had given KC a choice: stay on the Jaylex and go to Dramaltus, or take another "jump" and go to some unknown planet for some unclear reason. Krella had made it clear that she would go with KC, whatever his decision. Now KC had less than 40 time units to make a decision that would affect the rest of his life.

"Why can't I read anything in Zanatu's eyes?" asked KC. He was avoiding making a decision.

"He trained on Tambuki." Krella sounded tired. She was holding KC's hand—she held it tighter. "Ortans can learn to hide their feelings. Yes they can."

"Would you learn to hide your feelings from me if we went to Tambuki?"

"Yes, I would be trained to cover my feelings, and you would learn to block your feelings, but the eyes are only one path. Even though this path is the brightest, there are many others. I know you, and you know me. Tambuki will never change that. Never."

"Never," repeated KC.

◆

KC and Krella stood in the same room where KC had waited for his first meeting with Zanatu and the Venuvian. It seemed so long ago. Now, after meeting with Zanatu a second time, he and Krella looked at the visuals of the dome over the meandering river in a completely new light. Would this strange planet become their new home? Zanatu had explained that they would only spend a short time in the Tambuki domes. They would actually train in an area a quarter of the way around the globe.

Zanatu had also told them that, when the Venuvians had completed modifying Tambuki, they had removed all electronic devices from the planet. By terminating all electronic activity, the Venuvians had totally separated Tambuki from the Venuvian world. All food, clothing, and shelter were produced from the land. Communication was by an intricate system of mirrors. Transportation was by foot, domesticated animals, self-propelled vehicles, steam-assisted vehicles, and gliders. The Venuvians had hoped to create an area for open and unfettered studies and training. There was a Venuvian presence, but the Venuvians interceded only in cases of emergency.

"What about all this Tambuki training?" KC had asked Krella.

"When one masters The Way, one becomes eligible to become an Elder."

Krella had explained that becoming an Elder was the highest position anyone could attain. When KC questioned her further about it, she said that she knew no more.

For five time units, KC pored over the Venuvian archives searching for any information he could find on Tambuki. There was little. It was a planet in a seven-planet star system. It was a warm, lush planet with small polar ice caps. When the Venuvians arrived, it was uninhabited by any humanoid life forms. The Venuvians had established only one post on Tambuki—the domed area. KC read about the area that was set aside for open and unfettered studies and training. What did they mean by "open and unfettered"? Nowhere could KC find any reference as to what was being studied on Tambuki.

KC cross-referenced Tambuki with every branch of study he could think of from anthropology to zoology. The only bit of information he came up with was concerning a philosopher and spiritual leader named Stato, who was born and trained on Tambuki. The typically highly detailed Venuvian archives were scant when it came to the topic of Stato or Statoism. Statonian thought had a very strong influence on Venuvian philosophy. That was it. KC asked Krella if she had any knowledge of Statoism.

"I have heard that the Elders practice Statoism, but I know nothing of any of its principles, nothing at all," said Krella.

KC's frustration began to turn into anger. How was he supposed to make a decision with no information? Why would the Venuvians train him for years to be a V.I. and then ship him to some sparsely inhabited planet to train him in The Way? Then what? And, an Elder? What was an Elder? And what was Statoism? KC asked Krella what she thought about going to Tambuki.

"I have to make my decision alone, yes I do. You must make your decision alone. Then we will make our decision together."

"Well," KC said angrily, "if you will not help me decide, who the hell will?"

He immediately regretted having been so abrupt with her. He could feel her hurt without seeing her eyes. Krella understood. She had left without saying anything. With only 15 time units remaining before KC had to make up his mind, he did not seem to be able to think clearly. Thoughts of his "jump" experience, and of Krella, and of Tambuki flashed through his mind in a mingled mass of confusion, frustration and anger. Then he got a message on his computer.

It was from Krella, and it simply said, "You have made your decision, now you must accept it."

KC stared at the display for a moment and then turned away from it. He began to feel a calmness engulf him. Indeed, he had made his decision.

KC's biggest regret was that he would not have a chance to visit Dramaltus. He had seen preliminary visuals taken with an enlargement scope, but that was not the same as actually going to a viewing station and seeing an unenhanced view of the planet. KC wanted to look at Dramaltus just once, but that would certainly never be. Zanatu had told KC that if, for some reason, after going to Tambuki, he and Krella chose to abandon their training, their options would be limited. They could take a post in the domed area or take a post on a planet where one of the shuttles departing Tambuki was headed. The chance that there would be a shuttle to Dramaltus was slim, very slim. KC did not really care. Once he decided to go to Tambuki, the thoughts of Dramaltus faded. KC's biggest fear—the fear of another "jump"—did not fade.

The next few time units flew by. Krella and KC had to quickly arrange a vow ceremony. KC was shocked at the number of Ortans that attended. Ever since he met Krella, he had seen two or three hundred Ortans, mostly at work in their agricultural sector. Now there were well over a thousand Ortans at the ceremony—with eyes uncovered and happy to witness Krella's new life. The few V.I.s that KC knew well enough to invite sat to one side, intimidated by the mass of Ortans. After the ceremony, KC and Krella spent a few time units mingling with their guests and saying their good-byes. Then they collected their belongings and transferred to a shuttle ship. The shuttle separated from the Jayslex and, for the next six days, as the shuttle accelerated toward the Dramaltus sun, KC and Krella found a new oneness. The bliss they experienced was an altogether fitting beginning for their new life together.

Their second day on the shuttle, KC and Krella met Morbred and Jubley. Morbred could be as obnoxious as she was lovable. She was a large woman, even by the standards of her home planet. She stood two meters and weighed 90 kilos. Her physique could only be described as muscular. She had a flat nose, bushy eyebrows, thick lips, and a square chin. When she spread her lips—which she often did in boisterous laughter—she showed her large, white, prominent teeth. Her almond-shaped, steely-gray eyes were usually warm, but, when they were squinted in anger, they could send a chill through the bravest of souls. Crowning Morbred was a bizarre hairstyle. Its true color was unknown. She openly admitted she had tried various colors before settling on the current one. Her hair's current color was a brilliant gold. The color was eye catching, but that was not the most striking thing about her hair. With the aid of some of her special hair preparation, Morbred had enticed her hair to stand straight up evenly in all directions. The style added to her already enormous stature. Only her adoring mate, Jubley, knew how she managed to sleep without disturbing her hair.

Whoever said that opposites attract could not have found a better example than Morbred and Jubley. Jubley was quiet and withdrawn. He always had a subtle smile, as if he was aware of some joke no one else was getting. His 1.75 meters tall frame was slender—slender legs, slender arms, and long, slender, and delicate fingers. When standing, he had a habit of slowly pacing back and forth with his hands clasped behind him. Jet-black hair combed straight back topped his long, slender face. His facial features were delicate. His small upturned nose displayed the two narrow slits that served as nostrils. His eyes were small and round and rather close together.

Jubley's slight appearance belied his physical prowess. Morbred often spoke of how he had successfully dealt with her brothers who were friendly but enjoyed playful physical competition. They loved to run, jump, wrestle, and engage in activities that ended up with heavy breathing and minor bruises. They competed in the spirit of fun, and even perpetual losers enjoyed themselves. Jubley, Morbred bragged, seldom came out on the losing end of such competitions. Her brothers had constantly challenged him and derived great pleasure out of the fact that Jubley usually came out on top. KC and Krella became good friends with Morbred and Jubley.

"Why do you cover your eyes, woman?" Morbred had asked Krella only minutes after they first met.

"Why does your hair look like an exploding star?" Krella had replied with a smile.

Morbred had roared with laughter at the audacity of this woman.

"My hair is an extension of my mind and body—big. Now, why do you hide your eyes?"

Krella had answered without hesitation. "My eyes reveal thoughts that I do not wish to be revealed."

Krella's and Morbred's relationship could easily be characterized by their first meeting. Both asked straightforward and often personal questions, and both were quick to give honest answers. KC was somewhat surprised at Krella's talkativeness. She and Morbred usually dominated the conversation. Morbred liked to talk about family anecdotes that were usually humorous. Krella recounted agricultural projects she and her family had worked on, and KC discussed his Amazon Basin experiences. Jubley rarely spoke, but, when he did, it was to express a point of fact, logic, or reason. Of course, initially the topic had been about Tambuki.

"I wonder what kind of special training they have for us?" Morbred had asked.

No one had an answer. The Travelers would discover that, even after several years on Tambuki, there would be questions with no clear answers.

"We shall see. Yes, we shall," replied Krella.

"I know we shall see," said Morbred. "But I want to know now."

"None of us have any information on Tambuki, and the Venuvians say nothing," said Jubley.

"We know what we know," said Krella cryptically.

"What is that supposed to mean?" shot back Morbred.

"I mean, we shall examine what we know, not what we don't know."

"Do you know something we don't know?" Morbred was irritated.

"Whatever I knew before this conversation has definitely not increased," said Krella.

It was not until the Venuvians announced preparation for the "jump" that KC and Morbred revealed what they had in common. The two couples were drinking bevy, a hot beverage, after third meal.

"I am not looking forward to the 'jump,'" said KC.

"Why?" Morbred asked, looking intently at KC.

KC looked up from his steaming cup, surprised at Morbred's obvious interest. KC hesitated, suddenly realizing how much he had been suppressing the extreme fear he had experienced.

"I had some—some bad feelings," said KC.

"Frightening dreams?" asked Morbred.

"Yes, quite frightening," said KC.

He had wondered how Morbred knew. He glanced at Krella. Even though she concealed her eyes, a slight shrug of her shoulders and a movement of her head was enough to let KC know that she had revealed nothing.

"Did it involve being chased by a giant beast?" asked Morbred.

KC's shock was obvious, but, before he could say anything more, Morbred continued.

"I also had frightening visions. I do not think I have ever been so frightened. And you, Krella, did you also have visions?"

"No, I have been through two 'jumps,' and I have never had any such experiences. I am sure that is why the Venuvians selected you and KC to go to Tambuki," said Krella.

"What!" exclaimed KC. "You mean, you knew why I was asked to go to Tambuki, and you never told me?" KC could feel anger building.

"I have seen others leave for Tambuki after 'jumps.' I have been told that some of them had visions," said Krella in a calm and steady voice.

"Why didn't you tell me?" said KC, raising his voice.

"I do not know," she said sincerely.

As improbable as it sounded, KC knew she meant it. His anger subsided, while his curiosity grew. Something was at work here that none of them understood. Their questions would not be answered for many years, and it would not be by the Venuvians.

After KC and Morbred discovered that they both had frightening "jump" experiences, all they could talk about was their visions. Many of their visions were quite different, but one thing was the same—fear, uncontrollable fear, fear of a giant beast whose single-minded desire was to inflict unimaginable pain on its fleeing prey. Both admitted that it was the most terrifying experience they had ever had in their life. It was not just a fear of dying. There was something else, something unseen, something unspeakable.

"I guess I've been suppressing the whole thing." KC said pensively. "Just thinking about it still gives me the shakes. I almost didn't take this trip to Tambuki because I never wanted to make another 'jump.' But I can't get over the feeling that there is an answer somewhere, and that somehow the 'jump' and Tambuki are involved."

"Yes," said Morbred softly. "I feel compelled to go to the domed city. Something has entered my life that is unresolved, something that I must find."

"I must go to the domed city, even if I have to face the beast again," said KC.

◆

As the time to "jump" approached, KC and Morbred could see the apprehension in each other's eyes. All the Travelers were surprised that it only took five days to get the shuttle in position to "jump." When the rays from Dramaltus's sun became too intense, the shuttle's shields were activated on the observation deck. Even though the glare from the sun had long ago drowned out all other objects, the observation deck had been the only window into the vastness of outer space. With the shields up, there was a pervasive feeling of being trapped. The shuttle, a speck plunging toward a giant incinerator, was about to make an incomprehensible journey through space.

"The time will come and the time will pass. Yes it will," Krella said to KC.

She could feel his pain but she knew there was nothing she could do. What happened during the next "jump" was unexpected.

As the ship plunged toward Dramaltus's sun, it was accelerated by the sun's massive gravitational pull. The surface of the ship had reached incredibly high temperatures. KC, spinning on magnetically created axes, felt his consciousness slipping away as the sedative began to take over. Despite the numbness creeping over his body, he could feel himself tensing. The muscles in his jaw tightened as he tried to fight the inevitable.

And then, suddenly, nothingness.

SHUTTLE TO TAMBUKI

KC opened his eyes. For a few seconds his disorientation kept him from realizing where he was or what his condition was. Then, in a flash, it came to him. He was in his spinner, and it was no longer spinning! He was in recovery mode! The "jump" was over! No visions. No beast. No unrestrained fear. A smile spread over KC's face. The "jump" was over! Indeed the "jump" had been uneventful. Morbred had also come through the "jump" without an event.

When the two couples met after the "jump," both Morbred and KC—very excited and relieved that they had had no visions during the "jump"—shouted out "No visions! No visions!"

It would be years before they would ever mention the visions again, years before they found out what the visions signified, years before they were told why they were among the very few who had experienced visions.

Twenty days after the "jump," they achieved Tambuki orbit. On the last day, all electronic devices were turned off. The docking station, a strange looking ship in a stationary orbit, slowly came into view. It was small compared to the shuttle. It was merely a docking satellite, not a travel ship. Docking was a primitive affair. As the shuttle approached, the docking station shot three lines toward the shuttle. The ship captured the lines by means of magnets. When the lines were secure, the shuttle kept the lines taught by releasing a steady stream of pressurized gas toward the satellite. The docking station then reeled in the ship. The Travelers had arrived at the last stop before setting foot on the dome planet. No one had a chance to explore the Station. As soon as they had docked, things were transferred to a landing craft. The Travelers boarded the craft and were immediately issued protective headgear and strapped into heavily padded chairs.

"I don't know about you, but I feel like I'm being prepared for a crash landing," Morbred said, as an attendant was strapping her in.

"Not like Venuvian ship," a short, pudgy attendant had said.

He was the only person they had seen on the station.

"What is it like?" asked Morbred.

"Like bird," said the attendant, as he finished strapping in Krella. "You leave now." Then he turned and left.

"Wow!" said Morbred. "He sure was full of information," she said sarcastically. "'Not like Venuvian ship,'" she said, mocking the attendant.

"Like bird," said Jubley.

"Somehow, it doesn't give me a great deal of comfort knowing I am going to leave orbit and travel hundreds of kilometers after an uncommunicative assistant straps me in a landing craft that is something 'like bird,'" said Morbred, again mocking the attendant.

"He was confident we would land safely," said Krella. She offered no further explanation, but KC knew she had read his feelings.

The craft did indeed land safely, but not without some discomforts. As soon as the attendant had sealed the contraption, the temperature dropped precipitously and was almost intolerable.

"You think they have reverted to cryogenics?" KC muttered.

"No one told me to dress for winter," said Morbred.

All the Travelers were dressed in Venuvian-issued clothing that insulated them against both hot and cold—to a point. But the outfits were not sufficient for the cold that had engulfed the cabin. The birdlike ship released itself from the satellite and began its descent toward Tambuki. The reason for the cold interior became evident when the ship entered the atmosphere. As it began its downward plunge, the temperature began to rise until it became almost unbearable. The ship started to vibrate, and then shake, and then, as it picked up speed, violently buck. The Travelers felt every movement of the ship. When it seemed as if it must surely break apart, the landing craft threw the Travelers forward in their restraints as if brakes had been suddenly engaged. The bucking stopped and the temperature dropped. The Travelers only felt an occasional jerk. If they could have been on the outside of the craft, they would have seen giant birdlike wings spread. They were gliding!

After a few moments, Morbred began to laugh hysterically. "First they tried to freeze us, then they tried to cook us, and then they tried to shake our teeth out," she said. "What's next?"

"Let's not try to think up anything," said KC. "This may be some kind of test to see how much we can tolerate. We don't want to give them any more ideas." KC chuckled. "What have we gotten ourselves into? I feel like we are being sent back in time."

"Back in time?" asked Krella. "The first planet we visited did not even have its own satellite, no they didn't. This is a Venuvian planet. There must be a reason for these primitive conditions, there must be."

"I am sure all will be explained after we land on Tambuki," said Jubley in his reserved way.

After a while, the Travelers felt a few thuds and bumps, some twists and turns and what sounded like blasts of compressed gas. Then the ship came to a stop. The Travelers were finally on Tambuki!

DOME CITY

When the Travelers exited the ship, a short, portly, round-headed man greeted them. His cherub-like cheeks were deep brown. His wide fore-head hung in such a way that it almost obscured his twinkling, gray eyes. He held his thick blue lips in a perpetual grin. His stubby- fingered hands were the only other part of his body that showed. His clothing consisted of a hooded jalaba that reached the ground. It was made of a course material that could have been white at one time. Now it was the dull gray that comes with age.

"Welcome to Tambuki," said the round-headed greeter, Samtatu. "His name is Samtatu. He will be their guide until they are settled with the Outlanders." Samtatu could see the bewilderment on the faces of the Travelers. "Samtatu is the one who now stands before them," said Samtatu with a chuckle. "The Travelers will soon learn to understand the speaking ways of those who follow The Way."

Those who followed The Way always spoke in the third person.

"Can you tell us why we are here," asked KC?

"Yes, he can," said Samtatu. But he did not answer the question. "Someone will give the Travelers Outlander robes before the Travelers leave on their journey. The Travelers will need nothing else when they leave Dome City."

"Where are we going?" asked Morbred. "And *is* he going to tell us why we are here?" She strongly emphasized the word "he."

Samtatu let out a full belly laugh.

"Samtatu will answer all the Travelers' questions, no, *many* of the Travelers' questions. Samtatu cannot answer all questions. He does not know the answer to all questions."

"When exactly was Samtatu planning on answering many of the Travelers' questions?" Morbred asked. She was obviously irritated.

"He cannot say exactly when he will answer their questions," said Samtatu. "But he will answer questions at some time in the future."

With that, he turned and walked away from the Travelers and the landing craft. He moved with a gait that was brisk and steady but, at the same time, graceful. The Travelers quickly fell into step behind him. Samtatu had not answered any of the Travelers questions.

As the Travelers moved away from the landing craft, they got a better look at what brought them from the docking station to Tambuki. It looked like a giant creature with two wings that were at least 75 meters each. The body was a twenty-meter-long cylinder with tapered ends. It was charred black with a pattern of cracks that made it look like it had scales. Behind the landing craft were a series of what looked like giant spider webs. The webs were broken where the craft had flown through them. Evidently, the webs slowed the craft until it slid to a stop. There was already an army of workers rebuilding the webs, removing the charred, black scales from the landing craft and retracting the wings. It all looked very primitive.

Primitive, however, did not accurately describe the domed city. It did not have amenities such as electronics and towering buildings that the V.I.s expected from the Venuvians. But, as the Travelers approached a wide roadway, it became apparent that the designs of the transportation vehicles were Venuvian. Teams of long-haired animals with long powerful front legs and short, stubby rear legs provided much of the power for transportation. The roadway surfaces were earthen, but they were hard and smooth, and the long-haired animals trotted effortlessly back and forth pulling passenger-laden transports.

In contrast to the animal-powered transports, there were bi, tri, and quad pedicycles that were powered by the drivers pedaling. Some of the cycles belched out steam that filled the air with an odor that the Travelers had smelled on the landing craft. Odors from various food vendors also drifted through the air.

The buildings, which were flush against each other, were made of adobe bricks. There was not much variation in the design of the buildings. Some of the buildings were plain and were the same color as the roadways, but most were colored or in some way decorated. The colors varied from subtle to glaring. Some buildings had non-Venuvian writing on them, and some were covered with intricate or not so intricate designs. Building decorations ranged from child's play to sophisticated artwork.

Walkways were crowded with unhurried pedestrians and passive street vendors. Dress wear varied from intricate, flowing robes to brief loincloths. Only a few inhabitants wore Venuvian clothing. The Travelers had seen visuals of groups of people from many different planets, but here, on Tambuki, everyone the Travelers passed appeared to be of different origin. Morbred, who usually stood out with her imposing figure and unusual hairdo, went completely unnoticed.

The Travelers walked along a wide, busy thoroughfare for a while and then turned down a narrower, deserted street. Samtatu stopped in front of a building made of the plain adobe bricks. The building had two entrances.

"This will be their lodging for the night," Samtatu said. "Someone will bring their robes and meals. Feel free to explore the city, but get plenty of rest tonight. They will spend tomorrow exploring Dome City. The next day, they will leave Dome City with the first sign of light."

With that, Samtatu gave a slight bow with his head, turned and walked away.

"They will be leaving with the first sign of the sun," mimicked Morbred after Samtatu left. "Morbred will be sleeping in a mud hut tonight. She wonders what they will be feeding her."

"I believe Samtatu has good intentions," said Krella. "He has the ability to purposely conceal his feelings. I do not know if he was born with this ability."

Morbred and Jubley had come to understand that Krella had a special ability to interpret how people felt. They accepted her cryptic statements without question, but this was the first time they had seen her powers apparently fail. Morbred wanted to question Krella further, but she knew it would be useless.

"Well, let's have a look inside," said Morbred.

"Let *them* have a look," corrected Krella with a smile.

Morbred scowled and entered the living quarters with the others. The Travelers were pleasantly surprised—even Morbred. The rooms were spacious and opened with transparent, domed ceilings. The furniture was sparse, but there was an abundance of plants in every room.

"This is beautiful," said Morbred."

"It's certainly not what he expected," said KC.

"These plants," said Krella almost to herself. "I have never seen any of them before, no I haven't. I wonder where they come from."

"*She* wonders, yes *she* does," said Morbred looking straight at Krella. Krella turned to Morbred. She stood still for a moment and then, for the first time, Krella lifted her veil so Morbred could see her eyes. Morbred, who was usually unmoved by Krella's actions, let out a short gasp.

"Oh, Krella, I... she didn't mean anything. Please don't let her be a bother."

Krella lowered her veil. "She thanks Morbred for understanding."

"Come see this," said Jubley displaying uncharacteristic enthusiasm.

He was standing by a boulder in front of the far wall. Behind the boulder there was another opening. It was twice as wide as the door to the street. A short corridor led outside. On one side of the corridor, covering the entire wall, there was a map of Dome City and the five surrounding smaller domes. On the other wall was a map of the entire planet.

"They should see what's outside," said Jubley.

Outside, the Travelers discovered a lush, forest-garden park. For the next hour, they wandered through the park, admiring towering trees, beautiful shrubs, flowers, and ponds. Occasionally they heard voices in conversation, but they never saw anyone until they returned to their dwellings. There was a tall, slender, olive-skinned man sitting cross-legged outside of the corridor to their quarters. He rose as they approached.

"Are you the newly arrived Travelers who occupied these quarters?" He was soft spoken with a voice that gave an impression of intellectual prowess.

"We are staying here, yes," said Morbred.

"I am Tagu. I am your helper for tonight. I will be bringing you last meal—your evening meal. I shall also take measurements for your Outlander robes. If you are in need of any assistance, raise the white flag."

Tagu indicated a flagpole to the right of the rear entrance, which now flew a red flag.

"The red flag indicates that the residence is occupied, and the occupants do not wish to receive uninvited guests. If you raise the green flag, you are giving an invitation to all who wish to enter your dwelling. I must warn you, if you raise the green flag, you will be inundated with guests. There is a great deal of interest in Travelers. Does anyone have questions?"

"Why are we here?" asked Morbred immediately.

Tagu smiled. "You have been chosen to be trained."

"Trained for what?" asked Morbred. There was an obvious tinge of determination in her voice.

"To see, to listen, to move, and to speak—in The Way," said Tagu.

"Excuse me," said Morbred. "I do not mean to be rude, but are you saying the Venuvians brought us here to teach us to speak, to see, and to hear?" She asked incredulously.

"To listen," corrected Tagu. "And to move."

"After we are trained, then what?" asked Morbred.

"Many Outlanders spend their entire life training," said Tagu. "Others return to Dome City after only a few years. My grandmother was a trained Outlander. She talks of how beautiful life was in her compound. But none of her children chose to stay in the Outlander Domain. When the one child, who had remained in the Outlander Domain with my grandmother and grandfather, decided to move to Dome City and join my grandmother's other children, my grandmother left her training and came to Dome City with my grandfather."

"Tagu," said KC." I hate to break the news, but I think I have pretty well mastered hearing, seeing, moving, and speaking."

Tagu smiled broadly. "To listen," Tagu reminded again. "There is a fountain nearby. Before I spoke of the fountain, you could hear it, but you were not listening to it. Now you are listening."

The Travelers realized that Tagu had a point. They were now listening to the fountain.

"A well-trained Outlander masters these skills far beyond their everyday use. Those who reach the highest level of training are the Masters," continued Tagu. "If my grandmother sees me walk, looks into my eyes, or listens to me speak only a few words, she can tell me about my feelings. She needs only glance at me for a moment or speak my name to alter my mood. In some quarters of Tambuki, there are beliefs that Outlanders possess supernatural powers but the truth is they merely have enriched skills."

"Is Samtatu a trained Outlander?" asked Krella.

Tagu looked knowingly at Krella. "Yes he is."

There was a pause. The Travelers were waiting for Tagu or Krella to speak. Neither did.

"Why are the conditions on Tambuki so… so primitive?" asked Jubley, breaking the silence.

"Primitive?" said Tagu, musing. "I have never left Tambuki or boarded a Venuvian vehicle, so I have no experience with other worlds. But I have often heard Travelers speak of Venuvian technology and the amazing devices that can be found on Venuvian ships. My grandmother, who is a Traveler, has spoken of such devices. She says that when she reached a certain level of mastery, such devices created noise that interfered with her connection to The Way. She was not aware of the noise when she started training. She first noticed the noise during one of her Monthlies. She said that, after that point, the noise at the Monthlies did indeed become a distraction. One reason our city is domed is so that the noise created by the Monthlies is contained. Even though the Monthly equipment is located 200 meters underground and the city is domed, all Outlander villages are located far away from Dome City to avoid even the subtle noise that escapes. There are also transport machines that create noise but they are used only in cases of emergencies.

"What would be considered an emergency? Jubley asked.

"The most common emergencies are medical," said Tagu. "They occur two or three times every 100 years. There have been a few occasions when the Wild Ones or the Marauders had to be subdued, but that has never happened in my lifetime."

"Wild Ones, Marauders?" asked Morbred.

"There are those who live outside of Dome City but are not Outlanders and who do not take Monthlies," replied Tagu. "They are the Wild Ones. The transient Wild Ones are the Marauders. The Wild Ones usually keep to themselves, but occasionally they attack Outlanders and take what meager possessions the Outlanders have. Once, Marauders even attacked Dome City. According to stories, a trained Outlander commanded the attackers. The rebellion was so well organized, both on the outside and on the inside of the domes, that the Elders had to call for off-world Venuvian forces to squelch the attack. The Marauder Rebellion took place over 475 years ago, and nothing approaching such an attack has ever been repeated."

"It seems so peaceful and open here," said Morbred. "No locked doors or locked windows. What were the Marauders after?"

"Control, power, or some unexplainable desire to rule others," said Tagu solemnly. "Hundreds of people died in the rebellion. Today, many still continue to argue and discuss reasons for the rebellion. There are more questions than answers. Even though the Venuvians mounted a massive search, the Outlander who supposedly led the rebellion was never captured."

The group stood silent for a moment.

Jubley, who was intently interested in everything Tagu had to say, asked, "You said that only those trained and the Masters were bothered by the noise. What about others?"

"Most residents of Dome City are totally unaffected by the noise," said Tagu. "I only know what my grandmother told me, and she speaks infrequently of her actual training. She told me that the noise disturbs the calmness of Masters when they are in a state of deep meditation. Only by being in the presence of a Master can one even come close to understanding this sensitivity." He paused. "To answer your question, those who have reached a certain level of training are able to ignore the noise. Before that point, the noise is a distraction."

"How are Outlanders chosen?" asked Krella.

"Most Outlanders are mates or offspring of those who enter training," said Tagu. "However, there are villages that have gone years with no one in training. A dome dweller, who can find either an Outlander or a Master to train him, may become an Outlander. But the Outlanders who enter training are mostly Travelers. Evidently, if a Traveler has visions during a space 'jump,' then the Venuvians feel that the Traveler possesses special attributes."

Tagu scanned the Travelers' faces. KC and Morbred glanced at each other.

"I assume you have some knowledge of these visions," said Tagu, looking knowingly at KC and Morbed. "Occasionally, the Elders also choose an Outlander who is not in training, a dome dweller, or even a Wild One to enter training."

"What's our meal?" KC interrupted.

Tagu was relieved for the change in subject.

"You have a choice. You can try the standard Outlander meal—quite nutritious but it lacks any… excitement. Or, you may try my family's meal—a taste-treat in my opinion. You might want to try your luck in town. There is a fund for new arrivals for just such occasions. I will be glad to act as your guide if you choose to explore town. You will find a great variety of food in town. Most I am sure you would enjoy, but some food requires an acquired taste. Whatever your decision, simply raise the white flag and I shall return."

Tagu was about to leave when Morbred shot another question at him.

"What about these Elders, and how do they choose who enters training, and what do our visions mean, and… ?"

"Morbred," interrupted Krella gently. "We have plenty of time to ask questions."

Tagu looked at Krella's veiled face. "You must be an Ortan."

"I am," responded Krella.

"There are many Ortan Outlanders," said Tagu. Then he turned to Morbred. "If you can wait until after your meal, I will be glad to answer any question I am able to answer. Please excuse me for a short time." He turned back to the other Travelers. "I have a few duties to perform. When I return, you can let me know what your meal decisions are."

"I just want to know what we are getting into," said Morbred after Tagu left.

Her statement lacked the aggravated tone of her previous questions. Three of the Travelers sat down around a table. Morbred remained standing.

Morbred spoke again, "Walking, speaking, listening, moving—what's there to learn? And who are these almighty Elders?"

"I am sure Tagu will answer as many questions as he is able," Krella said.

Morbred's respect for Krella's insights was growing, and Krella's gentle responses were having a calming effect on Morbred.

The four were silent for a while, listening to the babbling fountain that was outside of the garden entrance. They were letting the events of the day soak in. KC and Krella sat close together, holding hands. Krella's head was resting on KC's shoulder. Jubley was now standing behind Morbred with his hands on her shoulders. The light coming through the dwelling's glass dome began to take on shades of orange. The day's end had arrived.

"Are we going to investigate Dome City?" asked Morbred.

Krella squeezed KC's hand in such a way that he knew she did not wish to leave.

"Well, Krella and I are going to try some of Tagu's cooking and retire early," said KC.

"Jubley, would you like to do a bit of exploring?" asked Morbred.

"Yes, very much," replied Jubley.

"We will report back with any interesting discoveries," said Morbred.

She stood and moved with Jubley toward the opening leading to the street.

"Don't wait up for us," said Morbred.

"We won't," smiled KC sheepishly.

◆

Tambuki, whose size and environments were not unlike those of Earth's, was located thousands of light years away from KC's blue planet. Here, as on Earth, the first signs of light signaled the approach of a new day. The early birds made their presence known and the sounds of a city coming to life slowly began to amplify.

KC and Krella lay in each other's arms blissfully unaware of the day that marked the opening of their new life, a life that was destined to see many new and amazing things. However, theirs was not the only new life that had begun that day. A life that had yet to take its first breath, or hear its first sound, or see the light of day passed its first few hours preparing for the time it would come into the world. It was small and, as yet, undetected. The miracle of life was preparing to create another soul in the universe.

KC's mind was dancing with thoughts of the previous night. Tagu had produced last meal—the last meal of the day—and it was indeed a taste treat. They started the meal with fresh, raw vegetables. Then they had some deliciously seasoned dumplings in an aromatic stew and slices of freshly baked, still-warm, dark-brown bread that they dipped in an oily, tangy sauce. Next, Tagu produced a variety of pastries and a pot of warm mint tea. When Tagu, who had answered as many questions as he could, departed, Krella and KC fell into each other's arms and...

KC was half awake and his mind danced with thoughts of the previous night. He thought about this new planet with no noise creating devices. He thought about the unforgettable meal Tagu had prepared. What was the most memorable from the previous night was the closeness he and Krella found in each other's arms.

Then Samtatu's booming voice brought KC back to the present. "TIME TO TAKE FIRST MEAL. THEY HAVE A LONG DAY AHEAD OF THEM." His strong, steady voice boomed throughout the dwelling. "THEY WILL BE STUDYING THE MAIN DOME TODAY."

After first meal, the Travelers prepared to look around Dome City.

"What happens after we explore Dome City?" asked KC.

"They will spend another night in Dome City," said Samtatu. "Tomorrow they will take a pediglide to the mountains. After two days of climbing and gliding, they will enter the Outlander Domain."

"*A pediglide?*" asked KC. "Are those the peds we saw on the roads?"

"What they saw on the roads were steampeds," answered Samtatu. "They are not equipped to glide."

"Are we going to *glide* to our village?" asked Morbred. She sounded doubtful.

Samtatu smiled. "The gliders are completely safe and extremely efficient," he said, sensing Morbred's doubts.

"How do they glide, and where do they get their power?" asked KC.

"Crews attach wings to the pediglides when the pediglides reach the launch area on a Glide Mountain," said Samtatu. "Pediglides and steampeds are both powered by pedaling and steam engines. The water for the steam is heated with rock nuts, which are very dense and, when they are ignited, burn very hot and very slow. The Venuvians planted groves of rock nut trees all over the planet. Rock nuts are one of the main sources of power on Tambuki. There are rock nut trees along all the roads that lead to Glide Mountains. Wells and windmill pumps provide water for the steam engines."

"What are Glide Mountains?" asked Jubley.

"There is a road that exits Dome City and goes to the beginning of a mountain range," said Samtatu. "The first Venuvians on Tambuki built six mountains in such a way that the mountains create tremendous updrafts. Three such mountains are used to travel away from Dome City to the Outlander Domain, and three are used to return to the domes. These mountains are called Glide Mountains. At the top of each Glide Mountain, crews remove part of the steam engines and attach gliding wings. The rock nuts remain in the gliders to produce heat, since, before the glider reaches the height where the glide path begins, the temperature falls to below freezing.

"Tomorrow, the Travelers will pump to the launch area of First Glide Mountain, catch the updrafts and spiral to the maximum height and then glide to near the base of Second Glide Mountain. They should be able to reach the top of Second Glide Mountain by the end of the day. They will spend the night at the compound on top of Glide Mountain Two. The next day, they will glide to near the base of Third Glide Mountain, climb the mountain, and then glide to the beginning of the Outlander

Domain. The Travelers should be prepared to peddle and glide from sunrise to sunset."

"Where did all this equipment come from?" asked KC who, along with the rest of the Travelers, was listening intently to Samtatu.

"The Venuvians brought all the peds and gliders to Tambuki before others arrived. Every 200 years, when a Venuvian ship lands, one of their activities is to pick up units that need repair and to deliver new and repaired units.

"The Venuvians only come here every 200 years?" asked Krella.

"Yes, regularly," said Samtatu. "Samtatu has yet to witness a landing, but older residents have told him that it is a time of great excitement. For one year, everyone, even some Wild Ones come to see the Venuvian marvels. The next arrival will be in 25 years."

"What happens when we get to the Outlander Domain?" KC asked, ignoring what Samtatu had to say about Venuvian visits.

"The Travelers will be trained," replied Samtatu.

"How will we be trained?" asked KC. Even as he asked the question, KC knew the answer would bring little satisfaction.

"Even those who live in the Outlander Domain do not know the exact nature of the training," said Samtatu. "Those who have been trained rarely speak of their experiences. There are rumors and superstitions, but Samtatu prefers not to deal with any of them."

"Tagu said his grandmother has received some training," said KC. "She implied that Outlanders can learn more about seeing, listening, speaking, and moving. Beyond that, she has said little to her grandson about her training. Apparently the code of silence has seldom been broken during the thousands of years of training on Tambuki."

Samtatu merely smiled and said, "Tagu is a very intelligent young man."

That day, Samtatu led the four Travelers on a walking tour of Tambuki. He told them that there was not enough time to cover every culture under the dome. As they studied the layout of the city, Samtatu was able to point out certain groups and cover the group's origins and the high points of their society. There was one group that appeared to have the most representatives—the Ortans.

At the end of the day, the Travelers returned to their dwellings. Morbred and Jubley decided to join KC and Krella for last meal. Morbred had enjoyed the meal she and Jubley had in town the night before, but Jubley was a little more reserved in his description of the food. Both Morbred and Jubley wanted to try the offerings of Tagu, which KC and Krella raved about. No one was disappointed in the meal. The four sipped tea after the meal, talked a while, and then went to bed with smiles on their faces.

◆

"THEIR PEDIGLIDES ARE WAITING."

Samtatu's booming voice awakened KC and Krella. It was still dark outside. When the Travelers were ready to start their journey, Samtatu spoke to them about the day ahead.

"Samtatu would like the Travelers to climb Glide Mountain One today and take their first glide," said Samtatu. "Then they will climb Glide Mountain Two. They are all V.I.s, so he expects them to keep pace. They will take first meal at sunrise."

As memorable and enjoyable as the last two days had been, the expectation of what was to come made the four Travelers anxious to leave. With only the clothes on their back and provisions for the journey, they mounted the waiting pediglides. Samtatu gave the Travelers a very few words on how to operate their machines, and then they began their journey into the pre-dawn darkness.

They followed a wide, still-quiet boulevard through the heart of the dome. The road narrowed as it approached the shell of the dome, and then it dipped downward into a tunnel. The torch-lit tunnel leveled then curved upward. When they exited the tunnel, they were outside of the dome. For a short time, the road followed the river that passed through Dome City, and then the road moved away from the river and into a forested area.

The only sound the Travelers heard was the chugging of the pediglides' engines. The engines alone propelled the tripeds at a good clip, but the Travelers had to pump vigorously to produce the additional momentum needed to keep up with Samtatu. By the time the first light of dawn began to appear on the horizon, they were ready for a break, but Samtatu pushed on. The sun had begun to show itself before Samtatu relented and pulled his pediglide to the side of the road.

"Excellent, excellent!" exclaimed Samtatu. "They are close to Glide Mountain One."

He seemed unaffected by the hours of heavy peddling.

"Off world V.I.s never cease to amaze him," said Samtatu. "At this rate, they should reach the base of Second Mountain before sunset. They should stop and take nourishment now. Is any V.I. having a problem?"

The Travelers let out a collective moan, but no one had a specific complaint. They were just tired. Samtatu smiled broadly and wrinkled his forehead revealing his sparkling gray eyes. He disappeared and soon returned with his shoulder bag full of fresh fruits and rock nuts.

"Good, very good," said Samtatu. "Eat now." Their meal consisted of balls of cooked, peppered grain that were held together with a sweet and tangy, sticky substance. They drank water to which Samtatu had added a few drops of dark-green liquid. The dark liquid gave the water a bitter taste, but it refreshed and invigorated the Travelers. They were silent while they ate. As they sat by the side of the road, others passed, sometimes in groups sometimes singularly, all on pediglides.

"Not a very interesting parade," mumbled Morbred.

After a time, the Travelers were beginning to feel rested and they contentedly sat cross-legged munching on fruit. Morbred broke the silence.

"Will Samtatu now tell us, ah, tell *them* what they are doing here?" asked Morbred.

Samtatu's face became serious. The smile faded, and his entire continence became gloomy.

"The time is short before they must continue their journey. Samtatu can tell them some things about the Travelers' purpose on Tambuki, but to know their future they must first know the past."

Samtatu shifted in his cross-legged position, straightened his back, put his hands in his lap with his fingertips touching, bowed his head, and sat still for a few moments. It seemed as if he were going into a trance.

The Travelers sat silently, eyes fixed upon this wonderful being. Samtatu slowly lifted his head and looked off into the distance.

"When the Venuvians arrived 2,375 years ago, Tambuki was uninhabited by any higher life forms," he began. His voice had taken on a hypnotic quality. "The ancient Venuvians modified the planet's climate and introduced a number of plants and animals to supplement the planet's existing varieties. The Venuvians had a very specific plan. As they spread their influence to different systems, they encountered groups that taught individuals how to harness and refine their energies to the point where they could exert control over others." Reacting to the perplexed looks on the Travelers' faces, Samtatu said, "There will be a time to ask questions. Please, now is the time to listen." Samtatu continued. "The Venuvians found that the societies that had reached the highest level of this controlling ability were found in two groups. The first and most obvious group was found in the civilizations that had refined controlling practices for hundreds or thousands of years. The other groups were the so-called primitive groups that were at or near the subsistence level. In addition to these two groups, there were some special individuals who, on their own, developed very powerful controlling abilities."

Samtatu paused and very briefly glanced at KC, then at Morbred. The Travelers, though listening to Samtatu's every word, let his glances go unnoticed. Samtatu continued in his drone monologue.

"These special individuals could be found in societies at any stage of the societies' development. They usually went unnoticed, but occasionally they reached great notoriety in their communities—they were sometimes revered and sometimes persecuted. The Venuvians, in an attempt to nurture those with these controlling abilities, discovered that special individuals from developed societies could follow the controlling practices of the more advanced societies and increase their abilities. Unfortunately, the controlling ability of those from the subsistence societies quickly deteriorated when they encountered the Venuvians. Tambuki was developed to supply these less developed people with a planet completely devoid of Venuvian influences."

So, thought KC, *this is why I have been brought to Tambuki.*

KC imagined that here, on Tambuki, he would make use of what he had learned from the Venuvians about primitive societies. KC would discover that his ruminations would prove to be far from what he had expected.

"Initially, the Tambuki experiment was a complete failure," continued Samtatu. "When individuals from primitive societies were removed from their birthland, their controlling abilities quickly died. Even when the Venuvians created areas as similar as possible to the area from which these primitive individuals had been extracted, the experiment with them failed. The Venuvians reckoned that the sun, or the position of the stars, or something else, over which they had no control, was the cause of the failure. To this day, the Venuvians have not discovered the reasons for their initial failure. They did find that control practitioners from developed societies flourished on Tambuki. They also discovered that any activity, manmade or natural, that caused any kind of electrical activity, affected the refinement of the control activities. Advanced practitioners integrated natural phenomena into their learning activities, but artificially created noise hindered their abilities. That is why the planet seems so primitive to the Travelers. Except for the Monthlies, nothing on Tambuki uses anything that causes electronic activity. The one who guides the Travelers knows that they have many questions, but now they must continue their journey."

Morbred did not try to conceal her irritation. Samtatu's short dissertation had only evoked more questions. She was about to speak, but a quick smile from Samtatu totally disarmed Morbred—and Morbred was not one who was easily disarmed.

"The time will come when more questions will be addressed," said Samtatu.

Samtatu's words had a calming effect on everyone, even Morbred. There was a quality about his voice that promised that rewarding things were to come.

The Travelers mounted their pediglides and, with no further words, began to ascend the mountain that had been constructed by the ancient Venuvians almost 3,000 years ago. The scenery was colorful but monotonous. Both sides of the road were dotted with groves of rock nut trees. A variety of fruit and nut trees grew between the groves of rock nuts. Food-bearing bushes and shrubs were everywhere. The monotony of the trees, bushes, and vines was periodically broken by an open area that contained huge windmills and large water tanks. At each watering area there were others taking food and replenishing the water in their pediglides.

The road zigzagged up the steep incline of the mountain. The sound of the steam engines changed as they worked harder to pull the pediglides up the hill. Several times, Samtatu had to wait for the Travelers to catch up. Every time he stopped, he would shoot each V.I. a cryptic glance that spurred them on. However, even with their renewed effort, other pediglides passed them with ease.

The sun was well above the horizon when the road began to level off and the alpine growth began to thin. Before the Travelers reached the top, their exertion and the sun had kept them warm, but they were beginning to feel the freezing air of the high altitude. Samtatu stopped and showed them the compartment that contained gloves, a thick poncho, a mask that covered their entire head, goggles, and a compact breathing apparatus—all items that were made by Venuvians.

"You will need these for the spiral up and much of the glide down," said Samtatu. "The roads are built over a heated water system that keeps ice from forming, but they are wet and slippery. Be careful."

As the Travelers approached the top of Glide Mountain One, they had a panoramic view of the area. They could see a twin mountain, Glide Mountain Six, which was the last mountain for pediglides heading for Dome City. The gliders above that mountain looked like birds lazily spiraling up into the sky. At the apex of the spiral, the gliders released and started their downward journey toward Dome City. The Travelers would soon be soaring above this mountain and taking a dive toward the next artificial mountain.

The Venuvian undergarments provided a great deal of protection from the cold, but as the Travelers climbed higher, the cold was beginning to affect their ability to pump. Samtatu pulled the Travelers to the side and instructed them on how to use their extra garments. He showed them how to attach their poncho to an area on the pediglide so that it could collect the heat from the steam engine.

The road began to take a slight descent when the Travelers saw a large clearing with a number of pediglides in a line. They could see four, two-person crews dismantling the pediglides and converting them into gliders. The Travelers took their places at the end of the line. What immediately caught the attention of the Travelers was the front of the line. After a pediglide had wings attached, the two-person crew rolled the pediglide down a ramp and off the side of the mountain! Moments later, the glider reappeared, spiraling upward in a spiral circle that was 100 meters wide. The Travelers watched as a succession of pediglides, which had become gliders, climbed higher and higher. Within minutes, the gliders were high above the launching area. Before long, they had become specks in the sky. Then, at the apex of their ascent, they peeled off the spiral and headed eastward. When a launched glider reached a height of five meters, the next glider in line rolled off the mountain's edge. KC and his fellow Travelers watched in awe as the gliders rose on the artificially created thermal updraft.

KC stopped thinking about why the Venuvians brought him to Tambuki. He forgot about his aching legs and tired arms. He looked at the gliders and realized that soon it would be his turn to climb high into the sky and dive toward some unknown horizon. The thought exhilarated him.

"It looks like we are going to get a little excitement," said Morbred.

She was right, very right. The Travelers stepped off their pediglides as two Outlanders expertly transformed the pediglides into gliders and set the gliders on a sled with wheels. Samtatu spoke to Morbred while the other Travelers listened.

"The lever between her feet is the only control she has," said Samtatu. "Pull the lever toward Morbred to go up, away from Morbred to go down. Push left to turn left and right to turn right. Follow Samtatu as closely as you can."

Those were the only instructions the Travelers received. KC slid into the glider. His legs, which were in the nose of the glider, were engulfed in a fur-like material. Outlanders adjusted his seat, tightened the material around his legs, and sealed his upper body to the glider. The Outlanders then pushed KC off the side of the mountain! The glider took a nosedive straight down! Instinctively, KC pulled back on the lever. Nothing happened. For a second, KC panicked and then the glider caught the updraft and jerked the glider to a stop. KC felt like he had hit a brick wall. Then the glider began to climb. KC's heart was still bounding as the glider began its ascent. He caught sight of Samtatu, leveled his glider, and began to follow him.

◆

Joe loved his job transforming pediglides into gliders. One after another, he and Javita, his mate, removed the pedal devices and part of the steam mechanism from the pediglides. Then they would attach lightweight wings that were each 50 meters long. The couple could convert the heavy pediglides to ultralight gliders in a matter of minutes. The precision Venuvian tools and the pediglides' exact specifications made each transformation exactly the same. Joe and Javita did not move through each operation—they danced. Repetitiveness and precision—Joe and Javita loved that.

Joe was born to Outlanders. His mother and father had trained in The Way. They saw, spoke, listened, and moved in The Way. Joe could never remember a time when a look and a few words from either of his parents were not enough to control his actions. He had no doubt that his parents loved him and that they would never do anything to harm him, but, whenever he was in in their presence, he was under their control. Only once had Joe felt in control—only once.

Abaraxus, Joe's father, would say, "Joe has to let go, clear his mind, breathe in emptiness."

Joe had heard some variation of this admonition hundreds of times: "Flow into nothingness." "Seek that which is not." "Until he releases he cannot hold."

Neither his father's words nor his penetrating stare were enough to enable Joe to deliver what his parents wished of him. It just did not click. What he *could* do was move like a Master. With imperceptible gestures, he could convey everything from intense fear to deep attachment. At the other three arts—listening, speaking, and seeing—he failed miserably.

Even his mastering of the movement techniques was more a mimicking of the trained ones than a true conquering of his inner balance.

Then, one day without warning, Joe said to his father, "He can't."

Joe's father immediately dropped his façade. A façade was the mode that trained ones were able to evoke when they shifted into practicing The Way. Joe had seen his father without his façade before, but on this particular occasion, for the first time, he saw his father as just another man. Joe was a young man, in his sixty-first year, but it was then—in that brief instant when he also saw the disappointment in his father's eyes—that Joe decided he did not need to master the four arts.

"He can't," Joe repeated.

That was the brief moment when Joe had felt in control.

Joe's father, still without his façade, looked directly at Joe with a blank expression, and tears forming in his blue-tinged eyes.

"He understands," his father said.

He warmly embraced Joe for several moments and then held him by his shoulders.

"Joe must follow his own path, not the path of others," said Joe's father. "Let him lead a good life and be a teacher to others." His father paused. "I love you, Joe."

His father's use of a direct expression of his love, universally avoided by Masters, sent a shock through Joe. His eyes met his father's briefly, and then Joe looked down. In those few seconds, he saw a genuine love in his father's eyes.

"Joe loves his father," was all Joe said.

He could not bring himself to use direct speech, even with his father, but, at that moment, Joe did indeed feel a strong love for him. Joe's mother had been just as understanding.

"Perhaps Joe can help grow crops," she said with an understanding smile.

Joe did work the fields for a few years. He liked the work, and, because so few sought to work in the fields, compensation was high. Joe herded a family of five guloks. Guloks were the eight- to twelve-meter high, gentle, slow-moving mollusks. He guided his family of brown and gray guloks over seed-covered fields by sowing the guloks' beloved gru-berries. The guloks would follow the sowed berries and leave a slimy, nutrient-rich trail over the seeded ground. The rains would wash the nutrients into the soil, and new crops would spring forth. The Venuvians had created the giant mollusks by modifying a native species, and, for thousands of years, the process with the guloks produced bountiful crops for Tambuki.

Joe spent many hours on top of one of the five guloks he herded. He passed the days reading, playing his lute, or just studying the plants and animals of the area. He became very adept at distinguishing between the species that were native to Tambuki and the ones that the Venuvians had imported. The Venuvians spent 200 years developing plants and animals that could live in harmony with Tambuki's own species. Joe had developed the ability to feel which plants and animals belonged to Tambuki. The silently moving guloks often came upon an unsuspecting creature. Joe could tell, just by the animal's movements, if it was a native or if it was imported.

In the years that Joe rode the guloks, he had never returned to the same spot. The pre-designated routes that he and his fellow riders followed took 10 years to complete. Joe never finished 10 years on one route. When a route opened that was farther from his dwelling, he would transfer to that route. Joe relished the daily routine of passing through familiar areas every day on his way to the guloks and then traveling to somewhere new.

Because Joe and his guloks passed through new areas every day, it was not unusual to encounter unfamiliar plants and animals. Joe would climb down the rungs that were implanted in the thick shell of the guloks, wade through a river of gulok slime, and walk ahead to examine an unfamiliar plant, insect, or animal. He would collect a flower, a leaf, a piece of bark, or some other plant part. Sometimes he would even retrieve small dead animals. Joe had an extensive library of Venuvian fauna and flora catalogs. He searched through the catalogs until he located the origin of the newly found specimen. He never found anything that the Venuvians had not already categorized. Joe rarely guessed incorrectly that a specimen was nonnative. He became an expert on the fauna and flora of Tambuki, and he loved studying them. He began to believe he had discovered his life trail. But life has a way of changing one's direction.

The morning had just begun to unfold. Light from the still hidden sun had barely begun to dissolve the darkness of night. Joe loved this part of the day. The only sounds were those of the chugging triped and the morning birds chattering to themselves. Joe wrapped himself in a shawl against the morning chill. He took a deep breath and filled his chest with the wonderful freshness of the dew-drenched world. He mounted his triped and began to pedal. His guloks were at a point on the route that was farthest from his dwelling. For the past few years, Joe had left earlier and returned later. After today, the trend would reverse as the route arched and the distances became shorter.

On this morning, Joe passed a group of High Gatherers. The High Gatherers were men and women who gathered food for Namtras, a group of Masters who had reached a high level of training. The Namtras only ate food that had fallen from trees or bushes—they did not eat anything that had been picked.

High Gatherers could be identified by their heavy flowing robes. The High Gatherers would move through the orchards, spinning in such a way that their robes would produce waves of turbulence. The turbulence caused branches and vines to dance with the High Gatherers. Their robes never touched the fruits, nuts, or berries, but the food that was ready to fall would do so. The High Gatherers would then collect the food that had fallen.

On this morning, Joe passed a group of 20 or so High Gatherers. One of the women turned toward him and their eyes locked. She was tall and slender with skin the color of the deep-red sky at sunset. Her long, jet-black hair, which was in a thick braid, curled around one side of her long, slender neck, ran over her shoulder, fell across her heart, and reached her waist. Her prominent nose, with its flaring nostrils and pronounced hook, jutted out over her thin, dark lips. Her narrow face was punctuated with large round eyes that were the color of dark earth. Joe did not know how long he had been staring at this High Gatherer when he felt his triped hit a bump. He jerked his head forward. His triped was already partially off the road and was heading for a ditch. He swerved back onto the road and came to a stop. He looked over his shoulder and saw that the High Gatherer he had been watching was looking at him with a look of concern. Then, her hand quickly came to her face and covered her mouth. Even though Joe could no longer see her mouth, her eyes had told him that she was concealing a smile. Joe was smitten.

He pedaled on. His heart was beating so hard that he thought he could hear it. He had passed High Gatherers daily. Had he passed her before? Would he ever see her again? Joe panicked and stopped his triped. Should he turn around and find her and tell her... tell her what? A voice jerked Joe from his quandary.

"His troubles seem great today but tomorrow they will fade."

Joe looked up and saw an Elder woman. Her clear, green eyes smiled at him from a face wrinkled with age. She appeared to be at least 200 years old, but she could have just as easily been 250. The Elder broke into laughter.

"It looks like love," she said. "If she could look forward to each breath she took with the same desire burning in him, she would become a great Elder Master."

She did not seem to be wearing a façade, but Joe could tell that she was able to read his every word, his every movement.

"Does the Elder Master know of the High Gatherers?" Joe blurted out.

He did not know if the old woman was manipulating him, and he did not care. The warmness of her being let him open up without trepidation.

"Are there any Outlanders who do not know of the High Gatherers?" asked the Elder. Again, the old Master broke into laughter.

Joe realized that he had asked a foolish question—most all Outlanders knew of High Gatherers. But her laughter still brought a smile to his face.

"If Hannah wanted to rest her old bones with the High Gatherers in this area," she continued, "she might find herself at Compound Galof, a meal and recreation compound. The young man, who has been captured by the spirit of love, can find Galof in Settlement 7 on Uhdini Road."

Joe knew that he had just passed Uhdini Road.

"If the one struck with love wishes to gaze upon the one who has ignited his desires, he might find himself at Galof compound, one iron strike after sunset. Many High Gatherers take their meals there, and, if the one who has grabbed the pedalist's attention is not present, there will certainly be someone there who knows of the one he seeks."

"He offers Elder Hannah great thanks for her guidance," said Joe.

"She accepts and prays her directions lead him to a place of joy."

Then the Elder's face assumed a different countenance. Her smile was less exuberant, and her eyes became more intense. She still exuded unmistakable warmth, but Joe sensed that she had put on a facade.

"This young one who now stands before Hannah has a singleness of mind. Many things he examines closely others never see. Someday he may see something no one else has ever seen. She hopes the discovery brings him comfort and not fear."

The Elder was correct. Though Joe somehow lacked the ability to master the learning arts, he did indeed have an ability to see things others missed.

Joe went to Galoff compound that evening after he left his guloks to graze. There he met Javita. He continued returning at the end of each day, and, every time he returned, he became closer to her. She told Joe that she had once followed The Way, but, even though her parents urged her to continue, she had decided she wanted a simple life. Joe told her of his love of plants and animals and of his inability to perform the practices of The Way.

Javita tried to teach Joe the fundamental dance of the High Gatherers. He was learning the moves, but his progress was slow. Joe gave Javita a ride on a gulok, but he had to carry her on his back through the slime. Both wanted to change their life situation. They soon found that they delighted in each other's company and needed no others. Their unity day was a large affair with family, friends, loved ones, High Gatherers, and Namtras attending. Joe gave up his guloks, and Javita left the High Gatherers. They settled atop Glide Mountain Three and lived in a compound with a team of pediglide converters and maintenance workers.

GLIDE MOUNTAINS

The Venuvians engineered six mountains between Dome City and the Outlander Domain: three mountains for gliders heading away from Dome City, and three mountains for gliders heading toward Dome City. Joe's and Javita's tasks were simple. Pediglides arrived at the top of Glide Mountain Three, the third mountain heading away from Dome City, and it was Joe's and Javita's job to transform the pediglides into gliders. Others looked upon the job as pure repetitive drudgery, but to Joe and Javita it was like a well-choreographed dance. The dance not only involved Joe and Javita but the pedalists as well. Unbeknownst to those who passed during the day, Joe and Javita involved each one of them in their dance. Every movement of the pediglide riders determined the next move in Joe and Javita's dance—always a rhythm to be kept, a flowing motion to follow. As the two mountain dwellers danced, they observed the people. They studied their movement, their composure, their every word. Even the Masters, with their strong façades, would occasionally loosen their grip on their control after pedaling up three mountains.

After their night's rest, the four Travelers prepared to leave Glide Mountain Two. When the sun, the reflective mirrors, the glaring white sand, and the specially contoured mountain created a sufficient updraft, gliders began to take off.

The slow spiraling climb before the dive off of Glide Mountain Two held less excitement for the Travelers than the first glide had held, but, halfway up the spiral, things changed. For the first time, the Travelers got a glimpse of what lay beyond Glide Mountain Three. In the distance, they could see what would soon be their home. At the height of the glide path, the Travelers were able to make out strings of smoke lazily rising into the air.

This is it, thought KC.

From high in the sky, it looked like some place one might find on Earth, but it was not Earth. How many light years away from Earth was KC? One hundred? One million? He had no idea. Would he ever see Earth again, or would he live out his life on this purposely undeveloped planet?

That day, Krella, KC, Morbred, and Jubley arrived on top of Glide Mountain Three—four Travelers on their first journey to the Outlander Domain. Joe and Javita had been on the mountain for 15 years. While Javita attached wings to Krella's glider, Joe removed the steam apparatus from her pediglide and made the final adjustments required to transform it into a glider.

"Her glider is now prepared," said Joe. "May it be the Venuvian wind's destiny to carry her gently and safely to her destination."

Krella lifted her still veiled face to Joe. Joe stumbled, lost the rhythm, almost fell. For a split second he froze.

"Thank y… *him*." Krella stammered, still not comfortable with Outlander's formal address.

"The pleasure is his," replied Joe, having regained his composure.

Javita saw that Joe had missed a beat. The female Traveler with the golden eyes had affected the changer's concentration. Later that night, Joe explained to Javita.

"The Ortan does not know what Joe saw. She only knows what he felt. There was something… ," Joe faltered, "something about her that… that was powerful. He has thought on what he felt today. Javita's mate is sure that the rider is with child, because what he felt was not her, it was of something that was to be."

Javita had only noticed that the Ortan was untrained in the arts, excited, anxious, and very attached to one of her fellow Travelers. Javita had no inkling of what Joe had seen. The Elder, who Joe had met that fateful day, the day he first saw Javita, had been correct in her prediction that Joe had been the first to see something no one else had seen. Although it brought him a certain comfort that he did not understand, Joe had little idea of what he had caught a glimpse of. Joe held Javita's hands, and then he lifted his eyes to stare at Javita.

"He feels comfort from the Ortan Traveler, but it is not, not… ," he sighed, and gently released Javita to stand. "He is sure the power is yet to be, and that the Ortan is unaware of the power growing within."

As the Travelers descended into the valley, two things became apparent. The shapes they had seen from high in the sky were indeed living compounds. Some blended in so well with their surroundings that they were hardly noticeable. Within the various compounds, there was abundant activity. People flowed in and out of the compounds, children played, and small animals moved about easily. Outside of the compound, in the agricultural areas, KC could see what looked like round, gray-brown structures. However, just before landing, KC got a close look at one of these objects—it was a giant snail!

By the time KC, Krella, Morbred, and Jubley had glided down from the top of Glide Mountain Three into the Outlander Domain, the sun had dropped to the horizon. Samtatu had pushed the Travelers hard all day. They were on schedule, and a crew was changing the gliders back into wingless pediglides.

"They have done well today. Tomorrow, they will pedal to their village. Sit now, and he will gather food for last meal. They should rest."

The four Travelers were anxious to get to their village, but now they were tired. They wanted to arrive refreshed and appreciated the break. They took refuge under a tree away from the road.

"Not much variety in the roadside attractions, is there?" said Morbred after a while.

"Yes, the scenery is *just as fabulous as ever*," said KC sarcastically.

"Did you notice how the Mountain Three changer looked at me?" said Krella, directing her question to KC.

"You mean looked at *her?*" said KC smiling. "No, I didn't."

"You mean no *he* didn't," said Krella. "It wasn't actually a look, it was his reaction. He acted as if he had seen something, something that amazed or shocked him."

"Him who?" interjected Morbred. "Him KC or him the changer? First we... *they* learn how to speak Venuvian, now they have to speak as if they are on the outside looking in. I, me, me, ME!" Morbred yelled defiantly. "Why can't they speak regular Venuvian like everyone else in the galaxy?"

"There is no place like this in the galaxy." It was Samtatu carrying a bundle of freshly picked fruits and nuts. "The Outlanders' first task is to step outside of their physical selves and become the puppeteer instead of the puppet. They speak not as the center but as the surrounding."

Samtatu spread the food out in front of the Travelers and continued speaking. "Words are tools, very powerful tools. Individuals can use words to help or to hinder. For the 3,775 years since the Venuvians arrived, the Elders have used this speech pattern as a tool to escape their physical being. Your guide has spoken thusly for his 103 years and has yet to depart his physical being." He paused, and then he said, "The Elders also teach patience." Samtatu smiled broadly, "The speaker hopes the new arrivals are able to become masters of their selves in a more timely fashion."

"What if Morbred decides to speak any way she wishes? Will she be put in detention or have her tongue pulled out?"

Samtatu chuckled.

"I, I, I — me, me, me," said Samtatu.

He smiled broadly, and then he began to laugh. As his laughter grew more boisterous, tears rolled down his cheeks and his whole body shook. The Travelers smiled, somewhat bewildered. They reacted more to the sight of Samtatu overcome with laughter than to anything he had said. Slowly, Samtatu regained his composure.

"Please forgive his loss of control," Samtatu said, still short of breath. "Neither Morbred nor the one caught with laughter need fear detention. Any Outlander may speak as he pleases. Besides, there are no detention facilities outside of Dome City. The few problems experienced in Outlander Domain are usually minor and handled by the Select Council. Occasionally a tribe of Wild Ones will cause trouble, but they are easily controlled and have long since learned to avoid disturbing Outlanders."

"What is a Select Council?" asked Jubley. "And how many Wild Ones are there?

The usually silent Jubley had his interest piqued.

"There are three councils that make decisions for the Outlander Domain," said Samtatu. "Every 10 years, someone is randomly selected from every compound. They form the Select Council. The Council of Elders elects 25 members from the Select Council to form the Elect Council. The Council of Elders is open to anyone over 250 years."

"As for the number of Wild Ones, this is not known exactly," said Samtatu. "There are frequent defectors from the Wild Ones, and the defectors have information that enables the Outlanders to make estimates. Every 200 years, the Venuvians also make estimates. The Venuvians' estimates do not vary much from those of the Outlanders. The last time the Venuvians visited, they estimated 10,700. The Wild Ones' growth has slowed as they start moving into the less temperate areas. Tambuki has a limited amount of land area, and the Outlander Domain occupies 80 percent of the temperate land mass.

"As one moves north, the climate rapidly becomes less hospitable. The Outlanders estimate that the Wild Ones' population will peak at 12,000. The lifespan of a Wild One is much shorter than that of an Outlander. A Wild One's average age is 68 years—only a few live more than 80 years. Their death and defection rates are approaching their birth rates. Most Wild Ones' tribes do not try to prevent their people from leaving, but a few tribes forbid contact with Outlanders. These tribes have become more and more isolated but have not been a problem since the Rebellion."

The Travelers immediately became more attentive, expecting Samtatu to discuss the Rebellion. He did not.

Jubley was silent for a few moments, his expressionless face musing over Samtatu's words.

"Tambuki seems like such a peaceful planet," said Jubley. "You spoke of a rebellion. Why would any group stage a rebellion?"

"Many have asked that question, and many theories have been posited," said Samtatu. "Perhaps power, perhaps greed, perhaps resentment, or maybe the result of one lunatic creating dissent among a tribe of Wild Ones."

Again, there was silence. The Travelers were obviously expecting Samtatu to elaborate, but he remained silent. Clearly, Samtatu was not eager to discuss the Rebellion. The Travelers were learning that Samtatu could end his conversations very abruptly. He had been willing to answer some of the Traveler's questions, but other answers they had to pry out of him.

"Come on Samtatu!" Morbred blurted. "Tell them all about the Rebellion."

Samtatu's face was expressionless. For a long moment, he said nothing. When at last he did speak, he was reciting to himself.

"The facts surrounding the Rebellion are few. On the third day of the second month in the 2,300th year of Tambuki time, a rebel group took control of Dome City. A few hundred Outlanders, who the Venuvians later exposed as former Wild Ones, disrupted life in Dome City. Their actions were well-planned and well-coordinated. The rebels halted traffic in and out of Dome City and detained members of the Three Councils and their families.

"The rebels attempted to capture the Monthly apparatus. They were able to control Dome City, but they were unable to enter the subterranean Monthly facility. The Venuvians had prepared the Monthly chamber so that the facility would automatically seal itself if problems arose. The rebels began killing the families of the Council members in an attempt to force the Council to open the Monthly facility. It soon became clear that only a Venuvian representative could unseal the facility.

"Four days after the Rebellion started, a Venuvian ship arrived. A small force of Venuvians restored order, rescued Council members, and detained the rebels. The Venuvians were able to restore Monthlies, six days after the start of the rebellion. Today it is very difficult for a Wild One or former Wild One to enter Dome City. Those are the facts of the Rebellion." Samtatu fell silent.

"What weapons did the rebels have and what were they after?" asked KC.

"He has asked two questions," said Samtatu. "One has an easy answer, and one has been answered in many ways. At the time of the Rebellion, Dome City was defenseless. Tambuki was a peaceful planet and had no need for weapons. The rebels not only had spears and arrows, they also had crude explosive devices that fired deadly projectiles. There are legends that, after the Rebellion, the Councils created a secret society inside Dome City. That society is trained, armed, and ready to protect Dome City against another uprising. Samtatu does not know if there is any truth in these stories. Samtatu does know that today there are troops of Outlanders, trained in the arts of defense, who are always ready to defend Dome City and the Outlander Domain. However, they use only simple weapons. Their role is to control disturbances until the Venuvians arrive.

"What did the rebels want?" asked Samtatu. "They wanted the Monthly apparatus. It is unknown why they would want equipment that they could not hope to operate. The Travelers will find out that the Monthly apparatus is the only advanced Venuvian technology on Tambuki. There are stories that the Rebels feared Venuvian technology and that they believed the Monthlies robbed people of their bodily essence. Many Wild Ones believe that the Monthlies add or remove something from people's blood and that the Monthlies enable the Venuvians to exert control over those who participate. Those are two of the many so called Blood Myths." Samtatu abruptly stopped speaking. Heavy silence greeted the words "Blood Myth."

Jubley stirred and asked, "What are the Blood Myths?"

Samtatu straightened and then gestured toward the fruit. "Samtatu is sure the Travelers know that, in the Venuvian world, V.I.s and Associates have substances added to their blood to balance their bodily systems. That is why the Monthlies enable those who take them to live at least 150 years longer than Wild Ones."

"There are fanatics on my... *his* planet, who claim that the Venuvians are stealing their blood," said KC matter-of-factly.

"The Ortans were the first civilization to come in contact with the Venuvians," added Krella. "Even from the earliest times, there have been superstitions about the Venuvians stealing blood. Our ancestors have always taught the Ortans that the Venuvians seek only to improve the conditions of the people they contact. Why these stupid superstitions persist is a mystery."

Even with her veil down, KC could see that Krella was agitated. He had never heard her speak about the ancient Ortans' encounter with the Venuvians. Indeed, this was the first time he heard that the Ortans were the first to encounter the Venuvians. KC and Krella would learn that there was more to the relationship between Ortans and Venuvians— much more.

KC thought of Krella. The thought of his life mate sent a feeling of joy through him. His would be a good life, and he knew it. But why had the Venuvians brought him to Tambuki? After years of training and studying primitive societies, he found himself on a planet that used no advanced technology. But Tambuki was far from primitive.

KC still felt uncomfortable recalling the visions he had during his first "jump," but he was sure that they were the reason he was on Tambuki. How were his visions and Tambuki connected? Why would the feelings of sheer terror he had experienced cause the Venuvians to rearrange his life? He was here to learn how to listen, to see, to hear, and to move—to what end?

His mind turned to the Adabuman shaman he had so closely studied. The young Adabuma men were strong and skilled in ways of survival. They had a keen and intuitive understanding of their environment. But the shaman had knowledge that transcended environment. He had an understanding of life and humanity that was timeless. Could the Venuvians teach what the shaman knew? Was the shaman's understanding of the human spirit something the shaman could share with another, or was it a gift that only a certain few received? KC felt that there were answers to these questions, and maybe they could be found on Tambuki.

◆

The Travelers had their gliders converted back into steampeds one more time. They would not see gliders again until they returned to Dome City for their Monthlies. KC and Krella had not shared Monthly days on spaceship Jaylex, but on Tambuki their Monthlies coincided.

They had grown together in more ways than their Monthlies. KC's love for Krella had continued to deepen from the day they first met. He felt warmth just watching her movements, the blithe way she moved her ample body, the rhythmical coordination of her short, thick fingers, even the contortions of her lips when they were puckered, pressed tightly together or slightly parted. Moreover, when he looked into those large, round, golden eyes, it was as if it were for the first time. He was flushed with a feeling of love and devotion he had never thought possible.

After the Travelers had their pediglides converted, Samtatu took them to a diamond-shaped compound. He introduced them to four young people and then said his farewell.

"Their paths shall cross again," was all he said, and he was gone.

It had only been four days since they met Samtatu, but the Travelers sincerely missed his stoic presence. The Travelers' new acquaintances, two males and two females, were to show the Travelers around the compound. All four helpers were under 30 years old. They spoke very little.

Krella's and KC's quarters were the same as Morbred's and Jubley's. They were simple diamond-shaped affairs with earthen walls, wooden doors, and glassless windows that were covered with a braided material. At one end of the diamond was a room used for sleeping, at the other end a smaller area for bathing. The living area was between the two end rooms with one door to the outside common area and another door to an outside private area.

The quarters were sparsely furnished. The living area had one large table, three small tables, and four chairs. The sleeping quarters had one large, very comfortable bed, two chairs, and two small tables. The bathing area, though not sumptuous, was certainly the most beautiful room in their quarters. It was the smallest of the three rooms and contained two chairs and a small table in one corner. There was a sunken tub at the other end of the room. The tub had been sculpted and polished from a large rock. The tub was easily large enough to accommodate four people. The ceiling was a dome made of non-symmetrically shaped, translucent, glass balls. From one corner, just below the ceiling and over the tub, a small stream of water meandered down moss-covered rocks. The trickle of water filled one small pool that spilled into another pool beneath it. The third and bottom pool fed the tub. Next to the tub there was a net made of braided ropes that held several smooth black rocks.

The net was connected to a lever that could pivot the rocks from an area where they were heated to the pond that fed water into the tub.

"Would the new arrivals like hot stones for a bath?" asked one of the youths.

"Yes!" said Krella immediately.

Both KC and Krella burst into laughter at Krella's abruptness.

"It's been a long day," said KC. "A hot bath would be wonderful."

"The bath rocks will be heated before last meal," said the female youth.

"There will also be towels and clean jalabas," added the male.

After surveying their living quarters, Krella and KC met Jubley and Morbred in the common area of the compound. Each of the Traveler couples was accompanied by two stoic youths—a male and a female.

"Did Krella and KC see the bathing area?" asked Morbred in her usual buoyant manner. "She can already feel that beautiful warm water surrounding Morbred's body. She hasn't had a decent bath since leaving her planet."

As the Travelers followed the youths, Morbred leaned close to Krella.

"Those two with Morbred and Jubley are very quiet, and Morbred doesn't think they smile. Are the two with KC and Krella the same?"

"Yes," said Krella. "They have taken a vow of some kind. They are actually happy and very excited to be with the new arrivals."

"They make Morbred uncomfortable," said Morbred. "People that age should be talking and laughing. When Morbred was their age, she was full of questions. But those, they just stand with blank expressions. It's weird."

"Krella is sure Morbred will become comfortable with them," said Krella. "Krella believes that part of their growing up includes a period of quietness and service. She thinks they will be Morbred's and Jubley's companions and helpers for some time."

Overhearing the conversation, KC spoke. "Servants, Krella and KC get human servants? Great!"

"They are not hired servants," said Krella. "They are doing service as helpers."

The youths showed the Travelers the working areas of the compound: cloth weaving and sewing area, laundry area, food preparation area, compound and agriculture maintenance area, and meeting and dining areas. Except for other stoic youths, the residents of the compound greeted the new arrivals with warm smiles. By the time the tour was over, the sun had set, and darkness began to engulf the compound. Fires were started, and gas and oil lamps were lit. Then a loud gong sounded.

"That is the first evening sounding," said one of the youths. "There will be three more tonight. The second sounding will be for giving thanks before last meal. The third sounding will be at story time, and fourth sounding marks day's end."

"Let's go bathe," said Krella to KC.

"I can hardly wait. Have their servants prepared the bath?" said KC, smiling from ear to ear.

Krella dampened his enthusiasm slightly. "The youths are here to assist KC. It is not their duty to respond to his every command."

Morbred, who was obviously excited about having even quasi-servants, looked a bit dismayed.

"What will they not do?" asked Morbred.

"Morbred and Krella will have to wait and see," said Krella.

"And so will KC and Jubley," said KC.

Jubley, his face as expressionless as ever, broke his silence. "I have little need for servants."

"Well," said KC jokingly, "KC has lived his life without servants, but the thought of having not one but two servants—he will suffer the indignity."

The Travelers' spirits were buoyant. In the last few days, they had landed on a new planet, a Venuvian-designed planet that lacked advanced technology. They had seen the domed city, with descendants of more star systems than they could have imagined. They had spent the better part of the last two days exhausting themselves on steampeds and exhilarating themselves on amazing gliders. Now they were in a friendly compound and looking forward to a relaxing bath.

"Magnificent!" said KC, luxuriating in the tub.

"Hmmmm," replied Krella, splashing water over her body.

The heated rocks had produced plenty of steam, which filled the entire room with a warm mist. The youths, who never gave their names, left a pot of warm mint tea and two cups next to the tub. The tea was invigorating and stimulated their palates.

"I love this place," said KC. "And I don't care how they speak here. When I'm alone with you, I will speak any way I please."

He leaned over and kissed Krella gently on the lips.

"Speak as KC wishes," said Krella. "But Krella finds a certain comfort in speaking as those training in The Way."

KC looked into her eyes and understood how she felt. He could feel the peace the new speech pattern was bringing to her. No other words were necessary. After that moment, KC rarely spoke in other than the traditional speech pattern of The Way.

KC and Krella reluctantly finished their bath, dressed in their clean jalabas, and went to the dining area. KC was shocked. More than half of those gathered in the hall were Ortans or part Ortan. Even more shocking, KC could look into their large golden eyes, and they revealed nothing. Only the young covered their eyes.

"Krella, there are so many Ortans here!" said KC.

"The Ortans have been with the Venuvians since the Venuvians began to expand their influence," said Krella. "Ortans started coming to Tambuki when the Venuvians first created a living environment here. KC's life mate has heard stories, supposedly from Elders, that the Venuvians have a plan for Ortans."

"What sort of plan?" asked KC, again surprised at the new information about Ortans.

"She does not know," said Krella. "Maybe Tambuki is part of the Venuvian plan."

Krella was more correct than she knew. There was a plan for the Ortans, but it was not a Venuvian plan. There was a plan for Tambuki, a plan that the Venuvians had not designed. There was also a plan for a part of the galaxy that could not be found on any Venuvian chart. And, though the Venuvians were an important part of those plans, most Venuvians had no idea what the plans were.

Giving thanks before evening meal was rather elaborate. It could have been called a prayer but it was not prayerlike. It was a recital of all the ingredients in the meal with thanks for each.

"And they thank the forest and the garden for giving of itself for the salad," intoned one youth.

"They are thankful," was the response from the crowd.

The participants responded with a certain reverence, but Krella and KC could hear people talking and laughing throughout the hall. The thanks were genuine but not all-consuming. The meal was simple—various greens tossed with a sweet-tangy sauce and covered with a mixture of small seeds, a thick stew, and slices of dense bread. The Travelers would find that most of the evening meals would be some variation of the meal they were having that night. The biggest change would come when one of the Guloks died. Its meat would be dry-cured and served as a condiment for those who ate flesh.

After their meal, KC and Krella returned to their quarters. They wrapped themselves with shawls they found in their sleeping area and sat outside in the private area of their quarters. The air was cool but not uncomfortable. The second of Tambuki's two moons sat on the horizon while the first had completed half of its journey toward the apex. The moons had waxed to their first quarter and presented an awesome sight to KC and Krella.

"The sky is so different here," said KC. "It's like being back on Jaylex. Nothing in the sky is familiar. And two moons! On Earth, there is only one moon. What about on Orta?"

"I have never been to Orta, but I have seen visuals—it only has one," replied Krella dreamily.

The hot bath and meal were having a sedative effect on her. The Third sounding reverberated through the compound. KC looked at Krella.

"It's Krella's and KC's first night," said KC. "He thinks it would be rude to miss story time."

"She agrees," smiled Krella. "But they shouldn't make new arrivals so comfortable."

On their way to the hall, KC and Krella noticed that there were groups of people gathered around the various fires, sitting in front of their own living quarters or strolling around the compound.

"I guess attendance is not mandatory," said Krella.

"Okay, just a quick appearance, and the sleepy one can go to bed," said KC.

He knew that all Krella really wanted to do was to curl up in their comfortable bed.

The hall now had only half as many people as it had at dinner. KC and Krella found seats near a door and waited. They lasted through the beginning of story time and found it entertaining, interesting, and informative. It began with a wonderful fable about a small, fast, and devious animal and a large, slow, and easy-going animal. It was told by a woman many years KC's senior. She was dark with a tinge of green and had a large, round, hairless head. Her yellow, oval eyes had pupils that could constrict to pinpoints or quickly grow to fill her entire eye. The lively woman captivated the audience with her wit, practiced voice changes, and delightful story-telling ability. The audience showed its approval by shouting "Whoooo, who, who, whoo!"

The fable was followed by an explanation by a very young boy, perhaps nine or ten years old, about what happens to teenagers when it is time for them to leave the compound and go into service for the community. KC and Krella learned that, at age 12, the community expelled the young people from the compound to live among themselves until they proved that they were able to rejoin the community. The little boy's candid innocence was charming and some of his obvious misconceptions produced laughter from the crowd.

The next speaker was a tall, thin, willowy woman with stringy, white hair and gray leather skin. She recited the female history of her family from the time the Venuvians arrived on their home planet until her female ancestors set foot on Tambuki. It was the Venuvian custom for women to trace their lineage and to accept the name of the female side of their family and for men to trace their lineage and use the name of the male side of their family. Thus, Krella's official Venuvian name was Krella Marson Kruga. Marson was KC's name from the males of his family, and Kruga was from the female side of Krella's family. KC's official name was KC Kruga Marson. The white-haired woman included every ship boarded and all the planets on which the women of her family had settled.

Though interesting, it was more than Krella could take. Her eyes became heavy and her glance at KC told him it was time to go. When the white-haired woman finished, KC and Krella exited amidst the "whooos." Shortly, both were in bed. Sleep came quickly. Tomorrow, another adventure would begin.

For the next 26 days, KC, Krella, Morbred, and Jubley toured some of the Outlander Domain past Glide Mountain Three. They saw other compounds, youth camps, agricultural areas, and various libraries and cultural centers. They even rode a Gulok and saw how crops were grown.

The Travelers spent a whole day observing the three councils. They discovered that the Council of Elders also contained an Inner Council of Elders. The Inner Council if Elders seemed to have no function at all and could only be viewed by members of the Council of Elders. The Inner Council of Elders was accountable only to the Venuvians. KC had heard that a Council of Elders existed on the Jaylex, but no one knew for sure.

Life in the Outlander Domain was vibrant as well as peaceful, but the Travelers had not heard one mention of teachers. When, the Travelers wondered, would there be someone to teach them how to listen, to see, to speak, and to move? It was time for their first Monthly on Tambuki, and not once had they met a teacher.

On the 29th day after their arrival, Krella, KC, Jubley, and Morbred made the return trip to Dome City. The scenery was no less monotonous than it had been on the original trip, but, after having spent a good deal of their 29 days on peds, they found the return journey much less taxing. The Travelers reached Dome City while the sun was still in the sky and they returned to the quarters they had occupied on their first two nights on Tambuki.

"Will they always be staying in the same quarters when they return to Dome City?" Morbred had asked when the Travelers were instructed on where to go when they returned to the dome.

"Yes, unless she wishes to make other arrangements," was the only response from the placid youth in her service.

"She may make any arrangements she wishes," mocked Morbred when the youths had withdrawn. "Those two are full of information."

"Krella is quite sure that after a few trips to Dome City, the system for arranging quarters will become clear," said Krella.

"Morbred is sure that those two aggravate her," said an irritated Morbred. "Sometimes Morbred wants to grab one and shake her until she is speaking more than one sentence at a time."

"Maybe the Outlander Domain will teach Morbred more patience," said Krella, smiling gently.

Krella suspected that that lesson would take Morbred some time to learn.

It was still light when KC and Krella reached Dome City. They now had steampeds, so they decided to explore more of the city with Morbred and Jubley. The Travelers had already seen a variety of peoples from other systems on the Jaylex, but they were amazed by the number of cultures they found in Dome City. Unlike the Jaylex, the people in Dome City had recreated much of the dress and culture of their home systems. Some sections of the city contained large areas with structures from one system. Other sections were a mishmash of different systems. KC was taken by the fact that, everywhere he went, he saw Ortans. Again, Krella pointed out that the Ortans had been in contact with the Venuvians for thousands of years.

After touring Dome City, KC and Krella returned to their quarters and enjoyed another exquisite meal. The Travelers were scheduled for an early-morning Monthly, which meant that, afterwards, they could take the rest of the day to continue their survey of Dome City.

The next morning, KC and Krella arrived at the building where they would be taking their Monthlies every 31 days—the length of the Tambuki month.

"Typical Venuvian," mumbled KC when he saw the exterior of the Monthly structure.

The building was circular with entrances evenly spaced around the structure. There was no vegetation. Once inside, the only light came from gas wall lamps. The dimly lit room was completely symmetrical with 40 entrances. Immediately inside each entrance, spiral staircases led down openings in the surface of the cold, hard, marble floor.

KC and Krella descended a spiral staircase for an indeterminate amount of time. The entrance to the staircase had become a small circle of light above their heads when they reached the bottom. The staircase ended at an open entrance with artificial light pouring from the opening. KC and Krella stepped through the opening, and, for the first time in 31 days, they felt like they were back in Venuvian territory.

The opening led to a door that opened automatically when KC and Krella approached. There was a Venuvian transport on the other side of the door that effortlessly zoomed the couple deeper into the underground. When the transport doors opened, KC and Krella saw what every V.I. and every Associate saw once a month—the Monthly room. The Monthly was something that those who enjoyed Venuvian services accepted as second nature—Monthlies from 10 years old until death. KC eyed the circular room with its smooth, polished-metallic surface that was interrupted only by the 40 openings. For a brief moment, it seemed alien. The Monthly rooms were so different from the rest of Tambuki.

KC wondered how his Monthly would work since his Personal had been disabled before he landed on Tambuki. The miniature device that had been implanted in KC's earlobe contained every bit of information that the Venuvians knew about KC, plus various bundles of data necessary to navigate through the Venuvian world—until Tambuki. Now there were no electronics—no credits, no information, no data.

KC removed all his clothing and lay on his back on the platform that had automatically slid out of the wall. It was hard but warm. The platform automatically slid his head and shoulders into the opening in the wall. A device was lowered to within one centimeter of his eye to read his cornea. Bands secured his head, chest, abdomen, legs, and arms. Small swabs extracted samples from all his orifices. Microscopic needles punctured his skin. Everything was automatic. Ten minutes and it was over. The swabs and needles retracted. Then an audio device came close to his ear.

"All readings are within specifications," said a soothing, male voice with a Hindu accent.

KC had programmed the Hindu voice into his ear-stud Personal after he removed Jacqueline's voice. His Personal must have been activated in the Monthly room. The platform slid out of the wall, and the restraining bands retracted. KC got off the table, dressed, and walked over to Krella just as she finished dressing. She turned to KC, threw back her veil, and looked into KC's eyes. KC saw the joy in Krella's eyes. The joy was so great he could see nothing else. The few tears in her eyes could not hide a radiance so bright she seemed to glow.

"Krella is with child."

◆

The Messenger opened his eyes, eyes that he had closed since... since he did not know when. He took a deep breath. His first? Again, his recollection failed. What the Messenger did know was that it was time to go to the Outlander Domain. He also knew it was urgent. He must find a certain Elder and he had to give that Elder a very important message. The Elder would know that the Messenger was coming and he would make arrangements. The Messenger stood. He could feel the strength in his legs. He knew that the strength would respond to his bidding.

Go now! The Messenger ordered himself.

The room was dark, but he knew where the door was and opened it. He was still in total darkness. He knew that there was a spiral stairway in front of him, a stairway that would take him to where he had to go. It would take him... somewhere. He just knew he had to go—now! He began climbing the stairs, slowly, tentatively at first, then quicker and quicker until he was bounding up the lightless stairway, away from his room. He was heading toward—toward the place where he would find Elder M'ase.

The stairs stopped. He opened the door, which he knew, even in the darkness, stood before him. The brilliant light shocked his senses. He stepped into a room that was obviously someone's sleeping quarters.

Has he ever slept? Has he always been asleep?

He could hear voices speaking softly in the living area. He did not recognize the voices. He just knew he must go. He stepped into the living area. A man and a woman looked up at him, obviously bewildered.

"Everything is alright," he said in a clear monotone voice. "He belongs here."

He spoke not only with his mouth but also with his eyes, his face, his whole body, his entire being. The two turned back to each other, now oblivious of his presence. The Messenger exited the front door onto a busy street. Crowds of people passed, and steam-powered vehicles chugged up and down the boulevard. Something was wrong.

What do I do next? he asked himself.

He returned to the dwelling. Again, he saw the surprised faces.

"He needs a pediglide," he said.

His voice was different. It conveyed a command as well as urgency.

"There is a pediglide outside the rear entrance," said the woman. "It belongs to an Outlander, but you must take it."

"I will use it, today and tomorrow," said the Messenger.

There was assurance in his voice.

"Yes." The woman and the man both answered, and then they returned to their conversation as if nothing had happened.

White-haired Elder M'ase sat cross-legged facing west. His unmoving eyes stared trancelike, fixed on a distant mountain peak. He sat at this spot every day from sunup until sundown since his 150th year—he was now 203. M'ase's tanned, lean, sinewy body was one with this spot. This was M'ase's life. Rise before sunup, bathe, eat, and walk to his spot. At sundown, return to the compound, eat, and, except on special occasions, retire. Why did M'ase spend his life as an Elder staring at a mountain peak? For many years M'ase had pondered this question, but he had long since given up searching for an answer. It was tradition. Many had done it before him and many would do it after him. Now he just flowed with his daily routine. Today, an event would alter M'ase's routine.

The sun was early in the sky, and the second moon had begun to set when M'ase saw the first flash of reflected light from the mountaintop. A series of flashes followed. When the flashes stopped, M'ase rose, stretched, and rushed to the Elder compound that contained the Inner Council of Elders.

"M'ase must have an audience with the Inner Council," M'ase said to Raibit, one of the Elders who monitored the compound.

Elder Raibit looked up and saw M'ase standing before him. Raibit had seen M'ase many times over the years, but he had never heard M'ase speak. He now realized that he had always taken M'ase for granted—just another Elder engaged in some ancient tradition, the origin and purpose of which was completely unknown to Raibit. Now M'ase was asking to meet with the Inner Council.

"What business does M'ase have with the Inner Council of Elders?" asked Raibit.

"Raibit must assemble the Council of Elders immediately," said M'ase. "M'ase must be given passage to the Council."

M'ase delivered the command with such power that Raibit quickly rose. Raibit was aware that M'ase was using his powers of The Way, but he did not think M'ase was manipulating him—or was he?

"It shall be done," said Raibit.

M'ase left without another word.

When the Messenger reached Glide Mountain Three, he announced, "I must be next to glide."

He had made this announcement at the previous two Glide Mountains. No one, not even the Masters, had questioned him. Afterwards, only a few Masters even remembered having seen the Messenger.

Then the Messenger saw Joe. Until that moment, his focus had been on finding Elder M'ase. For a moment, a very brief moment, the messenger looked at Joe. Joe felt a jolt of excitement. A change was coming to his life! He did not know what or when, but something, something very important, would be part of his destiny. Joe did not forget the Messenger.

M'ase watched as the gliders gracefully descended from Glide Mountain Three.

The time has come, he thought.

For thousands of years, Elders like M'ase had followed a tradition.

They spent their lives in the tradition's service. They waited for the signal. Until today, they had waited in vain. For the first time in years, M'ase allowed himself questions.

Who or what has come? Why must the Inner Council of Elders be informed?

When he first saw him, M'ase knew it was the Messenger. Even at a distance, the Messenger's every move exuded urgency and a sense of mission. M'ase hurried to greet him.

"Elder M'ase will take him to the Council of Elders," said M'ase.

He spoke no other words. The two hurried to the Council of Elders' chamber. The chamber was a round earthen structure, 40 meters in diameter and five meters high. It had a domed roof and stood alone on top of a small hill. A single row of tightly spaced trees encircled the base of the hill. Flowering shrubs and vines grew around the sides of the building. A dozen fountains were scattered around the well-manicured grounds. At the entrance, a three-meter obelisk spilled water into a pond that was stocked with a collection of fish and waterfowl.

When M'ase and the Messenger entered the Hall, it was half-full. Elders from the surrounding area had arrived and those from outlying areas were slowly filtering in. As soon as M'ase and the Messenger walked in, silence erupted. Mapraik, who was the senior Elder, greeted M'ase and the Messenger.

"Welcome to the Council of Elders," she said. "It is at the service of the new arrivals. The one speaking is Mapraik, the senior Elder. She personally welcomes you."

The Messenger greeted Mapraik and spoke. "Elder Mapraik, pardon his abruptness but the Messenger seeks an immediate audience with the Inner Council."

The intensity had left the Messenger's voice, but there was no mistaking the sincerity of his plea.

"It is the way of the Council to open Inner Council chambers only when all Elders are present," said Mapraik.

The Messenger turned and spoke to M'ase. "M'ase, please explain to the senior Elder."

"M'ase is a member of an order of Elders, whose only duty is to watch the hills for signs," said M'ase. "They train for 20 years, learning to recognize and interpret the signs. There are seven signs, and each sign requires them to take a certain course of action. Today's sign requires M'ase to lead the Messenger to the Inner Council. The urgency implied by the sign cannot be overstated."

Mapraik's face showed no emotion, her façade hid her inner thoughts. Her thin body, now approaching its 283rd year, concealed her decision. She looked at the Messenger.

"The door will not open until three quarters of the Elders have entered their key," said Mapraik. "Only the Venuvians can bypass the Elders. Mapraik is sorry but the Messenger must wait for additional Elders. There is great power in patience."

"Patience is sometimes action's enemy," replied the Messenger.

Without another word, he stepped around the senior Elder and went to the entrance of the Inner Council. He pulled out a brass object and inserted it into each of the Elder's locks. The door opened, and the Messenger was gone. He had entered the Inner Council of Elders' chamber without the aid of a single Elder.

The Messenger bounded down the dimly lit spiral stairway.

How had his key opened the door to the Inner Council chamber? The messenger asked himself. Where was he going?

He knew he was looking for the Inner Council of Elders and that he would find them at the bottom of the staircase.

What action should he take once he encountered the Elders of the Inner Council?

He knew he had the answer, but he just could not bring it into his consciousness.

The stairway ended, and the Messenger stepped into a circular room. There were twelve men and women evenly spaced around the room. The Messenger knew that these were not the Elders. Not one of the people standing looked to be over 100 years old. All their faces were expressionless, and no one seemed to be aware of the Messenger's entrance. On the side of each person there was half of an egg-shaped unit, one meter high and one meter in diameter. Each had its flat side resting on a square platform that was one meter high. The units were made of a brownish translucent plastic material. The Messenger knew that each of these translucent units held an Elder.

Suddenly, everything changed. The Messenger was in a brightly lit room. Everything was white. The floors, the walls, and the ceiling merged into each other with no indication of where one ended and the other began. There were no Elder units. The same men and women, who had stood next to the Elder units, now stared intently at the Messenger. Now the Messenger knew who he was! He knew who and what these 12 people were. He knew where the Elders were. He knew what his mission was and that he had completed it.

The Elders telepathically discussed the information that the Messenger had delivered to them.

"There is a new one."

"Yes, there is."

"He seems to be quite powerful."

"Good."

"Will he be given fluid?"

"Of course, he must be as powerful as possible."

"How large is their supply?"

"There is more than enough fluid to raise him and take him to the Frontier. The Power grows stronger by the day."

"When the day comes, will the Power be strong enough?"

"It must be."

"The new one may be special."

"Hopefully. Where is he from?"

"Sector 1037—Tambuki, a reconstructed planet for the Learning Project."

"The Learning Project, interesting. His lineage?"

"Ortan mother, Earth father."

"Yes, this one is special."

BB

Something was wrong. This was not supposed to be happening. He was afraid. No, not afraid, he was terrified. He knew it was not supposed to be like this. Something was after him. Something wanted to destroy him. He had lost control of his body. His arms and legs no longer worked. He could almost see what it was that he so feared—almost, but not quite. He wanted to run, but he could not move. He wanted to yell, but, try as he might, he could not force out a single sound.

He had no idea where he was or how long he had been there. This should not be happening. Then he saw it, a light—a warmth. Was it coming toward him or was he moving toward it? He could not tell. His fear was diminishing. He felt hope.

"BB, BB!"

Now the warm light was surrounding him. He could feel his arms and legs.

"BB alright? Look at me."

BB opened his eyes. There was his friend Jov, his head characteristically cocked to one side. Concern filled Jov's hazel eyes as they peered at BB through the fine, silver hair that covered his flat face.

"Bad berries, maybe," said Jov. "Maybe. You good now, BB? Make I go bring bitter. Jov go help you now now. Maybe bad berries."

"Thank you, Jov," said BB. "Yes, please bring me bitter."

BB wanted to forget what he had just experienced, but he could not. He could not forget the fear he had felt, the sense of unmitigated hatred focused at him. BB had never felt anything like this before.

BB thought of the words of Ogba, his Outlander teacher. *Every mo-*

ment is an experience. Every experience is a teacher. To grow, BB must learn from every experience.

BB felt a twinge of guilt. The first time he ate the small, green, foul-tasting berries, it had been for a new experience. It had been a wonderful experience. He had felt a warm, floating sensation—the feeling that all the pieces of a puzzle had been put together perfectly. Everything made sense. BB had felt as one with his world. The experience was so spectacular that BB had tried it again, and again, and again. The Outlander ways began to seem irrelevant. Even though Jov had given him roots and herbs and started him on an exacting exercise regimen, his Monthlies began to show imbalances. BB knew he should stop eating the berries, but he did not stop. Today's experience was so different, so unexpected. BB thought he would never eat the berries again.

"Drink, BB," said Jov. "Bitter go make you feel good now now. Maybe bad berries—maybe."

"Thank you, Jov," said BB.

BB sat up and sipped the bitter green liquid. He could feel the energy start to flow through his limbs.

"We go run now, BB. We go work now now," pleaded Jov.

"A moment please, Jov," said BB as he got to his feet. "I think I am through with berries."

"BB go leave berries? BB no want?" Jov's pointed nose twitched. "Maybe bad ones today. Next time, I go bring only good ones. You go see, BB. Only good ones!"

"No, Jov."

BB lifted the tall thick body that he had inherited from his Ortan mother. He was very weary.

"There will be no next time," said BB. "I have gone to the berries too many times. I must seek other teachers."

"BB great teacher. BB sees many things. Berries go show BB truth. Maybe berries bad today. BB very great teacher." Jov cocked his head again. "Where BB go now?"

"Wherever life takes him," said BB. "It is time to return to the Outlander life—The Way. He must seek, Jov. BB must seek."

"BB very great teacher," said Jov. "BB see truth. BB see many things. Make we go work now, BB? We go make too good Monthly."

Just as suddenly as the drained weary feeling had come on, it was gone. BB did not know if it was the bitter or his new feeling of direction that had lifted his spirits, but he now felt empowered. He was ready to return to the Outlander ways. He had almost lost his powers to listen, to speak, to see, and to move. He must again take up the daily postures. He must again speak in the Outlander way.

Open up, and let life in. Relax, and let life go, thought BB.

"We go now, BB?" asked Jov.

Yes, thought BB. *They must go.*

First, prepare for the Monthlies—balance the body's systems.

BB looked back on his life. He had spent his first 50 years in the Outlander Domain. He was born shortly after his parents arrived on Tambuki. His early life had been uneventful—carefree and open. But, even as a child, BB had been different. While others his age were physically active and playing games, he would spend a whole day engaged in activities like watching a flower's blossom open and close or listening to the subtle differences in the sounds a brook made.

When the time came for his temporary separation from his compound, he had already started to observe the ways of Master teachers. When his contemporaries reached their time to return to the compounds and learn the Outlander ways, he had already found Ogba, a reclusive Master teacher. Ogba spent most of his days in a sitting position, watching and listening to the ocean waves crash against a rocky shoreline. Ogba had used the ocean to teach BB how to see, listen, speak, and move. BB had learned to become one with the ocean. Ogba, who had spent most of his years alone, accepted BB as a student. Ogba said that, even before BB's arrival, the ocean had told Ogba that someone special was coming. Then the day came when Ogba told BB that it was time for BB to leave and seek other teachers.

"If he allows his eyes to see a leaf falling from a tree, then that will be a lesson for him," said Ogba. "If he feels the rhythm of his movement, he will know the story of which he is a part. If he speaks sparingly, he will create openings instead of barriers. Listen with all the skills he has learned, and each sound will be a teacher to him. Go and prepare him for the future. Ogba has felt with every part of his being that BB will someday be a part of destiny."

"Why has Ogba never chosen to join an Outlander community?" asked BB.

Ogba thought for a moment and then answered with a smile. "It is not yet Ogba's time."

Ogba was well over 200 years old, and BB considered asking if Ogba's death would come before Ogba's time. But BB knew there was no answer to this question. It was BB's time. BB left the Outlander Domain to take up residence in Dome City.

After making his farewells to his mother, father, and his few friends, BB made his way to Glide Mountain Three to see Joe and Javita, the ped to glider converters. For as long as BB could remember, Joe and Javita had been on Glide Mountain Three converting pediglides to gliders. They moved with such grace and ease they seemed to be dancing. Every time BB arrived, first with his father and mother, then by himself, Joe had broken the rhythm of his dance and, using only his eyes, had spoken to BB. Even before BB had learned the ways of the Outlanders, he could read Joe's movements and expressions. Joe saw something in BB. For years, BB acknowledged Joe's reactions but said nothing.

On this trip from the Outlander Domain to Dome City, BB decided to first go to Glide Mountain Three and speak with Joe. After the sun reached a certain position in the late afternoon, it no longer created the thermals necessary for gliders, and travel stopped until the next day. When BB arrived, Glide Mountain Three was nearing the end of its daily functions. Before Joe and Javita converted BB's pediglide into a glider, he moved it to the side and watched as Joe and Javita continued their dance with the last few pediglides. Although Joe and Javita continued to move with their same flowing rhythm and grace, BB's training allowed him to see changes, especially in Joe, whose movements showed that he was acutely aware of BB's presence.

As the sun slipped toward the horizon, its brilliance slowly faded, and its radiant warmth dropped precipitously. The thermals, which had been created by the Venuvians, used direct sunlight, sunlight that reflected from mirrors and white sand, heat-radiant boulders, and specially contoured mountains. When the sun's rays faded, the mountain lost its power to lift the gliders. When the shadow of a Venuvian-constructed obelisk touched a certain boulder on Glide Mountain Three, travel stopped. Late arrivals would be sharing their meals with the pediglide converters and their families. After travel had stopped, BB spoke to Joe.

"What is the dancing man's name?" asked BB.

Joe smiled at BB's question. He knew that BB could read his every movement.

"He is called Joe," Joe answered somewhat tentatively.

Joe was awed by the fact that the one he had watched for years expressed awareness of his existence.

"This seeker of truth who stands before Joe is known as BB. He hopes that Joe's day has brought him many good things."

Joe did not reply.

BB spoke. "A wise woman once said to BB, 'Every second gives him a lesson, he need only accept what he is given.' Joe needs to accept what life has given him."

"Joe has watched BB for many years," said Joe. "He can see that the learned one has gained many truths."

"Joe sees things others do not," said BB. "Even some Masters miss things that Joe sees."

Joe shifted self-consciously, not prepared for the compliment.

"Will he tell his story after meal tonight?" asked BB.

"Joe's story is very simple and probably of little interest to the learned one."

As he spoke, Joe could feel himself beaming from the unexpected attention he was receiving from the Master.

"A sunset is simple, but it contains the secrets of the universe," said BB.

"If it pleases the learned one, Joe will tell his story tonight," said Joe.

As the two men spoke, Javita approached and stood next to Joe. Although their lineages were from different systems, the two seem to be a perfectly balanced match. Javita's gaze told BB almost nothing. She was practiced in The Way.

"You look upon Javita," said Javita. "Joe is her mate. It is a pleasure to have someone who Joe has admired for years stop at Javita's and Joe's area. Perhaps the Traveler will tell his story after meal."

"You look upon BB, and it is his pleasure to make Javita's acquaintance, but today BB comes only to listen. He wishes to know what Joe sees in BB that inspires such admiration."

Joe blurted out his response. "The Master is different. Even in his mother's womb, Joe could feel that the one to be born had a special destiny."

Joe's eyes were blazing with excitement. "The ped converter would be honored if the learned one would visit their quarters after story time. He hopes Joe's mate will appreciate the Traveler's presence."

Joe looked at Javita with a youthful expression of delight. Despite Javita's training, an almost imperceptible flicker in her eyes, a very slight movement of her mouth, and a minute shift of her body told BB that Javita would indeed welcome him.

BB's ability to see the infinitesimal lapses in Javita's controlled expressions also revealed to him her deep love for Joe and the joy she received from his uncontrolled excitement. BB had become a master in The Way.

"Javita of course welcomes a visit from the Master."

BB immediately liked Javita and Joe. He liked them very much. At BB's urging, Joe told his story at last meal story time. Indeed, it was a simple story.

Like many others on Tambuki, Joe's father left his home system to go with the Venuvians to a new system. During the "jump," his father had visions and the Venuvians invited him to Tambuki. On Tambuki, he met Joe's mother during their early training period. Joe's mother, who is part Ortan, is a native of Tambuki. His mother and his father excelled in the arts. They completed their training and became Masters.

Joe talked about how he worked with guloks and collected specimens. He ended his story with a re-creation of the day he met Javita and how they had decided to work on the mountains.

Javita surprised Joe and BB by also telling her story. Three generations of women in her family spent their lives on Venuvian ships. The Venuvians invited her mother and father to Tambuki because they both had visions. They became Masters but, even though Javita trained and could have become a Master, she decided to become a High Gatherer instead. She ended by telling her version of the day she first saw Joe.

After story time, Javita, Joe, and BB went to the converters' quarters. They walked quietly under Tambuki's two moons. Not a word was spoken. Each was deep in thought.

BB was surprised by the living quarters. He had expected... he did not know what he had expected—maybe something simple, even austere. To BB's surprise, the place was alive with color—flowers everywhere, some growing, some fresh cut, some dried. In the middle of the room, there was an intricate, multicolored sand drawing, a rock garden, and a small fountain. In one corner of the room, the walls were covered with books that Joe had collected and journals he had written.

"Would BB like some of her specially blended tea?" Javita smiled. "It will make their guest's sleep pleasant." She had dropped her façade. BB could read her eyes, her every movement and gesture. Her genuine warmth was disarming. BB found himself irresistibly drawn to this couple.

"BB would be delighted," said BB. Joe and Javita disappeared into the cooking area. BB idly browsed through Joe's book collection. Most books were dedicated to Venuvian descriptions of the fauna and flora found on Tambuki. The journals contained Joe's observations of what he had encountered when he worked with guloks. In another corner stood a structure that at first baffled BB. Then he saw a pile of crude paper next to it and realized it was a rudimentary printing press.

"The Traveler's host got the design for the press from a proprietor of a print shop in Dome City," Joe said as he set down a platter with three mugs of steaming tea. "Joe borrowed some of the proprietor's print characters, which he used as models to carve his own characters. There are very few who are interested in the subjects in Joe's journals. Books on Tambuki fauna and flora are rare, so Joe decided to make his own. The Venuvian's books did not cover in depth some of the imported species. Some species were listed by name, but the Venuvian books did not always include a detailed description of them. The farther Joe and Javita explored outside roads and paths, the more plants and animals they found that the Venuvians had not adequately described."

"Does Joe or Javita fear encounters with the Wild Ones?" asked BB.

"They have seen a few hermits and one settlement," said Joe. "Most

Wild Ones only want to be left alone, so Javita and Joe have avoided direct contact."

BB replaced the journal he had been studying.

"Joe's work is truly amazing," said BB.

"Joe would be honored if the learned one would accept one of his books, perhaps one on oceanside plants."

BB recalled the years he had spent with Ogba by the Eastern Ocean. And BB remembered the many days he sat on the ground listening to the ocean reveal its secrets and watching a single plant perform its daily dance.

"BB is grateful for Joe's gift," said BB. "BB believes Joe's book will give Joe's guest a great pleasure."

BB sat on a rug and sipped Javita's sweet herb tea. For a few moments, the three sat quietly with their tea—BB studying his book, and Javita, legs folded under her, adding grains of sand to her design on the floor. Joe looked blankly into his cup. Then, simultaneously, Javita and BB snapped their attention to Joe. Both could feel a sudden change in his being.

"When BB leaves Tambuki, Joe wishes to go with him."

"Make we go working—now now," said Jov.

BB could hear the urgency and the concern in Jov's voice. BB began to laugh, he felt good, he felt... free.

"A moment, Jov, please," said BB. "The impatient one sacrifices that which can never be recovered."

Jov mumbled something. He was consumed with dread.

"Maybe bad berries, maybe. Jov love the berry. Jov no go leave berry."

"Jov, Jov, Jov," said BB. He paused. "Jov—Jov is BB's friend. Jov will always be BB's friend."

Jov's flat furry face lit up.

"BB Jov's friend? BB no go leave Jov?"

"BB is Jov's friend—good friend."

Jov beamed. Then his face again became gloomy.

"But Jov no go leave berry. Jov, he love berry." He perked up a little. "Maybe someday," Jov said quietly. "Maybe."

"Jov is Jov, BB is BB," said BB. "BB has his ways, Jov has his ways, but Jov and BB are friends.

"What thing BB go do now?"

"Now?" asked BB. "BB must awaken. Please Jov, we will work soon, but now BB must think."

"Good, BB go think," said Jov. "BB and Jov friends. Good, good."

Jov left BB to think, jauntiness in his step.

BB's thoughts drifted back to when he left the Outside domain and his first years in Dome City. Masters often spent a day or two in Dome City after their Monthly. At first, BB observed these masters as they meditated and contemplated. BB was himself a master, but he was many years younger than other masters. Whether it was the impatience of his young 50 years or some part of his personality that desired to seek the unknown, no one knew, least of all BB, but he found himself walking the streets of Dome City. He studied many of the cultures in Dome City but he knew he would never have time to acquaint himself with the thousands of cultures that had settled there.

Then he discovered Out Town. There were not many misfits in Dome City. There were a few former Associates and former V.I.s, but most of the inhabitants of Out Town were Dome City residents who avoided anything Venuvian, especially the one thing that the Venuvians required to become an Associate and part of the Venuvian system— Monthlies. One needed only to have good Monthlies to become an Associate. For those who chose to live outside of the Venuvian system, avoiding Monthlies meant that the Venuvians did not provide them with any of the Venuvian goods and services.

One could survive outside of the Venuvian world, but he or she would have to deal with problems with transportation, living quarters, and basic provisions. On Tambuki, one could exist without being an Associate. Food was abundant, most of it free for the picking. One could find some sort of clothing, but it was usually substandard. These Out Town residents had to rely on the goodness of an Associate or V.I. for their living quarters. They were, in essence, Wild Ones who live in

Dome City. Additionally, Out Town residents were not usually eligible to leave with one of the Venuvian ships that visited every 200 years.

BB was strangely attracted to Out Town. The variety of intoxicants available was staggering. They ranged from the very mild to the heavy and highly addictive. BB was not interested in the multitude of depravities that existed in Out Town, but he never tired of observing and reading the residents. Then he met Jov—and his berries.

Every 200 years, the Venuvians visited Tambuki. Their mother ships assumed stationary orbits and dispatched shuttle ships to and from Tambuki. Just as with newly encountered systems, Tambuki V.I.s had the option of joining ships and moving to other systems. Available destinations included systems with which the Venuvians had already made contact and created Academies, viable systems at various stages of human development, systems with no human presence, and systems with no human sustaining environments. Then there were some systems where the Venuvians had sent an advance probe. An advance probe collected information on a system, but it did not have the ability to transmit. Systems with only an advance probe were the Frontier Systems.

It never entered BB's mind to ever leave Tambuki. But Joe was certain that someday BB would leave. When Joe had told BB that Joe would accompany him, it started BB thinking. The more he thought about it, the more enticing the idea of exploring a new system became, especially now that the time was approaching when the Venuvians would arrive.

It was in the 2,780th year of Dome City—20 years before the Venuvians were to arrive on Tambuki for the 14th time—when BB first met the stranger. BB had spent the morning at the Western Ocean, something he did regularly ever since he first came to Dome City. There was calmness in the rhythmic crashing of the waves and anticipation in the air. Powerful ocean swells clashed with retreating waves and were drained of their energy in an explosion of surf. BB watched as a roaring wave tumbled over the retreat of the preceding wave. What had been a raging monster morphed into a tamed sliver of ocean, finishing its futile attempt to escape the boundary of the sandy shoreline. By the time the roaring surf reached BB's bare feet, the powerful wave had been reduced to a mere trickle. It was then that BB saw the stranger.

The stranger stood motionless, and BB found it impossible to read him. BB assumed his own façade. Then the stranger turned and looked directly at BB. His gaze was quiet and yet powerful. His steel gray eyes were unflinching. BB felt there was recognition in the stranger's eyes, but BB knew he had never seen this one before. The stranger was a person one would not forget. He was almost three meters tall and, even under his robes, one could tell that his gaunt body had a reservoir of power that was coiled and ready to strike. His skin was as gray as his eyes. His broad brow was smooth over his piercing eyes. His drooping jowls weighed down the corners of his mouth, which would make smiling difficult. His lips were the color of his skin and were set firmly in the deep furrows that framed the sides of his mouth. He was not a Venuvian.

"The ocean seems unusually calm." The stranger's voice was deep and raspy.

"Yes, yes it is," said BB.

BB was unexplainably drawn to this stranger.

"But, like the universe, its vastness can conceal turmoil," said the stranger.

"Turmoil in the universe?" asked BB. "The Venuvians have brought order to our universe,"

"The Venuvians serve a purpose, young Master, but the order they bring is only an attempt to avoid the inevitable conflict."

BB did not quite know what to make of this stranger.

"The Venuvian order has been here for thousands of years," said BB. "Why would the stranger say it is only temporary?

The stranger mused for a moment.

"Only eternity is forever. In comparison, a few thousand years is nothing—temporary," said the stranger. "A *million* years is temporary."

BB was intrigued.

"What happens when chaos confronts order? What then?"

"The inevitable conflict," said the stranger.

"How can conflict be avoided?" asked BB.

"It cannot. There are but two possible outcomes: either order succumbs to chaos or chaos succumbs to order."

BB felt the strength of truth in the stranger's words. The tall man of wisdom spoke of some inevitable future.

"Has the one who stands before the ocean seen the future?" asked BB.

The stranger's gaunt figure tensed.

"He has glimpsed the force of chaos," said the stranger. "And he has never known such fear before."

His words sent a chill through BB. His mind flashed back to the last time he had eaten berries; he had never known such fear before. For a second he lost his composure. For the briefest time his façade must have slipped.

"The young Master has seen the chaos and has felt the great fear, has he not?"

"Yes," replied BB, trying to distance himself from that terrible feeling. "BB has indeed felt the great fear."

BB was sure the stranger must know something more about that absolute terror BB had experienced—but what? Did the stranger hold a key that could unlock the door to this mystery? BB wanted to find out what lay behind his experience with the berries. Did this imposing Master hold an answer? BB would not question him now. He would wait—wait until he had better control of his feelings. The great fear BB had experienced was still affecting his emotions.

"BB must accept all emotions," BB's teacher, Ogba, had said. "Look at them from all sides. Feel them, embrace them, and then let them become part of BB's mind, body, and soul. No matter how distasteful, no part should be left untouched. Any part of any emotion that is kept out, ignored, or suppressed will leave BB incomplete."

BB had not yet accepted the great fear.

"What does the one who speaks of the future call himself?" asked BB.

"Gogandu," said the stranger.

For the next six years, BB and Gogandu saw each other regularly. Gogandu was a quiet type and seldom added more than a few words to the conversation. BB would relate an observation to Gogandu, and Gogandu would usually just nod. Then one day BB mentioned he had been thinking of leaving Tambuki.

"BB's destiny is on the frontier," Gogandu said.

Gogandu spoke not as if it were an option but as if it were a fact.

"Frontier?" asked BB. BB was truly puzzled. "Where is this Frontier?"

Gogandu stood. "The time has come for the young master to see part of the Plan," said Gogandu.

Then Gogandu turned and left without another word. BB followed, a bit confused. He fell into step beside Gogandu, his two strides for every one of Gogandu's. Gogandu led BB to a section of Dome City that BB had never been to before. The architecture was plain and unadorned. There were few windows. Doorways were closed. There was very little traffic either on foot or on peds. The area was not inviting. Gogandu approached one of the unmarked doors. He did not open the door immediately; instead he touched it a few times before it opened. Gogandu had a lock on his door! Though not unheard of, it was highly unusual for anyone to lock a door in Dome City, or anywhere on Tambuki for that matter. BB could not imagine what Gogandu might have that was so valuable he needed to lock it up.

They entered a dark room with no windows or skylights. Gogandu lit a candle. The starkness of the room shocked BB. The room contained one small table—hardly large enough for one to take a meal—one chair, one bed, and a small bookcase with 10 or 15 books. Nothing else. The room had an elliptical shape, and the walls were perforated with random holes that had no particular design. There was a small round hole in the center of the ceiling. Gogandu lit a lantern unlike one BB had ever seen. It did not have a wick or candle. Instead, it used rock nuts glowing brighter than any rock nuts BB had ever seen. Gogandu placed the rock nuts in a glass sphere that was inside the lantern. The thick glass magnified the light from the rock nuts to an extent that it hurt BB's eyes to look directly at the lantern. Gogandu stood on his bed and grabbed a rope, which he used to lower a wire through the middle of the ceiling. He attached the wire to the lantern. He then reeled the bright light thru the hole in the ceiling. When the lantern entered the hole, the walls were transformed. Each of the tiny holes in the walls, from ceiling to just above the floor, emitted a light. At first the spectacle of light merely surprised BB. Then he looked closer. The holes that had initially appeared random were not random at all. They were miniaturized depictions of star systems!

"Frontier systems," said Gogandu. "The stars are of course not to scale."

That was all that Gogandu said. BB was fascinated with not only the show on the walls and ceiling but also with the systems themselves. At least 10 worlds with different suns, planets, and moons lit up the room.

"How many systems are there?" asked BB.

"On my display, 12," said Gogandu. "But they are only a fraction of the frontier systems. There are over a hundred."

"Why does Gogandu keep his roomed locked?" asked BB.

Gogandu was silent for a moment. When he did continue, it was as if BB had not asked the question.

"In 14 years the Venuvians will visit Tambuki. There will be four ships. When they leave Tambuki, the ships will be headed to four different systems. Many Tambuki V.I.s will have the opportunity to relocate to another planet. The planets vary. One planet is almost dead, two have life but no humans, and one has a thriving society—much like the one the young master's father came from."

"How does he know about BB's father's planet?" asked BB.

BB had spoken of his parents only in passing and had never mentioned Earth, his father's home planet.

"Gogandu knows much about BB's father and mother and much about BB," said Gogandu.

He did not elaborate.

"The frontier systems need those who have mastered The Way," said Gogandu. "BB must not speak of these frontier systems. The Venuvians want only those whom they have chosen to go to the frontier to know any details about the frontier systems. BB has been chosen to go to the frontier."

BB remembered the words of Ogba: "When emotions are not controlled, they devour one's powers."

Right now BB's excitement was devouring his power. The thought of traveling to another system was intoxicating. Just the idea of boarding a Venuvian ship had already begun to exert control on BB's emotions.

"Why has BB been chosen?"

"Masters have been chosen because they have the power to recognize the unknown that might be encountered," said Gogandu.

"The unknown?" asked BB. "What unknown? Chaos?"

BB had questioned Gogandu further about why he had been chosen and what chaos was, but the only answers he got were not informative.

"In time, young master," Gogandu would say. Or, "There are many answers."

Gogandu would give no further information.

◆

Anticipation mounted as the time approached for the Venuvians to arrive. Those who were under 200 years old had never seen a Venuvian ship before. There was no advanced communication, no scouts, only the calendar that marked the Venuvian arrival day on Tambuki. The day of the Venuvian arrival was anti-climactic. Many eyes looked skyward, but there was little to be seen. It was not until the sun began to fade that the Venuvian presence unfolded. As darkness began to take its turn in the Tambuki sky, the four new specks of light were, at first, hardly visible. Then they slowly became the brightest lights in the sky. Four bright new stars had appeared over four sections of Tambuki. The Venuvians had arrived!

The next day, the real excitement began. A Venuvian ship landed near Dome City. Its landing was not the clumsy landing of winged shuttle ships experienced by most arrivals. Instead, the large landing craft floated smoothly to a pad outside of Dome City. Throngs of citizens surrounded the ship, and there were great cheers as the Venuvian visitors exited the ships. Joining the Venuvians were Travelers from many distant planets.

For the first few months, the Venuvians occupied themselves repairing peds and domes and servicing the Monthly station. Teams of observers surveyed the fauna and flora outside the dome to ensure that the artificial balance they had created was still intact. There were also teams whose sole duty was to take a census of the Unattached.

After the Venuvians and the assisting Travelers completed these initial tasks, the Venuvians concentrated on recruiting V.I.s for travel to other systems. For the next year, V.I.s from all over Tambuki explored the Venuvian ships—ships with never-before-seen electronic devices that, to the inhabitants of Tambuki, verged on magic. The Venuvians were seeking V.I.s to send to one of four different star systems. Three systems, which the Venuvians had already begun to modify, needed people to complete the awakening process. The fourth system had a planet with advanced civilizations. That planet would be receiving the benefits of Venuvian Academies and advanced technologies.

The residents of Tambuki knew nothing about eight ships that the Venuvians had hidden behind Tambuki's two moons. These were the ships headed for the frontier.

BB spent many days on the Venuvian ship marveling at the advanced technology. But it was Gogandu, inside his planetarium, who made the decision as to which system BB was headed.

"Of the 108 frontier systems, the Venuvians have successfully sent probes to 97. The remaining 11 are unknown quantities. The probes either never arrived or arrived and became nonfunctional. There are actually many more frontier systems, but these eight systems are about to have naturally occurring phenomena that will allow the Venuvians to arrive undetected."

"What sort of natural phenomena," asked BB?

"Asteroid belts and meteor showers," said Gogandu.

"Why do they want to arrive undetected?" Gogandu looked directly at BB and merely said, "Chaos."

BB had again attempted to get Gogandu to explain what he meant by chaos, but all Gogandu said was, "The time is not yet right."

Gogandu decided that BB would go to one of the 11 planets that currently had no surface data available.

"The Venuvians sent a probe to this planet, but it has not responded. They have sent a second probe, but BB will arrive before that probe," said Gogandu. "The planet is called Erlon."

BB wondered if Gogandu had somehow influenced his decision to leave Tambuki. Gogandu had an inner source of power that BB could not explain. He had seen Gogandu use this power to control others, and he was sure Gogandu had used it on him. To what extent had Gogandu used his powers on BB? BB did not know, and, curiously, he did not care.

A few days after BB accepted the decision, he and Gogandu sat on cliffs overlooking the ocean. They could feel waves crashing against the rocks below. Gogandu had a glazed continence about him. BB had often seen him in this state and was careful not to disturb him. Suddenly, with an air of immediacy, Gogandu spoke.

"BB must get a crew of at least 50. They must be people BB knows and trusts. It is very important that the operation to Erlon be kept completely secret."

Fifty? thought BB. BB's mind raced over all the V.I.s he knew, and he was sure he did not know 50.

"They need not be V.I.s or Associates," said Gogandu. "What is important is that BB knows them personally or knows of them from a trusted source. And they must take Monthlies."

"They do not have to be V.I.s?" BB asked incredulously.

The Venuvians had been recruiting exclusively from V.I.s for the four visible Venuvian ships. Not even Associates were eligible for the off-planet assignments.

"Go to Out Town, go to the Outlander Domain, go to the Wild Ones," said Gogandu. "Go where ever BB has to go, but he must find a crew of 50 who are willing to depart—soon."

BB began to assemble a crew. At first, he experienced a wave of sadness. He was now 67 years old, and he was not sure he even knew 50 people by name. Why had he chosen a life so devoid of contact with other people?

Again BB remembered Ogba's words: "Life gave BB his family, BB had no control. The path BB chose to follow, led him to Ogba. BB chose that path but did not always control where it took him. Life will send many things to BB over which he has no control, but he has full control over whom he calls a friend. A friend is a true reflection of what one calls one's self. Look to BB's friends to better see BB."

BB had only a few he could look to as true friends.

"Oh, Jov no know," said Jov. "Go some other place? What thing go happen in this other place? BB go make Jov leave his berries? I no know."

"You can take berries with you, Jov," said BB. "And you can grow them in the agricultural sector on the ship."

Jov thought for a moment. His deep friendship sealed his decision.

"I go new place with BB and take berries? Jov go! Jov go!"

The ped changer, Joe, was of course eager to go. It had been Joe who predicted BB's departure. Joe had planted the seed. BB traveled to the top of Glide Mountain Three. Before he could say a word, he read acceptance in Joe's face.

"Javita and Joe have agreed," said Joe. "They both wish to travel with BB."

"No one must know of the trip they are about to take," BB warned Joe and Javita.

Joe had wondered about the secrecy but said nothing.

"And BB needs more crew," said BB. "But only those who Joe trusts, and who will take Monthlies."

PLORV

Joe knew even fewer people than BB knew. Many years before BB's search for a crew, Joe befriended a Wild One named Plorv. Plorv had left his tribe of Wild Ones to join the Outlanders. He had quickly learned the practices of The Way, which had so eluded Joe. Plorv often visited Joe and Javita. He would spend days just observing the Outlanders that passed. Plorv knew of Joe's special relationship with BB. Joe found Plorv different in an indescribable way. Javita said she had a vague feeling that Plorv was hiding something, but she attributed her feeling to the many years Plorv had spent as a Wild One.

The truth was that Plorv was part of a Wild Ones' plot to destroy Venuvians. That was Plorv's secret. He had actually been practicing The Way long before he joined the Outlanders. Because Plorv had been a Wild One, he could not enter Dome City, but he could join a Venuvian crew that was headed for a different system.

Outlanders had to travel to Dome City at least once a month for their Monthlies. Plorv had systematically visited Joe and Javita and, by timing his visits, he was able to observe every Outlander as they had their pediglides converted. Plorv knew BB was a special Master. When Plorv found out that BB and Joe were going to leave with one of the Venuvian ships, he used his powers of The Way to sway Joe into selecting him to be a member of the crew. Plorv had a deadly secret, and Joe had innocently decided that Plorv could be a member of BB's mission.

BB's biggest surprise came when he visited his parents to say goodbye and to tell them of his plans to become a Traveler. KC, standing in his and Krella's private, enclosed area, looked over the surrounding landscape.

"This is a beautiful planet," said KC. "Your parents have spent many happy years here. Krella and KC have practiced The Way, and BB's father has found an inner peace he never imagined existed. But KC has a void that cannot be filled here on Tambuki. He will speak with BB's mother. If she agrees, they would like to accompany BB."

BB was stunned. He never imagined his father and mother might want to join him. Now BB had two more crewmembers and a future that included his mother and father.

BB spent the next few months looking for more crew. Since his mission had to be kept secret, the process of approaching a Tambukian with the proposal to travel to the frontier was involved and took time.

"The time grows near young Master," reminded Gogandu one day. "And the crew is not yet complete." He looked intently at BB. "BB has powers greater than he knows," said Gogandu. "Use his eyes and his heart. The head only observes what the heart already knows to be true. Go to Outland. There are V.I.s and Associates there who are seeking escape, but they do not know from what. BB and Gogandu have the answer. Do not speak, do not study—feel."

"But... " BB tried to object, but Gogandu cut him short.

"Do not worry young Master," said Gogandu. "The entire crew will be vetted by the Inner Circle of Elders. The unworthy will fail. The young Master must trust his heart."

The strange thing was that the first person BB had doubts about was Plorv. Plorv just did not feel right. Unfortunately, BB had to find new crewmembers, not release ones that had already been selected. BB did not listen to his heart.

The day finally arrived when the crew, which BB had so painstakingly recruited, boarded a Venuvian landing craft. Every member of the crew was assigned to a different post, but as soon as they arrived at the mother ship, they were relieved of their post and reported to a pre-arranged area of the ship. Then they were transferred to a shuttle that was attached to the mother ship. The mother ship's onboard manifest showed that 50 Tambukians had been found unacceptable because of unspecified reasons and that they had returned to Tambuki. The records on Tambuki still showed that the 50 were headed for their originally assigned systems. KC, Krella, Morbred, Jubley, and BB were the only V.I.s on the shuttle.

The electronic wizardry of the Venuvian ship amazed BB. The only electronic devices he had ever seen on Tambuki were in the Monthly room. The Venuvian spaceship, with its sliding doors, artificial lights, and audio and visual devices, seemed extraordinary to BB.

For KC, it was a return to his past life. His and Krella's Personals were activated, and they were given their travel modules. When KC opened his travel module, he was amazed by the old treasures he had brought from Earth. The Adabuma carvings and his hand made robes, which were once so prized, seemed so insignificant after all his years on Tambuki—time had changed KC.

Gogandu sat expressionlessly in front of the 50 crewmembers.

"There is a problem," said Gogandu. "One of the Elders from the mother ship's Inner Circle has expired. The crew will be unable to leave Tambuki orbit until the Inner Circle replaces her. If they do not replace her within the required time, the Venuvians will cancel this mission. For the time being, the crew is confined to the shuttle. Since the mission is secret, the crew will be unable to enter the mother ship. All mourn the passing of an Elder. Hopefully a replacement will be found on Tambuki."

There was a stunned silence. Then Plorv asked a question.

"Where will the crew go if no replacement is found?" asked Plorv.

"The assignment to a frontier mission is permanent," said Gogandu. "Tambuki has been producing Elders for thousands of years. A replacement Elder should be found within the acceptable time period. Since it is imperative that our frontier mission be kept a secret, the crew will remain in this shuttle until the mother ship to which it is attached departs."

"What if an Elder is not found within the accepted time period?" asked Plorv.

The crew could hear the edge in Plorv's voice. He was feeling trapped.

"Then they are prisoners on this shuttle," said Gogandu. "Spaceship Proxsina, the mother ship to which they are now attached, is slated to depart for Veltra, a planet near the frontier. The plan is to depart from Proxsina during the 'jump.'"

KC tensed at the thought of another "jump," but he was determined to join his son.

"Those who have had an uncomfortable experience during a 'jump' need not be apprehensive," assured Gogandu. "They will have no more such experiences."

KC wondered what Gogandu knew about the uncomfortable experiences but, as usual, Gogandu did not elucidate.

"The shuttle has all the necessary emergency systems," said Gogandu. "Basic necessities will be taken care of, but this small ship was not intended for long term occupancy. All must be patient."

◆

"I thought we weren't supposed to leave the area around the Dome," said La Mat as he and Juke entered the Venuvian land craft.

"I guess it must be important, but we're just on standby," said Juke. "If the package is not ready in time for the last transport departure, we abort. That is unless we want to be stuck on this backward planet for the next 200 years."

"No thanks," said La Mat. "It's amazing how these people live without power. Some of their gadgets are very ingenious, but I'll take Venuvian ingenuity every time." La Mat paused—thinking. "I thought the holy people here were disturbed by electronic equipment."

"Apparently, some are," said Juke. "That's why the Venuvians created this planet, so the monks, or whatever they are, could live without interference. But, if I get the order, interference or no interference, we go pick up the package."

◆

The room was dark. The Inner Circle of Elders began to meld their thoughts. There was absolute silence and no movement. The circle of encased Elders, each flanked by a personal BioDroid, was seeking to make a decision. The Elders from the Inner Circle had to choose one of their own to leave Tambuki.

There was a disquieting shift in the Inner Circle of Elders' harmony. The Inner Circle of Elders had never felt the need to rush to a decision before. Now they had to decide which one of their own would depart from Tambuki. What disturbed the Elders most was the time limit the Venuvians had set. In the past, decisions by the Inner Circle of Elders only involved choosing which Elder they would accept into their Inner Circle. But never, never had there been a time limit.

An Elder had expired on one of the spaceships that was preparing to travel to another system. The Venuvians needed a replacement. A ship could not travel without its full complement of 12 Elders. Now the Inner Circle of Elders was silently melding their thoughts.

It was Ubrota who returned the Inner Circle of Elders to its harmony. As an Outlander, she had often looked into the infinite sky and wondered what existed beyond the confines of Tambuki. Now, she chose to leave the comfort of the Inner Circle of Elders she had known for 187 years. The other Tambuki Elders felt Ubrota's desire and accepted it. Her BioDroid, which was a replica of Ubrota in her 59th year, immediately became activated and exited the underground chamber. The BioDroid had to alert the spaceship that the replacement Elder was available.

The Venuvians needed Ubrota to join 11 other Elders in another Inner Circle. Venuvian spaceships needed the psychokinetic energies of 12 Elders to propel Venuvian ships into another part of the galaxy.

◆

BB was trying to adjust to the fact that he might have to spend years in a cramped shuttle with 49 other crewmembers. A general feeling of dismay permeated the crew. Plorv began showing signs of a caged animal. Jov was at first quite agitated. Even if he rationed his berries, they would last no longer than two years.

"What Jov go do now?" moaned Jov. "Someday, no berries. Oh, this not good. What Jov go do now?"

Krella assured Jov that there would be more than enough waste products from a crew of 50 to create a growing medium for his berries. This news had a calming effect on Jov. However, for the first time in years, BB thought about the sweet escape of the foul tasting berries. But, even in the unlikely event that BB *did* consider seeking that escape, Jov would be unlikely to part with any of his precious treasure. Not until Jov actually saw a new crop of berries growing would he be willing to share.

Spending years on this tiny shuttle was not going to be easy. The shadow of resignation began to settle over the crew. Then news came that the Venuvians had found a replacement Elder. The crewmembers, who had been stoic when they first heard that they would be restricted to the shuttle, now made no attempt to conceal their excitement.

"We go now, big ship go now now," Jov repeated joyously.

PROXSINA

After the delivery of the Elder, things moved quickly. The crew had scarcely settled down when the announcement came to prepare for departure. Because the Inner Circle of Elders was involved in the integration of the Tambuki Elder, the vetting of the 50 crewmembers had been bypassed. Plorv's deadly secret went undetected.

BB took a few moments to view Tambuki. Proxsina, the spaceship that the frontier-bound shuttle was connected to, was still in its stationary orbit. Soon Proxsina would be headed toward the sun. This was the last time BB would be this close to Tambuki. It seemed immense and insignificant at the same time. The sight of his home planet elicited a feeling that BB would never forget and an emotion he could not explain. For a moment, he was one with the universe. Even though he had long ago mastered The Way, much of what he had learned from other Masters, crystallized at that moment. Everything fit together so perfectly. He was going to where he should be going. Everything felt right. Then another announcement came.

"The departure of Proxsina has been delayed. Proxsina will remain in orbit until further notice."

The shuttle was in an uproar. Crewmembers wanted answers to their questions.

"Is something wrong with Proxsina?"

"Is Proxsina safe?"

"Why can't Proxsina depart?"

"How long will Proxsina remain in orbit?"

BB remained calm. He accepted the situation as just another lesson in life.

The days dragged on. It was day 107. BB had learned more about his mother's and father's lives in those 107 days than he had in his previous 67 years.

Krella showed BB the agricultural sector. It was small compared to the agricultural sectors on mother ships, but it was big enough to supply the shuttle with basic food needs. Of course, Jov was there. He wanted to make sure that, in case of an emergency, there was somewhere he could grow his precious berries. Then there was another announcement.

"In nine time units, Proxsina will depart orbit. The ship will be traveling at a reduced speed for the next 20 days."

The crew came back to life. Proxsina was finally heading to another system. The first few days after departure from Tambuki orbit, BB visited the observation port every day, and every day his home planet grew smaller. Soon it was just another speck in a vast sea of stars. BB continued to spend his time assuming positions, and contemplating. He looked, listened, moved, and spoke in The Way. His inner peace was growing.

Gogandu did not let time go to waste. Daily, he put the entire crew through grueling activities to develop their physical, mental, and spiritual strengths. Each crewmember was also required to study courses from Venuvian Academies. By the time the Proxsina was preparing for a "jump," every crewmember had earned the title of Venuvian Integrate—V.I.

The twentieth month after leaving Tambuki orbit, the sun was all that anyone could see through the observation port. The Proxsina deployed its heat shields and the observation port no longer had a view. Spaceship Proxsina continued its plunge toward the sun—gaining speed and collecting energy. The time for the "jump" was approaching.

"Morbred, KC, and BB, please report to the multi-purpose room." It was Gogandu's voice.

The father and son met Morbred in the multi-purpose room, which was empty except for Gogandu.

"The Tambuki Elder is having a communication problem," said Gogandu. "It has been thousands of years since the Tambuki Elders communicated with any Elders who were not on Tambuki. Morbred, KC and BB will act as conduits for the information between the Tambuki Elder and the other 11 Elders in the Inner Council of Elders. When Proxsina makes a 'jump,' its Elder drive must be at full power to be precise. If communication among the Elders is not perfect, the ship could end up lost in deep space."

The three Masters were shocked at the turn of events. They had come to understand that KC's and Mobred's "jump" experiences and BB's experience with berries were proof that they could be affected by the Elders—but *communicate* with the Inner Circle of Elders?

"There is no need for concern," said Gogandu. "Elders have already communicated with Morbred, BB, and KC. Relax their minds, let their feelings flow and there will be no problem. They have powers that they are not yet aware of." Gogandu became very serious, "When they enter the mother ship, they must move as if they are invisible."

Gogandu gave Morbred, BB, and KC a reassuring look, and then he turned and went to the exit port that connected the shuttle to Proxsina. When the four entered Proxsina, no one noticed them, and no one re-membered seeing them. Gogandu headed toward the Venuvians' quar-ters. A door slid open, and the four entered a small area. Four Venuvians and one Ortan sat in front of monitors engaged in what appeared to be important activities. All five of the workers glanced at Gogandu and his three followers as they passed. The four Venuvians quickly returned to what they had been doing. The Ortan briefly examined BB's eyes. Neither BB nor the Ortan saw anything in the other's large golden eyes.

Another door slid open and Gogandu and the three Masters entered a dimly lit, circular chamber. Twelve semi-oval Elder containers were sitting on cube-shaped platforms and were equally spaced around the chamber. Each semi-oval had a male or female BioDroid standing be-hind it. Morbred, KC, and BB were in the presence of Proxsina's Inner Circle of Elders. Only a few non-Elders had entered this chamber since its creation.

"This way," said Gogandu softly.

He led the three visitors to one of the semi-ovals. The BioDroid standing behind the Elder, Ubrota, spoke.

"KC," said the BioDroid, "stand to her left. Morbred, stand to her right. BB, stand in front of her on the other side of the Elder. We will form a circle around the Elder, Ubrota. Relax their arms at their sides. Turn their left palms upward and their right palms downward. The four of them will now raise their hands and touch their fingertips."

The three complied with the BioDroid's instructions. When all the fingertips touched, there was a flash. Morbred, KC, and, BB felt a physical jolt and then they were in a white room. All three had seen the room before, but this time it was more inviting and less harsh. The room was silent but Morbred, KC and BB felt a turbulence. The turbulence slowly dissipated and the three became one with the Elders.

◆

The crew of the Proxsina and the crew of the shuttle were preparing for the "jump." They were strapped into their spinners. The ship's various compartments contracted until the Proxsina was one third of its original size. The crews began their two-axis spin as the ship increased its velocity. The soon-to-be Travelers, had a queasy feeling from simultaneously spinning head over heels and left to right at the same time.

Morbred, KC, and BB remained in the Inner Circle of Elders' chamber, which the Elders protected from outside forces during the "jump." Then it was over. There were no dry mouths, no dizziness, no disorientation—no visions.

The ship expanded until it was back to its original size. Everything was the same on Spaceship Proxsina except for the observation port. No longer was the observation port filled with a blazing sun. Now it was again filled with a vast array of stars. There was one other difference, one very big difference—a shuttle that had been part of Proxsina was no longer there.

When the shuttle that was headed for the frontier came out of the "jump," all the power on the ship was gone. Gogandu manually released each V.I. from their spinner. He assured each V.I. that there was no need to be alarmed and that there was a reason for the power interruption—there was no failure in the equipment. Excitement began to grow again. Gogandu held a meeting with the entire crew crammed into the multi-purpose.

"Unfortunately, the shuttle will be without power for a while," said

Gogandu. "There are ways to manually expand the ship, but there will be absolutely no use of electronic power. In 43 days, the shuttle will rendezvous with an asteroid belt. While inside the asteroid belt, the shuttle will have limited power restored. Fifty-eight days after the shuttle's rendezvous with the asteroid belt, Erlon will pass through the asteroid belt. Erlon is the inhabited planet in this system. Forty members of the crew will enter the landing craft and separate from the shuttle. The shuttle will take refuge behind Erlon's moon. The landing craft will enter the atmosphere as part of the meteor shower."

"Why must we disguise ourselves as a meteorite?" asked a V.I.

"It is of the utmost importance that the mission is carried out in total secrecy," said Gogandu. "The mission must go undetected until the investigation of the planet is complete."

"What if they are detected?" It was Plorv.

"If every V.I. follows orders, they will go undetected. There are indications that there is intelligent life on this planet, but it is unknown how intelligent."

◆

Some thought Miltok, the stargazer, was a fool. Others thought he used magic. Some even thought he was possessed by evil spirits. But Miltok always knew when the time was right to plant tufa, the root that was the staple of his people. If the people planted tufa too early, plants would dry up and die before the rain. If they planted it too late, they would produce crops that were small and immature. Many seasons ago, the people learned to heed Miltok's advice. Even distant villages sent individuals to find out what Miltok's predictions were. Those who did not follow Miltok's advice could go hungry during the long dry season—or worse.

Miltok kept to himself and seldom spoke. He spent most of his days sitting, thinking, and making drawings. His drawings were nothing more than dots on slates of rock. He had hundreds of these drawings. At night, Miltok looked at the sky and watched the movement of the stars. His slate drawings were his record of what he saw. It was the position of certain stars that enabled Miltok to predict the seasons and tell his people when to plant.

One night, while watching a display of meteors, Miltok saw something unusual. It looked like a meteor, but it was larger and it moved differently. Instead of disappearing in the night sky, it continued its descent until it disappeared behind the horizon. Others of his people saw the same thing, but to them it was just another meteor. Miltok had never seen anything like it before. He knew it was different. If a piece of the sky had fallen to Erlon, he must see it. The next day Miltok was gone.

◆

BB looked out over the barren land that was Erlon. All he could see for miles was dry grasses, dry scrub brush, and, occasionally, one of the gnarly trees that appeared to be barely hanging on to life. Unlike Tambuki, which had ice in the northern and southern polar areas and two oceans, Erlon had no oceans, the heat was deadly in the equatorial area, and ice was nowhere to be found on the planet. All Erlon's population was located in or near the northern polar area. Water was only available during the short, annual, rainy season. Similar conditions existed in the southern polar area. That area was unpopulated and the northerners had no means to cross the deadly equator. But there were still some groups on Erlon that were able to hold on to life in this wasteland that BB now studied.

The landing craft had landed south of most of the villages, far enough away to go undetected. Gogandu was very clear—the landing craft and its occupants must not be detected. Even though most of the dwellings were located north of where the ship's landing craft was located, there were signs that people lived even farther south of the landing area. There were reasons why some groups had settled in these desolated areas so far south, reasons that would soon become clear to the newly arrived crew.

"At one time there were large desert areas like this on Earth," said KC to his son. "The Venuvians revitalized Earth's deserts, but they left some desert areas as a reminder of what Earth was like before they arrived. Some ancients on Earth actually flourished in the deserts. Your father spent some of his off time exploring desert areas."

"But, without water, how can anything survive?" asked BB.

"Water in such areas is scarce," said KC. "But it can be found if one knows where and how to look. BB's father thinks that the end of the dry season on this planet will arrive shortly. Soon there will be rain on Erlon and things will come alive, if only for a short time. All life will busy itself collecting and storing food and water for the long dry season ahead."

"Why would people choose to live here instead of migrating towards the pole?" pondered BB.

BB spoke to himself as much as he spoke to his father. Both men fell silent absorbing the vast emptiness.

"Maybe the environment changed, and there were some who adapted, holding on to the dying land, and learning how to eke out a life," mused KC.

"The early reports say that the transportation routes in parts of the northern hemisphere are well developed," said BB. "What keeps these people away from the pole?"

"It does seem peculiar that, even with all the roads, there are so many of these dwellers who don't head toward the more fertile area in the north. Maybe there is something to the north that these people fear."

◆

Miltok, the stargazer, traveled only during the times of the day when the temperature allowed. He would start in the morning as soon as there was enough light to walk and push himself until the heat became unbearable. He would then erect his portable shade and wait until the blazing sun sank below the horizon. Then he would again push himself until it was too dark to navigate over the uneven terrain. He was sorry it was not the time of the moon, but he knew, if the moon had been out the night before, the object he saw might have passed unseen.

Miltok set up for the night. He put out his dew catcher to suck out a few drops of precious liquid from the night air. If only he had one of the four-legged beasts that the Northern Raiders had, he could have made the journey in one day. But the Northern Raiders, who controlled the polar area, jealously kept the animals under their control. Northern Raiders were the ones who held the power in the northern polar area. The gods gave them water year round, they had domesticated animals for food, and they had zwaps. Zwaps were the four-legged animals the Northern Raiders used to dominate the polar area. Only a few, those who were not Northern Raiders, saw these beasts and lived to tell about them.

Miltok did not worry about the Raiders this time of year. They did not usually sweep through the southern villages until after the rains, when the captives would be plump and suitable for sacrifice to the Northern Raiders' gods. Miltok was patient, he could survive for days away from his people, and he estimated he would reach the object that had fallen from the sky in one more day—and then what? Maybe he would find a big rock from the sky. Maybe he would find nothing. He would see tomorrow. No matter how small the possibility of finding something, he had to look. Miltok had to know.

Bijek, a landing craft V.I., was the first to sound the alarm. A figure was approaching their camp.

"V.I.s, capture and hold him long enough to gather his information and to run tests on him," said Gogandu. "Then he will be released to continue his trip."

Even though Gogandu gave his orders with every appearance of control, BB sensed a certain amount of apprehension.

"How will we prevent him from coming back with more of his people after he is released?" asked BB.

"The Elders will take care of that," said Gogandu.

Gogandu raised his eyes, and, for a long moment, he looked at BB.

"It is almost time for BB to stand with the Elders again."

Ogba, BB's Master teacher, had once said to BB, "Only when one has totally released the expected can one be free from the unexpected."

BB must not have totally released the expected, because Gogandu's words sent an unexpected shock through BB that BB wasn't prepared for. Stand with the Elders? BB had been a conduit with his father and

Morbred to facilitate communication among the Elders, but that had been an emergency. BB thought a V.I. could only become a part of the Inner Circle of Elders if they had reached their 250th year. BB was only 69. Once a V.I. became an Elder in the Inner Circle, they entered a world unknown to others. Only a very few were chosen to become part of the Inner Circle of Elders.

"Stand with the Elders?" BB asked incredulously.

Gogandu smiled, and then chuckled.

"There is much BB shall learn."

Then it was over. Gogandu returned to his usual countenance—the blank, expressionless face that seemed incapable of a smile.

BB must let go of the expected, BB thought to himself.

Miltok slowly trudged into his village. He was tired, more tired than he thought he would be when he started his journey. His head ached. It was not a pain he had experienced before. The pain felt as if he had tried very hard for a very long time to think of something or to remember something. The only thing he *could* remember was that his trip had been in vain. He had seen nothing—just the same bleak landscape everywhere he looked.

Miltok thought back to the night when he saw the object streak across the sky. He had been so sure he would find something, but he found nothing. Yet there was the uneasy feeling that something was not right, something was missing. He even entertained the idea of returning to the site. Maybe he had overlooked something, or maybe he had not traveled far enough. Miltok knew he had gone to where the object should have landed. He had spent two days scouring the area, or was it three days? Something was just not right.

Then there were the dreams he had been having for the last few nights. In the dreams, there were two men and a woman—three smiling faces. But there was something unusual about the faces. The three strangers just did not fit. Miltok had always had dreams, but they were filled with the night sky or the rains. He had never had the same dream night after night. Something was just not right.

The whole crew was abuzz about the native that the Zoltocs had captured. There were three V.I.s who bore a strong resemblance to the Erlon native. These V.I.s were Zoltocs. The Erlonian native was smaller and darker, but otherwise he bore a striking resemblance to the Zoltocs. It was the three Zoltocs that Gogandu sent to meet the native. They were able to disable the Erlonian before he knew what happened. When they returned with the native, V.I.s were amazed at how closely the Erlonian resembled the Zoltocs.

Gogandu took the unconscious captive to his quarters and did not emerge for two days. When the native exited the landing craft, he was conscious but unaware of his surroundings. Gogandu escorted him off the landing craft and the native walked away in a daze.

After the departure of the Erlon native, Gogandu addressed the crew.

"The greatest portion of the planet's population is located around the northern polar area," said Gogandu. "The native captive had no concept of the southern hemisphere. Some villages have settled outside of the northern polar area in an attempt to avoid the Northern Raiders. The Northern Raiders live in the central part of the polar area, and all year round they get water from their gods. Every five to seven years, the Northern Raiders, on their four-legged creatures called zwaps, sweep across the countryside capturing everyone in sight.

"According to the native, storytellers say that the Northern Raiders take their captives to a sacred area inhabited by the gods and high priests. In this sacred area, the priests sacrifice the captives to the water gods by draining the victims of their blood. Their bodies are then cremated on a funeral pyre. The Northern Raiders believe that, if they do not offer up sacrifices, the water gods will not deliver the precious water.

"The crew's mission is to investigate the area where victims are sacrificed. A small crew will stay behind with the landing craft. The rest of the V.I.s will head for the polar area. When the V.I.s reach the polar area, they will camp somewhere out of sight. The Zoltocs will continue, infiltrate the area, and gather information on the area where the victims are sacrificed. The other V.I.s will wait for the Zoltocs to return.

"According to the Erlonian native, rains should arrive in five to ten days. When the rains come, the entire population will be preoccupied with collecting water, and most of the natives will cover themselves while they work. After the rains start, V.I.s should cover themselves and move into the polar area."

"What are we looking for?" asked a V.I.

"The destination of the blood that is taken from those who are sacrificed," replied Gogandu.

"Are the Northern Raiders enemies of the Venuvians?" It was Plorv.

"Enemies?" Gogandu thought for a moment. "That is to be determined." Gogandu did not wait for another question. "Make preparations for the journey—they will start tonight."

The journey was arduous. The crew travelled by night and camped during the heat of the day. Since V.I.s had to carry their own provisions for the trip, food and water were at a premium.

On the eighth day, the landscape began to change. The crew spotted trees that actually looked alive. Green plants, though scarce, dotted the landscape. Then, on the tenth day, Gogandu spotted a settlement. The crew painstakingly avoided any contact with the inhabitants. The next day, Gogandu decided to set up a temporary camp and to have the Zoltocs continue.

Rima and her two fellow Zoltocs, TaRupi and Kolord, traveled at night and carefully avoided settlements. Gogandu told the three Zoltocs that, even though they greatly resembled the locals, the native, whom they had captured, noticed that the Zoltocs looked unusual.

After two days away from Gogandu, the settlements became so frequent that the Zoltocs had to limit their travel time to the dusk and dawn periods. Otherwise, the natives might notice three unusual-looking Erlonians passing by. Gogandu warned the Zoltocs that, even though they were wearing Erlonian garments, their chemically operated night-vision equipment would surely attract attention.

"You will have no means of communication," Gogandu told them. "In extreme emergency, fire the high-frequency-sound-emitting flares."

Gogandu's words instilled the Zoltoc woman and two Zoltoc men with a feeling of confidence and a sense of mission.

"You must not be captured. If necessary, use your sound flares as weapons—but you must not be captured. If escape is impossible, use the poison in your palate."

Every V.I. had been equipped with a dose of poison that was placed in their soft palate. If pressure was applied to the soft palate, a lethal dose of a fast acting poison would be administered.

"You must not be captured," Gogandu reiterated.

It was more than an order. Gogandu's powers of persuasion went beyond his words. He had used his movements and expressions to intensify the Zoltocs' sense of duty and urgency. The Zoltocs were motivated.

On the fourth day away from the temporary camp, the three Zoltocs encountered an abrupt change in the scenery. The dry and dusty landscape gave way to a dry and dusty wall of unattended growth. Trees, vines, and undergrowth made the living wall appear impenetrable. The Zoltocs followed the barrier of vegetation until they came to a road that led into the interior of the thick growth. The three scouts noticed that they had not spotted a settlement in some time.

"This must be the entrance to the Northern Raiders' area," said TaRupi.

"How do you know?" asked Rima.

"What else could it be?" asked TaRupi.

"It could just be an area that has not been cultivated," said Kolord, the third companion.

"Compared to most of the settlements we have seen, this area is expertly landscaped," said Rima, sarcastically.

"What would keep the natives away from this area if it isn't their fear of the Northern Raiders?" asked TaRupi. "And look at the road. Those gouges in the road were made by something heavy that was being pulled by large animals."

"Perhaps the tracks are from the zwaps that the native spoke of," said Rima. "They are not fresh. I think we should follow this road."

TaRupi and Kolord agreed. The three Zoltocs started down the mysterious road, heading toward the unknown. Even though the road passed through the first significant vegetation the Zoltocs had seen since they landed on the planet, the growth on both sides of the road looked foreboding. The road was straight and narrow. The only way to conceal oneself would be to burrow into the undergrowth that bordered the road. There was no escape route. Nonetheless, Gogandu's words spurred the three on. They headed down the road, tentatively at first, then increasing their pace until they were moving at a comfortable jog.

The Zoltoc's first indication that they were approaching life was the smell—a mixture of burning flesh, human sewage, and animals. They could also hear loud, boisterous conversations and raucous laughter coming from down road. The Zoltocs slowed their pace and continued cautiously. The smoke, the smell, and the verbosity continued to increase. The road entered an open area. The Zoltocs continued until they found a spot where they could observe the native Erlonians. After surveying the area, Rima, TaRupi, and Kolord prepared to pass through the enclave. They were acutely aware of the fact that they must not be discovered.

"We must assume a stature of confidence," said TaRupi. "We are not Masters, but we have some training."

Rima took a deep cleansing breath and stood tall.

"Apparently the women on this planet are treated like dirt, so I will look humble," said Rima. "But, if one of those primitive beasts tries to touch me, she will be sorry that blood every passed through her veins."

TaRupi and Kolord smiled. They both knew Rima was not exaggerating.

"Maybe we should not be speaking Venuvian," said Kolord. "Someone might hear us."

His companions nodded in agreement, and moved steadily along the rough road toward the opening ahead.

"This is it," said TaRupi. "From here on in we are Erlonians."

As they approached the open area, a woman carrying a stack of wood on her head passed near enough for the V.I.s to observe her. The woman could easily have been a Zoltoc. Her short stocky body, round red cheeks, dark deep-set eyes, and broad brow were so typical of the Zoltocs that TaRupi and Kolord almost stopped at the sight of her.

"Keep moving. Ignore her," Rima whispered.

Rima kept her eyes cast downward. The native gave the three a quick sideward glance and continued walking, apparently taking little or no notice.

"Should we stop and mix with the locals?" TaRupi whispered jokingly.

"Shut up, and keep walking," said Rima.

As they entered the clearing, they saw two bare-chested men brushing one of their zwaps. The men also took short notice of the three Zoltocs and continued in their loud conversation. There was a cluster of crude houses to the left of the V.I.s. The windowless structures had smoke curling from openings in each roof. The wood-carrying woman entered one of the houses. Small, evidently domesticated, animals scurried around the huts or crouched and gnawed on some morsel.

Feeling less conspicuous, the three scouts briskly continued down the road that again became bordered by thick vegetation. The three passed through five other clearings. The five enclaves differed from the first in that the structures had openings for windows and appeared much more habitable. The few Erlonians they did see ignored the three Erlonian lookalikes.

Except for the woman with wood and the two bare-chested men, not one of the inhabitants appeared to be engaged in any productive activity. After the sixth open area, the road widened. The three moved quickly. They had gone quite a ways without passing another opening.

"Why don't we stop and rest for a few." TaRupi made a statement rather than ask a question.

"No," snapped Rima. "We should not rest until we have completed our mission."

TaRupi smiled.

"Don't forget where we are, woman," said TaRupi jokingly.

"Shut up," Rima said casually.

Kolord looked at the sky.

"We have approximately 20 degrees before sunset," said Kolord. "Last night there was an early moon, about 15 degrees after sunset. We should be able to travel most of the night."

"We should be able to travel two days without rest, food, or water," said Rima. She was serious but not serious.

"And in the dark," added TaRupi with a smirk.

"Shut up!" said Rima, mocking herself.

The vegetation began to change. A canopy was starting to form over the road. The canopy looked even thicker ahead.

"We may be in darkness sooner than we thought." Rima grimaced. "Now see what you've done!" she said to TaRupi.

"Me? Why do you always blame me?" said TaRupi.

"Shut up!" said Rima, smiling.

The Travelers looked ahead. Indeed the growth had slowly begun to extend over the road, creating a tunnel-like effect. Moreover, the humidity was increasing. Humidity equaled water.

"Water," said Rima flatly. "Water on this arid planet? Water is a precious commodity here. So precious it will undoubtedly be guarded."

The three moved on cautiously.

"What about the sound flares? They will never make it through the overgrowth," said Kolord.

Just then, the Travelers heard voices. Kolord, always the most cautious, spoke.

"Someone should return to an area clear of the overhanging branches. The two who continue will signal if there is a problem ahead."

"I will go ahead," said Rima.

"No," said Kolord. "A woman would look more suspicious in a secured area."

"You are right," said Rima. "Kolord and TaRupi, go ahead. Signal me with your lasers if I can come forward."

TaRupi smiled.

"Rima, they don't have lasers on this planet."

"Shut up," said Rima. Then she became more concerned. "Be careful. These natives look rough."

"We are trained in self-defense." said TaRupi.

Rima was about to retort.

"Shut up," said TaRupi playfully before Rima could speak.

"We will return for you if we can." Kolord spoke with urgency. "We must hurry."

"He's right," said TaRupi. "We must go."

TaRupi and Kolord took off, moving quietly with an increased urgency. As the two moved on, the canopy became thicker, and the underbrush grew denser and closer to the road. The road began to curve to the left and upward. The voices grew louder. When the two saw light ahead, they slowed their pace. The road again curved to the left, this time abruptly.

A torchlit cavern came into view. What the two saw was a scene of what, for this planet, could be called extravagance and debauchery. Ten or fifteen men and women, who were eating and drinking, lounged in an area covered with swap skins. The men wore loincloths and ponchos. The cloth was made of a coarse, brown material. The women wore dresses made of the same material. It was obvious that the women were there for the pleasure of the men.

A group of men and women, eyes cast downward, stood on one side of the cavern. Their clothing had the same design and was made of the same course material as the clothing worn by those lounging on the zwap skins, but the standing group's clothing had deteriorated into rags. Periodically the standing group would respond to the lounging men's orders for food or drink. Conversation was subdued.

The V.I.s had received some training in the language that was spoken by the Erlonian they had captured, but the two Zoltocs did not understand most of the words used by the natives they were now observing. Nonetheless, Kolord and TaRupi agreed that the conversation was not of an intellectual nature.

Then, another attendant entered, and all the conversations stopped. The newly arrived attendant spoke with the other attendants. In unison, all the attendants faced the lounging men and women, bowed at the waist, and softly spoke a few words. Before the attendants completed their speech, the lounging men jumped to their feet, and the women scrambled away. Attendants bearing robes rushed to the men who had just been lounging and helped them into the robes. The hooded robes consisted of patches of a smooth, silver-gray material that was quite unlike the coarse material all the other natives wore. Kolord thought there was something vaguely familiar about the material, but it was too dirty to discern its original shade.

Before Kolord had a chance to think about the cloth, the sound of a distant rumbling interrupted his observation. Two attendants grabbed torches and headed straight for where Kolord and TaRupi were concealing themselves. Both Zoltocs did not hesitate. They dove head first into the thick brush that bordered the left side of the road. They had to burrow their way into the growth. Gogandu had somehow produced native clothing for the Zoltocs to wear over their Venuvian clothes. The Venuvian clothing protected most of their body, but the branches and thorns ripped through their native clothing and tore at their exposed hands and faces. Kolord and TaRupi continued digging into the thicket until they were out of view. Without the natives detecting them, the Zoltocs were able to twist their bodies and observe what followed.

The approaching rumble grew louder. Then a wagon, drawn by four zwaps, halted directly in front of the Zoltocs. The deafening rumble of the wagons ceased. All that the two V.I.s could hear was the heavy breathing of the animals and a few sharp commands from the wagon driver. Two cylinders in the wagon were visible to the Kolord and TaRupi. Each cylinder was 2 meters wide and 3 meters tall. They were made of animal hides wrapped with several strands of vine.

The robed men approached the wagons in a single file. The three men, who had arrived on the wagon, immediately fell to their knees and touched their foreheads to the ground. The robed men formed a line on an elevated ledge on the other side of the wagon that was in front of the Zoltocs. They all lifted their arms above their heads and, in unison, began to chant. One of the attendants yelled something at the kneeling men who immediately jumped to their feet. One scurried up the side of one of the containers and began unloading gourds, packets, and bales. Each item was lowered to a man on the road. The man on the road handed it to an attendant who disappeared into the cavern. The robed men continued chanting.

The attendants and the men from the wagon kept their eyes and heads down as they worked. After both containers had been unloaded, the wagon men returned to Kolord's and TaRupi's side of the wagon. The robed men stopped their chanting. Then, one of the robed men made a loud proclamation. A portion of the cavern wall smoothly slid open and revealed a polished metal surface. There was a circular hole in the middle of the metal surface that was one half meter in diameter. Again, Kolord felt he was looking at something familiar.

The wagon men immediately retrieved a crude shoot from the side of the wagon. They lifted one end of the shoot to the hole in the cavern wall, and the other end they held over one of the animal skin containers. There were a few moments of silence, then a torrent of water shot out of the hole, down the shoot, and into the container. After one container was full, the wagon moved forward so that the shoot was over the second container. When the second container was full, another wagon, which had been unloaded, moved under the shoot and repeated the process of filling the containers with water. The water-laden wagons used an open part of the cavern to turn around and exited with their precious cargo.

The water was constant, and the shoot was not 100 percent effective. Water splashed everywhere, and soon the area was saturated. As the ground became soft and muddy from the water, the beasts found it more difficult to pull the water-laden wagons. The drivers yelled at the animals and beat their flanks with wooden rods, but, as the road got muddier, the process slowed. TaRupi moved close to Kolord so they could communicate. The din of the activity made it unlikely that their conversation would be overheard.

"This must be where they get their water during the dry season," said TaRupi.

Kolord did not respond. He was staring intently at something.

TaRupi continued, "I don't think we can go farther without being detected."

Kolord was oblivious to what TaRupi said. He turned to TaRupi. The expression on his face was a cross between shock and bewilderment.

"The robes those men are wearing," said Kolord, "I am sure they are made with Venuvian cloth."

◆

Rima watched as the procession of wagons entered the canopy that covered the road. She counted 20. The wagons kept up a great deal of noise, so Rima was not worried about TaRupi and Kolord being surprised. She did worry that the Erlonians had trapped Kolord and TaRupi. She knew that everyone in the shuttle crew was well versed in self-protection and that TaRupi and Kolord were very resourceful. They could surely take care of themselves. Still, she worried.

The sun was beginning to hover over the horizon when Rima heard the wagons returning. She was able to find a hiding place with a good vantage point. She watched as the now water-laden wagons filed out of the tunnel of vegetation. The mud-caked animals strained under their burden while suffering physical and verbal abuse from the drivers. Rima counted the wagons: 18, 19… Her mind raced. What if one of those brutes had already discovered TaRupi and Kolord? Her comrades spoke a little Erlonian, but they would certainly arouse suspicion if they came in close contact with a native. Should she wait for Kolord and TaRupi, or should she leave and find Gogandu as soon as possible? Rima remembered Gogandu's admonition.

"You must not be captured."

What if her friends lay slain or wounded somewhere down this road? What if they had to use their sound flares? Should she follow the road and, at least, determine the status of the two V.I.s?

The twentieth wagon emerged. Light was fading and Rima knew she would have to make a decision. Then, from the rear of the last wagon, two figures unceremoniously disembarked. Rima knew immediately that it was TaRupi and Kolord. She ran toward them. The two men were drenched from the water that had splashed on them.

"Looks like you found the water supply," she said with a smile.

Kolord looked directly into her eyes. There was no humor in his face.

Kolord spoke, "I believe that there are Venuvians here or that the Venuvians have been here before."

◆

Gogandu sat motionless on the hard, dry ground and gazed steadily at the barren horizon. Everyone in the camp was still conserving their energy and their precious water. The Zoltocs had been gone for four days. The crew had nothing to do but wait for their return.

The days were hot and dry and passed at an achingly slow pace. Occasionally, a lookout detected a native on the road below the crew's spot. The camp could not be detected from the road, but spotting a passing native, even from a distance, was the most exciting thing that happened in the Travelers' dreary day.

Plorv casually walked up and sat near Gogandu.

"What if the Zoltocs have encountered a problem?" Plorv asked Gogandu.

Gogandu turned to Plorv. His eyes were steady and hard.

"If they have problems, they will overcome them," said Gogandu.

"How long will we wait?" asked Plorv.

Gogandu returned his attention to the horizon.

"We will wait until they return," said Gogandu.

"What if… "

"Quiet!" demanded Gogandu, as he held up his hand with his palm facing Plorv.

Plorv was about to protest when he heard a short high-pitched sound. It was the receiver for the sound flare. Then there was another sound blast, then another—three blasts. Gogandu told the Zoltocs to fire off one flare if there was a problem that might delay their return, two flares if they were in danger, and three flares for an extreme emergency. Gogandu jumped to his feet.

"We must find the Zoltocs—immediately!" Gogandu barked out the orders. "Break camp. The next few days are going to be very difficult. Gogandu must make contact with the Zoltocs and return to the ship. The crew's supplies will run out before they reach home base, but this crew can do it. Now they must hurry."

The crew hurriedly gathered their belongings and made ready to depart. There was an air of relief, even excitement among the V.I.s. Gogandu warned the crew that their supplies would run out before they returned to the ship. Despite Gogandu's dire warning, the crew felt that anything was better than spending another hot, dry day doing nothing.

Gogandu walked past the V.I.s, fixing his penetrating eyes on each one. Without a word being spoken, every V.I. knew that they must be strong to survive the days ahead. Even Gogandu's ominous prediction could not dampen the crew's spirits. They departed with a feeling of adventure, hoping that they would find the Zoltocs quickly.

After the first day, the sense of adventure began to fade. Gogandu insisted that they trek continually, stopping to rest only during the hottest time of the day. Gogandu was inexhaustible. He would rush ahead and check for natives, return to urge on the crew, and then rush ahead again. When Gogandu detected an Erlonian, he would lead the crew far enough away from the road to avoid being spotted. As Gogandu led the V.I.s away from the road, he would repeatedly reiterate that they must not make contact with the Erlonians.

When Gogandu began to detect natives too frequently, the crew had to travel away from the road where the terrain was sandy and uneven. Walking became much more difficult. On the second day, a V.I. approached Gogandu.

"We cannot keep up this pace Gogandu," said the V.I. "Our water is almost gone and the V.I.s are getting weak."

"We have no choice. We must continue until we find the Zoltocs," said Gogandu.

There was no emotion in his voice but it was obvious that he meant to continue regardless of the consequences. The density of vegetation began to increase as the dwellings decreased. A V.I. suggested a foray into one of the villages to get water and food.

"Absolutely not," said Gogandu. "The risk of encountering a native is much too great. Gogandu has trained these men and women to be strong. They will survive."

Water—they needed water. The food supplies, though low, had not yet presented a problem, but they were down to their last few sips of water. Lips were dry and parched, and tongues were beginning to swell. Each step took the crew farther away from the landing craft.

When the crew thought things could not get any worse, the wind began to pick up. It was not a cool refreshing wind. It was a hot dry wind that lifted the arid soil and flung it into the faces of the Travelers. Gogandu relented and let the crew rest until the wind died down. The wind did not die down, instead its ferocity increased. The V.I.s crouched down on the ground and huddled together in an attempt to shield themselves from the fierce winds.

The suffering of the men and women was so intense, they did not see the smile on Gogandu's face, nor did they notice him rise and stand full-faced toward the wind. It was not until he began to laugh that anyone took notice. It was not a faint laughter; it was a loud, boisterous laughter. The first reaction from the crew was shock. Gogandu rarely smiled. Unrestrained laughter was unheard of. Some of the V.I.s even became frightened. Was the exhaustion taking an unforeseen toll on their leader? Had the strain weakened the strongest one among them? Could the unbendable one snap?

Before any of the V.I.s' thoughts of Gogandu's condition had time to solidify, everyone, simultaneously, felt a change in the wind. There was no decrease in the magnitude of its ferocity, indeed the gusts of wind continued increasing in strength, but the harshness of the heat had notably decreased. The hot, dry winds had become cool and refreshing. The V.I.s stood, and froze in their spots. The only sounds were the whirling winds and Gogandu's continued laughter. Then it came like shots in the dark—too wish-fulfilling to be believed. At first, the V.I.s were unwilling to accept the reality. Then the resounding confirmation came. Someone yelled.

"Rain!"

After making the decision to fire off three sound flares, the Zoltocs headed for the entrance to the Northern Raiders' area. Rima, Kolord, and TaRupi moved as quickly as they could. They hoped their rapid movements would not create suspicion. The natives were much more active than they had been when the three Zoltocs first entered the area. Now the workers were feverishly building or repairing the carts that the zwaps pull. Even in the fading light of the day, the three could detect a great deal of urgency in the Erlonians' activity. Torch-bearing natives ran from place to place. Agitated conversation was punctuated with loud commands. By sunset, the three Zoltocs had reached the last enclave before leaving the Northern Raiders' encampment.

"Do you think they have discovered our presence?" TaRupi asked nervously.

"They must know that we are here," said Rima sarcastically. "That's why they blocked the only road to leave their area?"

"Of course, of course," conceded TaRupi. "I wonder what all the preparations are for. Those carts do not look like the ones that just carried out the water. "

"The carts look like they could hold captives," said Kolord. "The Erlonian native told Gogandu that the Northern Raiders periodically spread out over the countryside and capture people for sacrificial bloodletting. The Northern Raiders could be preparing to capture sacrifice victims."

"Gogandu said that the Raiders usually came after the rains," said TaRupi.

"Maybe this time it's unusual," said Rima. "We better hurry. If those brutes are about to start rounding up victims for sacrifice, I don't want to be one of the victims."

"Good point," said TaRupi.

The three began to jog at a moderate pace. They knew they could keep jogging at this speed for quite a while. After the Zoltocs reached the entrance to the Northern Raiders' area, they discussed the possibility of firing more sound flares.

"How could you be so sure it was Venuvian cloth?" questioned Rima.

"It was old, soiled, and in patches, but it was Venuvian," said Kolord. "There is nothing like Venuvian material. And the mechanism that delivered the water—it was not something from this planet. I am sure it was an advanced mechanical device. Even the metal had that Venuvian look."

"Why should we fire more flares?" asked Rima "We are in no danger. Gogandu said we were only to use three flares if there was an extreme problem. No one has even noticed that we are here. What danger are we in?"

Kolord paused. "I think there is a disabled Venuvian craft on this planet."

"What?!" said TaRupi. His voice went up an octave. "A disabled ship?! How did you come up with that idea?"

"I think he's right," said Rima.

"Have you two… what, how… ?" TaRupi was at a loss for words.

"Instead of exploding, why don't you relax," Rima said calmly.

"Think. If what Kolord saw was Venuvian, then the Venuvians have been here, or they are still here and there is a ship somewhere."

The three said nothing for a few moments.

Then Kolord continued. "I will look for the location of the ship and check for detection devices. I am assuming that the water source is near the ship. If my calculations are correct, I should be able to go to the origin of the water and return here in one day. When you meet Gogandu, you should assume I am one day behind you," Kolord hesitated. "I will not be captured."

The Zoltocs had avoided thinking about Gogandu's admonition to avoid detection and capture. Every V.I. knew that there was a point on their palate, which, if pressed, would result in the release of a potent poison resulting in instant death. Kolord and TaRupi had thought about the poison when they ventured into the canopy-covered portion of the road. Now, Rima and TaRupi had to face the fact that Kolord might possibly be forced to use the drug. Gogandu's insistence that they must not be captured meant there could be some kind of danger. If there were unfriendly Venuvians present, all three might have to use the poison in their palates to avoid capture.

"If I don't connect with you and Gogandu, in one day you will know what happened." Kolord embraced both of his fellow Zoltocs and left without another word.

LIBCHIC

Libchic finished the test on the pumping system. He had built the pumping station to draw water from the well, which he had also built. The well dropped 3400 meters into an underground aquifer and supplied water to the allies. All systems passed the daily tests as they had since he installed the pump 117 years, 3 months, and 4 days ago. Then Libchic checked the fluid extraction unit. The raw-material level was below moderate but at an acceptable range above critical. Lastly, he did a test on his internal systems.

Libchic limped back to the input station, entered the test data and then reported the malfunctions to his internal system. He had blurred vision in both eyes, his left eye had restricted mobility, his left forearm had restricted mobility, and his left leg's memory input system was locked. The level of effect of the malfunctions was moderate. Libchic had reported the same malfunctions since the ship's landing caused him to be flung across the maintenance cabin into some storage racks. Libchic did not know why this landing had been so different from the others.

Following the landing, the Elder instructed Libchic to repair a communication apparatus. This he was unable to do because of the unavailability of seven components. The replacement components had been destroyed during the landing. Nonetheless, Libchic input a list of components that he needed to repair the communication system. He reported that the level of the effect of the unavailability of the components was critical.

The Elder also instructed Libchic to gather information on the language and customs of the planet's inhabitants. The language gathering had been simple. Libchic placed some high-powered listening devices near inhabited areas. Within three days, he had gathered enough language data to enable the partially functioning computer to input the local language patterns into his memory.

Most of the native customs dealt with the scarce water supply. After Libchic input the data that he had collected on the natives' customs, the Elder instructed him to construct and maintain a well with a pump.

The Elder also instructed him to build a fluid extraction station and a solid waste disposal system. The raw materials would be supplied by the allies. Finally, Libchic was ordered to construct a detection system that would blast dire warnings at any intruder. Libchic had dutifully complied with all instructions.

On the third day of the second month in the 107th year after the landing, Libchic received an emergency alarm of the highest level. The Elders' life support system was failing. Libchic rushed to the Elder Chamber. His rate of movement had increased fivefold. He had never entered the Elder Chamber before, but he headed directly to the diagnostic output station. The breathing assistance system had failed. Libchic's algorithm presented two alternatives: alternative one—replace module 53, alternative two—replace damaged components in module 53.

At a speed he had never known, Libchic rushed to the room with parts for the Elders' chamber. Normally the door would have slid open at his approach, but the door did not budge. It only made a clicking sound, as if it were trying to open but was meeting resistance. Libchic ripped a panel off the wall next to the door and activated the manual mode. A handle sprang from the door. Libchic grabbed the handle and attempted to open the door. It opened slightly, but something on the other side of the door must have been wedged in tight enough to keep it from opening completely. Libchic reached through the slight opening of the door and, with a tremendous burst of strength, ripped the door open. There was a loud scraping sound made by a shelf that had been leaning against the door. Libchic flung the shelf aside and headed for the area where module 53 was located.

The deck was littered with various components that had fallen from overturned shelfs. Other shelves had partially torn loose from their bindings to the deck and leaned precariously in various directions. Libchic tossed aside any shelves blocking his way, sometimes causing more units to fall to the deck. Locating the breathing-assistance module was the only thing that mattered now.

An alarm sounded. It was the fluid low signal. Libchic knew that the Elder would not be able to pilot the ship without fluid, but he had to exchange the breathing-assistance module before concerning himself with the depletion of fluid.

Libchic came to the area where module 53 was located. The cabinet containing the module was still standing, but the front of the cabinet was smashed in by a large piece of equipment that the landing had flung across the room. Libchic grabbed the piece of equipment and tried to pull it away from the cabinet, but, even with his increased strength, he could not move the giant piece of machinery. He tried again to move the object. The low fluid alarm became incessant.

Then, suddenly, Libchic's left arm, the arm that had been damaged during the landing, ceased to function. The sudden burst of energy that had enabled Libchic to exert high levels of force was gone. The fluid that the Elder had used to take control of Libchic's system and give it enhanced strength had depleted the small fluid surplus that Libchic had been collecting over the last 116 years.

The low fluid alarm stopped. The Elder had ceased functioning. Libchic's internal circuits reset. He would try to repair the arm that his overexertion had damaged while he was trying to save the Elder. He would then return to his duties—maintaining the well pump, the intruder detection system and the fluid collection station. Libchic did not consider that, now that the Elder was non-functioning, there should be no one on the entire planet who would use the fluid. Libchic was not programmed to reason.

◆

Kolord burrowed his way through the thick brush. He had tried standing, but the vegetation was so thick he could hardly advance. He moved forward by crawling on his hands and knees or slithering on his belly. He was glad the crew decided to wear their Venuvian outfits under the native clothing that Gogandu had produced. Branches and thorns poked him constantly, but the Venuvian cloth kept the vegetation from ripping his flesh. Only his hands and face were unprotected.

Kolord hoped that he was heading in the right direction. He had calculated where he thought the water source was located. The moon had been up for a while so there was some light. But the overgrowth made it impossible to navigate by the stars, and he had no directional devices.

There was a slight uphill grade.

Good, thought Kolord.

He would be heading downhill if he had to make a quick exit.

Kolord did not feel threatened. The more he thought about it, the more he felt sure that what he had seen that day was somehow the result of a disabled Venuvian ship. The Venuvian material Kolord saw, the water dispenser, the whole mission seemed to point towards the existence of other Venuvians. But why the secrecy? If their arrival was a rescue mission, Gogandu would have been anxious to make his presence known. Was there a rogue group of Venuvian outlaws? Or maybe it was the chaos he had heard Gogandu and BB discussing. Kolord knew there was a piece missing from the puzzle. He had a burning desire to find that missing piece of information. His curiosity was a driving motivation for locating the ship—it was as strong as his desire to complete the mission.

The brush mercifully began to thin. Then, abruptly, it ended and opened to an expanse of dry desert landscape that resembled most of what Kolord had already seen on this planet. Kolord wiped the blood from his face and hands as best he could. The sun had not yet appeared, but the sky was ablaze with light. The rolling mounds of dry earth, occasionally interrupted by a weathered, dead-looking bush, extended for as far as he could see.

The early morning sunlight and the desolate scene gave Kolord a feeling of eerie unreality. He looked toward where he estimated the source of water might be. At first, he saw nothing but the same foreboding landscape. Then he noticed an uncharacteristic rise in the topography—it was the size of a Venuvian landing craft!

The brush had ripped Kolord's native clothing to the point where his Venuvian outfit was visible. He quickly removed the native clothing. Then he took off his Venuvian suit and replaced the suit with the native clothing. Kolord took his bearings and then concealed his Venuvian suit. The Erlonian cloth was uncomfortably scratchy, but Kolord's heart was pulsing with such excitement that he barely noticed the roughness of his outfit. Even his tender, shoeless feet did not slow Kolord's progress as he cautiously moved toward the large mound.

Then, three things happened almost simultaneously, things that would forever be etched in Kolord's memory. Any one of the events would have shocked Kolord, but coming in such rapid succession they almost overwhelmed him. First, as he came to within 50 meters of the mound, he saw what was unmistakably an entrance port to a Venuvian spaceship. Kolord had no time to process the information because, immediately following his discovery, loud voices began to yell at him in Erlonian. Kolord could understand enough Erlonian to figure out what was going on.

"Go away! You have offended The Giver of Water! You will be destroyed in a very painful way!"

The voices were meant to frighten away Erlonians, but they had little effect on Kolord. What happened next astounded Kolord. Exiting from what was obviously a Venuvian ship, was a figure whose features Kolord immediately recognized. Had it been a Venuvian, he would hardly have been surprised. Even an Erlonian on this wrecked Venuvian ship would have been understandable, but what Kolord saw sent chills through his body. The large golden eyes, which Kolord had seen so frequently on Tambuki, clearly identified the person exiting the Venuvian landing craft as an Ortan.

◆

Rima and TaRupi watched Kolord as he headed away from them. Rima fired three sound flares then she and TaRupi started back toward Gogandu. They were both tired. Food and water were running low. They wanted to stop and rest but the message that there could be Venuvians on the planet was too important to delay. TaRupi regretted not having sipped some of the water as it splashed from the containers in the wagon on which he and Kolord had grabbed a ride.

The sun was resting on the horizon waiting to be swallowed by the Erlonian desert, and still the Zoltocs pushed on. They continued through the night, keeping up their demanding pace. The next day their pace had slowed, but they persevered until finally the blazing sun forced them to stop. There was no shade, so they simply collapsed on the side of the road. TaRupi worried that he would be unable to stand up and start again. Rima worried that she and her fellow Traveler would not be able to complete their mission. They both worried about Kolord.

◆

Kolord looked at the Ortan, the Ortan looked at Kolord. He did not just look in Kolord's direction, he looked directly at Kolord. Those big golden eyes looked right into his. Kolord had heard stories about Ortans being able to mesmerize people with their eyes. He had seen many Ortans, but, except for the Masters, they always had their eyes concealed. He had never seen an unveiled Ortan until this mission. Krella, BB's mother and KC's mate, was an Ortan. She was a Master of The Way, and she could put up a façade, which she always did—except once.

The landing craft had docked the day before. Shortly after sunrise, Kolord walked to a boulder near the craft. He sat, leaned against the rock, faced away from the camp, and took in the vast barrenness of this new planet. The coolness of the night was fleeing the rays of the new day's sun. It was still and quiet. Then Kolord heard a slight rustling and turned to see a surprised Krella. She had quickly put up a façade, but, before she had drawn her induced vail, he had looked into those deep golden eyes. For an instant Kolord had peered into Krella's inner self. He felt her warmth, her wisdom, her feeling of awe at this lifeless planet. Kolord had been intrigued by the serendipitous encounter. He saw how one could imagine that an Ortan's gaze could bewitch someone. Before her quickly activated façade was in place, Kolord had sensed a vulnerability in Krella. He realized that Ortans hid their eyes because of this vulnerability. If someone felt enchanted by Ortan eyes, it was because the experience was unique and it could not be explained.

Now, for the second time, Kolord looked into the eyes of an Ortan. This time it was different, totally different. The Ortan who exited the Venuvian ship did not hide his eyes, and when Kolord looked into the Ortan's eyes, he saw nothing. There was no doubt that the Ortan saw him, but there was no sign of recognition on the Ortan's face. He just looked at Kolord for a moment then turned and continued walking. Was this Ortan a Master who could hide his feelings? He did not strike Kolord as a Master. The Ortan did not move like a Master. He did not have the bearing of a Master. Additionally, the Ortan walked with a limp, and he held his left arm unnaturally close to his body. Kolord had never seen anyone walk with an abnormality that Venuvian medical technology could not have easily repaired.

Kolord wanted more time to think. The Venuvian ship, the Ortan— more missing pieces of the puzzle. For an instant, he considered entering the ship, even though the voices were still yelling that he was about to meet a painful death. He desperately wanted to understand. His heart was pounding, there was a queasiness in his stomach and his breathing was unsteady. Kolord knew he did not have time to think, he had to act. His every inner desire urged him to keep going, enter the ship, and answer the questions flooding his mind. Instead, Kolord turned, retrieved his Venuvian uniform, and headed away from the ship as fast as he could.

◆

The heat from the blazing sun began to relent. Even though the two Zoltocs had lain baking under the midday sun, they began to regain some of their energy. They got to their feet and resumed their journey. When TaRupi and Rima reached the point where the road turned away from the Northern Raiders' protective wall of vegetation and headed south, the sun had lost much of its intensity. Except for the hottest time of the day, the Zoltocs had been moving at a steady jog—day and night—since they left the last Northern Raiders' enclave.

"Stop. We must talk," said Rima.

"I don't need to rest," replied TaRupi.

Both V.I.s were breathing heavily. Both were beginning to show signs of exhaustion.

"Well then just keep running," said Rima. "If you happen to pass Gogandu, let me know. Don't forget to waive at the bewildered Erlonians."

"You are right," said TaRupi. "Gogandu and the others will probably keep well-hidden and we shouldn't draw too much attention to ourselves. We could wait here for him."

"We don't have any time to waste," said Rima. "The sooner we connect with Gogandu the sooner we can go after Kolord." Rima thought for a moment, her chest still heaving. "It took us four days to get to the entrance. Gogandu and the crew will have to stay off the road, so their progress will be slower. We should make contact with them in a little over a day."

"How will we keep from missing them?" asked TaRupi.

"Before sunset today, we will fire another sound flare. Gogandu will find us."

"But, if we keep up our pace... "

The look on Rima's face stopped TaRupi in mid-sentence.

"Oh, of course, we don't want to draw attention to us, do we," said TaRupi.

It was not a question, it was a statement.

"I want to connect with the group as badly as you do," said Rima. "But it is still just as important that we are not detected, maybe even more so now."

Both Zoltocs were thinking about Kolord.

"Let's go," said Rima before their thoughts could dwell on their fellow Zoltoc.

◆

Treyak was feeling a mixture of excitement and fear. He had never gone on a hunt before. The last hunt had been over 12 years ago when he was very young. He could still remember how the old men, women, and other children stood on the edge of the road and watched as the strongest Raiders galloped out of the compound on the backs of zwaps. Zwap-drawn carts followed with three herders. For the next month, the carts would return packed with the Scrans, the unfortunate ones who lived outside of the Northern Raiders' area. The herders took the captured Scrans to the priests for sacrifice to the water gods.

"The gods must be fed!" was the Northern Raiders' mantra.

Treyak could still remember the mournful cries of the victims headed for sacrifice. Women, children, old, young—the hunters would capture anyone who crossed their path. For weeks, the compounds were filled with the wailing of victims when a cart returned.

Then the frequency would slowly diminish until the day came when carts returned empty. It was then that fears began. No one left a dwelling unless it was absolutely necessary. Women kept their children close to them and the old men waited. Old women had told Treyak frightening stories for as long as he could remember. If the sacrificial offerings of Scrans were not enough to appease the water gods, then the hunters would return and hunt their own people.

"The gods must be fed!"

The old men were particularly worried because they would be the first the Raiders would capture. Wives and daughters would betray the old ones in hopes of saving their children. Although no one could remember a time when the hunters had not captured a sufficient number of Scrans, there were stories, stories of how hunters had returned and began rounding up all the old men, then the old women, and then anyone until the priests declared that the gods were satisfied.

This time something was different, very different. Every story about capturing sacrifices always began: "After the rains when the Scrans were plump and ready for sacrifice… "

The rains had not yet come this year. The Scrans would not be plump with newly fallen water. Would their blood be sufficient?

The priests, who had only a vague idea of when the rains would come, decided that too much time had passed since the last hunt. The Raiders needed to keep their skills honed.

"The gods must be fed!"

Now Treyak made ready to leave on the cart he had prepared the night before. Treyak dreamed of becoming a hunter. hunters were the strongest, the fastest, and the bravest among the Northern Raiders. The whole compound revered the hunters. Most women wanted to mate with a hunter. Only the priests had more power—a priest could demand any-one's sacrifice.

Despite coaching from his eldest brother and his father and years of grueling practice, Treyak was never able to master the art of riding a zwap. He was stiff, awkward, and downright clumsy. After endless attempts to teach Treyak how to become one with the zwap, his broth-er and father gave up in frustration. Because of Treyak's inability to become proficient at riding a zwap, he could not become a hunter. He was assigned to the task of herding. The hunters would attack villages and bind most, if not all, of the inhabitants. The herders would follow with a cart, gather the hapless captives, and return them to the priests for sacrifice.

"The gods must be fed!"

Mossyek sat with Treyak on the back of the cart. Losstuv, the driv-er, guided the beast-drawn cart down the road to the Scran area. It was Losstuv's task to trail the hunters and find the captives. Mossyek and Treyak were assigned to the task of gathering the struggling victims and putting them in the cart. Besides making the carts ready, collecting the captives and delivering them to the priests, the herders had only one more obligation. Their other tasks had been merely assignments. Com-pliance was expected with little or no instruction. However, for the final duty, they had received repeated admonitions.

"Not one drop of Scran blood is to be spilled before reaching the priests."

"The gods must be fed!"

◆

Valiya sat listlessly in the corner of the thick-walled, mud-brick hut. This was the first year she had her own hut. After the rains, she would have a cistern with water. She slowly chewed on a piece of sunbaked jemo leaf and occasionally sipped the precious, bitter-herb tea.

When the rains come, everyone will be working nonstop and the time will fly, thought Valiya. Now the days are long with nothing to do.

Crops had been harvested and cooked, or dried, or powdered. The village had made mud bricks during the rainy season, and the blazing sun had baked the bricks during the long dry season. Builders had used the bricks to make new structures and to repair old ones. Villagers had cleaned and tanned the small animal hides and snakeskins. The precious animal hides had been carefully sewn and would be used to collect rainwater. The snakeskins were used to line the floors and walls of the underground cisterns, which protected the water during the long dry season.

Hunting for the scarce desert prey had ceased. It cost more in energy and water than the paltry bits of meat that were brought in could justify. The people of the village, who had gorged themselves following the rains with the temporary supply of plentiful food, now sought only to conserve water and energy. Energy required fuel, and fuel for the body was in short supply. Everyone in the village just waited—waited for the life giving rains.

Valiya's thoughts dwelled on harvest time. Not only was there plenty of eating and drinking, there was also singing and dancing. The old women told the stories of their families and their escape from the Northern Raiders. Men talked about the hugeness of their women after harvest. Most residents of the village were conceived during harvest time.

Valiya looked at the back of her right hand. The village matriarch had tattooed three parallel lines there during her coming-of-age ceremony. She was a woman now. After the next harvest, young men would visit her hut and bring bits of meat or a precious reptile skin. The skins, after years of collecting, would someday be part of a robe worn at special occasions. Her quiet beauty had already attracted the interest of several eligible males in the village. Unlike her counterparts, Valiya showed little interest in the subtle and sometimes not so subtle advances of the single, young men.

Then Valiya heard a rumbling sound. Was it thunder? Had the rains come? She rushed outside. The first thing she saw was a clear, blue sky. The second thing she saw was a Northern Raider. Valiya turned and ran back into her hut. She realized instantly that she was trapped. The Northern Raider adeptly slid off his beast and was inside the hut before Valiya could even turn around. In one, swift, seamless move, the Raider grabbed Valiya, bound her arms to her side, turned her upside down holding one calf and tied the rope around her ankle. The Raider was bigger and stronger than Valiya's people. Her attempts at escape were futile. In her last moments of freedom, two thoughts ran through Valiya's mind. First, despite his size and strength, the Northern Raider was incredibly gentle. Second, Valiya could not help thinking that she would not see the next rains.

◆

Treyak could hear the pandemonium that filled the air before he saw anything. What he heard was the yelling and screaming of the unfortunates who he was about to take to the priests for sacrifice. The sound was discomforting to Treyak. His mind pictured an unlucky victim staring into Treyak's eyes and begging for release. The thought sickened Treyak. The idea of releasing prisoners also crossed Treyak's mind, but he knew if he released even one captive, he would become a sacrifice victim himself.

"The gods must be fed!"

This was Treyak's first venture outside of the Northern Raiders' area where he had spent his entire life. He now saw what the world without water looked like. The sparseness amazed him. Even as he approached the village, there was no improvement in the landscape. Everything was dry and lifeless.

Then Treyak saw the madness. A terrified villager was running in his direction, with a Raider in pursuit. When the villager saw the cart, he abruptly halted. His chest was heaving as he tried to catch his breath. He instantly changed direction, but he was no match for the Raider. The zwap, on which the Raider rode, quickly reached the fleeing victim. The

Raider expertly tossed a rope over the runner's shoulders and around his arms. The zwap abruptly stopped and the runner was jerked off of his feet. The Raider dismounted, wrapped the rope around the victim's arms three times, lifted the captured villager from the ground, turned him upside down, wrapped the rope around the terrified villager's ankle, and then gently lowered the incapacitated capture to the ground.

Losstuv, the driver, guided the cart to the fallen native. Treyak and Mossyek jumped from the cart and retrieved the fallen villager. The villager begged for his freedom as Treyak hauled his convulsing body into the cart.

"Our first!" cried out Mossyek. "YES!"

Rain came quickly to this dry, desolate planet. First, the winds came, grabbing every unattached object and flinging it into the swirls of dust. Then a few giant drops of life giving water would pierce the air and plop on the thirsty, arid ground. Dark, rain-laden clouds would stomp across the sky and within minutes dump massive amounts of liquid onto the water-starved earth. The rain turned the dry, sunbaked landscape into a drenched morass.

The rains meant life. Shrieks of joy sounded throughout the village as every man, woman, and child feverishly attacked some task that would make use of the precious liquid. For a month, the natives worked non-stop. Even the small ones would run and jump in the mud pits to mix the mud with dried grasses and stems that the villagers had gathered after last year's rain. Workers would mold the mud mixture into bricks, which were set out to dry when the sun returned. The most important task, the task that would keep the village alive until the next rains, was collecting water. Every year, skins from the desert reptiles, which the men collected during the few months after the rains, were dried and carefully sewn together. The elderly painted the seams with the oil of a certain bean until the skins were sealed against water leakage. All over the village, the skin quilts collected rainwater and funneled it into underground cisterns. Skins were also used to cover the floors of new cisterns that had first been lined with hardened mud bricks. Builders built covers over the pits with thick bricks that they then plastered with more mud.

These were the water pits. The water pits held the water that the village would need during the long, hot, dry season. The more water pits a village had, the more stable it became. A leaking water pit in a village with only two or three water pits could mean doom for some by the end of a dry season. It took about 10 years to collect enough skins to make one water pit. What the water starved Erlonians did not know was that below the carefully built water pits lay a secret that would make the water pits useless.

It was time for Treyak to retrieve more captured Scrans. His response was feeble. He looked at the wretched creatures that had to be sacrificed so the gods would deliver water to his dry, sunbaked planet. The poor captives were only hours away from their sacrifice to the gods. Treyak wanted to vomit. After an hour, the cart was almost full.

"We have room for one more," Mossyek yelled above the din of the captives. It was then that Treyak saw the figure on the ground. Winds blew dust over her unmoving body. At first, Treyak wondered if she was dead. Unlike the others, she did not twist and fight against the inescapable restraints. He realized she was alive when she looked at him. She not only looked into his eyes, she looked into his soul, and into his heart. Treyak lifted her to her feet. Since her leg was bound, she had to lean against him. He felt the warmth of her body against his. When he lifted her to place her in the cart, he saw three lines on the back of her hand. They looked fresh. She had recently entered womanhood. She was so beautiful. Her eyes stayed locked on his even as the cart pulled away from her village and headed for the Sacred Area where she would be sacrificed. The winds began to whip wildly around the cart, inundating Treyak and the captives with dust kicked up by the zwaps.

"Treyak, Mossyek, come sit in front," said Losstuv, the driver. "The gods will guard their food."

Mossyek scrambled to the front of the cart, but Treyak stayed, unable to pull himself away from the woman. Then he felt it, a cool drop of moisture on his cheek, and then another. Then the sky opened, and the precious, life-giving nectar began to flow. Valiya smiled and, even as she headed toward her death, she broke into laughter. The gods gave her this one last exquisite pleasure—rain. Treyak's heart melted, and he also smiled. Treyak did not welcome the rain for the same reason as the captives. He was thankful for the rain because it hid the tears running down his face.

◆

The sun was beginning to take its toll on Rima and TaRupi. Even though their jog had become a brisk walk, they knew that they would have to stop and rest soon. Then the wind began to kick up. The air was full of dust, and breathing became difficult. TaRupi gave Rima a furtive side-glance.

"We must rest," he said with conviction.

Rima stopped and said nothing. Some part of her wanted to keep going and not stop until they met Gogandu and told him their story. But she knew that TaRupi was right. If they became over exhausted, bad things could happen.

"You are right TaRupi," said Rima. "We will stop here until we gain enough strength to continue. We can't be too far from Gogandu." Rima's chest heaved as she spoke "The sooner we find him, the sooner we can return for Kolord."

While Rima was speaking, TaRupi's face had turned skyward.

"I think it's starting to rain," he said in a matter-of-fact tone.

Rima held her breath for a moment as if the silence she gained would help her detect the rain. She too looked skyward in anticipation. Was that a drop of rain she felt on her cheek or was it her imagination? It took only seconds before it became obvious that it was not her imagination. The stray droplets quickly turned into a pitter-patter.

"We must set off a sound flare immediately," said Rima, still breathing heavily.

TaRupi realized her concern at once. Heavy rains would interfere with effectiveness of the sound waves generated by the flare. Rima quickly took off her pack, removed the flare gun, aimed it straight into the air, and fired. The sound flare, propelled by compressed air, streaked into the sky, which was now filled with giant, dark, cumulus clouds. Only a faint high-pitched whine was audible by humans. A receiving instrument could detect the sound, amplify it for humans, and indicate the approximate distance and direction of the source. Gogandu would hear the sound flare even before the receiver had amplified the sound.

The rain acted as a catalyst. The two Zoltocs' adrenalin began to flow, and, although they had been near exhaustion only moments earlier, they now felt a renewed energy. TaRupi was already prepared to continue when Rima spoke.

"We must go," said Rima.

Their energy level was still low and neither of the two Zoltocs knew how much further they could go before they reached their limit. They both had every intention of continuing until they reached that limit and, if possible, exceeding it.

Gogandu's laughter halted even more abruptly than it had started. He stood motionless and looked to the North. The V.I.s were still rejoicing at the onset of the rain. Their dry parched lips hungrily accepted the life-giving moisture.

"BB!" said Gogandu. "Gogandu and BB must leave immediately."

There was obvious urgency in Gogandu's voice. Before anyone could react to Gogandu's imperative, a V.I. yelled out.

"Sound flare detected three degrees east of due north. Distance—20 kilometers."

Gogandu began to bark out orders.

"Morbred, take control," said Gogandu. "Move at full speed. The natives will undoubtedly be too preoccupied to notice your movements, but avoid direct contact. Speed is more important than avoiding detection by the natives, but cover your faces as much as possible. BB!"

BB rushed to Gogandu's side. Gogandu lowered his voice so as to communicate only with BB.

"Take this," said Gogandu.

He handed BB a vile of green liquid.

"It will enable BB to focus his thoughts. BB will be moving at full speed until he contacts Gogandu and the Zoltocs. When he does encounter them, BB must immediately assume a posture of full relaxation. He must totally clear his mind. BB will not be able to keep pace with Gogandu. Just stay on the road. Gogandu will know where BB is."

BB had no time to think or question. Gogandu turned and sped away. BB could already feel the bitter green liquid taking affect. His body moved quickly but he was no longer a part of the motion. He felt like an observer, not a participant. Gogandu had already put quite a bit of distance between himself and BB. BB was amazed by the incredible speed at which Gogandu moved. BB just knew he must follow Gogandu.

◆

The rain was heavy now. At first, it had been refreshing and invigorating but now it felt more like a liquid barrier. The dusty road had turned into mud and the heavy rain severely hampered Rima's and TaRupi's vision. The two Zoltocs' already tired and aching bodies were now working harder than ever. They both knew that they could not go much farther, but, the more difficult their progress, the harder they pushed. With every step, their mud-caked feet took a greater effort to lift. TaRupi stumbled and fell. Rima continued. She was afraid that, if she stopped to help TaRupi, she might be unable to continue. TaRupi struggled to his feet and continued even as Rima increased the distance between them. Soon the driving rain had totally obscured Rima from TaRupi. He lost track of time. Had it been hours or days since the rains started and Rima fired the sound flare. Now TaRupi was nearing the end of his endurance. He just wanted to lie down, close his eyes, and sleep—sweet, eventless sleep.

"TaRupi." It was the unmistakable voice of Gogandu.

◆

BB was amazed that such a dry planet could produce so much rain. His detachment from his physical body had grown. He could feel his legs pumping hard through the mud, but he felt like he was floating above his body. He passed a few villages, but the natives were so frantically involved in their activities that they took no notice of the lone figure running along the road. Then he saw Gogandu standing ghostlike in the middle of the road, oblivious to the sheets of rain blanketing his body. Behind him on the side of the road lay the two Zoltocs, their chests heaving heavily. Gogandu did not waste a minute.

"Sit and clear BB's mind," said Gogandu.

His voice was soft but firm. All the while, Gogandu's eyes were intently focused on BB's eyes. BB assumed his mind-clearing posture. Still standing, Gogandu bent forward so his face was directly in front of BB's. Their faces almost touched.

"Look deep into Gogandu's eyes," said Gogandu. "Deeper."

BB could feel some invisible force pulling him into Gogandu's gaze. Everything around him began to fade away, even the pouring rain. Then there was a bright, blinding flash. It only lasted for a fraction of a second, but BB saw the white room, a room he had seen before—but where? Then total darkness. For a moment, BB felt fear. Then he heard, no, he did not hear, he felt Gogandu's soothing voice.

"There is nothing to fear. Cleanse BB's mind."

Although he could not see or hear anything, BB sensed a presence, a very powerful presence. Somewhere, there was a heated discussion, an imperative, an extreme imperative. All the while BB could feel a connection with Gogandu. All sense of time was gone. Then there was a consensus, a decision had been made.

"The Elders say a Zoltoc has made first contact," said Gogandu.

"Should Gogandu and BB make preparations?" asked BB. "Have the V.I.s been detected?"

"The Elders say BB should wait," said Gogandu.

"Wait for what?" asked BB.

"If the V.I. has made contact, the conflict is sure to come soon. The Freestones must make preparations." Gogandu's cryptic response was his only answer.

Kolord had to slow his pace. He had been running at high speed since he left the disabled Venuvian craft. He was running hard in order to get information to Gogandu as soon as possible. He was also running away from the temptation to return to the mysterious Venuvian craft with the limping Ortan. But now, Kolord had to regulate his running or he could collapse. It was more important than ever to get his information to Gogandu.

Kolord calculated that he was nearing the entrance to the Northern Raiders' area and that Gogandu would soon be connecting with Kolord's fellow Zoltocs. Once Gogandu heard Rima's and TaRupi's story, he would undoubtedly be eagerly searching for Kolord.

Kolord stopped long enough to take a sip of water and make a quick survey of his situation. He had not yet come to the entrance to the Northern Raiders' area, but he believed that he was getting near. He had a half day to get to Gogandu and the Zoltocs before they assumed that he had used his poison. As tired as he was, he decided to keep moving at high speed until he reached the entrance to the Raiders' area. He calculated how much more time he had and then decide at what speed he would move after he reached the entrance road.

Kolord took another sip of water and was about to resume running when he heard or felt a rumbling. He controlled his heavy breathing and listened intently. At once he realized what it was he was hearing. It was the sound of zwaps, the native beasts, moving at a fast pace. The sound was rapidly drawing nearer. Kolord was about to conceal himself in the brush when the hoof beats abruptly began to fade. He must be near the entrance! He cautiously moved forward and soon came to the opening in the brush.

Dust still hung heavily in the air. Kolord could see clouds of dry earth bellowing in the distance as the zwaps headed down the road. Kolord was ahead of schedule, so he decided to wait until the choking dust died down before he continued. He felt confident that he had enough time to reach Gogandu. When the dust died down, he could move at a moderate pace and connect with Gogandu and his fellow Zoltocs before his energy failed and his comrades assumed the worst. Then Kolord heard more hoof beats. He turned and, to his surprise, he saw a Northern Raider, rope in hand, bearing down on him.

Krelin was angry. His younger brother had overslept and arrived late to help him with his mount. Krelin cuffed his brother with the back of his hand. In addition to the physical attack that Krelin dealt to his sibling, he spewed an unending series of insults.

"You mindless bug!" said Krelin. "Do you not realize that today we feed the gods? You lay in your bed of zwap dung searching for your insignificant private parts while the gods contemplate withholding the water that keeps us alive. Your stupidity is only surpassed by your laziness. Your ugly face would frighten a blind Scran. It is my shame that we come from the same mother."

"Krelin," his mother meekly interceded. "Your brother is young, forgive his weakness."

Krelin's muscular body worked feverishly to secure his riding gear and ropes. He was ready to verbally attack his mother, but he was able to control himself.

"Mother, please leave me and your useless son to our work."

"But Krelin… "

"Mother!" Krelin shouted.

His mother slowly retreated. At that moment, a group of mounted Raiders went galloping by. It was the group that Krelin was supposed to accompany.

"Your blood should be wasted," muttered Krelin as he tightened the last rope. "Now, thanks to my weakling brother, I must eat dust until I overtake the others.

Krelin mounted his zwap and urged his ride onward. He was not far behind his fellow Raiders, which was good, but it meant that the clouds of dust were thicker. He felt a subtle reluctance from his beast that had to breathe the same particles of dry earth. Then, as Krelin exited the protected area, he saw something that made his heart race—a lone Scran in the distance. For the first time that day, Krelin felt a surge of joy. He would capture this Scran for the gods and, instead of the other Raiders laughing at him for being late to leave his compound—they would mention him in stories as the one who made the first capture.

For years, Krelin had trained for this moment. He urged his zwap onward as he grasped the end of one of his ropes in one hand and the hoop in the other. The Scran began to run. Krelin and the zwap moved as one. They would come close to the fleeing Scran and slip the hoop over the arms of the hapless victim. The zwap would halt abruptly and the Scran would be snapped off of his feet. The Raider would slide from his mount and lift the flailing Scran into the air. The hunter would wrap the rope around the hapless victim's arms three times and then secure the rope to the Scran's ankle, thus immobilizing the captive. This was the way the Northern Raiders had captured Scrans for hundreds of years, and this was what Krelin expected to do today. But today, Krelin's expectation would prove to be inaccurate.

Kolord turned and began to flee the oncoming Raider at full speed. He soon realized he could not escape by running. The hunter was rapidly closing in, and Kolord could tell by the determination and glee in the Raider's eyes that the rider had every reason to believe a successful capture was inevitable.

"When your pursuer is faster than you, seek an alternative that does not include speed." The words of a teacher shot through Kolord's head.

Kolord could only think of one alternative. Without warning, he stopped, turned, and ran with all his might directly at the Raider and his beast. In an instant, the confidence and glee drained from the Raider's face and was replaced by surprise—shocked surprise. Even the stride of the zwap was interrupted. Kolord caught the Raider and his animal completely off guard. Before the Raider could adjust, Kolord was at his side. The hunter tried to slip the loop around the Kolord but it was too late. Kolord grabbed the Raider by one arm and pulled him from the still moving zwap. Kolord delivered one well-placed blow to the back of the Erlonian's head. The Raider fell to the ground unconscious. Kolord, his chest heaving, used one of the Raider's own ropes to immobilize the Erlonian.

The flow of Kolord's adrenalin began to subside. He looked at the fallen Raider and was again amazed at this Erlonian's resemblance to his fellow Zoltocs. Kolord saw that he and his opponent were so far away from the entrance that the fallen Raider might go unnoticed for some time. On this planet, that meant death. Kolord decided to use the zwap to move the Raider closer to the entrance and perhaps ride the beast to meet Gogandu. He grabbed a handful of the beast's long, woolly fur and pulled himself onto the zwap's back. The animal reared its front legs and let out a cry. The feel of an unfamiliar rider made the animal stir for a few moments, then it became still. Kolord could hear the animal's bursts of heavy breathing, but otherwise it was motionless. Kolord took an instant liking to the docile creature.

"Now, will you hold still while I load your former rider onto your back?" said Kolord. He dismounted and lifted the dead weight of the native to his shoulder. The Raiders were heavier than the Zoltocs, but the well-conditioned V.I. had no trouble lifting his captive. Getting the Raider on the back of the zwap was another matter. Every time Kolord heaved his victim to the back of the beast, it would raise its front legs and the Raider would fall to the ground with a loud thump. By the third failed attempt, Kolord's fondness for the animal was growing thin. He stopped and wondered how else he might transport the Raider to the entrance. Waiting until he gained consciousness would waste precious time. Dragging him might result in unnecessary injury. Kolord decided he would carry his captive to the entrance. Hopefully, riding the zwap would erase any of Kolord's lost time. Kolord never once considered leaving the native to perish.

As he trudged across the arid landscape, Kolord noticed that the wind was picking up. The dust made the task of carrying the Raider while leading the tethered zwap more difficult. Kolord estimated that, in 50 more meters, the Raider would be within yelling distance of the entrance. If there was one Northern Raider, there was bound to be more to come. The captured Raider would be able to get help from one of his comrades.

The wind continued increasing, and the light began to fade. Kolord looked up and saw thick, black, clouds silently tumbling across the sky. Then the globs of wetness came. The raindrops' journey from the water-laden clouds, ended in random collisions with the thirsty landscape. The periodic drops soon became a steady downpour, then a torrent.

Rain—heavy, unrelenting rain! Rain in a land that looked like it had never seen rain.

So there is water on this planet, mused Kolord.

The rain came when he least needed it. It was heavy and it came on quickly. The dusty ground quickly turned into mud, which really slowed things down. Kolord decided to give the zwap one more try. He heaved the body over the animal's back. Surprisingly this time the beast barely moved. Kolord immediately grabbed its shaggy fur and pulled himself up. He urged the zwap forward, all the while hoping the animal would continue to cooperate.

◆

Gogandu straightened his tall, lanky frame. Rima and TaRupi, still breathing heavily, sat on the side of the road and stared intently at Gogandu and BB. The two Zoltocs observed as Gogandu placed his face in front of BB's face. They watched as the two Masters became frozen together for several moments. The Zoltocs did not know what they had witnessed, but they sensed it was something powerful and important.

"Gogandu must find Kolord as soon as possible," said Gogandu. "BB must follow Gogandu. Drink."

Gogandu handed him another vial of green liquid. BB was still dazed from his face-to-face experience with Gogandu. He stood and took the liquid. His legs were tired and weak, and he no longer felt a sense of detachment from his body.

"TaRupi and I should accompany BB to lessen his chance of detection," said Rima, getting to her feet.

"Yes, Rima is right," said Gogandu.

He handed Rima and TaRupi each a vial.

"These will aid their progress for a short time," said Gogandu. "They have already stressed their bodies and they may inflict damage, but it cannot be helped. Stay on the road, and Gogandu will find them."

Gogandu turned and headed down the road at an incredible speed. Rima helped TaRupi to his feet. The three V.I.s started down the road at a moderate speed. Soon, the liquid that Gogandu gave them began to have its effect, and their pace quickened. No one spoke. No one commented on what happened between Gogandu and BB or on Gogandu's super human speed. The trio just ran down the muddy road in the pouring rain, their minds detached from their bodies.

◆

Kolord deposited the hunter near the entrance to the Northern Raiders' area and then raced along the road on the back of the zwap. The rain and the muddy road had no effect on the animal. It moved effortlessly and with rhythmic grace. As he had hoped, the animal had no problem following the road. Kolord merely held a tuft of the zwap's rain-saturated fur as tightly as he could. He wondered how far he must go before he encountered Gogandu and the others. When he made his earlier calculation, he believed that he would be traveling by foot. Now that he was riding the zwap, he was unsure of the time it would take to reach Gogandu. Suddenly, the zwap stopped, almost throwing Kolord off its back. There stood Gogandu in the middle of the road.

"Tell me EVERYTHING you have seen," said Gogandu. The urgency in his voice was obvious. "Omit no detail no matter how small. I must know all that you remember."

The interrogation began before Kolord got off the zwap. At almost every point of his interrogation, Gogandu would interject with a request for more information. He was especially interested in the Ortan: "The Ortan looked directly into Kolord's eyes, and Kolord felt nothing?" and "Are you sure the Ortan walked with a limp and had an injured arm?"

After Kolord told Gogandu everything he could remember, Gogandu asked him to repeat the entire account. The repetition of the story and the questioning did not stop until BB and the other two Zoltocs arrived. BB and Gogandu placed their heads together and repeated the unusual procedure. Then Gogandu spoke to BB and the three Zoltocs.

"The V.I.s are on their way," said Gogandu. "Since they are no longer as concerned about detection, they should arrive soon." Gogandu paused. "The ship that Kolord discovered is most likely an Ortan ship." He ignored the shocked looks on the faces of the V.I.s and continued.

"If the disabled ship were even partially operative, the shuttle and the landing crew would have been detected by now and the Ortans would have captured at least one of the V.I.s. They have ways of inflicting pain that would cause anyone to give up all information."

"What information?" asked Rima. "That Venuvians exist? That they have spread throughout much of this galaxy? Or, have they always suspected the existence of the Venuvians? And, who are *they?*"

"What if it's a trap?" interjected TaRupi.

"The Ortans who stayed behind, called the Freestones, tell the Venuvians that most of those who live on Orta believe that the existence of escaped Ortans is a myth," said Gogandu. "They would not wait for over 32 hundred years to spring a trap. If the Third Family Ortans, the family that now controls the planet Orta, had even a hint that there were escaped Ortans on Erlon, they would not hesitate to completely destroy the entire planet. Erlon is very sparsely populated, and the shuttle has not detected any electronic communications. It is known from the Freestones that the Third Family still use primitive forms of electronics to communicate. Because of the way they use Elder energy, they have never investigated cerebral communication. There has been no communication from this planet."

"What about before the shuttle entered the system?" asked Rima. "And, who are *they?*"

"The probe has been monitoring the planet for 103 years," said Gogandu. "It detected something because it shut down all the shuttle's operations as soon as the shuttle entered the system. The probe allowed the deployment of the landing craft, so the probe hasn't detected any communication signals since its arrival. The shuttle has captured the probe, so as soon as Gogandu activates the shuttle, all the information that the probe gathered will be available. Nevertheless, the shuttle must be prepared to escape global destruction."

"What about the crew?" asked Kolord?

"Total destruction, including the Ortan ship that Kolord discovered," said Gogandu. "All V.I.s must be aboard the shuttle to escape destruction of the planet."

Gogandu had not answered Rima's question about who *they* were.

TaRupi and Rima lay on the side of the road still exhausted. BB, although not totally worn out, was not in much better shape than the two Zoltocs. Kolord discovered a few soft spots on his butt after his ride on the zwap, but he was otherwise rested. Gogandu looked as stoic as ever. The rain had almost ceased, but there was still a heavy mist in the air. The sun was losing its radiance to the moisture suspended in the air, and the orb's brilliance was muted as it dropped toward the horizon.

"BB and Gogandu will leave now," said Gogandu. "BB, take the beast."

BB was about to protest that he has no knowledge of riding such animals. Kolord, seeing BB's distress, quickly interjected.

"Don't worry BB," said Kolord. "The zwap is really a gentle animal. Hold a tuft of fur behind its neck and use your knees to keep you steady. Try to move with the animal's rhythm. You will be fine."

Gogandu continued giving directions.

"Zoltocs, wait here for the other V.I.s," said Gogandu. "When they arrive, head for the entrance to the Raiders' area. When the crew reaches the entrance, Kolord, take half of the crew and retrace Kolord's steps. Rima and TaRupi, take the other half and go to where the water is delivered. Do whatever is necessary to trace the source of the water. Everyone move at full speed or faster. Now go."

With that, Gogandu sped away. BB pulled himself onto the zwap.

"How does BB direct it?" asked BB.

"Just hold the fur, and use your knees to direct it," said Kolord. "It is amazingly responsive,"

BB turned the zwap around, and, at his urging, it took off down the road.

"I want one of those," said TaRupi as he watched BB and the zwap speed away down the road.

TaRupi and Rima sat on the side of the road and rested while they waited for the other V.I.s. The rain had stopped, and the mist was melting away. The sun grew brighter, and, for the first time since they had been on the planet, the rain-soaked Zoltocs welcomed its warming rays. Kolord paced nervously. He was anxious to return to the ship he had seen.

"Something very important is happening," said Kolord. "And it's more than just finding an Ortan ship that looks like a Venuvian ship."

"Ortan?" TaRupi asked. "Are you sure it's an Ortan ship?"

"I don't know if it's Ortan or Venuvian," said Kolord. "I just know I saw an Ortan walking out of the ship."

"Why are they making a fuss over an Ortan?" asked TaRupi.

"I don't know, but Gogandu... " Kolord stopped. "He's not human, is he?"

"I've never seen any human move like he did," said Rima. "Whatever he is, he's extremely interested in the disabled ship, and, until now, he was very careful that we were not detected."

"Maybe the Venuvians have some Ortan enemies," said TaRupi.

"The other V.I.s should be here soon," said Rima. "If we move at full speed we should be at the water supply early tomorrow."

The group fell silent for some moments. Then Kolord abruptly stopped his pacing.

"I'm going back to look for the crew," said Kolord. "If they take to the road and know they no longer have to worry about detection, they will be able to move much faster."

"Gogandu did not mention going back," said TaRupi.

"Gogandu is preoccupied," said Kolord. "I will return with the others."

Kolord departed without another word.

◆

Morbred and the other V.I.s were still in good spirits. The rain had refreshed them. Even though the dust had turned to mud and slowed them considerably, at least they were on the move. They all wondered what the three sound flares had indicated. Every crewmember felt he or she was well enough trained to handle any obstacle this planet could deliver.

"Morbred!"

Morbred halted the crew. It was Kolord.

"I have no time to explain, but we have discovered a Venuvian or an Ortan ship," said Kolord.

The V.I.s moved closer to Kolord.

"An Ortan in a Venuvian ship?" asked a V.I.

"Yes," replied Kolord. "We must move at full speed."

"Shouldn't the crew proceed cautiously?" asked Jubley.

"Gogandu said we should move at top speed, use the road, and don't worry about detection," said Kolord.

"But... "

Kolord interrupted Jubley.

"I have seen the ship and the Ortan," said Kolord. "If there is any danger, it would have struck by now."

Kolord, seeking agreement, focused on Morbred and her mate Jubley.

"Morbred?" asked Jubley.

"We will take to the road and move at full speed," said Morbred.

The crew headed down the road, racing forward. They now had a mission. The V.I.s only slowed when they connected with Rima and TaRupi.

The sun had set, but there was still some light when the crew reached the entrance to the Northern Raiders' area. Morbred was separating the crew into two groups when a cart drawn by two zwaps and full of captives arrived. The three herders, seeing the collection of aliens in their world, ran in fear. The captive natives assumed that these strange looking beings were the gods who had come to collect their sacrifices.

"Who are these people?" TaRupi asked, looking at the bound natives. "Even close up, they look like Zoltocs."

"They are probably for the Raiders," said Rima. "They will be killed for their blood."

"Bota and Johas, release these captives," ordered Morbred. "Joe, secure the animals and dispose of the cart."

"There may be other carts full of captives that have already past," said Rima. "If TaRupi and I take the animals, we may be able to help other captives who have already passed."

"What about the water source?" asked TaRupi. "I think the water source is the place where the captives will be taken."

"TaRupi is right," said Kolord. "I will take two V.I.s with me and retrace my path. Morbred, you stay here and intercept any more incoming carts. Send the next two zwaps to me."

As Kolord spoke, a din arose from the captured natives. The Erlonians' fears had turned to terror as the two V.I.s approached them, knives in hand.

"Go for the one who seems least resistant," Bota said to Johas. "Once they see that they are being released, they will be less trouble."

Johas opened the rear of the cart, and an old man exited, fell to his knees, and looked up at the Johas with an expression of sorrowful resignation. Bota and Johas lifted him and cut the rope that was bound to his leg. Then they cut the rope binding his arms. The old native looked bewildered. Bota motioned for him to go.

"Go home, go!" said Bota in his broken Erlonian.

The freed captive took a few steps away from the cart then ran back and embraced a gray-haired woman. Johas immediately cut her bindings. The old man, still tightly embracing the woman, stepped away from the cart and began to laugh. The other captives stopped their wailing and began to tentatively move forward. As the two V.I.s quickly cut the ropes, the sounds became joyous. After each Erlonian was released, the freed native would move away from the cart. No one left until every one of the captives had been freed. Then, still a bit bewildered, they all hurried off, casting back anxious glances as they left.

Rima and TaRupi took the zwaps and headed to the Sacred Area. Kolord left for the Ortan ship with two V.I.s. Morbred, with the rest of the crew, waited to intercept carts carrying captives. A new page in Erlon history was being written.

◆

Treyak vowed he would never retrieve captives again, even if it meant staying behind with the women, children, and old men—even if it meant being sacrificed.

The gods must be fed, thought Treyak.

The mantra sounded so hallow now. He looked again at the beautiful, young woman bound before him. She was on her way to be sacrificed, and yet there was a calmness about her. Treyak felt like she had cast a spell on him. He had first seen her only a short time ago, but it seemed like an eternity.

"What is your name?" asked Treyak.

"Valiya," she answered.

The sound of her voice only deepened his enchantment. He said nothing else. What could he say? He had taken her captive, and now she was on her way to her death. If only he could undo his deed.

Damn the gods! thought Treyak—words, which if spoken, would result in his sacrifice.

Their journey was nearing its end. Treyak passed the cheering crowds and entered the area where the living canopy covered the road. He looked ahead. Where the road curved, he could see light.

That must be where... Treyak pushed the thought from his mind.

"You are so beautiful, Valiya," was all Treyak could say.

There was no longer heavy rain to hide the tears in the eyes of Treyak, who had failed at being a Raider, and in the eyes of Valiya, who was headed for her death.

Then Treyak heard hoof beats. He turned to see two Raiders on zwaps rapidly gaining on them. When the riders were almost upon him, Treyak saw that one of them was a female. He had never seen a woman ride a zwap. When the zwaps passed the cart, Treyak thought that there was something strange looking about the two Raiders. What happened next was dreamlike. The Raiders stopped the two zwaps that were pulling the cart.

"What are you doing!" yelled Losstuv the driver.

The Raiders did not reply. Losstuv attempted to start the zwaps moving again. The female grabbed the driver's arm and pulled him from the cart. Losstuv tried to shove the new arrival, but she deflected his arm and delivered a blow to his mid-section. Losstuv fell to his knees in pain. Mossyek, the other herder, was frozen in fear. Who were these strange looking people? Should he help Losstuv? Mossyek saw how the female effortlessly defeat Losstuv. What would the male do? If Mossyek fled into the cavern, he might be mistaken for a sacrifice victim. Mossyek decided to make a run for it. He jumped from the cart and headed for enclaves as fast as he could. The strange looking Raiders ignored Mossyek's escape.

The male dismounted and came to the rear of the cart. Then Treyak saw it, a bright shiny knife. With one swipe, the knife cut through the rope holding the cart gate closed. The strange looking Erlonian opened the gate and was moving toward Valiya.

It must be the gods coming to collect their sacrifices, thought Treyak.

He threw himself at the strange looking native, fully expecting the knife to be plunged into his heart. Instead, the knife-wielding stranger, in one swift move, pulled Treyak past him, tripped him, and delivered a blow to the back of his head. Treyak fell, face first, onto the road. Immediately, he sprang to his feet. He was dazed and gasping for a breath, but, without a thought, he charged the god again. This time he was able to grab the god around his waist and pull him away from the cart. The strange looking god, using his elbow, delivered a blow to Treyak's bicep that paralyzed his arm for a moment. The god then went to one knee, releasing himself from Treyak's grip. When the god stood, he was behind Treyak. The god yelled something in a language that was foreign to Treyak. The female god headed toward the cart. She kept repeating a phrase. One word sounded like "home" to Treyak, but he was too agitated to listen closely.

The male was restraining Treyak when the female stopped next to Valiya and pulled a knife. Treyak struggled even harder, but the alien was much too strong. As soon as the female god cut Valiya's ropes, Valiya jumped from the cart and charged the male god. Using strength he did not know he had, Treyak broke away from the god, grabbed Valiya's hand and ran. One of the gods' zwaps was right in front of Valiya and Treyak. Treyak released Valiya's hand, grabbed a tuft of the woolly beast's fur and pulled himself up. He grabbed Valiya's hand and pulled her onto the zwap's back. Valiya wrapped her arms around Treyak and pressed her body so tightly to him he could feel her heart beating. He rode the zwap as he had never been able to before. For the first time in his life, Treyak felt free—really free.

◆

The Elders conferred telepathically.

"Is it a Third Family ship? Are there any Elders aboard?"

"It is a Third Family ship, but all but one of the Elders was destroyed when the ship crashed. The one that survived was injured and never recovered. She expired 107 years after the crash."

"Fluid?"

"There is a moderate amount. The Freestones said that the Third Family does not modify their fluid. They have never discovered how to increase volume by supplementing the fluid with additives. Since most of the ship's activities require Elder power, they use massive amounts of fluid for normal operation. The ship's BioDroid calculated that the amount remaining was low and he was initiating blood collection when Gogandu arrived. The crash destroyed the ship's blood-collecting equipment. Consequently, when the BioDroid extracted blood, the donors expired. In exchange for water, the natives offered victims for sacrifice."

"Can the ship be repaired?"

"Yes."

"This could be the vehicle that allows them to enter a system controlled by the Third Family. In 7 years the Spaceship Blastoc from Erlon will rendezvous with an asteroid belt. Valis, a planet that the Third Family planet has slated to be populated by those unfortunate Braks, will pass through the asteroid belt. Spaceship Blastoc could land on Valis during the meteor shower without being detected. An operative would then have to get to planet Onkor, where the Freestones have a pod. Perhaps the Freestones could... They shall see."

Kolord could feel himself getting tired, but he refused to slow his pace. He wanted to see the Ortan ship again and find out what Gogandu thought. The few landmarks that punctuated the monotonous landscape when Kolord first passed the area had been transformed. Now the scene was completely different. The powerful rains had washed the outcrops clean. Some rocks actually glistened with dull colors as if the water had brought them to life.

The crew had trouble keeping up with Kolord, and no one shared his enthusiasm. Kolord judged that they must be halfway between the entrance road and the disabled craft. He hoped a V.I. would show up soon with a zwap so he would be able to reach the site before nightfall. Two V.I.s fulfilled his wishes when they galloped up on zwaps. Kolord immediately relieved one of the V.I.s of his zwap.

"Tyzec, you lead the crew," said Kolord. "Follow the vegetation until you see... "

Before he could finish, Gogandu appeared.

"All V.I.s must return to the entrance at once," said Gogandu.

"But... "

Kolord was about to object, but the stern look on Gogandu's face halted his objection.

"I must speak with Kolord," said Gogandu.

The two men moved out of hearing range of the other V.I.s.

"Has Kolord spoken to anyone about the disabled craft?" asked Gogandu.

"I told Morbred, and I am sure most of the other V.I.s overheard me. Why?"

Gogandu ignored his question and was deep in thought for a few moments. Then he spoke to all the V.I.s.

"Return to the Northern Raiders' entrance road and join the other V.I.s," said Gogandu. "Go to the water source and remove all native personnel. Make sure the natives believe that the Zoltocs are giving the orders. The natives believe that the V.I.s are gods, so V.I.s should have no trouble controlling them. The crew will have a complete language translation when the shuttle is activated."

There was an audible expression of relief from the V.I.s. The thought of getting back to the comforts of the shuttle gave everyone's spirits an uplift—except for Kolord. His desire to revisit the craft outweighed any comforts the shuttle had to offer. As the others began retracing their steps, Kolord moved close to Gogandu.

"Will we be returning to the craft I saw?" asked Kolord.

Gogandu looked at Kolord for a moment, and then Gogandu's face, which had been hard and expressionless for so long, melted into a smile.

"In due time, Kolord. In due time."

KC sat on a rock in an area that had once witnessed the sacrifice of hundreds of thousands of unlucky natives. Most of the other V.I.s avoided this area because of its unsavory past, but KC found it peaceful. His years spent on Tambuki and the time spent traveling in the Erlon system gave him the opportunity to grow even closer to the ways of the Masters. He had come to better understand why Tambuki avoided electronics. From the time he entered Erlon's system until the discovery of the Ortan ship, there had been no electronic activity—no noise. When he assumed postures or practiced the Ways, there had been a background of quiet, a subtle peacefulness. Then the shuttle had been activated, and BB, his parents, and Morbred and Jubley—the masters—had to adjust to the electronic distractions.

The Venuvians were reshaping Erlon to make it a livable planet for everyone. Gogandu told the crew that the inhabitants of the planet no longer had to eke out a living. They were healthier and they were already living longer. There were no more sacrifices to the water gods. And the Northern Raiders and the Scrans have begun to live together, albeit not in complete harmony.

KC wondered what the planet looked like after six years of Venuvian influence. No one from the crew was allowed to leave the Sacred Area except Gogandu. Gogandu told the crew that it was imperative that no one, other than the crew, learn of the Ortan craft they had discovered on Erlon. Even the parts and equipment needed to make repairs on the ship were delivered by the Venuvians to an area away from the crash site. With the exception of eight Venuvians who were brought in to work on the Elders' section, V.I.s made all the repairs. With the restructuring of the planet and the repairing of the craft came the standard Venuvian electronic wizardry and an end to KC's quiet backdrop. KC now understood why the Venuvians kept Tambuki free of electronics.

"Kay Zee."

It was Krella, no façade, eyes uncovered, wearing the flowing white dress she had on when KC first met her. KC never failed to marvel at the emotions evoked by looking into those large, bottomless, golden eyes. KC knew Krella wanted to talk.

"She seems troubled," KC said as he held her hands between his.

"Krella has so many questions about the Ortan ship," said Krella.

"Krella has spoken of other Ortans," said KC. "What have Krella's people told her?"

"Only that there are powerful and merciless Ortans who want to destroy all Ortans who are not aligned with them," replied Krella. "Only the Elders know the true story."

For a brief moment, KC recalled the fear he had experienced during the jumps.

"What does that ship mean?" asked Krella looking deeply into KC's eyes to show her concern. "The crew is repairing the ship. It does not appear that the Venuvians are planning to evade our enemy. Will there be a war? Will Ortans be fighting Ortans?"

"Krella and KC can only wait and see if the thread that ties the universe together will provide them an answer," replied KC.

The Elders conferred telepahtically.

"The repairs on the craft are near completion. It should depart as soon as possible. The Elders don't want any information about the Third Family ship to get out."

"What about the V.I.s?"

"The woman or her son will be encouraged to infiltrate the Third Family System. If, for any reason, neither one decides to accept the assignment, the Elders can always find another Ortan who is more than willing to sacrifice all to restore the ways of the Elders to the System. Unfortunately, no one has the communication skills as powerful as the young Ortan Master."

"And the others?"

"They will try to erase certain memories, but that procedure is not foolproof—it can be dangerous. Gogandu will have to take the V.I.s to some uninhabited planet until after the…"

"The conflict?"

"Yes, there will be a conflict."

"And what shall happen to them if the Elders do not prevail?"

"If the Third Family defeats the Elders, an unpopulated planet would be the only safe place in the Exitir Galaxy."

The rains had recently ceased and the glorious days of Erlon were at hand. The desert vegetation was in full bloom. Plants and animals alike spent all their energy on storing the fruits of the season's rainfall. It was a beautiful time of the year. KC and Krella sat peacefully sipping on the local, bitter-herb tea and taking in the vast expanse of the planet that had been their home for the last seven years.

"Will he miss this place?" asked Krella.

"He has grown to like it here, but KC has never felt like he wanted to make it home," said KC. "And Krella?" asked KC.

"She will miss Erlon, yes she will," said Krella. "But the soil here is not inviting. The Venuvians will bring it to life but it will take time before the soil yields its natural goodness. Now growers must fight the soil."

"KC thinks most of the crew is ready to leave, even though Gogandu has not given a hint as to where the ship is going," said KC.

"Are all the ship's markings in Ortan?" asked Krella, abruptly changing the subject.

"There is not a trace of Venuvian anywhere on the ship," said KC. "Not one trace. There is not even a station for Monthlies. That is un-Venuvian, very un-Venuvian."

"What does KC think that means?"

"KC wishes he knew."

"Krella has heard stories saying that in ancient times there was a split among the Ortans and some families left the Ortan System," said Krella. "The Elders knew that, if they kept spreading The Way throughout the galaxy, someday they would again encounter those from the Ortan System. She hopes the Elders are fully prepared."

"After Krella leaves Erlon, she will learn much more about her people." It was Gogandu.

His arrival had been silent.

"There is much she needs to know," said Gogandu. "She will have to make many important decisions. Krella must be strong."

Gogandu turned and left as abruptly as he had arrived. His pronouncement still hung heavily in the air. During his brief appearance, Gogandu had not once recognized KC's presence.

Kolord was not satisfied. He thought that, once he had been able to board the Ortan ship, some of his questions would be answered. Only two questions had been answered. Was the spaceship an Ortan ship? It was. Secondly, what had happened to it? It had malfunctioned and crashed on Erlon. But there were still unanswered questions. Why did the spaceship look so Venuvian, and what did it have to do with the Northern Raiders' human sacrifices? Most of all, why were the Venuvians so secretive about the ship? For the past seven years, the entire crew except for Gogandu had been restricted to the Sacred Area and adjacent grounds. Now the crew was about to leave on the Ortan ship and no one knew where they were headed. Kolord had spoken with Krella. He hoped that an Ortan might have some information on the ship. Krella knew only a very little.

"Krella's ancestors withdrew from the other Ortan families many millennia ago," said Krella. "It has been so long, some Ortans believed the existence of other Ortans is nothing more than a myth. Now, of course, Krella knows there must be other Ortans who are almost as advanced as the Venuvians. They may even have known the Venuvians."

Kolord had even questioned Gogandu. Gogandu had smiled his mysterious smile and gave another answer that was not an answer.

"Some questions may be answered some may not." That was all that Gogandu said.

Kolord knew not to question him further. The time for departure had come and Kolord had grown tired of being restricted to the land around the Sacred Area. He had hoped to meet some of the natives who so closely resembled his fellow Zoltocs, but the only Native that he had come in close contact with, he had left partially conscious on the side of a road. Kolord now knew he would never see an Erlonian again. He did not look forward to spending another 14 years traveling to another system, but this was the life he chose.

ERLON POSTCRIPT

Castran sipped from his cool drink, leaned back in his chair, and relaxed. The scorching rays of the sun, filtered by an assortment of trees circling the compound, fell softly on vibrant gardens. Castran had grown fond of this planet. The rainy season was inconvenient but it was short and it produced the planet's spectacular show of colors. Within a few days, the seemingly lifeless desert would spring back to life.

Since the Venuvians came and tapped the underground water, the northern area of Erlon had blossomed. Thousands of tree-encircled wells were scattered all over the northern area. The unpopulated area around the southern pole was also being developed, and long tunnels and transport tubes were being built to connect the two areas.

Castran did not know what the planet was like before the Venuvians arrived. Most of the Erlonians told him that, before the Venuvians arrived, some of the Erlonians, the Scrans, eked out their existence by depending on the short rainy season. Younger Erlonians believe that the Northern Raiders, now integrated with the Scrans, would periodically capture Scrans and put them to work as slaves. There were a few Erlonians, mostly the older ones, who believed that it was the gods who gave water to the people and that the gods required human sacrifices. These older inhabitants believed that the Venuvians had chased the old gods away.

One day Castran spoke to the grandfather of one of the fishery project's co-workers.

"What was it like here before the Venuvians came?" asked Castran.

The gray-bearded old man poured himself a cup of tea, sat back in his chair, and made himself comfortable. He obviously relished telling stories about the old times.

"In those days there was little water except for the time of the rains," the old man began. "The Scrans led a dreadful life. They saved every drop of water they could. They even used their urine to make bricks. Have you ever heard of such a thing? Using one's own pee?"

Castran nodded, but he made no attempt to answer.

"What was even worse," said the old man, "every few years the Northern Raiders would swoop down upon unlucky villages and take victims to sacrifice to the gods. Did you know that my father was a Northern Raider? In those days, Northern Raiders were feared and respected. Not today. Now, people say the Northern Raiders were bad, that they took innocent Scrans to their death. Is it bad to obey the will of the gods?

"I remember the last raid. I was a young boy, but I remember. It was the only raid, I ever saw. I was very young, but I have heard Elders talk about it. Actually, it was not a real raid because the gods let all the captured Scrans go free.

"You know, I saw the gods. I did. I know they were the gods because of the way they looked. They looked like us but different. There were two of them. They were on zwaps, and one was a woman. In those days, the Northern Raiders did not allow women to ride zwaps, so I knew she was a god. Why else would she be allowed to ride a zwap?

"Nowadays they say that they were just aliens from other planets. Do you think I believe them? Did they see the gods? No they didn't! I saw the gods! I saw an army of strange looking beings join the gods. I think that the strange looking beings worked for the Venuvians, like you and the other strange looking off-worlders now living on our planet. I mean no disrespect to you Castran, but you must admit you are strange looking."

Castran chuckled but still did not interrupt the old man's story.

"Many of the old men and women ran away with their children when they saw the gods. They had heard stories about the gods taking victims for sacrifice from inside the protected circle that surrounded the Northern Raiders' area. The old ones thought the gods were coming to take them, even though the rains had started that very day.

"I was not old enough to be brave, but I was young enough to be foolish. I stayed and watched as the gods rushed into the priests' Sacred Area. Later, I saw the bewildered Scrans huddled together leaving the Sacred Area. A Raider on a zwap preceded them. There was a woman on the zwap behind the Raider—the second woman I had seen on a zwap that day. This woman was not a god, she was a Scran! In those days, the Scrans were much smaller than those who lived in the protected circle, so I know she was a Scran. This Scran, this woman, she held on to the Raider with her arms tightly around him. She pressed one side of her face firmly against his back. It looked like she feared she would be separated from the Raider.

"That day was the beginning of the change, especially for the Scrans. In the Sacred Area, before the Venuvians arrived, the priests spoke with the gods, and we got our water from the gods. We did not suffer like the Scrans. Then the Venuvians built wells. Now, everyone has water all year.

"After the Venuvians chased away the old gods, things changed for us, things changed for everyone. The Venuvians brought all these strange plants and animals. You know, before the Venuvians, there were no flying creatures on Erlon. I do not understand how these flying creatures stay in the sky. The Venuvians also brought their strange looking water creatures that my grandson studies all day. The water creatures are as strange as the flying creatures. Before the Venuvians, there was no place on Erlon for these creatures. How do the water creatures move so quickly in the water? I have asked my grandson many times, but I cannot understand his answers. Can you explain how these creatures move so quickly?"

"No, no I cannot," admitted Castran.

"Of course, today, there are no more sacrifices to the gods," said the old man. "For many years, the Scrans continued to fear the Northern Raiders. Even today, some who are as old as I am think the Raiders will strike again. Why would the Raiders want to capture more Scrans? We all have water and food. There are no more priests in the Sacred Area to carry out sacrifices, and the Northern Raiders no longer train. My father trained every day before the Venuvians came. After the Venuvians came, my father, like most of the Raiders, got lazy and fat. There are a few who still train with zwaps. Now they have competitions. Would you believe that, today, even women and Scrans train with zwaps?

"Now, everyone is a V.I. or an Associate—Scrans, Raiders, even women. In addition, we are healthy. Look at me! If it were not for the Venuvians, I would be dust in the desert wind. I go to my Monthly, train with the other old ones, and eat the strange food. The Venuvian way is good."

"Where do you think the old gods went," asked Castran.

"No one really knows, but something strange happened in the Sacred Area. For one thing, no gods or aliens ever returned after they entered the Sacred Area—only Venuvians were allowed to enter. The Venuvians would not allow anyone else, not even priests or other aliens, to enter.

"The Venuvians were building something. They took many crates into the Sacred Area. One day, a line of Venuvians carrying crates and moving faster than any Raiders ever had, ran into the Sacred Area. I was still a young boy and I had time to watch what went into the Sacred Area. Then all the traffic stopped. Soon after that, the Venuvians opened the Sacred Area. I remember the day because, the night before, I saw a very bright light shoot across the sky. Some of the old ones said it was a sign that the gods were returning, but I think it was a signal for the gods to leave. You wonder how I know this? It was just a feeling I had, a feeling that something new was about to happen."

The departure of the repaired Ortan ship, Spaceship Blastoc, was uneventful. There were no briefings or meetings of any kind. Five Venuvians joined Gogandu and the 50 V.I. crewmembers. The V.I.s were assigned quarters and told what time to report. They deposited their few precious belongings in travel modules, and the Blastoc unceremoniously departed Erlon.

Spaceship Blastoc closely resembled Venuvian spaceships with one glaring exception: there was no Monthly station on the Blastoc, only a blood *donation* area. Spaceship Blastoc's landing craft had to be replaced with the Venuvian landing craft that Gogandu had used to land on Erlon. Of course, all the Venuvian markings had to be replaced with Ortan markings. There were also a few technological advances made by the Venuvians that were not found on Spaceship Blastoc. To avoid suspicion, all technical advances had to be stripped from the landing craft.

Most V.I.s were not looking forward to spending months on Spaceship Blastoc as it traveled toward Erlon's sun. There was grumbling among the V.I.s until they learned the biggest surprise of all: the Blastoc would be jumping from the Erlon system directly to a new system—wherever that was. The Blastoc would not be taking the 19-month journey toward Erlon's sun in order to use the sun's gigantic mass to gain speed and collect energy. Instead, only days after departure, the V.I.s were instructed to prepare for a "jump."

After the "jump," the observation deck provided another delightful surprise. The viewing port was filled with thousands of sparkling lights that were not stars. The sizes varied from pinpoints to chunks larger than the ship. The Blastoc was in the heart of an asteroid belt!

On the second day in the belt, Gogandu spoke to the V.I.s.

"The V.I.s now know that the Blastoc is an Ortan ship, even though it looks like a Venuvian ship," said Gogandu. "The truth is, all Venuvian ships follow a design created by Ortans thousands of years ago."

There was a stunned silence among the V.I.s.

"Three millennium ago there was a schism between two factions on Orta," said Gogandu. "One group, the Ortans that the V.I.s know, decided to depart from their home system. As many V.I.s also know, untrained Ortans are unable to conceal their emotions from non-Ortans. Because of this trait, the Ortans chose the Venuvians to act as their proxies. Fortunately, the Venuvians were one of the first groups that the escaping Ortans encountered. One Venuvian trait was their lack of expression. Ortans liked the fact that Venuvians did not show their emotions. The two peoples have had a special bond ever since.

"Over the years, the Ortans who left Orta have expanded their influence in this part of the galaxy, which they call Exitir. The Ortans have worked in tandem with the Venuvians as the Venuvians' silent ally. Few, very few, Ortans or Venuvians know that the Elders make the most important decisions. The Inner Council of Elders is made up of Venuvians and Ortans with one or two members from the planet where the mother ship was constructed."

Gogandu's often-stern features softened as if a burden was being lifted from his shoulders. He had given every V.I. a feeling of comfort along with a keen understanding of the importance of his message.

KC, Krella, and their son BB perceived the subtle feeling that Gogandu was holding back something. The noise from the ship's electronics and Gogandu's powers, kept them from solidifying their perceptions.

Gogandu continued. "The ship that the crewmember found on Erlon belonged to the Third Family, one of the three Ortan Families that remain in control of Orta."

Gogandu's revelations continued to amaze the V.I.s.

"The Third Family is committed to the total annihilation of all Ortans who are not allied with the Third Family. After thousands of years, the Third Family Ortans came to believe that all Ortans were under the control of the Third Family or their two allies. Some Third Family Ortans believe that, even if there ever were any other Ortans, they are now extinct. Most Ortans feel that the idea of the existence of other Ortans is merely a myth. But the Third Family leaders have tried to convince the populace that there are indeed other Ortans and that these other Ortans are a threat to The Three Families. The leaders maintain that, because of this outside threat, it is necessary to maintain large military and police agencies in all systems controlled by The Three Families.

"The Elders have told Gogandu that someday the two Ortan factions would collide. What the discovery of Spaceship Blastoc means is that contact has been made with the Third Family. Soon, very soon, there will be a conflict. The survivor of the conflict will determine who controls the Ortan and Venuvian portion of the galaxy, Exitir."

"Where will the V.I.s be during your conflict?" It was Plorv.

"The conflict is not Gogandu's," said Gogandu. "Gogandu will be accompanying the V.I.s. The location cannot be divulged—even to Gogandu. The V.I.s may be wondering at the extreme secrecy that Gogandu has been maintaining. The V.Is must be warned—if anyone should fall into the hands of the Third Family, they will be tortured. Third Family Ortans can inflict unimaginable pain. Even Gogandu could not withhold information if the Third Family subjected him to a Third Family interrogation. The V.I.s should be safe regardless of the outcome of the conflict, but not the slightest chance can be taken that they possess any information that could be of use to the Third Family."

"Where did you get your super human abilities?" asked TaRupi.

Gogandu did not answer right away. He seemed to be searching for a response. For a moment, he tensed. Then he relaxed and appeared to be amused.

"Gogandu has no answer," said Gogandu. "He is what he is."

There were obviously more questions, but an announcement over the audio system brought the meeting to a sudden halt. It was in Ortan, so only Krella and Gogandu understood. Gogandu's countenance changed immediately. His face became expressionless and, without another word, he rushed from the room.

Krella turned to KC and whispered, "Another ship has been detected."

SPACESHIP LUMKOF

Welvek and Stuven were worried. Somehow Welvek had made a mis-calculation. They were supposed to have entered System Bravin, but now they were nowhere near Bravin. Fortunately, they did not land in deep space, and they had detected a system that was within range. The ship had enough fluid to reach the system, plant Braks and harvest the fluid from their blood, and then return to Orta with a shipment of fluid. Braks were a race of genetically modified giants that the Third Family created for the sole purpose of fluid production.

What if there was no planet capable of supporting Braks, thought Welvek?

Stuven did not think—he just worried.

Welvek and Stuven did find a suitable planet. If they had a good harvest, the Third Family would forgive their miscalculation. Now a new problem had arisen. They had detected another ship in the area. If there were already a ship assigned to the planet that the Lumkof had recently found, how would Welvek explain the Lumkof's presence to the other ship?

"Should we try to contact them?" said the short and pudgy Stuven.

Stuven slouched in his chair and folded his arms over his midsec-tion, but he could not conceal the fact that his gut cascaded over his belt.

"NO!" replied Welvek.

Unlike Stuven, Welvek was thin. His short-cropped black and gray hair framed his worried face.

"Let them contact us first," said Welvek. "We can ask them what they are doing in a Third Family system."

The pupils of Welvek's large, golden, Ortan eyes expanded and contracted, revealing his apprehension. It was Welvek who had set the incorrect coordinance, so he would receive the brunt of Third Family's punishment.

"Maybe they will not detect us," said Stuven.

"Have you lost your blood?" Welvek said angrily. "If we can detect them, they can detect us."

"What if it's a Fourth Family ship?" asked Stuven nervously.

Welvek shook his head in disgust.

"Do you believe those stupid superstitions?" said Welvek. "Those crazies who claim the Families are headed for another decline are the only ones screaming about how the Fourth Family is going to return and destroy the Third Family. Honestly Stuven, I don't know what you are doing on a Third Family ship. You should be back on Orta testing beds."

Welvek knew that the only reason Stuven had a position on a Third Family ship was that he had connections with someone high in the Family. Stuven pretended not to know how he got his position.

There were other navigators who were not connected to the Third Family. They were called "drivers." Any Ortan not connected to the Third Family was called a "driver," even if they had never set foot on a spaceship. Since Welvek and Stuven were part of the Third Family, they did not suffer from the physical discomfort during the jumps like the drivers did. Welvek hoped that the unidentified ship had Third Family navigators. Driver navigators resented Third Family navigators and would be much less cooperative.

Welvek watched the display. It indicated that the unidentified ship was drawing nearer. The unknown ship was in a cluster of other objects, probably asteroids. If the Lumkof had been in another star system, this unknown ship would have gone undetected. Why was the ship traveling inside a group of asteroids? Was it *trying* to go undetected? For a moment, Welvek thought about the superstitions surrounding the Ortans who had left Orta over 3,000 years ago. The Third Family simply called these escaped Ortans "enemies of the Families." To others, they were known as "the Fourth Family." He felt ridiculous even considering the possibility that some ancient, mythical group was returning to wreak revenge on The Three Families. But why did the ship not reveal itself or seek Lumkof's identification?

◆

Gogandu could not understand why this unexpected ship did not ask Spaceship Blastoc to identify itself. If it did, he knew exactly how he would respond. The unidentified ship had been a total surprise to Gogandu. He expected to find a livable planet that was uninhabited. There were some Ortans who stayed behind when the other Ortans escaped. The reports from the Ortans that were left behind, called "the Freestones," indicated that the Third Family would not explore this star system for another 150 years. Gogandu believed that he and the V.I.s would be able to conceal themselves until the Elders prevailed, or… The alternative was unthinkable. Gogandu decided to take action.

"This is the Spaceship Blastoc, Third Family. Please identify yourself."

There was a long pause.

"This is Spaceship Lumkof with the United Families, friends of the Third Family." It was Welvek.

Again silence. There were three families that had joined forces to control Orta. Gogandu knew that, during a period when The Three Families' power was in decline, an unidentified ship would have been attacked. But that was hundreds of years ago. The Three Families had regained power. The Third Family was the most influential of The Three Families. There should have been immediate cooperation between the two ships. But Spaceship Lumkof did not seem willing to divulge any further information. Gogandu again broke the silence.

"We had a malfunction that caused a forced landing on some planet outside of The Third Family's control," said Gogandu. "The ship has been repaired and is in route to Orta."

This time the reply was immediate.

"This star system is assigned to United Families," said Welvek. "We are here to initiate a colony of Braks. How long has your ship been in repair?"

Gogandu could detect relief in Welvek's voice.

"We were able to complete repairs in seven years," said Gogandu. "But it has taken us over 98 years to collect enough fluid from the sparse population on the planet where we crashed."

Gogandu spoke perfect modern Ortan, which was somewhat different from the dialect spoken by Krella and the other Tambuki Ortans.

"When we left on our mission, there were still some hostilities among the Families," said Gogandu. "We have information stating that all the Families are now cooperating."

"The Families are completely at peace now," said Welvek. "That was such a wasteful period in our history. I hope we never display such foolishness again."

There was another pause.

"Will you be reporting to the Third Family on your return?" asked Welvek.

Gogandu could again hear apprehension in the Ortan's voice.

"Yes, of course," said Gogandu. "But our navigational equipment lost most of its memory. If we could get some coordinates from you for our return, it would be very helpful."

Welvek did not immediately respond. Finally, he spoke.

"We had a malfunction of our own," said Welvek. "We do not have the exact data now, but, as soon as we identify of the surrounding sun system, we will have that exact information."

The Lumkof is lost! Gogandu now realized why he had detected apprehension in Welvek's voice. If Welvek's Family found out about his mistake, he would be in serious trouble. The situation fit perfectly into Gogandu's plan of action.

"It seems as though we both have encountered incidents that could prove unfortunate if they were discovered by our Families," said Gogandu.

Again, Welvek's voice was relieved.

"Yes! Quite right!" said Welvek. "Were you planning on landing on or orbiting the planet?"

"We must conserve fluid, so we have no choice but to stay in orbit," said Gogandu. There was a short pause. "Unless we could obtain more fluid."

Welvek's voice tensed.

"We could never transfer any of our fluid," said Welvek. "That would be treason. The Family would destroy us.

"Of course, we would never expect you to part with even a drop of fluid." Gogandu's voice had an immediate calming effect on Welvek. "I assume you are here to plant."

"Yes," replied Welvek.

"Are you planning on taking the normal 40 years to bring your crop to maturity?"

"Yes, of course," said Welvek.

"Since our ship is presumed lost, we could land, help tend to your plantings, and more than double your harvest," Gogandu said convincingly. "We could both fill our cargo space and have enough stock remaining for a quick second harvest."

The idea pleased Welvek.

"We could return with full cargos?" Welvek's response was part question and part musing. "The Families are not happy when a ship returns with cargo space that is not completely full."

Gogandu used his persuasive voice.

"You can cultivate the northern hemisphere, and my ship can work the southern hemisphere," said Gogandu. "I believe that the usable land masses are equivalent." Gogandu's voice had a further calming effect on Welvek.

"Yes, yes, wonderful!" said Welvek.

Gogandu had enlisted a co-conspirator who was unaware of how he had just been manipulated. The Lumkof was an unexpected addition to the first-strike Plan. But now the crew would have to be told certain things, things that the Elders had wanted to keep from them until The Third Family's unspeakable acts had been terminated forever.

VALIS

KC and Krella looked across the expansive valley. The warm breeze carried the sickly sweet odor of the ubiquitous limcra tree. KC thought of his home planet Earth. This could be a scene from some forested area on Earth except for the smell. Even though during this time of the year the limcra trees' scent was at its lightest, KC and Krella could only stand the smell for a short time. Then they had to return to the purified environment of Spaceship Blastoc.

KC looked over an outcrop to a clearing below. He saw a scene that was duplicated tens of thousands of places on planet Valis. A group of about 20 giant Braks—men, women, and children—were lying motionless in the afternoon sun. Even the children did not move. None of the young ones were running and jumping or playing any of the games that KC had seen children play on Earth or Tambuki. At first glance, the large extended family looked like they had been afflicted with some fast-acting, deadly malady. It was not death that had befallen these nearly naked, blood-engorged giants. It was the fruit of the limcra tree.

"They look so helpless," said Krella, her voice was weighted down with sadness.

"They are," said KC. "Without the addictive fruit, they would all die withdrawing from limcra—even the babies."

"They age so quickly," said Krella. "Their Elders were babies 40 years ago." Krella paused. "Does KC think that what KC and Krella are doing is right?"

KC and Krella had both dropped their learned façades. Like Krella, KC was troubled.

"They have to trust Gogandu," said KC. "The slaughter of these people has been going on for thousands of years. There have to be more sacrifices before the Elders can stop the evil. If the Elders tried to intervene and the other Families found out, they would eliminate everyone on Valis, and the slaughter of innocents would continue."

◆

Plorv was confused when he heard about the killing that was going to take place. When he first heard Gogandu explain why the crew was staying on Valis and what Gogandu would be doing, Plorv had felt a surge of gratification. It was too bad for the creatures that the Venuvians were going to slaughter, but now he knew that his beliefs for the past 82 years had been justified. The Venuvians and the Ortans were part of a conspiracy to suck the life out of the victims who thought the Venuvians were there to help them.

There had been moments on Erlon when Plorv had wavered and when he had wondered if the Venuvians were as evil as he believed. They seemed to be genuinely concerned about the people. They had ended suffering and turned Erlon, a desert planet, into a habitable place.

But Plorv's training had been too overpowering. His mentor, Wildon, had told him on a daily basis that the Venuvians were only cultivating others for their own use. Wildon had drilled that thought into Plorv before Plorv could even speak. Wildon, who had taught Plorv the Ways, was a wonderful teacher, a great teacher. He told Plorv that the gods had chosen him to save the living from the terrible fate of domination by a few. Wildon told Plorv that Plorv was special—every morning, every night, every day. Plorv could even remember awakening, and finding Wildon kneeling by his bed chanting repeatedly, "you will save us," or, "you have been chosen."

What about the other ship they had encountered, the one allied with the so-called Third Family? Gogandu said that the practice of slaughtering victims for blood was something that the escaped Ortans had always abhorred. Yet Gogandu stood by and did nothing while the Braks gorged on limcra, a fruit that contained a highly addictive narcotic and a strong aphrodisiac.

The Braks reproduced rapidly. They grew to a massive three meters and weighted up to 200 kilos. From before birth, every Brak lived in a drug-induced stupor. So, who were the enemies—the Venuvians, the Ortans, or the Third Family?

Plorv's teacher had continually said, "It is the nature of things—every being has at least one enemy, seen or unseen. Every enemy will always have a weak spot. Use the enemy's eyes and ears as well as your own to find this weakness."

Plorv decided that the Venuvians were the enemy. He must now find their weakness.

◆

The idea had entered Welvek's mind at the first meeting on Spaceship Blastoc, a Third Family ship. In some respects, Spaceship Blastoc's crew resembled Spaceship Lumkof's crew. They both had non-Ortans in their crew. Even the Third Family's uniforms could easily be mistaken for those of the United Families. Welvek was not sure what the ever-present Gogandu's role was, but two Ortans seemed to be in control of the ship. However, two distinctions separated this Third Family's crew from the United Families' crew. First of all, one of the Ortan navigators was a female. Even though Stuven could not stop blabbering about how beautiful she was, Welvek found it very uncomfortable dealing with a woman navigator in control.

As unusual as it was dealing with the lovely Krella, that difference paled in comparison to the other glaring difference—the difference that had first planted the seed of betrayal in Welvek's mind. The seed had grown over the years, and now, as the time for harvest neared, he thought of little else. Welvek had only been on the Blastoc once, but he would never forget what he saw—the Third Family's leaders did not wear weapons. Welvek was convinced that, if the leaders did not wear weapons, it would have been unthinkable for other crewmembers to possess even rudimentary devices. What if there were no way that Spaceship Blastoc could defend itself?

When the Blastoc left the area controlled by the Third Family, the

Families had been at peace for hundreds of years. Now, even though the Families worked well together, the United Families still carried weapons that they considered ceremonial—but they were still weapons. Welvek could not stop wondering what his rewards would be if he returned with two ships loaded with the precious fluid. He could easily return to one of the outlying sun systems, store his ill-gotten goods, and then return to Orta. He would tell his superior that the harvest was so plentiful it was necessary to return for a second load. If the Blastoc crew had not yet contacted the Third Family—and they had good reason not to—then the Third Family would not miss Spaceship Blastoc.

◆

"If the Third Family finds out we pirated one of their ships, it could mean another war!" Stuven had said.

Welvek knew immediately it had been a mistake to tell Stuven. Even though Stuven agreed that the Families would reward them handsomely if they were able to bring in two shipments of fluid, he was terrified that the authorities would discover their illegal activities.

"I could lose my position, and then where would I be?" said Stuven.

It had taken Stuven's father years of pressure and bribes to make Stuven a navigator. Stuven had tried to become a navigator on his own, but he had failed every test—miserably.

"Stuven," Welvek had pleaded. "How will anyone find out? The Blastoc has been out of contact for years. We can quickly eliminate the crew and no one will be the wiser. Think of all the extra credits we can earn."

"What about the Elders? Who will power the ship?" asked Stuven, who was obviously terrified.

"Without a crew, the Elders will be powerless," said Welvek. "If they refuse to cooperate, we will eliminate them."

"Kill an Elder?! That would be high treason. We would be executed! And, without the Elders, how would we move Blastoc?"

"Stuven!" Welvek put on his best smile and used his most convincing tone of voice. "Do you think the United Families would punish us for bringing in more fluid at the expense of the Third Family Elders? We would be heroes! If we have to eliminate the Elders, we simply return to Valis and transfer the fluid to our ship. The extra trip would cost us one third of our profit, but we would still make a tidy sum. We could even salvage Blastoc. There are traders who would pay handsomely for parts, no questions asked."

"I don't know, Welvek," said Stuven. "Steal a ship, kill the Elders and the crew? I would hate to see that beautiful Krella destroyed."

Welvek immediately saw the solution.

"The woman can be yours, Stuven," said Welvek. "Just think how grateful she will be if you step in and save her. She will be yours. You can do anything you wish."

Welvek could see his suggestion had worked. Stuven's eyes glowed with lustful anticipation. The thought of possessing the beautiful Krella, obscured any doubts he held. Stuven was ready to do Welvek's bidding. Welvek began to plan his diabolical mission in earnest.

The V.I.s waited in the multi-purpose room. Some sat, some moved from one V.I. to another, others quietly leaned against a wall or stood motionless, showing little or no interest in their surroundings. The hum of casual conversation filled the hall. It was the bi-annual meeting, and all the Blastoc V.I.s were present. No one expected Gogandu to present anything new or interesting, just the usual admonitions to avoid contact with the Braks and to never, never touch limcras. There might be a change in work detail assignments or a reprimand for some infraction of a rule. No one expected anything new. Nothing new had happened in the last 40 years. Then Gogandu entered. Immediately there was a change in the hall's atmosphere. Gogandu replaced his usual enigmatic countenance with an air of heavy sadness. Even before he had spoken one word, every V.I. had fallen completely silent.

Gogandu broke the silence. "The crew must make preparations for the arrival of the United Families' aircrafts," said Gogandu. "After the aircrafts arrive, the scene on this planet will be one of death. Genetically engineered winged insects will scour the surface of the planet. Every man, woman, or child these creatures find will have their blood drained. All V.I.s are confined to the ship. If any of the crewmembers wish, they may leave the ship after the blood collection is complete. There may be a few Braks who survive, but any V.I. who witnesses the carnage will be haunted by the sight for life." Gogandu took on a countenance that convoyed the magnitude of the horror that was to come. "No one is required to witness the deaths of these innocents, but for those who do, never forget that this is what the Great Conflict will be all about."

Gogandu could have planted ideas in the minds of the V.I.s, but he wanted them free from his control. What they would see would be the horror that the Third Families and their allies have been perpetrating on the Braks for more than 3,000 years.

◆

Plorv knew what he had to do. He must tell the Lumkof navigators that those who controlled Spaceship Blastoc were not Third Family at all— they were the so-called Fourth Family. He would tell Welvek that the Fourth Family's goal was to destroy the Third Family and all their allies. Even if the Lumkof crew did not believe him at first, they would surely investigate. Since every crewmember of the Blastoc now knew the real story behind the Blastoc's recovery, the United Families crew was bound to find something.

How could Plorv get the information to the Lumkof? Even if he could get into the tightly secured communication center, he had no idea how to operate any of the equipment. Everyone had learned the routine Ortan markings, but Plorv was sure that the technical symbols inside the communication room would be unintelligible to him.

Spaceship Blastoc had landed in the southern hemisphere and the Lumkof had landed in the north. There was very limited travel between the two ships. Word was that on rare occasions, aircrafts from the Lumkof would visit the Blastoc, or Gogandu would go to the north with Krella and BB. No one knew when an aircraft would arrive or depart. Plorv was at a loss. The solution to Plorv's dilemma came shortly after Gogandu announced the approaching slaughter.

The crew needed to make preparations on the Blastoc for 20 aircraft from the Lumkof. They would be arriving with the collectors. The Blastoc was buzzing with anticipation. Who or what were the collectors? Plorv only thought about how he could get on one of those aircraft and return with it to the Lumkof. He began to formulate a plan.

◆

Welvek kept running over his plans to take over the Blastoc. The key would be to destroy the Ortans before they could retaliate. He would wait until after the Third Family ship had harvested the blood and extracted the fluid. When the Lumkof's air ships came to the Blastoc to retrieve the collectors, Stuven and Welvek would meet with Gogandu, the woman, and her son. He would then eliminate them.

Welvek knew he would have to commit the deed himself, because Stuven did not have the strength to help. Stuven believed that he would return to the Lumkof with the beautiful Ortan woman. He would not. If Stuven had even a half functioning brain, he would have realized that to return to Orta with the woman would be the height of stupidity. She would have watched her son being killed and her ship being stolen—and possibly witnessed the elimination of the Elders. Except to satisfy Stuven's ridiculous desires, there was no good reason to keep the woman alive.

Welvek knew Stuven. He knew that Stuven would object, then pout, and possibly even threaten to reveal what happened. What could Stuven do? If he reported anything, he was sure to suffer the same consequence as Welvek—death. Welvek knew that Stuven would get over his loss, especially after they collected the extra credits for delivering the pirated fluid and then collecting even more credits for selling the Blastoc for parts. Welvek smiled at the cleverness of his scheme. What could possibly go wrong?

◆

From the moment Plorv learned that there would be airships arriving from the Lumkof, he spent every spare moment investigating Blastoc's exits and loading areas. He could tell by the work that was going on in a certain area where the United Family planned to deliver the collectors. Plorv assumed that Gogandu would have all exits secured after the arrival of the collectors. He searched for places where he could conceal himself before the collectors arrived and the Blastoc became inescapable. Plorv spent hours observing the cargo bay where he believed Spaceship Blastoc would receive the collectors.

Once, Plorv concealed himself behind one of the many empty shipping containers. He noticed that on several occasions, V.I.s stationed at the exit to the loading dock would leave their post for a few moments. Once, impulsively, Plorv decided to see if he could exit the area without being detected. He could, and he did. Plorv casually walked through the cargo area, opened the exit door, and stepped outside. The exit door closed behind him.

The powerful, sickly sweet smell of the limcra trees immediately struck Plorv. He had spent very little time off the ship since it landed and, the few times he had, the scent of the limcras had been light. But now, it was the season when the drug-laden trees were at their most potent. The narcotic was so powerful that the Braks spent most of their day in a drug-induced stupor. Plorv knew that when the time came for his escape, he would have to board the cargo airship immediately or he may fall victim to the intoxicating fumes of the limcra. He knew what he had to do, but he was worried—so many things could go wrong.

◆

Gogandu watched as the first of twenty United Families' crafts transferred the collectors to the Blastoc. Everything looked so sterile and innocent. The Lumkof's aircraft mechanically slid the gleaming, silver cylinders into the Blastoc. The Blastoc silently transferred each container into the receiving hull where several rows of perfectly shaped receptacles awaited them. To the untrained eye, the Blastoc appeared to be loading up some harmless cargo. Gogandu knew better. He knew that the shiny containers held an untold terror, something that was the greatest evil to have been unleashed on the galaxy. He soon would be ordering creatures to destroy innocent people. Gogandu knew that what he was doing had to be done, but he could not stop feeling that he had become a servant of evil.

Anticipation on the Blastoc had grown to a fever pitch. Morbid curiosity had drawn most of the crew to the observation area. Discussions centered on what the collectors would look like. An underlying tension permeated the ship. What was the disaster that lay ahead?

Krella, KC, and BB sat quietly at a table.

Krella broke the silence. "She doesn't understand why there is no way around slaughtering hundreds of thousands of innocent people."

KC turned and faced the woman he so loved.

"If there were another way, Gogandu would find it," said KC. "There must be no other way."

"His mother has a wonderful heart," said BB, still holding his façade. "There are times when even precious belongings must be lost before the truth is revealed."

Krella's voice verged on anger, "Your teacher's wise words will mean nothing to those who die today. No, they won't."

She had dropped her façade and BB and KC could see the sadness in the golden expanses of Krella's eyes. She was already feeling the pain of the upcoming tragedy.

"Please forgive Krella, but she must return to their quarters," said Krella.

Her apprehension had grown. The whole idea of what was about to happed was overwhelming.

"I do not know why she even came here," said Krella. "There is nothing she wants to see, nothing she wants to remember."

KC took Krella's hand.

"He must witness what is about to happen," said KC. "Please go. Don't let this horror infect Krella's mind."

KC looked away from Krella. He was deep in thought.

KC spoke softly. "The future of the galaxy may be determined by what happens here today."

"Why is that?" queried BB. "And why are the son and his father here?"

"If what Gogandu says is true, what happens here may be the prelude to mass destruction," said KC. "Your father has to know, he has to see with his own eyes why this war is necessary."

Krella stood and placed her hand on KC's. She leaned over and kissed his cheek.

"Krella understands," said Krella.

She turned and left. KC turned to BB.

"Why is my son here?" said KC. There was a challenge in KC's voice.

BB looked straight into his father's eyes, which were still hidden by KC's façade, and simply replied, "BB does not know."

◆

Plorv knew why he was here. He had to reveal to the United Families' crew that the Blastoc was not what it appeared to be. It was an Ortan ship, but the Ortans were puppets of the evil Venuvians. Plorv knew that luck had brought him this far without anyone detecting his true feelings. But the Venuvians were not stupid. There would be only one chance to contact the Lumkof and expose the Venuvians. That chance would come when the Lumkof delivered the collectors.

Plorv concealed himself in the cargo bay and listened to the muted sounds of the Lumkof crafts unloading their collectors. Unfortunately for Plorv, unlike every other time he had observed the cargo exit door, the V.I.s did not leave the station. The maddening frustration of being unable to do anything had only increased Plorv's determination. He vowed to himself that, when the crafts returned to retrieve the collectors, he would be prepared. He began to develop a plan, but Plorv felt uneasy. If the Ortans from the Lumkof were part of the plan to destroy the innocent Braks, were they not as evil as the Venuvians? Plorv did not understand, but he had no reservations.

Wildon, Plorv's Wild One mentor, had taught Plorv from the day he was born that he must stop the Venuvians. Now he, Plorv, was the only one who could defeat the Venuvians' desires. He had only one more chance. He decided that, instead of waiting for the crafts to return and then trying to escape from the Blastoc, he would leave the first time he had a chance and wait outside.

First, he had to construct a breathing apparatus. His last experience outside had made him aware of the power of the limcra. Finding the material for the breathing apparatus had not been easy. The Blastoc recycled every bit of material used on the ship. Plorv had only a few sources for the material he needed for his breathing apparatus. One source was the area where items were stored waiting to be repaired. Plorv constantly monitored this area and on occasion was able to pilfer a few usable items. Plorv was also able to obtain material used in the ships air filtration system that was waiting to get cleaned and reused. After a few weeks, he had fashioned a crude breathing device that he believed would protect him from the limcra fumes for at least 10 days.

Out of necessity, Plorv started spending longer and longer periods away from his quarters. Sometimes he spent days waiting for an opportunity to secretly enter an area and search for material. After he had completed constructing his air filtration device, Plorv continued to stay away from his quarters and avoid anyone who might notice his absence. He had always kept to himself, but now he wanted to make sure that, when he left the Blastoc, his absence would go unnoticed.

Plorv stowed his breathing apparatus and his food supplies near the exit. He continued to move about the Blastoc until the time came when he could make his move. He planned to conceal himself outside the Blastoc until the Lumkof aircrafts came to retrieve the collectors. Then he would make contact with the crew from Lumkof. His plan had one near-fatal miscalculation.

◆

Everything was going as Welvek had planned. It was almost harvest time. As Gogandu predicted, planting the northern and southern hemispheres simultaneously had produced enough Braks to fill both ships with fluid. The collectors had already filled the Lumkof. Now, Welvek was ready to deliver his creatures to the Blastoc—and to wait.

Welvek was sure Gogandu believed that, after the collectors filled Blastoc with fluid, Welvek would retrieve his collectors and depart. Welvek did not intend to leave Blastoc's fortune under anyone's control but his. Once he had loaded the collectors, he would board the Blastoc on the pretext of wanting to celebrate both ships' good fortune. Instead of celebrating, he would eliminate the Blastoc's leaders, enter the Elders' quarters and give the Elders a choice—cooperate or be destroyed.

It was the last part of the plan that disturbed Welvek. Elder power ran and controlled the Ortan system. If there was one thing that all the Families were united on, it was the preservation of Elders. As valuable as the extra fluid would be, if the Third Family or any of the Third Families' allies found out what Welvek was planning, they would execute him immediately—or worse.

After he finished with the Elders, Welvek planned on returning to the Lumkof. He would make sure that during the entire operation, the Lumkof would be locked down. On the outside chance that the Blastoc crew had weapons, Welvek wanted to be sure that no one could enter the Lumkof—no one.

Gogandu sat alone in his quarters. He did not understand the new feelings he was experiencing. He knew that the massacre of Valis's artificially created population was eminent. He felt regret, apprehension, and disgust—but he was fulfilling his destiny. He had little choice. He had *no* choice! His success would mark the beginning of a new Ortan system. It would reverse the fate of millions—born and unborn. Gogandu also felt relief. This distasteful part of his life would soon be over.

Then there was Welvek. Welvek's Ortan eyes and his voice held few secrets, and Gogandu knew early on that Welvek had some treacherous scheme planned. Gogandu had only to drop a few loaded remarks to discover that Welvek was planning on stealing Blastoc's cargo of precious fluid. Even worse, Welvek had thoughts of killing the Elders. Surprisingly, the knowledge of Welvek's transparent plans was evoking a sense of amusement in Gogandu, a feeling he seldom had.

Gogandu was finding it difficult to process this mixture of seldom-felt emotions. He wished that he could control these feelings and deal only with those emotions with which he was familiar. He wanted the slaughter to be finished, even though he knew that, if the plans were successful, there could follow an even greater carnage. The decision to embark on that endeavor would not be his. The unsuspecting soul who would have to initiate this great conflict was still mercifully unaware of his destiny.

◆

"What does BB's father think of Gogandu?" asked BB.

BB was wondering about the upcoming horror. He kept returning to one thought—Gogandu had the power to stop it.

"Why?" asked KC, who also had questions about Gogandu's role in the slaughter.

"There's something about him," said BB. "Has my father ever seen Gogandu without his façade? He always seems to be in control. Back on Erlon, he did, he did… things BB can't explain."

KC looked at his son who so resembled his Ortan mother. BB was now 114 years old. Except for 101 days when they were attached to the Proxsina, BB and KC had not spent much time together. On Tambuki, BB had passed his early years studying with Ogba. Then he went to Dome City where he stayed for several years. BB had spent most of his time by himself or with his friend Jov. When KC and his son were together, Krella was usually present. Now, here they were, waiting for a catastrophe, and BB was seeking his father's advice.

"Gogandu is a strong man, well skilled in the Ways," answered KC. "He can do a great many things that BB and KC cannot."

BB's eyes, without façade, met his father's eyes.

"BB can also do things that his father cannot do," said KC. "Your father does not know all his son's capabilities. But Gogandu is truly different. KC has lived on a moon and four planets. He has seen what Venuvians can do. Gogandu is more than impressive, he is extraordinary."

"BB knows that Gogandu could stop what's about to happen," said

BB. "Gogandu wants to stop the massacre, but he won't. Your son wishes he could understand why."

Both men fell silent.

"He is on a mission," said KC.

"Yes, he must be on a mission," said BB. "But for whom?"

An announcement from the public address system abruptly ended their conversation.

"The collection operation will begin in two minutes."

The hall fell silent. Lights dimmed and the audiovisual systems flashed to life. The scene was a familiar one—expansive views of limcra trees and groups of Braks trapped in a narcotic-induced stupor. A dull hum that grew to a loud buzz broke the silence. Then they appeared—the collectors. What followed was a scene, the sight of which every person watching would carry to their deaths.

◆

Plorv was frantic. The plan he had worked on had fallen apart. The first few days had gone by smoothly. He had managed to slip off Blastoc without being detected and to conceal himself in a clump of limcra trees. His food supply was sufficient, and his hand-constructed breathing apparatus worked perfectly. He had one big problem—eating. He would remove the makeshift air filter and gobble down his food as fast as he could, but, no matter how hard he tried, he would inhale some of the sickly sweet limcra fumes.

The first time he removed his mask to eat, he had not been prepared. His lungs quickly filled with the powerful narcotic. Before he could replace his mask, his senses began to dull. Even after he had replaced the air-filtering mask, he could feel a warm, sensual sensation engulfing his body. His tensions slipped away and all was good with the world. The experience had not been at all unpleasant.

Plorv wondered what it would be like to spend all of one's life intoxicated by limcra fumes. But he could not allow himself to be sidetracked by the comforting feeling induced by the trees' hypnotic fumes. He had to make contact with the Lumkof. He had to let them know that Gogandu and the Blastoc crew were not what they appeared to be. He had a mission to complete.

Plorv had just finished gobbling down a meal. He was still feeling the effects of the limcra trees when he first heard the sound. It was a low frequency hum that steadily grew in volume. Plorv could not tell if the sound was getting louder or just getting closer. He had hoped to board one of the aircrafts from the Lumkof before the crew released the collectors, but now he had to wait until the collectors were through.

Plorv situated himself as close to the entrance of one of Lumkof's aircrafts as he could. He made plans to protect himself if the collectors were released before he was safely on board an aircraft. He fashioned a domed-shaped structure, barely large enough for him and his supplies. Gogandu told the V.I.s that the collectors were winged insects. Plorv assumed that the recycled Venuvian metal would stand up to any insect's attack. His protective gear was about to be tested.

When the hum began to grow stronger, Plorv feared he had miscalculated. The hum became a roar, the roar became deafening. Plorv hoped that he would be able to lift his protective shelter long enough to have a look at the collectors. His curiosity quickly morphed into fear. His only thought now was to hold tightly to his protection and hope he would go unnoticed. He did not go unnoticed. Moments after he first heard the hum, a barbed spear half a meter long pierced his shelter. Plorv realized that if the size of the spear was any indication of the size of the insects, the collectors must be enormous. That was his last clear thought.

The giant spear jerked Plorv's shelter into the air with Plorv hanging on for his life. The insect flung Plorv and his shelter through the air. Plorv crashed into the branches of a tree and fell to the ground. The next few moments became indelibly etched in Plorv's memory. The fall dazed him and the limcra fumes began to seize his entire body. Then he heard the sound of ripping metal. He could see nothing.

Plorv began slipping into a warm, comfortable, narcotic-induced sleep. He wanted to let go and fall into the sensual abyss, but, somewhere deep inside, he heard a voice telling him to hold on and pull himself out of the stupor. Was it the voice of his Tambuki mentor, or was it his own voice, telling him to fulfill a promise? Whoever was calling him awakened the last bit of resistance in his being and gave him the strength to force open his eyes. What he saw was so terrible it jolted him back into a foggy reality.

Plorv saw a giant creature 10 meters away. It was undoubtedly a collector. It was a winged insect, and its dimensions were staggering. The proportions were similar to that of a common biting insect, but its size—its body was at least six meters long with a wingspan of four meters. The barbed spear protruded from its body another meter. Its grayish, translucent body was an unfilled reservoir. The creature's legs were covered with short coarse spikes of hair. They dangled uselessly under the giant insect's body. The gigantic protruding eyes sent shivers through Plorv. They dominated the collector's black leathery face. The eyes were examining Plorv. There was no expression, no feeling, just an unthinking stare.

The beast shot straight toward Plorv. Plorv had no time to react. The limcra intoxication left him paralyzed in the hypnotic trance. Plorv had no doubt his life was about to end. The collector abruptly stopped right in front of his face. He could feel the wind from the rapidly pulsating wings. Then, in a flash, the collector was gone.

Plorv's racing heart and his uncontrolled breathing assured him that his life had not yet been snatched away. His heart began to slow as his breathing returned to normal, but the fear was slow to fade. Then Plorv realized what was happening. The fog of the limcra vapors was reasserting its control over his mind and body.

Escape! I must escape.

His mind yelled at him but his unsteady legs refused to respond. He lost control and fell to the ground.

Escape, escape! Find a ship—find the sanctuary of a ship, thought Plorv.

It did not matter to Plorv whether he got to the Blastoc or to one of the Lumkof's aircrafts. As he vainly tried to pull himself to his feet, a group of Braks appeared. They were running in his direction. He could see the absolute terror in their eyes. He watched in horror as a collector appeared from nowhere. The giant insect, without hesitation, pierced the back of a Brak. In an instant, the color drained from the innocent giant's body as it shriveled into a lifeless heap. The bug shot backwards a few meters causing the Brak to fall from the collector's stinger. Immediately the collector darted forward and stabbed another victim. In a matter of minutes, the same monster had pierced 15 to 20 Braks and drained them of their blood.

The last to fall was a woman. She was only a few meters away from Plorv when the collector struck. Before she fell victim to the blood-engorged insect, Plorv got a good look at her. He could see the fear in her eyes. His eyes fell from her eyes to the supple smoothness of her giant, full-figured body. He found the sight of her bare undulating breasts extremely exciting.

The limcra tree was also a powerful aphrodisiac. For those few seconds he was totally engrossed in her beauty. Then, in an instant, the beauty was gone and a shriveled and lifeless body lay in front of him. Her fear-stricken eyes were wide open and staring into space. One of the collectors appeared centimeters in front of Plorv's face and just as quickly disappeared. That was Plorv's last memory. He slipped into a limcra-induced sleep.

◆

"Her mate's stay was a short one," said Krella.

Both Krella and KC had dropped their façades. They had grown so close over the years that they had become as one.

"Your mate had to see for himself," said KC. "Even the little he did see was more terrible than he imagined. It was a full-scale massacre of innocent beings. How could Gogandu allow this to happen? How could he order it to happen?"

"These collectors, are they terrible creatures?" asked Krella.

Krella was distressed by what the collectors were letting loose on the Braks. She was also worried by what she saw in KC's eyes.

"The creatures are not terrible," said KC. "They are doing what Krella's people have created them to do."

"These are not Krella's people," said Krella. "Why would you call them Krella's people? Why?" Krella did not wait for a response. "These Ortans have been separated from Ortan Travelers for thousands of years. No Ortan that Krella knows would ever condone the creation of such evil."

Krella had put on her façade and spoke in a calm, even voice, but KC knew he had inadvertently struck a sensitive nerve.

"Krella thinks the myths about the existence of escaped Ortans may have some truth," said Krella.

"Myths, what myths?" KC was immediately interested. "KC's love has never told him of any Ortan myths."

"As a child, Krella did not like the stories. They frightened her," said Krella. "She never thought the myths had any truth, but now Krella wonders."

"What were the myths?" asked KC.

"Children were told stories of how, in ancient times, some Ortans were driven from their home planet by their blood-sucking enemies. The stories said that the enemies have been searching for the escaped Ortans for one million years, and, when they find them, they will wait for them to go to sleep, and then they will suck out all their blood. The stories were so silly. As a child, Krella did not believe them. But now… , KC says these insects, these collectors, suck the blood from the Braks?"

"Yes."

"Krella is afraid," said Krella. Her façade was gone.

"Are there other stories?" asked KC.

"There are many. They are mostly the same. The Wikkas are always hiding."

"Wikkas?" asked KC.

"Yes, they call these ancient ones Wikkas. They will hide in every conceivable place—in trees, under rocks, in one's bed. Most stories say they will wait for one to fall asleep. They can also jump out, grab an unsuspecting victim and drag them away to suck out all their blood. Children pretended to be a Wikka to frighten other children."

"Was there ever any mention of winged insects sucking blood?" asked KC.

"No, no winged insects." Krella looked hopefully at KC. "What shall Krella and KC do?"

"They shall wait," said KC. "They shall wait."

Plorv felt waves of warm undulating pleasure wash over his body as the sweet vapors of the limcra tree filled his lungs. His mission felt so far away now. Then, slowly, the sweet dreams began to slip away. His stomach began to have spasms of pain that were growing more intense. A small pain in his head was expanding and taking over his consciousness. His head throbbed with every heartbeat. He opened his eyes, and the light from the late afternoon sun sent sharp pains shooting through his skull. His eyes were dry and scratchy, his mouth even dryer. He closed his eyes and took a deep breath. That helped for a few seconds but then he felt even worse.

Suddenly, he felt the blasts of air from another giant insect. It was right in front of him. He was afraid to open his eyes. Another spasm of pain attacked his stomach. He thought he was going to be sick. Plorv's newly exposed body was going through limcra over-intoxication. He felt like he was going to die. He wanted to die. Plorv would never forget what happened next. A firm hand grabbed his shoulder. Plorv turned and immediately felt a sense of relief. There stood Gogandu.

The dream of the towering white haired leader caused Plorv to bolt from the bed. He had to warn someone about Gogandu—but who? Plorv wondered where he was. He had to escape, but he did not even know if he was a prisoner. There was no time to think. He had to leave. Franticly, he began to search for an exit. He approached a wall, and a door slid opened. The light was blinding. He fell back into the room holding his throbbing head. The door closed behind him. After a few seconds, he stepped back into the brightly lit corridor. This time he shielded his eyes with a hand.

"The way you move is as important as the look in your eyes," Plorv's Tambuki mentor, Wildon, had said. "Each step you take reveals your thoughts. Control even the flicker of your fingers. Controlling the façade is power. Control, control, control."

The words of his mentor took control of Plorv. He removed his hand from his eyes and stood erect.

"Even if you have the vision of your own death, you must not let calmness leave your being, even for a second," Wildon had said.

Plorv wondered what had happened to him. How had he so completely lost control? Then he remembered the limcra fumes. They had taken control of him and dragged him into a stupor. He remembered the life-draining creature hovering in front of his face. Even as he recalled the terrifying vision of his death, his eyes remained calm.

◆

Welvek was nervous. He passed a few strange-looking non-Ortans in the corridors as he headed for the meeting with Gogandu. On his Ortan ship, the crew never mixed with the leaders. What if they had weapons? Since he was sure Gogandu did not have a weapon, it was inconceivable that the crew would be armed. Stuven's babbling snapped Welvek out of his thoughts.

"We are almost there," said Stuven. "Are you sure we are prepared? Is your weapon fully loaded? There are crew members everywhere." Stuven leaned close to Welvek and spoke in a conspiratorial whisper. "After you do the thing to Gogandu, these horrid creatures may turn against us. Oh, I wish we were back with our own Ortans."

Welvek glared at Stuven.

"If you don't be quiet, I will do THE THING to you before I do it to Gogandu." Stuven's eyes widened.

"What are you saying?" said Stuven.

"Just be quiet. Don't say another word until we are finished."

"Well," said Stuven.

His pudgy face tried to express a feeling of anger and insult. He was about to convey his feelings but the menacingly, stern look on Welvek's face stopped him before he could say a word. Instead, Stuven sank back into a state of anxiety. Welvek cautiously felt the weapon under his robe. In a few moments, he would do the deed. Then, without warning, Gogandu appeared.

"Greetings Welvek, greetings Stuven. Please relax."

What happened next seemed like a dream—or a nightmare. Before

Gogandu's words were completed, his hand had firmly grabbed Welvek's arm and twisted it inward. His other hand reached into Welvek's robes and pulled out the weapon. It happened so quickly. Welvek had no time to move, no time to think. Stuven let out a frightened shriek.

"Step inside the chambers," said Gogandu.

Gogandu stashed the weapon and directed Welvek and Stuven through an opening.

Besides Welvek and Stuven, there was only one person who knew what Gogandu had removed from Welvek's robes. That person was Plorv. He had decided to head towards Gogandu's chambers. He hoped he could unobtrusively observe Gogandu's activities. Maybe he would see something that would help him decide what his next move would be. The spaceship's sparse designs left few places for Plorv to secretly observe Gogandu. He was still wondering what he would do after he reached Gogandu's chambers when he saw something that almost caused his composure to slip. Gogandu approached Welvek and Stuven, and, in one quick and smooth, motion he touched Welvek's arm and removed a weapon from Welvek's robes.

Plorv's mind raced. What did this mean? Gogandu had disarmed the only ones Plorv thought could help him.

I must make the Ortan's aware of the truth—Gogandu is not a friend, thought Plorv. *He has an ulterior motive that would put the Ortans in danger.*

Now Welvek and Stuven were apparently Gogandu's prisoners. Plorv recalled his mentor's words.

"Surprise is the most powerful weapon a combatant can possess," Wildon had said. "A well-thought-out plan is the best when doing battle, but, when no plan exists—attack."

Plorv, without a thought of what he might do, walked purposefully toward Gogandu's quarters.

BB and Krella, façades in place, sat motionless watching Gogandu and the other two Ortans. Welvek dejectedly looked at the floor, head in hands.

Stuven rocked back and forth in his chair, repeatedly muttering, "Oh dear, oh my."

"There should be another arrival soon," said Gogandu, using Third Family dialect.

As usual, his demeanor was unreadable. The door slid open and Plorv walked in. Without breaking his stride, he headed straight toward Gogandu.

"I must speak with you Gogandu, and with you Welvek, and you also Stuven," said Plorv.

Welvek looked up with a look of distained puzzlement, and Stuven became even more nervous. Gogandu held up an outstretched arm, palm facing Plorv.

"Stop, Plorv. Sit and listen. When I am finished, you may speak with whomever you please."

Plorv stopped in his tracks. Not only Gogandu's outstretched arm but also his eyes, his words, his very being completely disarmed Plorv. Plorv sat. Gogandu turned to BB.

"We are preparing for a great battle," said Gogandu.

Though he was able to conceal his apprehension, BB felt as if Gogandu had taken control of him. Then, in an instant, Gogandu's features softened.

"BB has been chosen to play a most important part in that battle," said Gogandu.

"It is true, then!" Plorv said as he bolted to his feet. "You mean harm to the Ortans." Plorv turned to Welvek and Stuven. "You must stop him. He wants power for himself. He wants to control you and destroy you. I have known of his treachery since we left Tambuki." Plorv turned back to Gogandu. "My mission since birth has been to stop you, Gogandu, even before I knew who you were, even before I had ever seen your face. This is the moment I have trained for my whole life."

As he spoke, Plorv maneuvered himself into a position to attack Gogandu. Plorv was coiled like a tightly wound spring. Gogandu was nonplussed. Plorv's fist shot towards Gogandu's heart. Gogandu effortlessly picked off Plorv's attempted blow. He grabbed Plorv's wrist. With an iron tight grip, he twisted Plorv's arm to his side and grabbed a spot between his shoulder and his neck. Plorv let out a cry of pain.

"Please sit," said Gogandu.

Plorv, in an instant, was defeated. The pain in his shoulder and neck was intense, but it was the feeling of defeat that completely deflated Plorv. His life, his whole existence had become meaningless. Gogandu released his iron grip on Plorv. The cessation of pain bathed his body in unfamiliar warmth. He knew he had fallen under the control of Gogandu. He did not care. Gogandu continued talking as if there had not been an interruption.

"Stuven, tell us the story of the First Family," said Gogandu.

Stuven looked up at Gogandu. Gogandu had a trace of a smile. Stuven looked puzzled.

"There is no First Family." Stuven replied haltingly, "Only Second Family and Third Family."

Gogandu's smile, though still slight, broadened.

"Have you heard of the First Family?" asked Gogandu.

"There are stories, myths that there was a First Family but no one believes them," said Stuven.

"Tell us one of the stories," said Gogandu.

"I don't know, it has been so long," said Stuven. "Only young school boys talk about the First Family."

Stuven was searching his memory to recall what he could about the First Family.

"The first to discover blood fluid was Xytus," said Stuven. "He was a god who became the ruler of the first Ortans many thousands of years ago. He gave the Ortan's blood fluid. That must have been the First Family!"

Stuven had a look of accomplishment, as if he had just discovered something.

"Once Ortans learned how to prolong life and harness the power of fluid, an element in blood, Xytus returned to his Family of gods. There are other stories," said Stuven, looking questioningly at Gogandu.

"Yes, go ahead," said Gogandu.

Gogandu was enjoying Stuven's story. Not only was he smiling, he had a twinkle in his eyes.

"These are only stories," said Stuven. "I don't believe them myself. Some say Xytus actually stole the blood fluid from the gods and that he is still alive and lives underground in a secret place. He is waiting for the Ortans to become powerful enough to overthrow the gods so he can become all-powerful. Xytus cannot breathe because, if he does, the other gods will hear him, seek him out, and destroy him. So, every 1,000 years, he takes one deep breath. He holds that breath for another 1,000 years. They say, if you look into Xytus's eyes while he is taking his deep breath, you can gain the power of the gods. Of course these are only children's stories, and I don't believe them, but… "

"Thank you, Stuven," said Gogandu.

Stuven was warming up to his storytelling. He looked disappointed when Gogandu preempted him.

"There was indeed a man named Xytus," began Gogandu. "But he was not a god. He lived 5,000 years ago and he was a very wealthy and powerful Ortan. He was never the ruler of the Ortans, but his wealth was so great he exerted a great deal of influence on Orta. What is true now was true then—there are some things money cannot buy. For Xytus, it was good health. He was cursed with a rare malady, and the best doctors on the planet could not cure him. It was his blood. It degraded to a point where his body could no longer use it. His own blood became an enemy. All his blood-fed organs began to deteriorate. His doctors performed a number of blood transfusions that produced temporary relief, but the relief was short lived.

"His doctors made the decision to have Xytus's blood totally replaced on a regular basis—first once a day, then twice a day—until he was continually having his blood exchanged for new blood. His body stabilized, except for his eyes. His sight slowly faded. He had eye transplants. Then he added an artificial heart and had a liver replacement. His body parts continued to fail, and the doctors continued to replace them with transplants or artificial units. His body began to shrivel, his limbs atrophied, and he became chair bound. Yet he lived, and lived, and lived. An implanted voice box allowed him to communicate verbally. He used an eye movement recognition device to transmit data. New blood continued to flow."

Gogandu stopped. The twinkle had left his eyes. His face had become cold and gray.

"And then it happened," said Gogandu. "Xytus had reached his 178th year. His mind remained sharp. Some insisted his brilliance had grown more focused. Xytus had a 1000-year-old vase, which was one of his favorite possessions. Jokus, Xytus's personal aid for the last 70 years, for some reason, fainted, and, in an attempt to break his fall, he instinctively grabbed the nearest object to him—the vase. Xytus watched the whole incident transpire. He wanted to reach out and grab the vase but it was all the way across the room, and, more importantly, his arms were useless. However, instead of crashing on the floor, the treasured vase floated inches above the floor and then slowly moved back to its original position.

"As he passed into his 178th year, Xytus discovered that he had developed psychokinetic energies. The blood feeding continued, and Xytus's kinetic powers grew. By the time he reached 200 years, he could effortlessly move objects weighing hundreds of kilos. His body, which had shriveled to a skin-covered skeleton, was now encapsulated. If he desired, his capsule could travel faster than anything could on the planet, but there was a price to pay. The more he used his powers, the faster the blood flowing through his artificial veins deteriorated. His first attempt to accelerate speeds had almost killed him. His blood became unusable before he could return and replenish it. Until his death at 307 years, he was never again without access to large amounts of replacement blood."

"He died?" Stuven blurted. "He was not a god?"

"He was no god, Stuven, only a mortal like you," said Gogandu. "His death was sudden and unexpected. But the power to create fear in any who opposed him had not died."

"Where did Xytus get the blood to help keep him alive and feed his power?" asked Stuven.

"Don't be a fool, Stuven!" Welvek spat, still brooding over the failure of his plan. "He is just filling you with more silly stories."

Gogandu shot one of his harder than steel glances at Welvek who then returned to sullenly staring at the floor.

"Every minion, in all his many enterprises, was required to give blood monthly or risk being unemployed—or worse," continued Gogandu. "Xytus had an army of scientists working on his malady. As with many scientific endeavors, the scientist made discoveries that were unexpected. Scientists discovered that there was a very small area of Xytus's brain that became extremely active when he used his psychokinetic powers. They then found the element in blood that fed this area in his brain—Xytus fluid. Within 20 years of Xytus's death, scientists had learned how to extract the fluid from blood.

"Xytus's scientists were not the only ones working with the fluid. There were others. The leaders of three powerful Families believed that together they could form the most powerful Ortan union in the history of the planet. For 152 years, The Three Families combined their skills. They did not flitter away their powers flying through the air or moving mountains. In fact, they seldom left their secret underground bunker—they did not need to. Brilliant minds had long ago discovered how to focus kinetic energies into one power source. They used that energy to power their machines—machines that moved mountains, machines that flew through the air, machines that made other machines.

"The psychokinetic power of the three powerful Families energized legions of machines that were at their disposal. The Families had been secretly developing powers that they believed would help them take control of Orta. They had not yet fully tested these powers—until that monumental day. On that day, the planet witnessed an event that marked a change in Orta's history. On that day, the reign of Xytus ended. The powerful Xytus, who had controlled the planet with an iron grip for the last 200 years, was gone. Now there was no known force that could stand against The Three Families.

"Their power takeover was quick, effortless, and complete—almost complete. When The Three Families demonstrated their greater-than-Xytus powers, the ruling structures obediently fell under their control. People had become so accustomed to the rule of Xytus that few stood up to the takeover, but there were some who stayed hidden after the death of Xytus.

"For two hundred and eight years, another group of families had secretly collected fluid. For two hundred and eight years, their power grew. Then, after two hundred and eight years, they tried to take the control of Orta from The Three Families. That is when the First Blood War broke out. Other groups, which had also been secretly collecting fluid, also tried to exert their power. Treaties were created and broken. Then the two most powerful groups on Orta became one—The First Family. The First Family lasted for one hundred and two fitful years and then splintered into three competing rivals. Over the next three hundred and seventeen years, another group, the Second Family, ruled Orta. Then The Three Families reasserted their dominance over Orta. When fluid levels dropped to unacceptable levels, the smaller families had to submit to the control of The Three Families, later to become the Third Family.

"The Third Family reigned in the time of Gogandu's arrival. The Third Family rulers were tyrants. They mercilessly destroyed their rivals and suppressed any activity that in any way opposed their control. The Third Family forcibly extracted fluid from every living Ortan. In the seven hundredth year of the Third Family rule, a schism developed between those who though that fluid should be forcibly extracted and those who felt it should be given freely. Those who felt that blood was a personal possession called themselves the Freestones. The Third Family was preparing to crush the Freestones when the Freestones disappeared.

"For hundreds of years the Third Family believed that someday the Freestones, known to some as the Fourth Family, would return. There were groups from the Fourth Family, the Freestones, that stayed behind while the others made a massive exodus into deep, unexplored space. The few who remained behind went deep underground. They believed that someday the Fourth Family would return for those who had stayed.

"Highly disciplined and well-trained Freestone sects kept the memories of the Fourth Family alive. They studied and trained and waited for the return of the Fourth Family. There was very little communication among the Freestones. 'Every second of every day be prepared for our return,' was the instruction left by the Elders. The Freestones who were left behind have waited, and waited, and waited. Their perseverance will soon be rewarded, and their waiting will end."

Stuven sat enthralled with Gogandu's story. Even Welvek had shown some interest. The story meant nothing to Plorv. He was still confused and conflicted.

"Are Gogandu and BB part of the Forth Family's Plan?" asked BB.

"Yes," said Gogandu emotionlessly. "And the time draws near when the Fourth Family must take action. BB will be asked to make a decision that could determine the future of the galaxy."

"Will BB be part of a carnage as great as what has happened here on Valis?" asked BB.

"Greater," replied Gogandu without hesitation.

"And, if this V.I. refuses to be a part of the Plan... ?" asked BB.

"Then the battle will take place without BB, and the chances of success will be diminished."

"What is Gogandu's Plan?" asked BB.

"It is not Gogandu's Plan," said Gogandu. "Gogandu is only a facilitator. Those who he serves have one very strong tenet: every V.I. and every Associate shall have freedom of choice except for the one requirement."

"Monthlies?" asked BB.

"Monthlies," said Gogandu.

◆

BB just wanted to keep listening to Gogandu's voice. He was falling, falling from nowhere to nowhere, and he did not care. The feeling was unusual, but he had experienced it before. What had been frightening now felt mildly comfortable. Then he was in the white, endlessly expansive room. Was it a room? He could not see the walls or the ceiling or the floor, just white.

"BB has questions?"

BB did not hear an audible voice, yet he heard every word telepathically and knew exactly what someone or something was communicating to him. He could not move or speak.

Gogandu has put me in a trance, thought BB. *He has hypnotized me.*

"Gogandu is only a conduit to the Elders," again the non-audible telepathic voice, which actually was not just one voice. *"Indeed there are five voices."*

"Where is BB?" BB spoke voicelessly and in the Way, as did the voices.

"They do not know. It could be dangerous for them to know."

"What is the Plan?" BB wondered.

"They will return to Orta to support those left behind—the Free-stones. There is only one way to return—destroy the Third Family."

"Is there no chance for peace?"

"There is none. The carnage you have seen on Valis, the Third Family Ortans regularly duplicate in 137 other systems. The Third Family has cloned over eight billion Braks solely for the purpose of extracting fluid. On Orta, billions of Braks spend their entire lives in robotic boxes. From birth until death, these beings never see real life. Their only purpose is to feed blood fluid to Third Family Ortans."

"What is his part in the Plan?" queried BB. *"BB thought the Free-stones were peaceful Ortans."*

"They are seeking peace for the many at the expense of a few."

"Why do they think he would agree to destroy even a few?"

"He has seen the unfeeling mass destruction of the Braks with his own eyes. The Third Family regularly engages in hundreds of such destructions on other worlds. On Orta, the Third Family breeds Braks who will never see the light of day—solely for their fluid. Billions of lost souls are milked of their blood to feed the Third Family's unstoppable thirst for fluid."

"What is their Plan?"

The unseen voices had so far replied without hesitation. This time BB sensed a controlled reluctance.

"Once they have revealed their Plan, they must put a control on BB's free will. They may find it necessary to erase memories, supplant them with different memories, and place controls on his future actions."

"They can control thoughts and actions?"

"Yes," came the reply. *"He must agree to permit such controls before he sees the Plan."*

"Could they control BB's actions and commit him to the Plan against his will?" asked BB.

"They could, but that is not the Way, and forced actions are not as secure. BB has powers he is not yet aware of, powers that could defeat forced control."

BB thought of Gogandu and how his words and demeanor could control others. Moreover, Gogandu's physical strength—where did it come from? Did BB have such powers? BB did not know the Plan yet, but, from the beginning, he had never considered not being part of it.

"He understands and submits to their control," said BB. *"He has felt their presence before in conjunction with great fear. If these feelings were his own and not those of others, he accepts their stipulations."*

"BB's visions were a result of his ability to communicate with Elders. That is why he was chosen."

The white immediately faded and was replaced with a black, star-sprinkled sky. Prominent in the sky were brightly glowing asteroids.

The voices continued. *"Every 172 years these asteroids pass through the Third Family-controlled system of Onkor. Occasionally, one of the larger asteroids enters the atmosphere of Onkor. One such piece of the space debris will be BB. After he has landed on Onkor, he will go through some training, and then he will board a Third Family ship that will take him to planet Orta."*

"How will he do that?"

"His powers are immense. The Elders will channel energies through BB that they have created over the last 2,007 years. After he arrives on Orta, he will lose all conscious awareness of his powers."

"Will he have the ability to subdue the Third Family pilots?"

"Effortlessly. BB will proceed to the heart of the Third Family's power and initiate the Plan."

"The Plan," BB mused. *"And what is the Plan?"*

"The Plan will be revealed to him when he reaches the destination."

There was a sudden change in the communication.

"Now the Elders will give him the past and present conditions on Orta," said the voices.

The stars and the asteroids dissolved. In that instant, BB knew the beginning of the Third Family Ortans' lust for the life-extending element in blood. He knew of the beginning Families, of the wars, the waste, and the slavery.

Ortan Families started as a quasi-volunteer network of Ortans who regularly donated blood to the few who, with the help of fluid, grew more powerful as they aged. Different groups recruited volunteers with the promise of protection from other groups. Competing groups formed alliances to become more powerful—the more blood, the more fluid; the more Elders, the more power.

Certain events radically altered the fluid paradigm. First, three powerful groups secretly united their powers. Once their connections were complete, the new group, in one fell swoop, destroyed any groups that had even a minute chance of opposing their power.

The second change followed the Ortan scientists' creation of genetically engineered giants capable of reproducing. This new race of people became a major source of fluid. They were the Braks. The Third Family placed the Braks on limcra-tree planets to breed and multiply. The addictive limcra fruit stimulated and nourished them. They were not volunteers.

The Braks on the limcra-tree planets were the lucky ones. They at least had a chance to see the sky and breathe fresh air and have a family. Billions more never left Orta. From birth until their eventual death, they were the primary segment of the Ortan fluid production. They spent their entire lives suspended in liquid, nourished through a tube, and continually drained of their blood. They were living, breathing, thinking, and even dreaming beings. They were not volunteers.

The Braks' production of fluid enabled larger and larger numbers of Ortans to obtain fluid and to live longer lives. These longer-living Ortans, who controlled fluid, became the Third Family aristocracy. They ruthlessly guarded their power and brutally crushed opposition to the enslavement of the Braks. Only the Freestones or the Fourth Family managed to survive. For a hundred years, they refused to accept any fluid from the giant Braks. They could see that it was only a matter of time before the Third Family crushed them, so they fled en masse. A few from the Fourth Family remained behind. They went underground and formed small, dedicated, secret societies that followed the Fourth Family Way. They are called "Freestones."

After the departure of the Fourth Family, the Third Family Ortan aristocracy became more powerful and more rigid than ever. *Donations* of blood became universal and mandatory. Those who were not part of the aristocracy received little benefit from the energy generated by the flu-id-fed Elders. The Third Family used massive amounts of the fluid for Elder energy to protect Orta from what the Third Family said would be the eventual return of the Fourth Family. After thousands of years, most believed that the return of the Fourth Family was a myth, but the Ortan aristocracy used the fear of the return of the Fourth Family to justify their rigid control of power. After 1,000 years, the Third Family Ortans cautiously expanded to other systems to plant the Braks. The planting, collection, and transportation of fluid used half of what was collected, but limcra planets still accounted for an important source of fluid.

The Third Family expansion into new planetary systems for the pur-pose of planting limcra trees and Braks was slow and limited by the distances between the systems. In contrast, the escaping Fourth Fami-ly, in their desire for rapid escape, discovered that, if a number of El-ders focused their kinetic powers, they could jump long distances, light years, and travel through rips in the space-time continuum. The Fourth Family still does not know exactly how this process works, but they know it requires huge amounts of fluid. The more the Elders use their kinetic powers, the more fluid they expend. They learned to use other forms of energy and used fluid primarily for jumps. The Fourth Family also learned how to produce one molecule of synthetic fluid for every naturally produced molecule of fluid. The process doubled the amount of available fluid. The Fourth Family stored vast surpluses of fluid in preparation for their return to Orta.

"Who are the volunteer fluid donors?" BB continued the commu-nication.

There was again a pause in the thought flow.

"When a new planet becomes part of the Fourth Family, the Fourth Family collects all the available medical data," came an answer. *"They share the medical advances that have been gathered from every system they encounter, medical advances that allow the inhabitants to live three to four times longer than before the Ortans arrival."*

"Monthlies?"

"Yes," came the response. *"All organs are monitored and rejuve-nated, external and internal bodily secretions are analyzed, and fluid is removed.*

"Not voluntarily."

"All those who come in contact with the Fourth Family have a choice to become an Associate or a Venuvian Integrate. But the fluid removed at the Monthlies is not voluntarily."

BB understood the rationale behind this breach in Fourth Family Ways, but he knew that they could be controlling his thoughts with their nonverbal communication powers.

"Some of the fluid that is recovered is used for Elders chosen from the planets where mother ships are being built," continued the voices. *"BB's planet, Tambuki, because of its special status, receives considerably more fluid than other planets. The Venuvians have fed fluid to BB and other Masters of the Way for many years. Someday he will become an Elder. The war is drawing near. If the Fourth Family and the Freestones fail, BB will die, or worse."*

"Worse?"

"The Third Family Ortans have mastered the ability to activate and control the body's pain centers," said the voices. *"That power enables them to inflict unimaginable pain. Even with BB's Tambuki training, he could not resist the powerful Third Family."*

"The Elders must know of some power that BB possesses," said BB.

"Yes, he has great powers, but he is young. As he ages, his powers will grow. Until that time, BB must protect his identity. Without his help there is less of a chance for the Plan to succeed."

The Plan... , the Plan. BB was back in the room with Gogandu and the others. No time had passed, but BB had become a different person. BB's eyes met Gogandu's eyes, and BB knew that Gogandu was aware of BB's change.

◆

"Stuven and Welvek must prepare to leave," said Gogandu.

"Leave?" said Stuven anxiously. "Where are we going?"

"Welvek and Stuven will never see Orta again," said Gogandu.

Welvek jolted from his deep thoughts.

"Will we die?" he said with no sign of emotion.

"Someday all that lives must die," said Gogandu. "The crew of Space-ship Blastoc will remain here and work on a project to rehabilitate the remaining Braks and to rid the planet of the limcra trees. Of course, Welvek and Stuven will have some limitations on their freedom, but otherwise they will live their lives in peace."

"And me?" asked Plorv. He had awakened from his reverie.

"The same is true for Plorv, but, before Plorv can find peace, the Tambukian will have to overcome the poison that has been pumped into him since birth."

Plorv's head dropped back into his hands, and he again fell into the stupor of depression. Gogandu looked at BB.

"It is time for BB to prepare for another journey, one that may well determine the future of our galaxy."

◆

BB sat in Gogandu's private quarters. The plain gray Venuvian walls were bare except for two blank video displays. These were not Gogandu's sleeping quarters. Did Gogandu sleep? BB only knew that this was the only room that was reserved for Gogandu. BB had long ago given up trying to understand who Gogandu was or where he came from. BB was sure Gogandu now knew what the Plan was.

"BB will have to cut short the lives of hundreds of millions of Ortans." Gogandu spoke softly to BB and paused while BB digested his words. "He will take the Lumkof and pilot it to an outlying area of the Third Family. When the path of the spaceship passes though the asteroid belt, he will leave the ship, become a piece of asteroid debris and land on Onkor as it passes though the asteroid belt. The Freestones will meet BB. After some training, BB will board an Ortan ship that will take him to planet Orta. He will infiltrate Orta and set off a series of actions that will eventually destroy the fluid-fed Ortans. That is the Plan."

"Why was this V.I. chosen?"

"BB was born of an Ortan, and he has the appearance of an Ortan," said Gogandu. "He was also chosen by the Elders because he possesses certain innate abilities."

"What innate abilities?

"This, Gogandu does not know."

BB wondered if the horrifying visions he had during his first "jump" had anything to do with his innate abilities.

◆

Luku was doing the same thing his father had done. His father had done what Luku's grandmother had done. His grandmother had done what her aunt had done. From every generation, for hundreds of generations, Luku's family had chosen someone as a Sky Watcher. Luku was the pick of his generation. He had been the one in the family to whom the Elders gave this sacred duty. It was more than a tradition, and it was more than a ritual—it was part of the Plan for the return of the Fourth Family.

Luku was a Sky Watcher. He scoured the night sky looking for anything unusual. Some night, something would appear in the sky, something that signaled the return of the Fourth Family, something that would start the Plan in motion. Luku had been studying the skies for 73 years. He was 100 years old before members brought him into the secret society that awaited the Fourth Family's return, and 150 years old before he learned of the Sky Watchers. He now knew every object in the nighttime sky.

The Plan said that the Freestones would not need visual aids to spot the sign. Luku knew the shifts and the cycles of every object in the sky. He understood the invisible clockwork that followed every movement in the sky. The two Sky Watchers, who had trained Luku, passed on to him the changes that would take place in the evening sky, even the changes that would not happen in his lifetime. There were always two Sky Watchers in every area, and they were never in the same place— part of the Plan.

There had been false signs in the past, such as an unexpected piece of debris from a past millennium that blazed a fiery trail across the sky and crashed onto Onkor. Nothing had proved to be the true signal. Nothing initiated the engagement of the Plan.

Luku was growing old. He was already training a new one to become a Sky Watcher. Someday, Luku would tell the new one about the

Plan, and, if the Elders approved, the new one would become fully accepted into Onkor's oldest, most secret society.

Luku had begun reflecting on his life. He even let himself question the necessity of his duty. What if the Fourth Family never returns? What if circumstances had somehow destroyed his fleeing ancestors? The younger Luku would never have allowed these thoughts to enter his mind. Now, as the remaining years of his life dwindled, he had let doubt seep into the outer reaches of his consciousness. Then, when his doubt was about to take form, something happened. It was after his second donation. First *donation* was to the Third Family. Second donation was to the secret Freestone Elders. On that day, a very young boy, not even in his manhood, appeared at Luku's side. When he looked up at Luku, the boy's eyes were not those of a boy but those of a wise one.

"Do not fear your doubts," said the boy. "Keep your thoughts clear."

As quickly as he appeared, he was gone. Was he real or a vision? Luku did not know what to do. Did the Elders send a spirit to help him open his thoughts or was it just a boy who was wise for his age? Luku would never know.

One night Luku took his spot on the mountain peak that allowed him a full view of the western sky. As was his habit, he began to identify every constellation. Botes Bear to the south, Two Dogs in the west, the Mighty Hand, Sisters' Eyes—distant galaxies, stars, and planets he had watched nightly for years—always in their places, never an exception.

And then it happened. The corner of his eye caught a movement in the sky. He watched as the object's tail flashed across the sky. The object could have been a piece of debris from the asteroid belt that had for millenniums been destined to end its life in the Onkor atmosphere. Or the Forth Family could have made it look like a piece of space junk. Then, in a fraction of a second, the streak of light turned bright green and abruptly ended. Luku knew what it was. The unique bright green color was the sign. He had to perform the ritual that he and those before him knew how to perform flawlessly. This time Luku knew it was not a ritual. It was a key part of the Plan.

After Luku carefully took note of the trajectory of the object, he jumped to his feet and swiftly and gracefully raced down the hill. He had to go to Satua, an Elder Sky Watcher, and seek—no, *demand* presence with the Elders. Satua was the Gate Keeper for the entrance to the Elders' chambers. Another Sky Watcher would immediately understand the urgency of the matter.

"I must be present with the Elders, I have seen the object." Satua looked at Luku for only a moment and then Satua sprang to her feet and disappeared into the chamber. Luku was still standing, breathing heavily. His heart was pounding from his run down the mountainside and from the realization of what was happening. He had put the wheels of the Plan in motion. After thousands of years, what his people had prepared for had arrived.

"The Elders await," said Satua.

Luku quickly walked down a dimly lit corridor. Even coming in from the night air, he felt a chill. Luku entered the Elders' chambers. The chill and the silence hid the underlying power contained in the room. But Luku knew that there was indeed great power present. In the dim light, he could see the chamber's circular shape. Twelve tinted, semi-capsules bordered the walls of the chambers. A BioDroid stood behind each semi-capsule. Luku knew that, in each capsule, there was an Elder. Every one of these Elders was at least 300 years old. Their bodies were barely more than a memory, but the fluid of millions had fed their brains. Each capsule contained an entity with more contained energy than the galaxy had ever seen in one being. Even the Elders themselves did not yet know the magnitude of their power.

The chamber Luku stood in was replicated tens of thousands of times throughout that part of the galaxy. Together, these chambers were the only force that could rescue the Freestones from the Third Family. Before Luku arrived, all but one of the Elders had been in a state of suspended animation. Because the fluid that extended their life and that gave their power was so precious, only one Elder stayed active until there was a real need for all 12. Luku stood in the center of the room.

"They have arrived," said Satu.

Luku felt a shift in the chamber—not a physical shift, but an indescribable change in some unseen balances. Then, from the shadows behind one of the capsules stepped a tall sinewy figure. His white, braided hair hung behind him to his waist, his bushy white eyebrows loomed above his golden Ortan eyes. The giant round eyes revealed nothing, even to a trained non-Ortan. Luku's teacher told him that every Elder had a BioDroid clone. Each clone was a stand-in for an Elder.

"We are sure that you saw the item and that the Third Family did not detect it," said the BioDroid. "We must greet them and make them safe."

Them, it was always *them*. Not *he* or *she*, but *them*. They, the Freestones, would arrive in great numbers. A league of Ortans would return to free their suppressed tribe. At some point in ancient history, the Freestones had become the Fourth Family. But there was not a league of Freestone warriors ready to battle for freedom. There was only one person sent to do battle with the powerful Third Family. That person was BB.

◆

"You have calculated the impact of the object," said Parl, an expert on oceans. It was not a question. "We will leave now and arrive at the contact spot before the sun rises. Plans are being made to infiltrate the arrivals into a Third Family vehicle."

"What is my role?" asked Luku.

"You will teach them our ways and the ways of the Third Family," said Parl.

"And my sky watching?"

"If they have arrived, there will be no further need for Sky Watchers."

◆

Torzerg watched the display monitoring all incoming objects.

"There's another big blip entering the perimeter, it's the 23rd since I came on," said Torzerg.

"More junk from the asteroid belt. Ignore it," said Maskin.

"But we are supposed to report every incursion," said Torzerg.

"Those archaic regulations have been around forever. They are supposed to protect us from some long lost mythical enemies who are going to descend on the Third Family someday. It's just the leaders trying to keep us occupied. We have an equipment check. Send in a report after we finish the equipment check, if you want to waste your time."

A Freestone had entered the Onkor boundary—undetected. The Plan was under way.

BB waited for the color change on the indicator of his entry cocoon. The cocoon had protected him from the freezing cold of deep space and the fiery entrance into Onkor's atmosphere. It had only partially protected him from intense vibration and the jarring halt. His body ached all over, but he had survived. He had entered without any mechanical devices that might have aroused the Third Family's suspicions.

Even though it felt like this vehicle had collided with a solid object, BB knew he had hit the surface of the ocean and was now deep in ocean water off an Onkorian coast. The temperature color-indicator had quickly changed from entry heat to ocean cold. Now all that BB had to do was to wait for the Onkorians to retrieve him and release him from his cucumber-shaped prison. Then, for the first time, it occurred to him that, if the next step in the Plan failed, he would be taking his last breaths in this unimpressive space vehicle. The entry vehicle would become his tomb.

The Plan was clear and well designed. He assumed that the Freestones would perform all tasks with the highest possible precision. But what if he had entered the airspace so stealthily that he had not only been undetected by the Third Family but also been unseen by those who were supposed to rescue him? It had been over 3,000 years. What if they had stopped looking or, over the millennium, had forgotten the Freestones' duty? What if people had come to think of them as a myth? In that case, no one would come to free BB. BB felt very alone.

Parl and Luku slipped into the icy ocean waters. The inky darkness was beginning to retreat from the onslaught of the new day. Based on Luku's observations, the calculations had placed the unit nearby. Three other teams were converging on the suspected landing site. Luku could not fully contain his excitement. He was about to become part of Ortan history. The Freestones had been waiting for thousands of years for this event. He was about to set in motion a chain reaction from which there could be no turning back. The Freestones were about to rise up and challenge a system that most thought was invincible. When they discovered the object they were looking for, the Plan would be set in motion. Luku did not know the details of the Plan, no one but the Elders knew.

Parl, Luku's companion, stopped the descent toward the ocean bottom. He was motioning toward an unobtrusive object on the ocean floor. Parl spent as much time scouring the ocean floor as Luku spent watching the skies. At first, Luku saw nothing unusual, only the rocky outcrops scattered below. An occasional banubub lazily swam by. Though banububs were large and fierce-looking fish, Luku knew they were harmless. Then he saw why Parl had stopped. Amid the random debris of rocks and the towering coastal sea plants swaying with the movements of water, he saw an object that was out of place. It had the same colorless appearance as the surrounding landscape, but its shape was unusual. It was an ellipse with one tapered end. It was lodged between two boulders. His perspective from under water made it difficult for Luku to judge the exact size of the object, but, even from a distance, it was possible to see that the object was not very large. A bizarre thought flashed through Luku's mind. What if the Forth Family had created a way to miniaturize themselves? Luku was so giddy with anticipation that he laughed to himself for having such an outlandish thought. But how could a craft that could hold no more than two people help his people get from under the yoke of the callous Third Family? This was not the league of Elder warriors Luku had expected. In fact, no one with whom Luku had ever dared discuss the Plan expected less. What could so few do against so many? How could the Plan succeed?

◆

Asel and Bekas prepared to take off for Orta. They had informed the Elders of the destination coordinates. Flight time to outer atmosphere was 17.45 home time units. The drivers dreaded the trip, the painful reaction to sudden accelerations, the brain rattling vibration, the incredible headaches that followed the trip. They were only drivers. They were expendable. They were less valuable than the machines and equipment that they had delivered to Onkor. They were only there in case there was a minor malfunction. The Elders would handle major failures.

"Are you ready for the trip?" Asel asked Bekas sarcastically.

"No," Bekas replied bluntly. "Let's make our final check so we can get the ride over with."

Bekas began to study the three panels that displayed the ship's system status. Asel started checking the cargo containers and the bay hatches to ensure that all hatches were sealed and all transport containers were secure and ready for the trip. One insufficiently closed hatch or loose container and the resulting vibration during the trip could damage the ship and make the trip even more painful for the minimally protected drivers. The Elders, of course, had a liquid cushion that protected them from the vibrations. Asel knew that the Third Family and the Elders were always protected.

Asel was about to check the last row of containers when he heard a noise—a noise he had heard many times before—the sound of a container door sealing. He should have already sealed all the doors. Instinctively, his hand felt for the key at his side. It was there. Without the key, which he now clutched tightly, only the control room could seal a door remotely. Neither Asel nor Bekas had ever sealed a door remotely. On the final inspection, a driver had to personally secure every door. Asel was sure he had checked every door, but, if he heard a door seal, it meant he had left one open. Had he forgotten to seal a door?

"Bekas, did you just now seal a door?"

"What do you mean?" said Bekas.

"I just heard a door seal," said Asel.

"You must have missed one." As soon as he said it, Bekas realized how unrealistic his statement was. It was next to impossible for an unclosed door to go undetected.

"No," replied Asel, his mind searching for possible answers. "Maybe there was a malfunction."

It was almost a question. Both men were thinking the same thing. If a door came open during the trip, the vibrations would damage the ship, and they could be severely injured—or worse. Neither man cared about the ship.

"I'm going to check every door again, Bekas. I will inform the Elders of the delay, then I will come back to help."

They checked and double-checked every door. They did not detect any malfunctions. All doors were secure. No doors were open. A door that had been closed had been opened and then closed—but not by either of the drivers.

◆

BB slowly sank to the floor. He had made it aboard the ship and successfully stowed away. Everything had gone according to the Plan.

"When you approach the ship's loading area, assume the all superior mode," said Vope who was appraising BB on how to board the ship that would be departing for Orta.

"The standing superior position?" asked BB.

"Yes," said Vope. "You must tell the personnel stationed at the entrance that you are to be allowed to board. You do assume the Way positions on a regular basis?"

"BB takes the positions every day," replied BB.

"You will disarm the person with your stance. Use all your power to direct the driver. Instruct him to open a storage door, allow you to enter, and then to forget, forget all that has happened."

BB heard the words and understood their meaning, but what was he supposed to do with them. Everything had happened so quickly. His removal from the coffin-like vehicle, in which he had arrived, had been quick and precise. He changed his clothes to fit Ortan style while Vope instructed him on his immediate itinerary.

Then the world stopped. BB was in the white nothingness, the glaringly quiet white room. He could feel power swelling within him, but, at the same time, he felt powerless and frozen.

Again spoke the five Elder voices. *"BB has been trained to focus his powers until they are laser sharp. BB will use these powers to board a ship bound for Orta. Once BB has reached Orta, all his powers will become dormant. They will replace all memory of BB's previous life with new memories. If any hint of BB's abilities is detected, the Plan will be aborted."*

"What will BB do when he arrives on Orta?" As soon as his words came out, BB knew the answer would be waiting.

"The answer will be waiting."

BB was back. What had happened? Where had he been? He now stood in front of an Ortan ship. As a driver approached him, he assumed the superior stance. His whole being radiated a force that engulfed the driver.

"I will board your ship, you will open a door to an empty storage area, and you will lose all your memory of my presence."

Asel did not say a word. Later he wondered why he had left the ship. He felt as if he had just missed something. Then he heard the sound of a door sealing.

BB continued to hold his posture until he had entered the storage room. He immediately relaxed his posture. BB was surprised at the energy he had expended to assume a posture for such a short time. He let the tension drain from his body—then he sealed the door.

ORTA

Loosk had been ruminating on how long he would live. His mother and father had made it into their seventies—a feat for drivers who actually made jumps in Third Family spaceships. Loosk was lucky. Unlike other drivers, whose jobs contributed to their short lives, he worked in one of the thousands of fluid production centers. Anyone who did work that no Third Family member would do was called a "driver."

It was Loosk's and his crew's job to make sure that 95 percent of the 20,000 Brak units continually produced the quota of fluid for the Third Family. Eventhough equipment failure was rare, Loosk had become quite proficient at repairs. Daily disposal of the hundreds of expired and terminated units was what wore on him. Capsules, which contained the gelatinous masses that had been a supplier of blood for 40 or 50 years, had to be flushed, sterilized, and made ready for the next Brak *donor*. Loosk had long since given up regarding the units as living beings. They were just chunks of flesh that the Third Family had sentenced to supplying fluid to the Ortans lucky enough to be born into the aristocracy. Drivers, like Loosk, got none of the life-extending fluid. Except for their *donated* blood, drivers like Loosk were expendable. Moric stuck his head into the cramped room that served as the center's headquarters.

"We have 137 expired," said Moric, Loosk's number one assistant.

Loosk looked up from his table. Loosk had stuffed the room with tools and parts. A single light hung from the ceiling.

"You and Kay flush and stuff," said Loosk. "Do we have enough replacements?"

"Receiving got 100 replacement units in today, all producing," said Moric. The pupils of his big golden eyes expanded and contracted.

"We were supposed to get 200!" shouted Loosk. "How do they expect us to make our quota if they don't send us enough units?"

Moric shrugged and turned to leave.

"Moric, "said Loosk.

"Yes."

"How old are you?"

"Fifty-seven," Moric replied with a slight look of surprise. "Why?"

"How long do you expect to live?" asked Loosk.

"As long as I can, maybe 20 or 30 more years," said Moric. "Is this a survey the Family is taking? Maybe now they think we count for something."

"Do you know how long a member of the Third Family lives?" asked Loosk.

"Two hundred, maybe two hundred fifty years," said Moric.

"Do you ever think of Braks as living beings?" asked Loosk, more to himself than to Moric. Moric's eyes began to shutter.

"No," answered Moric.

For a brief moment, Loosk felt as if he could feel Moric's thoughts.

"Watch what you say Loosk," said Moric. "If the Family detected your words, they might think that you are an ancient one returning to release the Braks."

"Do you believe those stories?" asked Loosk.

"Of course not."

Moric's eyes shuttered again. He turned to leave.

"Moric," said Loosk.

Moric stopped, but he did not face Loosk.

"What?"

"I'll be gone for a while," said Loosk.

"What?!" said Moric.

Moric spun and faced Loosk. His countenance had gone from irritation to surprise.

"Who is going to work on the equipment?" asked Moric. He looked worried.

"You."

"I can't repair things like you," said Moric. "We won't be able to make the quota."

Moric's voice had turned to panic. "If I drop below the quota, I could be transferred. I'll never make another 20 years if Family moves me to some other job. How long will you be gone?"

"Family wants me to help out the centers that are below quota."

"That would be every center!" said Moric.

"You are going to take my place someday," said Loosk.

"I'm not ready yet," said Moric. "I have a mate and two offspring." He was beginning to sound desperate. "They could put me on one of those transport jumpers. Have you ever seen one of those drivers after 20 jumps? They might as well be dead. I'm just not ready yet."

"You will be. You have to be," said Loosk.

"Loosk, you have some special talent," said Moric. "I have always marveled at how quickly you repair things. You're different, Loosk." Loosk was indeed different, very different.

◆

It was late. Loosk was tired. He had been working non-stop for 715 days. He had been to over 7,000 centers, repairing units, and briefing techs. He was ready to go back to his home center. Moric had been running problems by Loosk almost every day, and Moric was starting to fall apart. Loosk was worried about Moric. Moric had held up, but he needed Loosk's help.

"Moric, how is the station?" asked Loosk on his communication device.

"Is that you, Loosk?" Moric spat out his words. "We need you. We were below the quota on the last three audits. Please come back."

"I just have to complete a few tests and go over some data. I'll be back to celebrate Victory. I can't wait."

"Let's really celebrate," Moric said, greatly relieved.

"This Victory celebration, everything is on me," said Loosk.

◆

Loosk was glad to be back. The trip home had taken less time than he had expected, but he felt physically and mentally drained. As the transport neared his home site, he began to think about the millions of *donors* inside the underground structure that stretched for kilometers. For years, he had managed to suppress his thoughts about the giant creatures who supplied most of the blood from which Ortans extracted fluid. Today, for some reason, his mind's eye was conjuring up images of the innocent victims. The Third Family considered it treason to speak of Braks as anything but willing volunteers, sacrificing themselves for the good of the Third Family.

Loosk was looking forward to meeting with Moric. Loosk welcomed the time to relax, even if Moric would be going on and on about how much he missed Loosk. Loosk relished the idea of not having to think about work, even if it would only be for a few hours.

◆

Primis examined the latest purity readings. He always paid attention to every detail, a trait that had put him in an extremely important position.

"Learn everything you can about fluid," Primis's mother would say. "We will always need fluid."

Primis had listened. He had studied every aspect of fluid. He was the leading expert on the subject. He knew where fluid went, and he knew where it came from. Others active in the field came to Primis to learn more. Before any Third Family member received a drop of fluid, Primis had examined hundreds of samples. As important as his job was, others in his field found its repetitive nature boring. Not Primis, he loved the fact that every single sample was exactly the same.

That is why Primis was concerned. Today he noticed that there was a minute deviation in one of the samples. The result was within specifications but it was slightly different. It could have been caused by a trace of a substance left by the sterilization process, a slightly out-of-calibration testing apparatus or a failing component. Whatever the reason, Primis had to solve the mystery—something was different.

First, he tested the final step of fluid production—purification assessment. He used different test substances in the high-precision instruments. All results were exactly the same—perfectly within specification. Next, he tested the instruments that washed out all impurities from fluid. Again, the same exact results. Primis tested and retested every step of the process that produced fluid. All that Primis had left to test was the source of fluid—blood. The task was enormous. There were 7,031 Brak donation stations on Orta supplying blood with over 2,000 Braks per station. And there were over 4.353 billion drivers who gave monthly *donations*. The task was daunting, but Primis was determined.

◆

"Primis, you've been working too hard, why don't you take a break? The lab can do without you for a few hours," said Zremus.

Zremus was the only technician who even tried to communicate with Primis.

"The Miras Group is having a night gathering in two days to celebrate Victory," said Zremus.

Victory was short for Third Family Victory of Peace, Unity, and Order.

"There will be hundreds there," said Zremus. "No one will even know you. You won't even have to talk. You just need to get away from the lab."

"I have been getting some odd readings. I really need to find the problem," said Primis.

"I know. Everybody knows," said Zremus. "The problem that isn't even a problem. I'm beginning to worry about you. I know you are a fanatic, but spending all your time examining a problem that is well within specification is extreme even for you."

"I have never seen any deviation, even one this small. I must find the cause," said Primis.

"It could be an insignificant component that is starting to decay."

"No!" Primis slammed his fist on a table. "It is not a component."

The anger quickly left Primis's words. He was thinking, thinking out loud.

"There is some kind of pattern," said Primis. "Individual batches changed at different times. A failing component could not explain that. There has to be some other explanation. Some batches have not changed. I have examined all the batches three times, and every time there are more batches that have failed."

"Primis!" said Zremus. "They have not failed! There are only differences that don't matter."

Zremus could see that he was not getting through to Primis. He could see that faraway look in Primis's large golden eyes.

"We could go to a driver celebration," said Zremus. "I am sure you could find a driver who would do anything you wanted for a shot of fluid."

"What!" shouted Primis. "That is treason to even think such a thing."

Primis did not notice the smile on Zremus's face.

"I know, I know," said Zremus. "Even I wouldn't be that foolish. I was just trying to get your attention. I know that you account for every molecule of your precious fluid."

Zremus could see Primis frowning and see his eyes expanding and contracting.

"It was only a joke." Zremus gave a forced chuckle.

"It wasn't funny," said Primis.

"Yes it was," said Zremus.

"It was not!" There was anger again in Primis's voice.

"It was too!" said Zremus, mocking Primis.

Primis finally realized that Zremus was only toying with him. He summoned up a weak smile.

"Why don't you just go away and let me work?" asked Primis.

"Why don't you just go to a Victory celebration?" said Zremus.

"All right, I'll go," said Primis. "Just leave me alone."

As soon as he said it, Primis was sorry. Primis hated social events. But Zremus was his best friend, maybe his only friend, so he knew he would be going to the Victory event.

Maybe I can solve the puzzle before Victory celebrations, thought Primis. *Maybe.*

Every year at this time, Ortans celebrated the Third Family's ascension to total power. Traditionally, celebrations took place outside. Large crowds gathered at various monuments that were dedicated to the Third Family. There were crowds everywhere. It was a time when one could find a Third Family member standing next to a driver singing patriotic songs or retelling stories of the great triumphs of the Third Family. Walkways were crowded, and anyone who wanted to get anywhere had to press their way through masses of people. This was the time of year when physical contact was encouraged. Attendance at these events was not mandatory, but failure to participate could lead to one's being looked at askance. It could even lead to one's being investigated.

Primis looked around. He did not like gatherings. There were people all around him, touching him, bumping him, pushing and pulling him. The Miras Group gathering was a little more civilized, but Primis could not stop thinking about the abnormal readings. He attempted to find Zremus, but, after pushing his way through crowds in all directions, he was unable to locate him. Even though Zremus was a good friend, Primis was glad that he was unable to find him.

Seventy years ago, Primis and Zremus had some wild times together. Primis was always the one who yielded to Zremus's crazy escapades. Tonight, all he wanted to do was to make sure the Miras Group bosses were aware of his attendance. He had seen a few who had acknowledged his presence with a nod or a smile. Primis was ready to leave. His only hope was that Zremus would not sabotage his retreat.

Sabotage. The word jumped out at him. What if someone were trying to interfere with the production of fluid? He had been focusing too closely on the variations—only on the variations. He studied charts and graphs and looked for patterns in numbers. All Primis had been looking at was data. He needed to step back and look at the whole picture. He needed to study the human element. Sabotage. Maybe a disgruntled driver was trying to affect the life-prolonging fluid from which they never receive any benefits. Sabotage? Why would anyone risk facing the wrath of the Third Family? Elders could inflict unbearable pain that could last for years, decades, a lifetime. The Elders could keep one alive long past the normal life span, just to inflict more excruciating pain. Who would be so foolish? Primis was going to examine every Ortan, Third Family, or driver who had any part in the production of fluid.

Primis left the event and went straight to his lab. He immediately began to pull data on all those involved in the production of fluid. He started with the Third Family, the smallest group. Primis had no idea what he was looking for—an oddity, a misfit, or even a pattern, a pattern that could point to the solution. He studied through the night, checking the profiles of every person at every site at every level.

He wanted to go to his quarters, but it was the last day of Victory, and there would be revelers everywhere. Some waited for the last day of Victory to celebrate—and to enjoy the spectacular displays of Victory's Last Night. Others had been going for days, their spirits lifted by some intoxicant or other. Primis could not bear the thought of facing the inevitable crowds through which he would have to navigate if he left the lab, so he continued to search through the data.

He grew tired, very tired. He realized that he was going to have to admit that Zremus was right. Primis was chasing an imagined shadow. He was about to leave his display when a search result at the bottom of a data column caught his eye. MATCH/REPEAT: Loosk. What did that mean? Primis looked at other data pages. Every site page terminated with MATCH/REPEAT: Loosk. Who is Loosk? It was not a typical Third Family name. This driver had gone to every site on the planet. There was a direct connection between when Loosk left a site and when the anomaly displayed itself. There was a definite connection. Where is this Loosk? He has to be found. There could be a catastrophe of the greatest magnitude. The Family must find this Loosk immediately.

Who should I contact? thought Primis. At first he drew a blank. Then, it came to him. *Zremus!*

Zremus would know what to do and who to contact. He was good at that sort of thing. But how could he get ahold of Zremus? He was probably still celebrating Last Night without his tracker. Primis had to find Zremus. He had to put aside his personal distastes and deal with the crowds. But where should he look? Zremus disliked the people at Miras even more than Primis did, so he would have already left their gathering. Zremus might even be at a driver gathering. Primis could not, would not search driver gatherings looking for Zremus. The celebrating would end, and Zremus would be in his quarters tomorrow—Rest Day. Primis did not want to wait for another day. His finding was much too important. The Third Family's entire fluid supply might be at risk. Perhaps he could contact a Third Family site representative. What could some Third Family appointee with no power accomplish? Primis tried to think of a way to alert someone. In the end, he had to admit to himself that there was nothing he could do. He would have to wait until tomorrow when all the Ortans had finished celebrating Third Family's Victory of Peace, Unity, and Order.

◆

"It's wonderful to finally have you back, Loosk," said Moric, grinning from ear to ear.

"He did a good job while Loosk was gone," said Loosk.

"Who? What?" Moric was obviously confused.

"I'm sorry Moric," said Loosk. "I am so worn from the last few months my mind is in a different world. Our site just needs a few minor adjustments, and things will be fine. You will be able to catch up on your quotas in no time."

"I am so relieved now that you are back," said Moric. "I don't know what I would do without you."

BB smiled and looked into Moric's round golden eyes. For the first time he could feel Moric's thoughts. BB could not help but think of Krella, his mother.

"A very wise old woman once told BB that what BB is at this moment is a perfect expression of the universe," said BB to Moric.

BB looked at Moric again, this time calling forth his powers as a well-trained Master. "Never forget that. Moric will forget Loosk, but Moric will never forget what he has learned from Loosk."

BB raised his mug in a toast. "Happy Victory's Last Night," said BB.

Moric looked perplexed for a moment and then looked at BB.

"And to you, stranger, a very happy Last Night."